THE HUNTERS, THE HUNTED . . .

James Victor Lynde. World War II's most valuable spy and top agent for the CIA, he designed the ultimate cover for his subversive strategies: the perfect home, a happy marriage—and the ultimate betrayal. He never expected anyone could undermine the façade he created. But his bond with his own daughter would place his cover—and his life—in jeopardy . . .

Jaime Victoria Lynde. She inherited more from her father than just his name. Her fierce determination would lead her on a dangerous search for the one person she trusted—even at the risk of her own life . . .

Jack Forrester. Lynde's former partner, code-named "Minotaur." He held the secret to Lynde's past—but someone was determined to keep him from Jaime Lynde and the truth.

Nicholas Kendall. He knew the risks involved, and still he was willing to help Jaime on her quest. But she had known the despair of betrayal too many times. Would she dare to trust him . . . ?

Berkley Books by Norma Beishir

ANGELS AT MIDNIGHT
DANCE OF THE GODS
A TIME FOR LEGENDS

A TIME FOR LEGENDS

NORMA BEISHIR

BERKLEY BOOKS, NEW YORK

A TIME FOR LEGENDS

A Berkley Book / published by arrangement with
the author

PRINTING HISTORY
Berkley edition / February 1990

ISBN: 0-425-12069-4

A BERKLEY BOOK® TM 757,375
Berkley Books are published by The Berkley Publishing Group,
200 Madison Avenue, New York, New York 10016.
The name ''BERKLEY'' and the ''B'' logo
are trademarks belonging to Berkley Publishing Corporation.

PRINTED IN THE UNITED STATES OF AMERICA

10 9 8 7 6 5 4 3 2 1

All competent men should have some ambition, for ambition is like the temper in steel. If there's too much, the product is brittle; if there's too little, the steel is soft; and without a certain amount of hardness, a man cannot achieve what he sets out to do.

—*Dwight D. Eisenhower*

In memory of
Eleanor M. Bird
whose strength and courage
    touched my life in ways
    she never knew . . .

and with deepest
    affection for her sister,
Maria Carvainis,
who's helped to make a
    lifelong dream come
    true

Author's Note

The background for a novel of this nature was difficult to research. At times it was virtually impossible. Certain government agencies don't open doors to the public, and so it was necessary to draw from the works of other authors for the information needed to make my backdrop as authentic as possible.

The sources most often used were the works of Gayle Rivers—*The Specialist* (Stein and Day hardcover, 1985) and *The War Against the Terrorists: How to Win It* (Stein and Day, 1986); *Manhunt*, by Peter Maas (Random House, 1986), *Spycatcher*, by Peter Wright (Viking Penguin, 1987), and *The Secret War*, from Time-Life Books' World War II series. The background material on the U.S. air strike against Libya on April 15, 1986, came from published accounts in *The New York Times*, the *St. Louis Post-Dispatch*, *Time* magazine, and *Newsweek*. As always, I took literary license where necessary in order to enhance the story; any factual errors are mine and mine alone.

As always, special thanks are due the team that makes it all happen: Maria Carvainis, my agent, without whom none of this would be possible; Damaris Rowland, my editor, who constantly challenges me to be a better writer; Sybil Pincus, my copy editor, who doesn't let me get by with anything; Joni Friedman, who consistently gives me gorgeous cover art; Sabra Elliott, who masterminds unbeatable promotions; Liselle Gottlieb, who always provides me with wonderful advertising; Donna Gould, Amy Barron, and Kirsten Kreimeier, who have the dubious task of arranging my publicity; and Christie and Carol at the Boyle Secretarial Service, who relieve me of the most unpleasant task of all—typing the manuscripts. All of them have my deepest respect and appreciation.

Norma Beishir
St. Louis, Missouri
April 15, 1989

PROLOGUE

Washington, D.C., September 1985.

There was no record of his death.

Jaime switched off the microfilm viewer and stared at the blackened screen for a long time. It was all so incredible. No wonder no one believed her. Here she was, so close—dangerously close—to blowing the lid off a conspiracy of silence that had existed now for almost nineteen years, and nobody would listen to her. Nobody took her wild claims seriously. They all saw her as a desperate woman who was unable to accept reality, who had fabricated this outrageous claim about spies and secret deals and . . . Jaime slammed her fist against the table in frustration. There *had* to be someone—someone who would listen to her and help her.

It was difficult to believe, even for Jaime, that someone in the highest echelons of the United States government had been willing to go to such lengths to keep the story quiet. They had gone to a great deal of trouble, but someone had been careless. Details had been overlooked. Loose ends had not been tied up. There was no grave, at least not according to these records. No death certificate. Sloppy. Very sloppy. God . . . was it possible that he might still be alive? Jaime asked herself. Could she even dare to hope?

If he really were dead, Jaime reasoned, why should they still be going to so much trouble to keep the secret? Why would it matter to anyone? It didn't make any sense. Why would it matter to them that she was trying to find out what happened to him? And if he were *not* dead? If he were still alive somewhere, why did they want everyone—even her—to think he was dead? Why had they tried to frighten her into giving up the search?

What did it all mean?

She took the reel of film off the viewer and put it back into its box. She slipped on her dark green suede jacket and swung her oversize shoulder bag over her left shoulder. Collecting her things, she returned the film to the front desk.

"Thank you for your help," she told the desk clerk. She began rummaging through her bag for her car keys.

"Find what you were looking for?" he asked casually.

"I hope so." She looked at him. "That is, I think I have. I'll know soon."

He grinned. "Have a good day, ma'am."

Jaime nodded. "You, too."

"I sure aim to try." He watched her as she headed for the exit, moving in a long, quick, graceful stride. *There goes one good-looking woman,* he thought appreciatively. She was tall, maybe five-ten, and reed-thin, like a fashion model. Her long, thick hair was a combination of maybe forty shades of red, depending upon the way she stood in the light. Its glossy sheen reminded him of an Irish setter's coat. Her eyes were green, so dark they were the color of pine. The clerk shook his head as he turned to put the box containing the film back onto the cart he used to take materials back to their proper storage areas. *What I wouldn't give to get to know her better,* he thought.

As Jaime emerged from the building, she noticed the blue Ford Escort parked across the street. She smiled to herself. So he had waited for her again. She tried to get a closer look at the driver, but his face was hidden behind the newspaper he was pretending to read. *He's trying to look inconspicuous,* she mused wryly. *Who does he think he's fooling?* She hurried down the steep concrete steps to her car, parked at a meter in front of the building. She slipped the key into the lock and opened the door, then threw her briefcase into the back seat and slid behind the wheel. *Damned rental cars,* she thought. The seats were always adjusted for people shorter than herself. She always felt cramped in compact cars. She glanced in the rearview mirror as she backed the car out of the parking stall. The man in the Escort had put his newspaper away and was starting his engine. She still couldn't see his face clearly. He was wearing dark glasses.

Jaime thought about him as she headed for the Veterans Administration building over on Vermont Avenue. Did he work for *them*? He was certainly determined, she'd give him that. He had been following her since she left Dulles Airport that morning. She had seen him in the airport parking lot; then she'd noticed him again when she was crossing the Potomac River. He'd been right behind her on the Mason Memorial Bridge. She had not given it much thought until she noticed him parked across the street as she was leaving Congressman Blackwell's office earlier. She'd realized that he was following her when she came out of the restaurant where she'd had lunch. *I hope I don't keep you waiting long at the VA building,* she thought as she glanced up at her rearview mirror again.

The people at the Veterans Administration had not been able to help her any more than anyone else had so far. As she was leaving, she wondered who had gotten there first. Who had gotten to the files ahead of her and managed to remove all of the military service records she was looking for, records of possible pension or burial benefits paid out? She looked across the street. The Escort was still waiting. *You bastard,* Jaime thought irritably. *I'm no threat to you, can't you see that? All I want to know is what happened to my father!*

Jaime was exhausted. It had been a long day. An infuriating day. She wanted to go to her hotel, take a long, hot bath, maybe order from room service, and get to bed early. But there was one more stop she had to make before she could call it a day. It couldn't wait until morning.

If Jaime were not so angry, she would have laughed. The

idea of the government placing her under surveillance was so
ridiculous that if she did not know it for sure, she would have
laughed in their faces! She caught sight of the Escort in her
mirror. As she turned on Constitution Avenue, he was practically on her bumper. *You're supposed to look inconspicuous, you fool,* she thought as she headed east, toward the
Capitol. *I'm not supposed to know you're following me, or
didn't anybody bother to tell you that?*

This had only confirmed Jaime's belief that there was more
to her father's disappearance than met the eye. He had been
gone almost nineteen years. If he were dead, if the things
she'd been told were true, then why the tail? she wondered.
Why would it matter? Why would anyone—least of all the
U.S. government—care how much probing and digging she
might do? Jaime's instincts smelled trouble. Big trouble.

She turned on First Street and found a parking place near
the office building. She thought about leaving her briefcase
in the car, but these days she couldn't be sure it would still
be there when she returned. She took the briefcase and locked
the car. As she climbed the stairs to the old but still
impressive-looking building that housed the offices of several
senators and congressmen, she turned and quickly glanced
over her shoulder. There was the Escort, just as she had
known it would be, parked a discreet distance down the street.
The driver's face was once again hidden behind his newspaper.

She entered the lobby of the building and rang for an elevator. She was alone in the car as it made its ascent to the
fourth floor. As she entered Congressman William Blackwell's offices, she noticed that his secretary was not at her
desk. Jaime looked at her watch. Five-thirty. She had probably gone home for the day. The congressman's door was
closed, so Jaime tapped lightly to announce herself.

"Come in," called a voice from inside.

Jaime opened the door. Congressman Blackwell was at his
desk. His high-backed leather chair was turned away from
the desk, and he was staring thoughtfully at the Capitol's
dome. William Blackwell was a distinguished-looking gentleman in his sixties, with thinning white hair and a mustache.

He's always dressed as though he'd just stepped out of the pages of GQ, Jaime thought now as she stepped forward. Many of the politicians she knew came from the old, mon-eyed families. Their poise and charm came from generations of breeding and culture. As a rule, only very wealthy men could afford to enter the political arena.

The congressman looked up. "Ah . . . Miss Lynde," he greeted her. "I was not expecting you until tomorrow."

"I couldn't wait," Jaime confessed. "Did you find out anything at all?"

He nodded. "Sit down—please."

Jaime took a seat in one of the chairs opposite the desk, elegant antiques the congressman's wife had brought back with her from her latest trip abroad. Jaime liked the feel of the royal blue velvet that covered the seats. It reminded her of the chair in her bedroom when she was a little girl. Her father had brought it back with him when he'd taken one of his business trips to Paris. *What were those trips really for, Daddy?* she wondered now.

"What did you find?" Jaime asked finally. He was looking at her oddly, as if it might be bad news.

"You're not going to like it," he began.

"There's a lot about this whole business I don't like," she admitted, taking a deep breath. "Something's rotten in the state of our government." She forced a smile. "Things are getting pretty bad when private citizens are placed under con-stant surveillance. Some character's been following me since my plane landed. Here, the Hall of Records, the Veterans Administration, even to the restaurant where I had lunch. At least they can't follow me into the ladies' room."

"I wouldn't be too sure about that," Blackwell said grimly.

"You're serious, aren't you." Jaime sat ramrod straight and eyed him cautiously. "Please . . . what is it you've learned?"

He paused. "Are you sure you want me to tell you what I've got? Some things are best left buried, you know."

Jaime shook her head emphatically. "No. The past nine-teen years have been hell for me. You have no idea what it's been like. One day, my father just disappeared. He left me at school and went away on one of those business trips, and he just never came back. I didn't know if he was dead or alive, if he would ever come back. Nothing. There were rumors, of course, that he had embezzled a lot of money from Grandfather's firm and bought himself a new life in Europe. I never believed that for a minute. I *knew* my father—I knew he would never have abandoned me like that if he'd had a choice." There were tears in Jaime's eyes. "Then, when I talked to Kate, she told me something . . . she said there had been stories, that my father had been involved in some sort of undercover work during the war, that he'd been given a medal for his work with the French Resistance . . ." Jaime's voice trailed off.

"That's true," Blackwell said quietly.

Jaime's heart leaped. "You have proof?"

"Well, not quite proof . . . but let's say the indications are strong."

"Tell me!" Jaime insisted. "I have to know!"

"Your father joined the Army just after Pearl Harbor was bombed—in January of 1942, I believe. He was not in the service very long, though. It seems that he was an exceptional man, both physically and mentally." Blackwell paused. "He was recruited to work for the OSS. Have you ever heard of it?"

Jaime nodded. "Sure. Some sort of intelligence outfit, wasn't it?"

Blackwell nodded and opened a manila file folder he had taken from the drawer. "He was sent to France at the end of 1942, according to this report. He spent the next two years there, leading a group connected with the Resistance, coordinating their activities with the military operations taking place in Europe at the time. He was quite a colorful fellow, from what I've been able to learn about him."

"You're telling me my father was a *spy*," Jaime said quietly.

"There's a little more to it than that," Blackwell told her. "He was a spy during the war, yes . . . and afterward as well."

Jaime shook her head. She still couldn't accept it. "Oh,

no . . . you've got to be wrong there. I lived with him. I knew him better than anybody else could have. He would have told me," she said with certainty. "There's just no way—"

"You were only a child then," Blackwell cut in softly.

She stood up and paced the floor. "No, you *have* to be mistaken. If he were a spy, and he got caught—"

"He *was* a spy," Blackwell said. "His position with your grandfather's firm—it was just a cover."

Jaime was silent for a long moment, trying to take it all in, to digest what the congressman was telling her. "I suppose I should be relieved," she said at last. "At least he wasn't an embezzler."

"I'm afraid it's a bit more serious than that," Blackwell said gently.

She turned to look at him. "What do you mean?"

"Your father wasn't an embezzler. He was a traitor to his country. He was found guilty of treason."

ONE

Washington, D.C., September 1942.

"Would you be willing to jump from a plane behind enemy lines if you knew in advance that you would be tortured—possibly even put to death—if you were caught?"

The question had raised scattered chuckles and wisecracks among the servicemen at Andrews Air Base, but it had not been intended as a joke. Quite the contrary. The U.S. Army captain addressing the group assured them that he was quite serious. He was, he explained, a recruiter for the newly founded Office of Strategic Services, the first intelligence agency in United States history. He told them that he had visited a number of military bases across the country in the past few weeks and had received similar responses to his question at each stop. From past experience, he knew that many of those same men who had laughed at his opening remarks would end up volunteering for what would become a most dangerous mission. What he did not bother to tell them then was that out of the four or five thousand men who would volunteer during the recruiting drive, only a handful—fifty, if he were lucky—would be found acceptable for the highly specialized duties of an OSS agent.

At the back of the crowded auditorium, James Victor Lynde

shifted uncomfortably in his seat. At six feet four, he had long ago concluded that the standard folding chair had *not* been designed with someone of his physical proportions in mind. Nor had a man of his large frame been considered when the width of the spaces between rows of chairs had been determined. The aisles were barely wide enough to accommodate his long, muscular legs. Invariably, he found that when he was forced to remain seated in this most uncomfortable position for any great length of time, the muscles in the back of his legs would ache for hours afterward. Normally, this discomfort would have made it impossible for him to concentrate on what the speaker was saying, but today had been different. He had been able to tolerate the pain, for he found the cloak-and-dagger world of the OSS more fascinating than anything he could have imagined. He sat amidst the muffled laughter and whispered commentary, silent, unsmiling—and intrigued by the possibilities.

From the time he had arrived at Andrews, nine months earlier, Lynde had established himself as the official black sheep of his platoon. He had been a loner from day one, a man who had consistently kept to himself and discouraged all attempts at friendship, even from the men who shared his barracks. None of his fellow servicemen knew anything about him because he had been adamant in his refusal to talk about himself. They knew nothing of his family or where he had come from. As far as anyone at Andrews knew, he had not had any kind of contact with anyone from his hometown since he'd been stationed here. There was no regular woman in his life, of that they had been reasonably certain. He had been spotted on several occasions around the nation's capital, each time with a different woman on his arm. This had come as no surprise to anyone at the base, for James Lynde was an extraordinarily handsome man. His height and his lean, athletic build cut an impressive figure, and the stern, serious expression he normally wore gave the appearance of a warrior. His features were strong and regular, offering no clues as to his ethnic background. His eyes were the dark, cool green of a pine forest, and his hair was thick and wavy, a rich, dark red in color. He was the type of man most women would find devastatingly attractive.

The men at Andrews knew that James Lynde was in peak physical condition: he hadn't been sick a day since his arrival and had not had so much as a mild head cold. He was an expert marksman who could handle any kind of firearm with remarkable ease. He possessed a cool, calculating manner that had led his fellow servicemen to nickname him "Iceman." They were puzzled by his cold, detached attitude and often commented on it when he was not around. "Lynde has ice water flowing through his veins," they joked behind his back.

What they didn't know about Lynde, what they could not have known, was that he was a man who loved to gamble, not in the traditional sense of betting on the horses or playing poker or roulette, but in the sense that he thoroughly enjoyed taking calculated risks, living on the edge of danger. He loved nothing quite so much as a real challenge, and the prospect of working undercover for the government was a challenge greater than any he had ever known before. As he sat in the crowded auditorium, listening to the OSS recruiter's pitch and ignoring the men who remarked about the insanity of what the government was asking of them, Lynde found himself licking his lips in anticipation. Before the captain had finished his speech to the potential recruits, Lynde had made his decision. He was going to volunteer his services to the OSS.

It was a decision that would change his life irrevocably.

As he studied the young private before him, the OSS recruiter decided that James Lynde looked older than his twenty-four years. In fact, he could easily pass for thirty. He was an impressive-looking man, one who would find it almost impossible to blend into a crowd. Maybe, the recruiter thought, it was the proud, regal bearing with which he carried himself, or the strong, aristocratic face, or the arrogance that seemed to come through in every look, every gesture.

"At ease, Private," the captain told him. "Sit down. There are a few things I'd like to ask you about."

"Yes, sir." Lynde seated himself across from the captain.

"I've been going over your records, Private Lynde," the captain went on. "I'm impressed. I'm really impressed."

Lynde's face was expressionless. "Thank you—sir."

"You're quite a man of mystery, aren't you?"

"I'm afraid I don't understand, sir." Even his voice gave no indication of what might be going through his mind as he spoke.

"Nobody seems to know very much about you—like where you come from, who you associate with, if you have any family, things like that." The captain stared at him expectantly, waiting for a response.

Lynde paused thoughtfully. "Well, sir, the Army didn't ask for my pedigree when I signed on, and I didn't figure it was anybody else's business," he said honestly.

"I see." The recruiter was taking notes. "Well, Private Lynde, the OSS *does* care about your pedigree, as you call it. We're picky about who we accept within our ranks. We do thorough security checks on all prospective personnel— can't be too careful with the government's secrets now, can we?"

Lynde remained silent, wondering what the man was leading up to.

"Where *are* you from, anyway?" the captain asked then.

"Baltimore."

"No family?"

"None that I care to claim," Lynde responded without hesitation.

The captain looked up. "No close confidants?"

"I've never needed any," Lynde said simply.

The recruiter made some more notes. "You will have to be screened, of course," he said finally. "In addition to the routine security checks, you will be tested to determine your suitability . . ."

James Lynde was sent to a place known only as Station S, a suburban Washington facility, where he and other potential recruits were slated to undergo a rigorous three-day screening of physical and mental agility. The battery of tests included psychological examinations and timed exercises designed to gauge each candidate's ability to think and act under pressure. This specialized testing was extremely difficult, but necessary to reveal the presence or absence of that essential combination of qualities the OSS sought in its agents: cool nerves, good physical condition, and linguistic flair.

It became apparent early on to the OSS personnel at Station S that James Victor Lynde was all they could have hoped for in an agent—and more. Here, they agreed unanimously, was a man who could not have been more ideally suited to the life of a spy if he had been born into it. He was physically superior to the other recruits in his group, with a strength and coordination that was rare. He was unusually bright: he'd received a master's degree in business administration from George Washington University in 1941 and had graduated at the top of his class. He had a photographic memory and a natural aptitude for foreign languages. He was, they found, fluent in French, Italian, and German.

They agreed that the nickname he'd been given in the early days of his military training—"Iceman"—provided a most accurate assessment of his personality. Lynde was, by his own admission, a man who preferred to live and work alone. He had no close personal friends, no romantic attachments. Through the routine security check done on all potential agents, they'd learned that he had severed all ties with his family in Baltimore long before he enlisted in the Army. It appeared that Lynde was a man who resisted the need to form any deep, lasting feelings for anyone.

"He's perfect," one of the Station S instructors told Captain Harry Warner, an OSS commander, as they reviewed Lynde's test results at the end of the three-day screening. "He couldn't be more ideal for what we need if we'd had Research and Development *create* him for us!"

Harry Warner reviewed Lynde's test results over and over. On the plus side, he was quick-thinking and fast on his feet. He had the physical strength and coordination of a professional athlete. He was cool, detached—a man not likely to lose his head in a crisis situation. He could think without emotion, reason without passion. He had no emotional attachments that might hold him back or get in the way of his duties. He was a quick study with an amazing facility for absorbing and retaining information. On the minus side, there was his age. He was barely twenty-four, and Warner saw that as a disadvantage. He was not comfortable with the idea of using men so young; he saw them all as unpredictable and irresponsible. However, General William Donovan, head of the OSS, did not share his opinion. The general preferred younger agents. Donovan wanted bright, agile young men who were calculatingly reckless, possessed a disciplined daring, and could be trained for aggressive action. That description, Warner thought now, described no one quite as precisely as it did Private James Victor Lynde.

And that, in the end, had been the deciding factor.

The OSS training camp was located in the Catoctin Mountains of Maryland. The basic training given new agents consisted of an unbroken succession of twenty-one eighteen-hour days focusing on such skills as code work, interrogation exercises, and memory tests that, according to the official *OSS War Report*, had been specifically designed to prepare trainees for the reality that the life of an agent was a constant, continuing gamble with detection. They were educated in the fundamentals of intelligence work: espionage, sabotage, and survival. They received instruction in the sending of Morse code and the repair of radio transmitters. They were taught to kill silently and swiftly with a knife or a garotte. They learned to use both Allied and Axis firearms—essential to agents operating behind enemy lines. They were taught to parachute into any kind of terrain under any conditions.

One afternoon early in October, Lynde was part of a group of trainees receiving instruction in various techniques employed in hand-to-hand combat. The instructor had just finished demonstrating a method of killing silently and almost casually with a scalpel-thin dagger and called upon Lynde and another recruit to try using the techniques they had just learned. With his opponent armed with a dagger, Lynde was to attempt to assault the other man. His opponent was to demonstrate how the dagger could be used to bring his assailant down. Lynde had used all of his strength to overcome the other man and disarm him. Then he had brought his opponent down with his own dagger, coming dangerously close to causing serious injury to the other trainee. It had been a most unsettling experience, not only for the defeated agent but for the other trainees who had been looking on wondering if Lynde were going to go too far.

"I think he could have terminated the other guy without batting an eye," the instructor told Harry Warner afterward. "He's an odd one, that fellow. I think he really does have ice water for blood."

"That's what we're training them to do, isn't it?" Warner was intrigued by the scene taking place several yards away. Lynde had just overcome two of the other recruits simultaneously with only his bare hands, and with an ease that suggested to Warner a mastery of martial arts techniques.

"Lynde's different from the other men," the instructor said, lighting a cigarette. "From day one, we've been pounding it into the heads of all the other trainees that they had to learn to keep their emotions in check, to not let their feelings of right and wrong get in the way of the job they're doing. But with Lynde, I don't think he really feels much of anything. He just reacts."

Warner grinned. "He'll be better off that way when he's out in the field," he said quietly.

"Sometimes I wonder if he's even human," the instructor said with a shrug.

As Lynde moved on to the more advanced training, designed to train and toughen OSS recruits for more specialized operations, those responsible for his "education" began to feel that, in Lynde, the OSS had found its master spy, the superagent William Donovan had had in mind when he created the agency. In spite of his youth and lack of experience, he was surprisingly mature and level-headed. He was, they discovered, like a chameleon, able to adapt quickly and totally to any situation. Here was a man who could probably survive almost anywhere in the world, living totally by his wits. Over a period of weeks, he had mastered the most basic of survival skills, those skills that would enable him to live off the land. He had learned lock picking, a talent that would aid him in situations where he would find it necessary to break into enemy strongholds in order to steal important documents. He had mastered sabotage, one of the most important skills of all, since a successful sabotage mission done in the right place at the right time could place the enemy at a grave disadvantage. He proved to be exceptionally good at forging signatures. He also demonstrated talents not taught at the OSS camp—most notably the ability to disguise himself, changing his appearance so dramatically that he was unrecognizable.

"Your own mother wouldn't know you," Warner told him, impressed by Lynde's impression of a wino. "Where did you learn the makeup tricks?"

Lynde grinned. "I used to date a girl who'd worked in the makeup department at MGM for a while," he explained. "She taught me everything she knew. At the time, I didn't really give a damn about it. I was just humoring her. I never figured I'd ever have any reason to make use of any of it."

Warner studied him for a moment, wondering if there were no end to this man's talents. Who *was* Lynde, really?

"Learn all there is to know about your radio. Know how to use it and how to repair it," the instructor told the trainees. "Whatever information you may get is useless if you can't communicate it. Get it accurate and get it through—as quickly as possible." While other recruits fumbled through the exercises in transmitting coded messages, frantically checking and double-checking their code books, Lynde confidently keyed in message after message with lightning speed.

"Use your camera," the instructors stressed. "Valuable information will often be extremely complicated and technical. Don't even try to rely on your memory alone. There's no way it can compete with a photograph." Lynde learned to use the miniature camera that had been specially designed for use by OSS agents. He learned how to conceal the completed rolls of film in various ways so that they would not be easily detected, even if he were to be detained and searched.

"Most important of all, you will have to forget everything

you've learned about fair play and sportsmanship,'' the new
agents were told. ''You'll have to forget everything except the
fact that your country is literally fighting for its life. You're
going to be forever on the spot—the enemy will have you at
a disadvantage. It's kill or be killed out there—and your only
chance is to beat him to the punch.''

Lynde thought about it. He was still thinking about it, long
after he had returned to his quarters that night and the lights
were out. He lay in bed, contemplating what was going to
happen and what role he might be playing in it. War, he
decided, was much like a game . . . a costly, deadly game
in which the stakes were the highest of all.

Life and death.

Lynde and two other OSS agents parachuted into northern
France on a cold, windy night early in February 1943, em-
barking on a mission that was not to end until Allied troops
crossed the enemy lines. Under the code name Unicorn, he
would spend the next two and a half years in France, mostly
in the northern part of the country, living and working undercover. As it turned out, his mission was twofold: first, to
collect information—movements of Axis troops, locations of
key military installations, and plans for top-secret Nazi weapons—and transmit them to his OSS commander, Harry
Warner, who would be stationed in London for the duration
of the war; second, he was to work with the French Resistance, supplying them with weapons and materials that were
to be dropped into northern France by air and coordinating
their raids with the advances of the Allied troops. He was to
play a key role in many of their sabotage missions, mostly in
the area between Le Havre and Paris, the most important of
those being the destruction of the French railway system,
which now carried weapons and ammunition to German
troops throughout the country.

As a spy, James Lynde was in his element. He treated
espionage as though it were a game and he were its master.
Nothing, he found, could compare to the exhilaration he felt
when he watched a bridge blowing up as two Axis ammuni-
tions trucks crossed, en route to waiting troops. He looked

for ways to combine his targets. Often, he found it was possible for him to knock out a bridge and a train at the same time and, in the process, pull down power lines and block river traffic below as well. He used explosives that had been developed for the OSS to resemble innocent substances such as flour, coal, or manure, and that enabled him to knock out any target he could get near. His favorite explosive was a device called "the mole," which could be attached to the exterior parts of a train and detonated only when the train entered a tunnel. His ingenuity and his imagination made it extremely difficult for the Nazis to identify him as an Allied agent, or even to connect him with any of the bombings, for he had assumed a number of convincing disguises on various occasions. Once, he had successfully blown up a railroad yard and walked away without arousing the Gestapo's attention by donning the look and mannerisms of a clochard, the vagabonds who lived on the streets of France. On another occasion he disguised himself as a man of the cloth. He entered a village church conveniently situated near to a building used by German military commanders and made his way to the bell tower. From there, it had been a simple matter to cross over to the Nazis' stronghold and plant a cleverly constructed bomb that would bring down the building before anything could be done to salvage its contents. Working with another OSS agent, a man known only as Minotaur, he succeeded in transmitting to their OSS commander in London without detection by posing as a wine vendor. Securing a large hogshead mounted on wheels, the kind the local vendors used to push through town, they inserted a partition halfway down the cask. They filled the lower half of the cask with wine, which was drawn through a bung positioned at the bottom of the cask. In the upper half, Lynde and his transmitter were concealed, sending out information, while his partner, dressed as a peddler, traveled the streets. If a German truck approached, his partner would stop in his tracks, a signal to Lynde to stop transmitting. Their charade had continued for months while they forwarded intelligence to OSS/London on movements of enemy troops and pinpointed bomber targets.

Possibly the most notorious of Unicorn's escapades in
France, however, was his use of the French fire department
in order to gain entry into Nazi fortresses. The fire department—called Pompiers—had fallen under the jurisdiction of
the German army at the time. Lynde had questioned Julien
Armand, a leader in the Resistance who was finally convinced that his outrageous plan might work, learning all he
could about the Pompiers and how far the Germans might be
pressed to trust them. When he was certain that he had covered every angle and anticipated every possible problem that
might be encountered, he put that plan into action. He assem-
bled a number of small incendiary bombs, which were to
serve as part of his ruse. He would drive through a town,
tossing one of those bombs that would start the fire through
a window of a Nazi-occupied building. When the Pompiers
were called in to put it out, Lynde would enter as one of
them. While the firefighters used their axes and high-pressure
hoses to further the destruction—which from the bomb alone
was minor—Lynde managed to lift important documents he
could not have touched otherwise and made his escape
through a window or a rear exit. It had taken the German
High Command over six months to figure out what was happening, and even then they had no real proof. Nevertheless,
every member of the Pompiers was rounded up and sent to
the eastern front—except, of course, the man responsible for
wreaking havoc on the Nazi leaders.

The Germans had never been able to identify their neme-
sis. They thought they were dealing with a group rather than
one man. There were two theories among the German troops
as to exactly what was happening. One was that the foes they
sought were members of the Maquis, a band of freedom-
loving French patriots. Another stated that the bombings and
thefts had been the work of a small group of British and
American intelligence agents. The French people regarded
their faceless ally as a folk hero, the man who was going to
help them in their quest for victory over the dark forces of
Axis domination. But to those in command of the OSS, who
alone knew the truth, Unicorn had become something of a
legend. He was a rakehell, a daredevil who would do any-

thing to sabotage enemy power and morale. He was driving the Germans to distraction, for they never knew when or how he would strike next.

If only they had more men like him, OSS leaders lamented.

"Our double agents have infiltrated the Abwehr," Lynde explained. "They've been feeding the Germans information for months now. They've had to give out just enough accurate information to gain the Krauts' trust. Hitler's got to believe it when they pass the word along that the Allies will launch their invasion force along the coast of Bordeaux."

"And where will this invasion you speak of really take place?" Julien Armand asked.

"Normandy." Lynde paused. "So while Hitler's concentrating all of his efforts over on the Atlantic coast, our troops are going to catch him with his pants—and his defenses—down to the north."

"And do you feel that this invasion will be a success?" Armand did not sound convinced.

Lynde grinned. "It had better work," he said as he rolled up the map that had been stretched out on the table. "This is our best shot—possibly our last. If the Allies fail now, we could all end up speaking the Führer's German."

"Those of us who survive," Armand said grimly.

During that first week of June 1944, the Allied-backed Resistance fighters launched a massive assault on Nazi troops in an attempt to disable them as much as possible before the scheduled Allied invasion. In that seven-day period, from the thirtieth of May until the fifth of June, Resistance groups aided by OSS agents would sabotage well over eight hundred German targets, including trucks, trains, and bridges in the northern part of France. They were convinced that they had done all that could be done. Now they could only wait.

And pray.

On the morning of June 6, Major Friedrich-August Baron von der Heydte, commander of the German Sixth Parachute Regiment, at the time located thirty miles to the south of Cherbourg, caught his first glimpse of the invasion fleet when he climbed the steeple of the village church at dawn in the village of Saint Come-du-Mont and saw the fleet before him, filling the Channel from shore to horizon. The German troops had not been prepared for the invasion force that included some five thousand transports, six hundred warships, and ten thousand aircraft that delivered the countless troops to the beaches of Normandy that morning, but they had nevertheless put up a good fight. Few knew how close the Normandy campaign had actually come to failing, in spite of the Allies' careful preparation.

Normandy had been one of the major turning points of the war. Less than a year after the first Allied troops had landed on the beaches of Normandy, on May 7, 1945, Germany surrendered to the Allies unconditionally at Reims, France. With the United States still fighting valiantly to reclaim its territories in the Pacific, Lynde had been certain that it was only a matter of time before he and other OSS agents still in Europe would be shipped off to the Philippines or one of the other South Pacific outposts, but it had never happened. On August 6, the Americans dropped the first atomic bomb on the Japanese city of Hiroshima. Then, three days later, on the ninth, the second bomb leveled the city of Nagasaki. Damage in both cities was reported as "devastating." Never before had the world witnessed such a destructive force.

On August 14, aboard the battleship *Missouri*, General Douglas MacArthur received the unconditional surrender of Japan. When the news was first broadcast, it was received with momentary disbelief around the world. Then, for one long moment, the world seemed to hold its breath, waiting . . . and praying. This silence was followed by wild, grateful rejoicing. In New York City and in London, crowds went wild in the streets.

The war was finally over!

TWO

At war's end, the OSS closed up shop, and Lynde returned to Washington to find himself temporarily out of a job. Until now, he had not given much thought to what he was going to do with his life. Now that there was no longer a war going on and no need for undercover agents like himself, he realized, with mild amusement, that there wasn't much call for out-of-work spies. At least not in this country. He had his degree, of course—he'd completed his MBA just before his life had been so rudely interrupted by the war—but he wasn't at all sure he could spend his life closeted in some tiny office working regular office hours and punching a time clock. At one time, maybe, but not now. Not after he'd lived the life he'd lived in France, knowing the thrill of matching wits with the Germans, existing on the edge of danger every minute of his life. He had enjoyed that life, more than he had realized at the time.

Like many of the men and women who had signed on with the OSS, Lynde had entered into it with the idealistic beliefs that he was fighting on the side of right, that he and other OSS agents like himself were out there to change the world. Though he had never been quite as idealistic as some of his fellow agents, Lynde nevertheless thought of himself as a patriot. He believed in American ideals and values. But war, he had discovered, did things to those who had experienced the full force of its horror. It left its mark on their minds. It hardened their souls. After a while, for most of them, it had stopped being a matter of right or wrong. They just went all out to win, no matter what the cost. Winning became all-important, the only thing that really mattered.

For some of them, there had been no turning back.

Lynde received the Distinguished Service Cross for his work with the French Resistance. That day, he had realized for the first time just how many people—wealthy, influential people—had been willing to lay their lives on the line in the service of their country. There had been a number of scions of rich Social Register families, like Quentin Roosevelt, a grandson of Teddy himself, who had served as special representative to Chiang Kai-shek; movie stars like Sterling Hayden, who, as John Hamilton, had been running guns to partisans in Yugoslavia; and men and women of especially useful talents, such as Hollywood stuntman René Dussaq, known as the Human Fly, who had worked with the French Resistance.

"Looks like I'm in good company," Lynde said lightly as Harry Warner joined him.

Warner looked at him. "You were one of the most valuable men we had in France—possibly *the* most valuable," he said.

"Yeah," Lynde said with a grin. "I guess the OSS didn't have too many people over there who were quite crazy enough to try some of the things I did."

Warner grinned back. "I'll admit that you had me on the edge of my chair more than I care to remember. The word around OSS headquarters in London was that Unicorn was a real straitjacket case. We used to wonder what would happen if you ever did get caught."

Lynde looked at him. "Why would you wonder that?"

"It was so damned hard to second-guess you, to know what was going on in your head or what you might do next. We all wondered how you'd manage to talk your way out of it." Warner paused. "You're still valuable to the government, Jim."

"How?" Lynde asked. "The war is over. There's not much use for spies here in Washington."

"There's talk that the OSS may be revived. If it is, we want you back on the team."

Lynde furrowed his brow. "Why would they want to—"

"There's talk that the Russians have been working on an atomic bomb of their own," Warner said quietly. "We need to know what they're planning."

Lynde stared at him. "You're planning to send American agents into Russia?" he asked, dumbfounded. "And they thought *I* was insane!"

"If anybody can get into Russia and get the information we need, I'm betting that you can, Jim," Warner told him. "After all, how many of our men were able to don a Gestapo uniform and waltz right into their headquarters? If you were able to fool the Germans, I'd be willing to bet that you could put it over on the Russians, too."

"You'd be willing to bet *my* life on it, right?" Lynde asked, laughing. "You know what, Harry? I've really underestimated you. You've got more nerve than I thought."

"Tell the truth, Jim," Warner urged. "You'd like nothing better than to be back in action—in Russia or anywhere else."

Lynde hesitated for a moment. "You've got me there. I've come to realize that I'm just not the executive type."

"Then we can count on you?"

"Well—yeah. But there's just one thing—what am I going to be doing while I'm waiting for Uncle Sam to decide when and where Unicorn will resume active duty? I'm not the type to sit around twiddling my thumbs."

Warner thought about it for a moment. "Would you consider an office job on a temporary basis?" he asked finally. "Some of the people from the old Research and Analysis department are still operating out of those old buildings that used to house the old labs of the National Health Institute. I know it's not exactly something you're trained for, but they could use help, and—"

"You're right—it's not something I'm trained for," Lynde agreed. "But I can do just about anything if I have to. Just make sure it doesn't turn into anything permanent, okay?"

Warner grinned. "There's no chance of that," he said re- assuringly. "As I've already told you, you're much too valu- able to us out in the field."

Lynde wondered what they really had in mind for him.

In the next two years, the OSS was replaced by the newly created National Intelligence Authority and its later succes- sor, the Central Intelligence Group. As those two organiza- tions came and went, Lynde remained in Washington, tied to a job he hated and furious that Warner had not yet lived up to the promises he had made after the war. The job he'd been saddled with was worse than anything he could have imagined when he first returned to the States, uncertain about his future or his goals. Not only was he not using his training as an espionage agent, he was not using the things he'd learned in college, the education that had been intended to prepare him for a career in the business world.

Lynde was never quite sure which he hated most—the idea of being trapped in an office all day, every day, or the paper- work that went with the job. God, he hated paperwork! Sur- prisingly, no one within the department ever knew just how dissatisfied he was, for he proved to be surprisingly good at his work and even better at concealing his feelings. *After three years of learning to put up a good front, I should be good at it,* he thought bitterly.

How much longer before Warner and his people bailed him out of here? he wondered.

In 1947, with growing concern over the cold war and the steadily increasing hostility between the United States and Russia, those in the executive branch of the government were worried about the possibility of another surprise attack like the one that had taken place at Pearl Harbor. That year, Con- gress passed the National Security Act of 1947, a motion that was to establish the Central Intelligence Agency, an organi- zation that was authorized at the time to collect and analyze intelligence information. They were given the green light to interfere with the internal affairs of other nations when it was deemed necessary, but it was made quite clear that they would not be permitted to engage in such activities within the United States itself.

Sounds like they don't even trust their own people, Lynde thought, amused.

One of the first actions taken by the CIA was the massive support of guerrilla movements in Eastern Europe in an attempt to roll back the Iron Curtain. Lynde had been a part of that movement, performing much the same as he had when he'd worked with the French Resistance. Through him and a number of other agents, the guerrillas received arms and matériel, as well as financial support in their campaign. He had divided his time between West Germany and Italy, where the CIA had begun to infuse large sums of money into Italy's Christian Democratic Party, hoping to prevent a Communist victory in the 1948 elections there. It seemed to him at the time that the United States government was willing to go to any length—and expense—to prevent the spread of Communism throughout the world.

In the course of his travels throughout Europe, Lynde had developed a taste for good liquor, fine food, and exotic women—though not always in that order. He discovered that it was much easier to have an affair with a woman he would probably never see again, someone he could walk away from without regret, than to involve himself with someone who might expect more from a relationship than he had been willing—or able—to give. Lynde had never been able to cultivate a serious, lasting relationship with any woman. While he was not inclined to try to analyze his feelings—or rather the absence of those feelings—he had always suspected that his ambivalence stemmed from the fact that he had never had any positive relationships with women in his past. In childhood, there had been no fond memories of a mother or sisters to lay the groundwork for later involvements. When he grew older, he came to think of women as little more than instruments to be used for sexual release.

It was just as well, he decided now. He had neither the time nor the temperament to be a family man. He had never been able to picture himself married with a couple of kids, settled in suburbia in a monotonous existence. Besides, in his line of work, he would be spending most of his time abroad, which was hardly conducive to a good marriage and family relationship.

Better, he thought, *to remain a loner. Better and less complicated.*

Lynde returned to Washington in February 1949 for a meeting with Harry Warner. "We want you to start making regular trips to Russia," Warner told him. "We've learned that the Soviets are ready to begin testing their bomb, and we intend to keep a close watch on them."

"Getting into Russia is not going to be all that easy, Harry," Lynde told him. "The NKVD is especially suspicious of Americans traveling in Russia. If they have any idea that everything's not exactly as it's been presented to be, they'll use any excuse to detain a person. The covers we use have got to be pretty good to keep them off our asses."

"How long will it take you to come up with a convincing cover?" Warner asked.

Lynde shrugged. "I haven't really given it much thought. Like I said, it's going to have to be airtight. Something that can be corroborated if they decide to have one of their people over here check me out."

Warner nodded slowly. "I'll leave that up to you," he said finally. "But bear in mind that time is of the essence, Jim. We need you over there as soon as you can develop your cover and put it into operation."

Lynde nodded. He hadn't the faintest idea where to begin.

Over the next few weeks, Lynde gave serious consideration to his problem. He needed a cover that would give him a valid reason to be traveling in the Soviet Union, something that would appear legitimate, no matter how thoroughly they might decide to check him out. He needed a profession, a position that would explain what could be frequent trips into Russia. He had his degree in business administration, so he felt that landing such a position would not be as difficult as finding one that would suit his needs. How many professions would give him such an opportunity and place him above

suspicion? Public relations? No . . . no American PR firm
had offices in the Soviet Union, therefore there would be no
opportunities for travel within that country under those pre-
texts. Manufacturing firms? A possibility, but how many
American industrialists also conducted business in the Soviet
Union? Not many. Media? Hardly. He suspected that they
would really keep tabs on anyone from the U.S. media. Airlines? Not too many great opportunities in that field. Fi-
nance? That was a definite possibility. There were a number
of international banking firms that had offices in New York
City—and in Moscow. Their people traveled all over the
world, many of them living abroad at least half of the time.
They conducted business in every part of the world. It was
perfect, he thought.

He checked out all of those international firms having offices in New York City or anywhere along the East Coast,
and he discovered that there was a large number of them. He
wasted no time in contacting several of them, seeking em-
ployment. Unfortunately, he found, there had been a number
of young, well-educated men like himself who had served
during the war and had returned home in need of jobs. Open-
ings were few and applicants many. It was not going to be as
easy to get a job as Lynde had expected it to be.

The answer to his dilemma had come to him quite unexpectedly. He had developed the habit of reading the local
newspapers every evening, from first page to last. He had
done this every night, three hundred sixty-five nights a year,
since he was a freshman at George Washington University.
Now, as he performed this ritual one evening in February
1949, he came across an item in the society pages that caught
his eye. A prominent U.S. Senator, Harrison Colby of New
York, had announced that morning that he would not seek
reelection at the end of his present term in office. He was
making plans to return to his home on Long Island and take
over the running of the international banking firm founded
by his father-in-law in the early part of the century. The senator's father-in-law had passed away recently and had no sons
of his own to succeed him.

Along with the article was a photograph of the senator and

his family: his wife of twenty-six years, Colleen O'Donnell
Colby, and their two daughters, Frances and Kathryn. Frances was the eldest, an attractive blonde in her early twenties,
a recent Vassar graduate. Kathryn, her younger sister, was
just twenty and a student at Wellesley, a brunette who was
also quite attractive. Lynde stared at the photograph for a
long time, and an idea began to form in the back of his mind.
How many times had he heard that the easiest way to get a
foot in the door in any kind of business was to marry the
boss's daughter? A wife would sure as hell make his cover
more convincing. A foreign government would probably be
less suspicious of a man who was married to the daughter of
a man who'd hired him. They'd figure nobody was going to
allow his own daughter to be part of a cover-up—at least not
if the father were aware of that cover-up. Hell, even the
Americans were generally suspicious of a man his age who
had never married!

He studied the two young women in the picture, trying to
decide which of them was going to be the object of his supposed affection. Kathryn was too young for him. She was
quite beautiful, but he could not see himself with a girl of
twenty. Not when he'd just celebrated his thirty-first birthday.
Frances Colby was twenty-two or twenty-three, probably.
That was more like it. He would go all out to charm Frances.

He lay awake that night, thinking about it. He knew that
what he was doing was morally wrong, that he did not have
the right to use an innocent person as part of the elaborate
smoke screen he'd create for himself. He did not have the
right to use Frances Colby to get her father to give him a job
in his firm. Still, he knew that as an intelligence agent, his
first and most important obligation was to the government
who had hired him. His first consideration had to be the CIA,
and he justified what he was going to do in his own mind by
telling himself that he was acting on behalf of the United
States.

Besides, he reminded himself, he had to be so convincing
that everyone involved would believe that his intentions were
strictly honorable. Even the young woman herself could never
know that he was not in love with her, that he might have

married her for any reason other than love. It had to appear to be a real marriage—to all concerned.

I've really got my work cut out for me this time, Lynde thought, lying awake in the darkness. *This is going to be harder than trying to convince the Nazis that I was part of the Gestapo.*

If he could pull this off, he could do anything.

He phoned Harry Warner the next morning. "I need to talk to you," he announced without preamble. "It's important."

"You've come up with your cover," Warner guessed.

"Yeah—but there's a problem," Lynde told him. "I'm going to need your help."

"I told you before, you'll get our cooperation on anything you need," Warner reminded him. "Anything at all."

"This may be a little difficult—even for the guys at the CIA," Lynde warned.

"Don't bet on it."

"When can we talk?"

"This afternoon okay for you?" Warner asked.

"I'm free all afternoon."

"Fine. Why don't you stop by around three-thirty?" he suggested. "Whatever the problem is, I'm sure it can be worked out."

"Tell me everything you know about Senator Harrison Colby."

"Senator Colby?" Warner laughed. "Not much to tell. He's squeaky-clean."

"What about his personal life?"

Warner stared at him for a moment. "First, why don't you tell me why you're so interested."

"Didn't you see last night's paper?" Lynde asked.

Warner shook his head. "I was at a formal dinner last night—my wife's idea, of course," he said. "Why? What about it?"

"It seems the senator's decided not to run for reelection. His father-in-law just died and he's going home to New York to take over the family business—an international banking firm.''

''And you think this might be an opportunity to establish your cover,'' Warner concluded.

''It might. You know, of course, that the senator has two lovely, quite unattached daughters.''

''Yeah.'' Warner thought about it. ''I see what you've got in mind—romance one of the Colby girls and Daddy just might give you a good job in his firm.''

''Bingo,'' Lynde said with a grin.

''Good idea. I'm proud of you, Jim—as always you've got it all figured out,'' Warner said.

''I need to learn as much as I can about the Colbys—all of them. Then I need someone from their inner circle of friends to arrange an introduction.''

''Easy enough,'' Warner said. ''Colby's from a good family, but one without a large bank account. His wife's family had all the money. In fact, it was Colleen Colby's father who bankrolled the senator's campaign when he ran for office the first time, twenty-odd years ago. I guess that's why the senator feels obliged to take charge of the old man's business now that he's gone.''

''So Mrs. Colby comes from a wealthy family?''

''The wealthiest,'' Warner replied, nodding. ''The cream of Long Island society, you might say.''

''What about their two daughters? What can you tell me about them?'' Lynde asked.

''Well . . . Frances is the oldest—twenty-one or twenty-two, I think. She just graduated from Vassar. She's a lovely young woman, blond, blue-eyed, an aspiring artist, I hear. She's a pretty quiet reserved young lady. Her younger sister, Kathryn, is a bit of a hell-raiser. She's been kicked out of three private schools and almost got herself kicked out of Wellesley. She seems to think life's one big party. The Colbys are worried about her, and with good reason, I think.''

''I see,'' Lynde said thoughtfully.

''Which of the girls have you set your sights on?'' Warner wanted to know. ''Or shouldn't I ask?''

"Why not?" Lynde chuckled. "I think Frances Colby will make a perfect wife for an up-and-coming banker."

Harry Warner had promised to introduce him to someone who could arrange for him to meet the Colbys. Lynde was not concerned. Warner had contacts coming out of the woodwork. It might take him a while to come up with just the right one, but he'd do it. Lynde stared at the newspaper photograph and thought about what he was about to do. He was good, but he was not sure he was *that* good.

Would he really be able to pull it off?

Harry Warner phoned Lynde on Thursday evening and told him to stop by his office on Friday morning. "I've found someone who can introduce you to the Colbys," he said. "I'll introduce him to you in the morning."

"I'll be there."

Lewis Baldwin was about Lynde's age, a tall, attractive man with curly dark hair and brown eyes. He looked like a rich young scholar. It seemed to Lynde that Warner had called some theatrical casting agent and said, "Send me an Ivy League type—good-looking, but not *too* good-looking, good bearing, aristocratic, with perfect teeth." Lynde suppressed a grin as he shook the other man's hand. Probably has a degree from a good Eastern university, too.

"Lewis worked for the OSS," Warner was saying. "As a matter of fact, he was in France about the same time you were. He was south. Provence."

"You were with the OSS?" Lynde didn't bother to hide his amazement.

"Does that surprise you?" Baldwin asked.

"Quite frankly, yes. I suppose it shouldn't—there's very little that does, these days, but—"

"Lewis is also a good friend of the Colby family," Warner said then. "He's one of Kathryn Colby's former escorts."

"Oh?" Lynde turned to Baldwin again. "You know her well?"

Baldwin grinned. "Quite well." He took a pack of cigarettes from his pocket and offered Lynde one.

There goes the Ivy League image, Lynde thought. "No thanks," he said aloud. "I don't smoke."

"Since when?" Warner wanted to know.

"Since France," Lynde replied with an easy grin. "It got to be too hazardous. Every time I threw down a match or tossed away a butt, I ran the risk of blowing up something."

"The Colbys have no idea that Lewis works for us," Warner told him. "They know only that he was in the Army and that he fought in France—*after* the Normandy invasion."

"I'm going to tell them that you and I met then, that we were part of the same platoon," Lewis Baldwin explained. "We're good friends as far as the Colbys are concerned, so we're going to have to get together and work on it. Our stories have got to match."

"Sounds fair enough," Lynde agreed. "Leave it to Harry to come up with a perfect plan."

"I think we should get started on it immediately," Baldwin suggested. "After all, we *don't* have a great deal of time."

"Where and when is this introduction going to take place?" Lynde wanted to know.

"Next Saturday," Baldwin told him as he lit a cigarette. "Have you ever been to the Lake Forest Country Club?"

Lynde shook his head. "No."

"It's one of the best private clubs in Washington. Actually, it's in Georgetown," Baldwin told him. "You almost have to have been born to one of its founding families in order to be accepted for membership. Or you have to marry a daughter of one of those founding fathers."

"Upper class stuffy," Lynde concluded.

"That's an accurate assessment," Baldwin said with a laugh.

Lynde hated the idea already. Country club . . . elegant restaurants . . . socialite families . . . they were all part of a world he had rejected years ago. He took a deep breath. "Okay, friend," he said, looking at Baldwin, "suppose we get started right away. What are you doing for lunch today?"

Baldwin grinned. "I'm meeting an old friend."

THREE

"You're sure Senator Colby is going to be here?" Lynde asked as he and Lewis Baldwin entered the crowded ballroom at the Lake Forest Country Club.

"Trust me," Baldwin said confidently. "He hasn't missed a Saturday night here in almost thirty years. Anybody who is anybody in this town turns out for these dances. Colleen Colby—the senator's wife—is a real class-conscious lady. I think she comes here just to make sure she gets her picture in all the local society pages. And the senator's not one to object to being center stage either."

"Isn't that true of all politicians?" Lynde asked with a smile.

"Maybe . . . but more so of Harrison Colby than others, I think. He's one ambitious man." Baldwin looked around the room for a moment, then nudged Lynde. "What did I tell you? There he is—over there."

Lynde looked in the direction Baldwin had indicated. It was Colby, all right. He was an imposing figure of a man, of medium height but husky, with thick hair that had turned partially gray. He had alert, intelligent eyes, and he looked exactly like his photographs.

They made their way across the ballroom, pushing through

the crowd until they reached the senator and his wife. Colby
greeted Baldwin warmly. "Where have you been keeping
yourself, Lew?" he wanted to know. "It's been a long time."

"Too long," Baldwin agreed. Then he introduced Lynde.
"Jim and I were in France together during the war," he explained to the Colbys. "You may have seen his pictures in
the papers—he was awarded the Distinguished Service Cross,
you know."

"Ah, yes." Colby's face brightened with recognition. "I
believe I *did* see it. It's a pleasure to meet you," he told
Lynde.

"I assure you, the pleasure is mine," Lynde insisted.

"And where are those two lovely daughters of yours?"
Baldwin asked Colleen Colby. "They *are* here tonight—"

"Of course. I'm surprised you didn't see Kathryn over at
the piano when you came in." She nodded toward the piano
on one side of the room. The orchestra was taking a break,
and Kathryn Colby, an attractive brunette, sat at the keyboard
playing current show tunes with a cluster of admiring men
around her. "Sometimes I wonder what I'm ever going to do
with that girl."

"What about Frannie?" Baldwin asked.

"Frances is in the powder room. You know how it is with
young ladies, Lew." She smiled a positively perfect smile,
and Lynde guessed that anything Mrs. Colby did would have
to be perfect. She probably wouldn't have it any other way.
She reminded him of—no, that was a long time ago, he told
himself. He studied Colleen Colby for a moment. He esti-
mated her to be in her early fifties. Her gown was elegantly
understated, with exactly the right finishing touches: a single
strand of pearls around her neck, small pearl earrings, and a
diamond on her left hand that looked large enough to choke
an elephant. She was the genuine made-to-order politician's
wife.

"Lewis Baldwin!" called out a female voice from behind
him. They all turned as Kathryn Colby, who had spotted
Baldwin with her parents, sailed across the room and into his
arms, greeting him enthusiastically. "Where on earth have
you been hiding yourself?"

"I haven't been hiding, Kate—you've just been too busy with all of your other admirers to notice me," Baldwin told her as he gently pried her loose. "Jim, this is Kate Colby—Katie, this is Jim Lynde. He's a very good friend of mine."

Kate smiled warmly. "Good to meet you, Jim Lynde," she told him. "Any friend of Lew's is definitely a friend of mine."

"Kathryn—" her mother said in a low voice.

"Oh, Mother, don't be so stuffy. If I weren't around to liven things up here, this place would be about as much fun as a mausoleum!" She turned to Baldwin. "Does Frannie know you're here?"

"I haven't seen her yet."

"She'll be happy to see you."

Lynde smiled appreciatively at the young woman. She was small and petite, but with a soft, full figure. Her features were delicate, her eyes a soft, velvety brown. She wore her luxuriant black hair up. Her strapless white gown showed off her splendid figure. He wondered what the other sister was like.

"I haven't seen Frannie since she came home from Vassar," Baldwin said to Senator Colby then. "I guess the fellows are beating the doors down, now that she's back."

"Oh, you know Frannie," the senator said with a smile. "That's not her style. She likes things slow and tranquil. The cave-man approach is more Kate's style."

"Daddy!"

"We both know it's the truth, honey," he said gently. "God knows why you seem to enjoy that sort of romance, if you can call it romance, but—"

"Harrison." Colleen Colby put her hand on his arm, an unspoken signal to drop it.

"Yes, dear," he said.

"Here's Frannie now," Kate said as her older sister crossed the room to join them. Frances Colby looked nothing at all like her sister, yet each was quite lovely in her own way, Lynde decided. Frances was taller than her sister, with a leaner, more athletic figure. Where Kate was dark, Frances's hair was a sun-streaked ash blond and her eyes a pale blue;

Kate's features were softer, but Frances's were also delicate for someone of her build.

"Jim, this is Frannie Colby," Baldwin introduced them. "Frannie, I'd like you to meet a good friend of mine, Jim Lynde."

"I've very happy to meet you," she said in a low voice.

He took her hand, bowed slightly, and kissed it. "The pleasure is all mine, I assure you, Miss Colby," he said gallantly.

Frances Colby blushed. Her eyes darted nervously from her sister to her parents and back to her sister again.

"Come on, Kate," Baldwin said, taking her hand. "Let's go out there and show this crowd how to dance."

She looked up at him and smiled wickedly. "I'd love to."

As they strode off, arm in arm, Lynde looked at Frances and smiled. "Would you do me the honor?" he asked, extending his arm to her.

"I would enjoy nothing more."

He led her onto the dance floor and took her in his arms. She was tense at first, slowly relaxing against him. "So you're a friend of Lew's," she said finally, attempting to make conversation with him. "How long have the two of you known one another?"

"Since the war." He grinned. "You really get to know a guy when the two of you fight side by side, day after day, getting shot at from all sides."

"You make the war sound like a sporting match," she said with a slight smile.

"In a way, it is," he said. "It's a lot like chess."

"Oh?"

"It's a game of strategy—and a lot of people don't realize it, but it's more mental than physical."

"You sound as if you enjoyed it."

"No one enjoys war, Miss Colby," he told her.

"I'm sorry," she said, embarrassed. "I didn't mean to—"

He grinned. "Let's just forget about it, okay?" he suggested. "Lew tells me you just graduated from Vassar. What was your major?"

"Art history."

"You're interested in art?"

"Very." She paused. "There was a time I wanted to become an artist myself. A painter. But my talents weren't equal to my ambitions."

There was skepticism on his face. "I'm sure you're just being modest," he insisted.

"Oh, no—no, I'm not," she said quickly. "The most unfortunate thing about having an eye for truly good art is that it's impossible for me to overlook my own shortcomings as a painter."

"You shouldn't be so critical of yourself," he told her with a mischievous gleam in his green eyes. "I'd say it's really a matter of personal preference, wouldn't you—really?"

"Only to an extent."

"Like you, for instance. You and your sister are both beautiful women, but beautiful in different ways," he told her. "That white dress looks great on her, but it would make you look washed out. But you look marvelous in mauve—a color that would not suit Kate at all."

Her eyes narrowed suspiciously. "I think you're making fun of me."

"Not at all. I'm merely trying to make you see that what might not look beautiful to you might appeal to someone else." He smiled. "I would love to see your work."

"Are you an art lover, Mr. Lynde?" she asked.

His eyes met hers. "You might say that. I like to think that I have an eye for anything of beauty."

During the war, the rich, fashion-conscious women who normally made at least two trips to Paris each year to view the latest collections by the top French couturiers had turned to the better-known crop of American designers. Though many of those women would flock back to Paris once the war was over and life on the Continent had returned to normal, hungry for something new—anything new—from those great legends of haute couture, including Dior, Balmain, and Chanel, Colleen Colby and her daughters would not be part of that exodus. Mrs. Colby, who had always favored the designs of Hattie

Carnegie and had worn exclusively the charming hats that had
been designed for her by Titiana of Saks Fifth Avenue, found
it was rarely necessary to go any further than New York to
find exactly what she was looking for. Only when she accompanied her husband on one of his diplomatic missions abroad
did Colleen Colby treat herself to an extravagant ball gown
from either Dior or Chanel, the two designers she felt created
gowns most flattering to her figure and taste.

In the past two years, her daughters had had their clothes
designed for them by a young designer in Washington who
became known only by his first name: Sebastian. Both Fran
and Kate felt that Sebastian, more than any other designer,
understood their particular taste and need for a more contem-
porary look. Colleen watched as Fran admired a suit worn
by one of the house models, a tightly fitted, dark blue suit,
double-breasted, with black velvet lapels. It was a lovely creation, and Fran would look marvelous in it. The jacket was
nipped in severely at the waist, and the roundness of the hips
was exaggerated by a buckram lining above the rather slim
skirt, which stopped just a few inches above the model's ankles. It was accented perfectly by the black kidskin gloves
and high-heeled pumps, but most striking of all was the hat:
small, elegant, of the best black velvet, with a sheet veil that
stopped just below the model's nose.

"Are you thinking of taking it?" Mrs. Colby asked idly.
"It is quite lovely."

"I don't know, Mother," Fran answered with a shrug. "I
can't really make up my mind."

Colleen Colby watched silently as the house models moved
about in the richly decorated salon, dressed to kill in Sebastian's newest and most spectacular creations. She had had the
feeling all day that Fran was not feeling well. Her mind certainly was not on the selection of new additions to her already
extensive wardrobe. No, Frances had not been herself all day.
They had had lunch at Cassello's, Fran's favorite restaurant,
and she had done little more than pick at her lunch, pushing
it around on her plate with her fork to make it look as though
she had eaten. Mrs. Colby wondered what was wrong. Fran
didn't appear to be ill, and she didn't have a temperature.

"Are you all right, Frances?" she asked finally. "You've been so quiet. If you're not up to this today, we can leave and come back some other time—"

"I'm fine, Mother," Fran said quickly. "I guess I'm just in a quiet mood today."

"She's just in love, that's all," Kate said then, still admiring a strapless, sea-green chiffon ball gown Sebastian had brought out. "She's quite taken with that dashing gentleman Lew introduced us to at Lake Forest last Saturday night—James Lynde."

Fran glared at her sister, embarrassed. "Really, Kate! All I said—and you did agree with me—was that I thought he was most attractive—and charming!"

Her mother thought about it for a moment. "Perhaps, then, it might be a good idea to invite him to dinner one evening," she suggested. "It would give us all a chance to get to know him better."

"I would truly enjoy that," Fran admitted with a smile. "But how could I? It wouldn't be proper to call and ask him, would it?"

"No, I suppose that it wouldn't," Colleen Colby said thoughtfully. "But it would be entirely proper for your father to extend the invitation."

There was an eagerness in Fran's manner and voice that betrayed her emotions. "Do you think he would?"

"Of course he would," Colleen Colby said confidently. "I'll speak to him about it this evening."

The Colbys lived in Georgetown, in an elegant old four-story Georgian mansion that Lynde guessed to be at least two centuries old. He was admitted to the house by a butler in an immaculate white jacket and black trousers. The reception hall brought back memories of another time, he thought, eyeing the white marble floors, the burnished oak staircase, and the elegant old crystal chandelier. He followed the butler into Colby's study where the senator was waiting for him.

"Good evening," he greeted Lynde, smiling. "The ladies are still upstairs, I'm afraid—you know how women are—so I thought we could take this time to get to know one another better. We didn't have much time to talk out at Lake Forest, I'm afraid.''

Lynde nodded, wondering what he was leading up to.

"Frances is not by nature an impulsive young woman," Colby was saying. "She's always been so practical, so level-headed. Much more so than her sister, I'm afraid.''

"Yes, that was my impression too," Lynde agreed.

"Frankly, that's why it comes as such a surprise to my wife and myself—the way she'd taken such a fancy to you after only one meeting,'' Colby went on. "She's quite smitten with you.''

"I must confess, sir, that the feeling is mutual," Lynde said quietly. "I'm quite taken with her, also.''

Colby nodded. "I see." He poured a scotch for each of them. "I'm sure you can understand why I'd be concerned. My daughter is very important to me. I would not want to see her hurt—''

"Nor would I," Lynde assured him.

The door opened then, and Colleen Colby and her daughters appeared. Frances's face lit up when she saw Lynde. She rushed forward to greet him. "I'm so glad you could come, Jim,'' she told him, not bothering to hide her excitement.

"I wouldn't have missed it for anything," he assured her, taking both her hands in his. "You look especially lovely tonight, Frances.''

"Would you please call me Fran?" she begged. "I detest being called Frances—it reminds me of that dreadful mule in those movies!''

"Fran it is," he promised.

They dined by candlelight in the large, old-fashioned dining room. The elegant silver candlesticks, the heavy linen tablecloth and napkins, the polished silver and expensive china, the liveried butler, they all reminded Lynde of a past he wanted more than anything to forget. He immediately pushed the thoughts from his mind and turned his attention to Fran, who was seated to his right. She *was* a lovely woman.

I hope I'm doing the right thing, Lynde thought miserably.

• • •

"I am glad you could make it, Jim." Fran and Lynde stood on the steps in front of the mansion after dinner.

"I'd like to see you again, Fran," he told her.

Her heart skipped a beat. She looked up at him, her cheeks flushed with color. "When?" she asked.

"Would Thursday evening be all right?"

"It would be wonderful."

"I've been thinking . . . there's a new gallery opening over in Arlington. They're featuring a one-man show by a new artist. I think the newspaper said he's been called 'the greatest new talent of the decade.' "

"That would be Tom Kelly," Fran said.

"Oh—so you've heard about the exhibit," he said.

"Yes, I have, and I would *love* to see it."

"Great. How would it be if I came to call for you around seven, then?" Lynde asked. "We could go to the gallery and maybe have a late supper afterward. I know a great little place across the river."

Fran smiled. "It sounds delightful," she told him. Impulsively, she kissed him lightly on the cheek. "Then I'll see you on Thursday?"

"It's a date."

Long after Fran had gone back into the house, Lynde sat in his car, thinking about what he was doing and why.

It was something he was not proud of.

"You still haven't told me," Lynde began. "What's your expert opinion of Tom Kelly—as an artist, I mean?"

Fran thought about it for a moment, sipping her wine. "Well, first of all, I'm hardly an expert, though I do know art," she said slowly. "But I did enjoy it. It was much better than I had expected."

"Oh?" he raised an eyebrow. "Why do you say that?"

"I normally don't expect much from the smaller galleries," she explained. "They're wonderful for showcasing new talent—but there's so little new talent on the horizon these days."

"Maybe you're just spoiled by the old masters," he suggested, remembering the paintings that hung in the Colby mansion.

"Maybe," she agreed. "I do have a preference for the French Impressionists. Monet, Renoir . . . they're my favorites." She looked at his plate. "You're not eating. Isn't the veal scallopini good?"

"Oh, no . . . it's not that at all. In fact, it's excellent." He smiled at her. "It's just that I find it difficult to think about food while in the company of such a beautiful and charming lady."

Fran's cheeks colored visibly. "I'm flattered."

He reached across the table and took her hand. "You're a very special lady, Fran Colby—do you know that?"

"I feel special when I'm with you," she confessed, feeling slightly embarrassed.

"I'm very happy to hear that," he said softly, "because I'd like very much to go on seeing you."

"I'd like that, too," she said.

For the next six months, Lynde saw Fran Colby almost every day. They went to art exhibits and prowled the local galleries. They went sailing. They spent their Saturday evenings with her family at Lake Forest. They took long walks together along the Potomac. Lynde bought her expensive gifts and courted her on a grand scale, one befitting a princess. He knew that his plan was working, and he felt good about it. He also knew that Fran was falling in love with him, and he felt bad about that.

He did not like the idea of using Fran Colby to get to her father now any more than he did when he first began seeing her. She was a wonderful young woman, and Lynde knew that she would make a great wife . . . for someone. But not for him. He was not the marrying kind. He could not imagine himself married—to Fran or to anyone else—and tied down with two or three children. That was not his style. He had to be free, had to be able to pick up and go when he wanted.

But it was too late to turn back now.

• • •

"You never talk very much about yourself, Jim," Fran said one afternoon as they walked hand in hand along the Potomac River. "Why?"

"There's not a lot to talk about," he said with a shrug. "I live a very unglamorous life. I work for the government."

Fran laughed, and he realized how ridiculous his remark had sounded. "I didn't mean it that way," he said quickly. "I—"

"I know what you meant, Jim," she assured him. "It's just that it sounded so funny."

"Yeah—I guess it did," he agreed. He'd have to remember to tell Harry Warner that one.

"I wouldn't think your life would be dull at all," Fran was saying. "After all, you were a big war hero. You were awarded the Distinguished Service Cross. That's quite an honor."

"I was doing my job. That's all," he insisted.

"It was your job to risk your life aiding the French Resistance?" she asked.

He looked at her. "How did you know about that?"

"Well . . . I really don't want to make you uncomfortable or anything, but Daddy checked you out when we first started seeing one another," she confided. "He's a bit overprotective of his daughters. He likes to know what kind of men we're seeing . . . although I'm afraid if he were to check out all of Kate's dates, he wouldn't have much time to do anything else."

"And what did he learn about me?" Lynde asked tightly.

She took his face in her hands. "Please don't be angry, darling," she said softly. "Actually, he was quite pleased with what he learned. He said you were quite a man." She kissed him. "And of course, I agreed with him one hundred percent."

"I'm not angry," he insisted. He had to keep himself under control. He could not afford to make Colby suspicious of him now. Obviously Colby hadn't been able to unearth anything of any real importance. "And I suppose I *do* understand his position."

"Thank you for understanding," Fran said in a low voice. "I do so want you and Daddy to like each other."

"The first time I came here," he recalled, "your father told me he was concerned that I might break your heart or something to that effect. I think we should put his mind at ease, once and for all."

She laughed. "And how would we do that? Daddy won't be satisfied until both Kate and I are settled down, married, and—" She stopped short and looked at him for a moment. "Are you—"

He nodded. "Fran, I want to marry you," he said simply.

She threw her arms around his neck and hugged him tightly. "Oh, yes, Jim, yes!"

Lynde held her close and stroked her hair. *This should satisfy Colby.*

"You proposed?" Harry Warner was grinning from ear to ear. "That's wonderful! You're a fast operator, Jim."

"I don't like this, Harry," Lynde admitted. "I don't like doing this to her. She's in love with me, dammit. I guess I never considered the possibility that it could happen—"

"It means it's going to be a helluva lot easier to get the senator to offer you a plum of a job in the family business," Warner said sharply. "Do I have to keep reminding you how important this is? Do I have to keep reminding you—"

"No, dammit, you *don't*!" Lynde snapped. "I walked into this with my eyes wide open, remember?"

"We all have to do things we don't particularly enjoy doing at one time or another in our lifetimes," Warner said then.

"Even you?"

"Yeah. Even me. Does that surprise you?" Warner asked. "I've done many things I didn't like having to do in the years I was with the OSS. But that was my duty, and I accepted it, because I knew it wasn't my choice to make. Do you think I enjoyed recruiting all those young GIs, knowing that a large number of them were going to have to sacrifice their lives in the line of duty?"

"I never thought of it that way," Lynde admitted.

"I used to think about some of those men, men who were

captured and tortured before they were finally allowed to die.
I used to feel guilty about it because I knew it was my big
pitch that convinced them to sign on with the OSS to begin
with," Warner recalled. "I used to feel as responsible for
their deaths as the Germans or the Japanese had been. I did
not sleep well at night, in case you've ever wondered."

Lynde was silent for a long moment. "This is not the
same, Harry. Fran's fallen in love with me—"

"Half of the mademoiselles in France were in love with
you, my friend, but you walked away from them without feeling guilty."

"That was different, Harry," Lynde said again. "I didn't
really know any of them. They didn't really know me—"

"Neither does Fran Colby," Warner reminded him. "I
don't see how you can think you're hurting her. She loves
you, she wants to marry you—that should make her real
happy."

"It should. But what if I can't be a good husband to her?
You know how hard it is for me to—"

"I've got faith in you," Warner said confidently.

Lynde looked at him. He wished he could share that faith.

"Are you sure this is really what you want, honey?" Senator
Colby asked his daughter.

Fran smiled at him, and her whole face was aglow.
"Daddy, I have never been more certain about anything in
my life," she assured him. "I love him, and I know that he
loves me. No one could make me as happy as I know he
will."

"How well do you really know him?" Colby wanted to
know. "I mean, the two of you have only been seeing one
another for a matter of months—"

"I know him as well as I need to," Fran insisted. "Oh, I
know he doesn't talk about himself much, but that doesn't
mean anything. You told me yourself that he was quite a hero
during the war."

"That doesn't necessarily mean he's going to be an ideal
husband," her father reminded her.

Fran laughed. "I think you worry too much, Daddy," she

told him. "Jim and I will have a wonderful marriage. You'll see."

"I hope so." Colby had to admit, if only to himself, that he had never seen her so happy. "Does he plan to stay with the government, or does he have other plans for the future?"

Fran thought about it for a moment. "I don't really know. We haven't discussed it," she admitted. "Why do you ask?"

"I was thinking about offering him a job."

Fran looked at him. "You mean in New York?"

"He does have a graduate degree in business, doesn't he?"

"Daddy, that would be wonderful!" Fran declared. "We could all be together then, and—oh, maybe I'm being presumptuous. I don't know if that's what Jim wants."

"Maybe you should ask him," Colby suggested. "Or better still, maybe I should ask him."

"Would you, Daddy?"

"I'd be happy to," Colby told her. "Why don't I give him a call and invite him to lunch at the club . . ."

"The Jefferson Club?" Lynde asked. "Yes, I know where it is. What time shall I be there? . . . One will be fine. . . . Sure, no problem . . . I'll see you then, Senator." He replaced the receiver slowly and looked up at Harry Warner, who stood in the doorway of his office.

"Senator Colby?" Warner asked.

Lynde nodded. "He wants to meet for lunch. He says he'd like to discuss a business proposition with me."

The Jefferson Club, located on F Street, was the most exclusive club in a city full of exclusive clubs. The easiest way for one to become a member was to be the son of one of the members, but if one had not had the good fortune to have qualified by birth, it was always possible to be accepted for membership by being recommended by three members in good standing. This, however, was something of a gamble, since being blackballed by just one of the members could keep someone out for life. No prospective member could be considered again after having been turned down.

The interior of the club was spectacular by anyone's standards. It had been decorated by one of the world's leading interior decorators, with meticulous care taken to make sure the color and lighting were just perfect. It was especially flattering to the women, who found their beauty enhanced by the soft candlelight glow. The cuisine was superb, and the club's wine cellar was considered by those who would know to be the third best in the United States.

Lynde looked around the room as he was escorted to Senator Colby's table. He spotted several senators, two Supreme Court justices, a group of Cabinet members, and an assortment of high-powered industrialists, men who currently controlled some of the largest corporate empires in the world. In one of the booths, he spotted one of President Truman's aides with a Washington columnist. *If the Russians ever wanted to wipe out the top power brokers in this country,* Lynde thought with mild amusement, *all they'd have to do is drop a bomb on this place.*

He forced a smile when he saw Senator Colby. The senator stood up as he approached. "Good of you to come on such short notice, Jim," he said as they seated themselves. "I thought you might have had other plans."

"I rarely get out at lunchtime," Lynde said vaguely. "There's always too much to do and too little time to do it in."

"Do you like working for the government?" Colby asked then. ' Is it something you want to do for the rest of your life?"

Lynde studied him for a moment. "I hadn't really thought about it," he said carefully. "After the war, I needed a job, and they made me an offer—"

"Would you consider leaving if you were to receive a better offer?" Colby asked.

Lynde laughed. "I suppose I'd be a fool not to, wouldn't I," he chuckled. "But then, I'd have to say that would depend upon the offer."

"How would you feel about living in New York?" Colby wanted to know.

Lynde paused. "Are you offering me a job, Senator?"

"I might be."

He smiled. "Something tells me Fran's told you about our plans," he said slowly.

"Yes, yes, she has," Colby admitted. "Fran practically grew up in New York, Jim. She loves it there."

Lynde nodded. "She's talked about it often."

"As you know, I'm retiring at the end of my present term in the Senate to take over Colleen's father's firm. It's an international banking firm. He founded it years ago, before the Depression."

"And it's still going strong?"

"Yes, fortunately, it is." Colby studied the younger man thoughtfully before going on. "I could use a bright young man like yourself—and I think Fran would be happier if she were in New York, near her family."

Lynde smiled. "I think Fran and I would be happy anywhere we're together."

Colby looked at him for a moment. "I'm sure you're right," he agreed, "but I think it would be worth your while to at least consider what I'm offering. It will be a wonderful opportunity for you, a chance for a career in a most promising field. And Fran would be happy."

Lynde smiled. "Okay. Suppose you tell me exactly what it is you're offering us," he suggested. "Tell me what's involved in this position, how much it pays, things like that. I'll talk it over with Fran and give you an answer within, say, a week?"

"Fair enough." Colby started to talk, and Lynde listened with interest, but was careful not to appear too eager.

He didn't want Colby to know he had already made up his mind.

FOUR

Frances Colby's engagement to James Victor Lynde was announced officially in December, just before Christmas. Predictably, her photograph appeared in newspapers in both Washington and New York, along with the announcement that the wedding would take place in April at the Colbys' New York home on Long Island.

Though Lynde would have preferred a small wedding without fanfare, he knew that it would be out of the question. People like the Colbys did not have small weddings. They had major productions. They had large, lavish affairs with orchestras and the most prestigious caterers in town and a platform of bridesmaids dressed to their eyeballs in the finest designer gowns and hats. They had the best of everything, and they invited half the state to see it. Of course, all the "best" people came, as well as the leading society columnists, since that lavish splendor would be wasted if it did not get into all the newspapers. *It's like being placed on display,* Lynde thought with distaste. It was definitely not his style, but he had committed himself and there was no turning back now.

Lynde displayed an interest he didn't really feel when Fran, bubbling with enthusiasm, talked to him about the wedding

dress Sebastian was designing for her or the china and silver
patterns she had selected. He went with her to formal dinner
parties he found dull and boring and forced himself to make
small talk with people he didn't know—and didn't want to
know. No one ever knew how uncomfortable he was, for he
played his role well. He made several trips to New York where
he met other members of the firm, selected office furniture
for an office he would probably not be spending much time
in, and went with Fran to meet with the decorators working
on their new home. The Colbys had given them the house—
a grand old Colonial-style home overlooking Long Island
Sound, near Sound Beach—as a wedding gift. Lynde and Fran
spent an entire day in Manhattan, selecting wedding rings at
Cartier, lunching at L'Aiglon, and making plans for their
honeymoon in Paris. Back in Washington, he went with her
to Sebastian's salon and was convincingly enthusiastic as he
helped her select ensembles for her trousseau. He met Fran's
friends and their husbands or escorts at parties given in honor
of the engaged couple. The women were invariably young,
attractive in a subdued way, elegantly understated, and properly conservative. The men all looked as though they had
been cut from the same mold—clean-cut, all-American, Ivy
League types. *Some of them don't even look old enough to
shave,* he thought wryly. Lynde recalled how he had once
faced spending his life as one of them, how he had rebelled
against it. It was ironic, he thought, that he was marrying
into that way of life now.

Especially after fighting so hard to break away from it.

Lynde stood at the window, watching the caterers and the
florists and the musicians move about unobtrusively as the first of
the guests began to arrive. From the guest room he now occupied at the Colby estate, he had a clear view of the area
where the ceremony and reception would take place. Stepping
away from the window, he took the small gold circlet from
his pocket and stared at it for a long moment. Fran's wedding
ring. Lynde had managed to justify his reasons for marrying
Fran almost from the very beginning. He had realized that
what he was about to do was morally wrong, that it was not

fair to her, but then he had reminded himself he was not the first man to enter into a marriage of convenience, nor would he be the last. He was simply doing what had to be done, he thought as he returned the ring to his pocket.

He paused in front of the mirror and nervously ran his fingers through his thick red hair. *Okay,* he said to himself as he studied his own reflection. *You've given yourself a role to play—and so far you've played it to the hilt. Now go out there and give the best performance of your life.*

As he opened the door and went out into the hallway, he saw Colleen Colby at the top of the staircase. She wore a pale yellow dress several shades lighter than those selected for the bridesmaids. How predictable, keeping with Fran's choice of yellow and white for the wedding party and the flowers. He grinned. Above all, society weddings were color coordinated. God forbid anything should clash.

When he reached the bottom of the staircase, he found his best man, Lewis Baldwin, waiting for him. He gave Baldwin the ring. "Is Harry here?" he wanted to know.

Baldwin nodded. "Why did you decide to pass Harry off as your uncle?" he asked in a low voice.

Lynde grinned. "I figured it would look fishy to my new in-laws if I didn't produce at least one member of my family to attend my wedding."

"Don't you have any family of your own?" Baldwin asked.

"None worth mentioning," Lynde said coldly. He turned on his heel and walked away, with Baldwin following close behind.

They went through the French doors at the rear of the house and made their way across the lawn to where Lynde and Fran would take their vows. The guests had all seated themselves, and the orchestra had begun to play. Lynde flashed a smile at Colleen Colby, seated in the front row with Fran's grandmother, a woman of eighty who still looked surprisingly lovely. Rich women had a real knack for keeping themselves well-preserved, he noted.

The six bridesmaids appeared wearing identical buttercup yellow, full-length gowns and made their way down the aisle that had been covered with white carpeting. Lynde turned his attention to the French doors. Kate appeared, dressed in a gown that was a darker yellow than the others, with puffed sleeves that were just off her shoulders. Her gown was silk, with a full skirt and tiny white flowers embroidered all over the skirt. She wore her hair up, with a cluster of yellow flowers at the back of her head. As she reached the end of her walk, the orchestra launched into the bridal theme, and Fran stepped through the French doors on her father's arm. She had never looked more beautiful, Lynde thought as he watched her moving toward him, her face glowing with love behind the sheer veil she wore. Her dress was like something out of a fairy tale—high-necked, Victorian in style, made of the finest silk, and covered in antique lace and tiny pearls. Pinned to the wide band of white velvet encircling her throat was an elegant-looking gold brooch Fran had once told him was well over a hundred years old. Her blond hair was pulled up in a loose knot on top of her head and adorned with a cluster of babies'-breath. He smiled as she took her place at his side. "Nervous?" he asked in a voice so low that only she could hear.

She shook her head. "I love you, Jim," she whispered.

"I love you, too."

As the minister began the ceremony, Lynde's mind wandered. He thought about his first venture into the Soviet Union—which would undoubtedly be soon—thought about his new position with Colby's firm in Manhattan, the new role he had created for himself. Automatically, he repeated the vows as the minister spoke them to him, slipping the ring on Fran's finger when he was told to do so. He barely heard the minister pronounce them man and wife. "You may kiss the bride," the minister said, beaming.

Lynde turned to Fran, slowly pulling the veil back, away from her face. He took her in his arms and kissed her tenderly.

The first leg of his mission was now completed.

"Normally, the ship doesn't make any stops between New York and Southampton," Lynde told his bride as they boarded the *Queen Mary*, "but we'll be getting off at Cherbourg. I've made arrangements to rent one of those oversize Delahaye touring cars—with an English-speaking driver, of course. I thought you might enjoy driving to Paris. The route from Cherbourg is really quite lovely. The roads are lined with poplar most of the way.''

Fran looked up at him, beaming. "I'm sure I'll love it,'' she told him. "I'd be happy anywhere as long as we're together.''

They were escorted to their cabin by the ship's purser. The first thing they noticed as they entered were the flowers—yellow and white flowers, everywhere. On the bureau was a large basket of exotic fruit and a platter of caviar and Melba toast. Chilling in an ice bucket was a bottle of Dom Perignon. Lynde wondered who had sent them, but Fran had no doubts. "Daddy thinks of everything,'' she laughed.

"Of course,'' he said, nodding in agreement. "They must be from your parents.'' But he wasn't so sure. They could have been from Harry Warner.

They had dinner in the ship's dining room that evening, having been invited to sit at the captain's table. Fran was excited, telling Lynde that she had a special dress that would be perfect for the occasion. He waited as she dressed, idly wondering what this special dress could be. He thought he'd seen everything she'd bought, but she insisted that he had not seen this one. Women were so funny about their clothes, he thought. He remembered a time when . . . no, he didn't want to think about that now. He'd promised himself he would never let it bother him again. Never.

Fran emerged from the cabin then, and her face was glowing. "Well, what do you think?'' she asked. "Will you be embarrassed to introduce me as your wife?''

The dress was a floor-length chiffon evening gown with a strapless bodice held up by tiny bones, the fabric draped softly across her bosom. The bottom layer of chiffon was a sky blue, with each successive layer just a shade lighter until the fifth layer was a pure white. Draped over her shoulders was a stole of the same multilayered chiffon, ornamented here and there with sprays of pale blue flowers. She wore her hair up, as she had at the wedding, with pale blue flowers pinned to the back of her head, and a single strand of Burmese pearls—the same pearls she told him her father had given her for her eighteenth birthday—around her neck.

"Embarrassed?" Lynde laughed. "Frannie, I would never be embarrassed to introduce you as my wife—here or anywhere else," he assured her.

When they returned to their cabin after dinner, Lynde sensed Fran's nervousness. Like most other young women of her breeding and social class, she had never been to bed with a man before. Lynde was not surprised that he had married a virgin. He had grown up in a time in which men expected the women they married to be virgins. *You're going to have to go easy on her,* he reminded himself. *She's not like the women you knew in France and Italy.*

"Why don't we open that bottle of Dom Perignon?" he suggested when they were alone. "The evening's still young. Besides, it'll help you relax."

She looked up at him. "Does it show?"

Lynde smiled. "Yes, it shows. But don't worry about it," he told her. "Everybody's nervous the first time."

She opened her mouth to say something, then changed her mind. "Why don't you pour?" she asked. "I think I'll go change into something more comfortable." She paused, then smiled. "That sounds terribly cliché, doesn't it."

He grinned. "Yes, it does . . . but who cares?"

She nodded. "I'll be right back."

As she disappeared into the bathroom, he took the bottle from the ice bucket and opened it. He poured two glasses and left them on the table beside the bed. He turned down the sheets on the bed and took off his clothes. He slipped on the blue silk robe he'd bought for this occasion—normally, he did not even wear pajamas and had never owned a robe—and stretched out on the bed, waiting for his bride.

The bathroom door opened, and for a moment the room was flooded with the brilliant light coming from within. Fran stood in the doorway wearing a filmy, ice-blue negligee. In the harsh light, he could see her body outlined clearly through the sheer fabric. She had a better figure than he'd expected.

But Fran was the outdoorsy type. She enjoyed sailing and swimming and all the things that would keep her in good shape. Silently, he extended his arms to her, and she came forward, her lips trembling slightly as she lowered herself to the bed beside him.

"Not much of a seductress, am I," she asked, trying to make her voice light.

He handed her one of the glasses he'd filled. "You're beautiful, Fran," he said in a low voice. "Even more so than I'd expected."

"Do you really think so?" she asked, not believing him.

"I wouldn't say it if I didn't mean it," he said, watching her intently as she drank the wine, almost too quickly. She was like a frightened little animal as she handed him the empty glass and asked for another. He obliged and finished his own. The second time she gave him her glass, he put it on the nightstand. "That's enough," he told her. "I don't want you passing out on me tonight." His mouth came down on hers, tender yet urgent. "I've wanted to make love to you for so long," he whispered as his hands roamed over her body, touching her through her filmy negligee. He took one of her nipples between his thumb and forefinger, as the sheer silk slid off her right shoulder, and began to squeeze it gently. Fran trembled as his lips moved down her neck to her exposed breast. She stroked his hair, not sure what else she was expected to do at a time like this. She shivered as he took her nipple into his mouth and began to suck at it. He pulled away from her abruptly and sat up, pulling her into his arms. He kept kissing her as he finished undressing her. "Oh, Fran," he whispered as he shed his own robe. She looked at him, naked now, his organ standing erect against his abdomen. He came back to her, hovering over her as he whispered endearments, stroking her exposed flesh, setting her on fire at his touch.

"Make love to me, Jim," she whispered as he covered her body with his own.

"You're so beautiful," he muttered in the darkness as he explored her with his hands, his lips, his tongue. "My lovely Frannie . . ."

"I love you, Jim . . . I want to make you happy . . ." she moaned as he kept touching her between her legs, making her wet with desire.

"You are making me happy . . . very happy . . ." Finally, when he was sure that she was ready for him, he insinuated himself between her legs, barely touching the throbbing warmth of her. "Just relax, honey . . . relax . . ."

Fran bit her lower lip in the darkness as he entered her. He felt enormous, and his thrusts were painful, but she was determined not to let it show. She clung to him, digging her nails into his shoulders as he moved deeper, faster inside her, taking her quickly, urgently. Then she felt his body suddenly tense and his breathing became a gasp. "Oh, Jim!" she cried out as a strange, dizzying sensation swept through her body. He went limp on top of her, burying his face in her breasts.

They lay there in silence for a long time, neither of them moving a muscle, neither of them speaking. Finally, Lynde pulled himself up on his elbows and stared down at her with an odd look in his eyes. Then he bent his head and kissed her tenderly. "Are you okay?" he asked in a low voice.

She nodded. "It's such a strange feeling," she began slowly. "I felt as though my whole body were shaking, as if the room had begun to spin—"

He smiled. "What you had, darling, was an orgasm," he told her, kissing her again. "I'm surprised. Knowing how nervous you were and all—"

"I love you," she said simply. "Just being with you makes me feel like the world is spinning." She touched his cheek. "I hope I didn't disappoint you."

He kissed the tip of her nose. "Never," he told her.

He thought, *How could I ever be disappointed? After all, this is supposed to be a perfect marriage.*

By the time they returned from their honeymoon in May, Fran was still glowing like a bride on her wedding day. Paris was wonderful, she reported to her parents, and her husband was even more so. She could not possibly be happier than she was at that moment, she insisted, as they headed out on Long Island toward their new home.

While Fran settled into blissful domesticity at Sound Beach, Lynde began the process of familiarizing himself with his new position as an executive of his father-in-law's Manhattan firm. He accustomed himself to the routine of two-hour lunches with other banking executives, having martinis with those lunches and listening to the other men talk about their mortgages or their children's orthodonture bills or the mistresses they kept conveniently in Manhattan while their wives were hidden away in Connecticut or out on Long Island. Though the idea of keeping a mistress had appealed greatly to Lynde, who had always enjoyed variety in his sexual relationships, he knew that to try it would be suicide. Colby would find out, and he'd be dead. Harrison Colby was a shrewd businessman and an ambitious one as well, and he would understand frequent absences for business reasons. He would not understand his son-in-law keeping a mistress. No . . . Lynde had realized that, once he married Fran, he would have to be a faithful husband. He decided it was not as bad as he'd expected it to be. Fran was lovely, and she adored him.

Lynde proved to be good at his job, and Colby was open with his praise. "You're doing a great job, Jim," Colby told him more than once. "Keep up the good work, and soon you'll be a full partner in the firm." Lynde knew what Colby wanted from him. Colby had been selected as his father-in-law's heir years ago because Colleen Colby's father had had no sons to take his place. Now Harrison Colby was in the same position, a man with only two daughters to inherit from him. Lynde was not fooled for a minute by Colby's lavish praise of him. A partnership? Of course it was inevitable. Colby expected him to become his successor. *Fine,* he thought. *That means he trusts me.*

At the office, Colby spoke of the sons Lynde and Fran would produce as if it were a foregone conclusion that they would have at least two, preferably more. At home, Fran spoke with wistful longing of a friend's new baby, anxious to have one of her own. Lynde did not want any children. He felt it was enough to be tied to a woman he didn't love for the sake of his job. He did not feel that children could possibly add anything to his cover. Besides, it wasn't fair to a child to grow up with a parent who spent most of his time off in another country, putting his life on the line at the request of his government. It wasn't fair to a child to grow up in a home with a parent who didn't want him—nobody knew that better than he did. Maybe if his own past, his own childhood, had been different, he would feel differently now. But it was too late to think about what might have been. He could only hope that his frequent absences would prevent Fran from becoming pregnant too easily. He couldn't just tell her he didn't want to have any children. He had to act as though he did. It was expected of him.

Sometimes he wondered if they did not all expect too much.

New York City, August 1954. Harrison Colby got to his feet, smiling, as his daughter approached his table at El Morocco on that hot summer afternoon. "It's good to see you, Frannie," he told her as they seated themselves. "What brings you into Manhattan?"

"I had a doctor's appointment," she said quietly.

"Oh?" His eyebrows raised in concern. "Nothing serious, I hope."

"I don't think so," she said. "I had to see a gynecologist—just for tests. I think there may be something wrong with me, some reason why I can't seem to get pregnant."

"And what does the doctor say?" her father wanted to know.

Fran's smile was weak. "He just took some tests, cultures, things like that. He said he wouldn't know anything for a few days." She paused. "I suppose I'm worrying for nothing."

Colby looked at her. "What makes you say that?"

"Oh, Daddy—how much chance do I have of getting pregnant when my husband is almost never home?" she lamented. "Jim spends more time in Europe than he does at home."

"Honey, we've been over this before," Colby reminded her. "It's his job. He travels because he has to. Jim's a very important part of the firm, and—"

"He's a very important part of our marriage, too, Daddy—though that doesn't seem to matter much anymore," Fran said, her voice rising slightly in anger. "I feel like I'm living in that dinosaur of a house alone! Do you realize that in the four years we've been married, we've never been together on our anniversary?"

They both fell silent as the waiter came to their table, asking if they would like a drink before ordering. Colby ordered a martini. Fran asked for a daiquiri. After the waiter had gone, Colby looked at his daughter, disapproval on his face. "I'm surprised at you, Frances. You're not a child anymore," he told her.

"No, I'm not a child," she agreed. "I'm a married woman—a happily married woman—who desperately misses her husband and would like very much to have more time with him, to have a child with him if that's possible. Is that too much to ask?"

Colby shook his head. "Fran, I was away more than I was home while you and Kate were growing up. Do you recall your mother ever carrying on the way you are right now?"

"No—but Mother has never been one to openly display her feelings," Fran reminded him.

"I don't think your mother has ever been unhappy with me," Colby told her. "She learned to manage quite well and to bring up you and your sister with relatively few problems. Tell me—did you ever feel as though I rejected you?"

"No," Fran said slowly, "but I do remember wishing you were around more often."

"Do you feel as though Jim is neglecting you?" Colby asked.

Fran paused as the waiter returned with their drinks. After he had gone, she looked at her father. "I'm not blaming Jim for any of this," she said. "I think he'd like to be home more often. And I also think you could do something about it—if you really wanted to."

"As I've already told you, Frances, this is your husband's job, his responsibility," Colby said quietly, sipping his martini. "He has to take his work seriously and do the best he possibly can if you expect him to take care of you in the manner to which you've always been accustomed. Jim is good at what he does. One day he'll be running the firm."

"Wonderful," Fran said sarcastically. "Sometimes, Daddy, I think I may have been better off if I had fallen in love with a dockworker or a door-to-door salesman."

"I've got to fly to Paris next week," Lynde told Fran as they dressed for dinner one evening. They were dining at the home of one of his colleagues from the firm.

Fran stopped what she was doing. "But you just came home yesterday," she protested.

He frowned. "I know, but it's something that just couldn't be avoided."

"This isn't fair," she said angrily, slamming her hairbrush down onto the dressing table. "You're almost never home anymore."

"You know I'd be here with you if I could," he told her. "God, Fran—you, of all people, should know—"

"You sound like my father!" she snapped. "You know, Jim—sometimes I get the feeling that you really enjoy taking all those trips, that you really want to be away from me!"

"You know that's not true," he said quietly.

"The rational part of me tells me that—but the frustrated wife in me says I have a husband in name only these days!" she cried.

He paused for a moment. "Maybe we'd better cancel our dinner plans," he said finally. "I think it's more important for us to be alone tonight, to talk things out."

She nodded. "I really don't think I could face the Shermans tonight," she admitted.

"Fine. I'll give them a call." He went to the phone and dialed the number. She was barely listening as he explained that Fran was feeling a bit under the weather and that they would have to ask for a rain check. *God, he even sounds like Daddy sometimes,* she thought wearily.

When he hung up, he turned to face her again. "Think we can get Sadie to whip up something simple for dinner?" he asked. "I'm famished."

"I'll do it," Fran said quietly, remembering that she'd

given their housekeeper the evening off. "Sadie's already gone. She won't be back until late, I'm afraid."

Lynde grinned. "Honey, we both know you can't boil water," he said gently. "Nobody ever expected you to. Know how to cook, I mean."

She nodded. "Maybe we could send out for something."

"How many places around here deliver?" he asked.

She nodded again. "I don't know what I could have been thinking of," she said, slightly embarrassed.

He looked at her for a moment. "What's bothering you? You haven't been yourself since I got home. You seemed so quiet at the airport—"

"It's a lot of things adding up," she sighed. "You being away so much, Daddy being so insensitive about it." She paused. "I went to see Dr. Ellerman while you were away."

He turned to stare at her. "The gynecologist?" he asked. "What for? There's nothing wrong—"

"Oh, no," she said quickly. "I just went to see him to find out if there was something wrong with me, some reason why I haven't gotten pregnant yet."

"And?"

"He says I'm in perfect health. No problems, no reason why I can't have a dozen children if I want them—provided my husband spends enough time with me to make it happen." She crossed the room and put her arms around him. "I want a baby, Jim," she said in a low voice, gazing up into his dark green eyes. "Everyone I know is having babies now or already has them. I want a child—your child. It's lonely around here when you're gone. If I had a baby, then I wouldn't be lonely when you're away."

He looked at her for a moment. Maybe she was right. Maybe it was just what she needed. "Well," he said as a slow smile came to his lips, "you're not going to get that baby by hanging around doctors' offices." He began slowly unbuttoning her blouse.

"Jim! What are you doing?" Fran looked shocked.

He grinned. "Now what does it look like I'm doing?"

"But it's only six o'clock!"

"Where is it written that lovemaking has to be restricted

to specific time periods?'' he asked, sitting on the edge of
the bed. He reached behind her to unhook her bra and pulled
it off. ''If you want a baby, we've got to put forth a little extra
effort,'' he told her as he cupped her breasts in his hands. She
shivered involuntarily as he put his mouth to her nipple and
began to suck at it fiercely. His hands moved lower, unzipping
her skirt and pushing it down over her hips. It fell to the floor
and was quickly followed by her slip, underpants, garter belt
and stockings. He pulled her down on the bed beside him and
held her close, stroking her breasts, her thighs, his fingers moving between her legs, touching her, arousing her . . .

Realizing he had pulled away from her, Fran opened her
eyes and looked up. He was tearing off his clothes. He came
back to her, covering her body with his own, setting her on
fire with his hands and his mouth. Since Lynde had realized
it would be too risky to involve himself in extramarital affairs,
he had established a satisfying sexual relationship with his
wife—which he found fulfilled his needs quite nicely. Fran
had never been much of a sexual adventuress, but she was
available to him whenever he wanted her, and he found her
quite desirable.

He gazed down at her for a moment as if he wanted to tell
her something, then changed his mind. He pulled away from
her, sliding down on the bed until his head was directly above
the triangle of soft golden hair. Gently, he parted her legs and
buried his face in her thighs. Fran began to squirm frantically.
He grabbed her buttocks in his hands and held on to her as he
brought her to a sharp orgasm with his tongue. Then he reared
up over her again, launching himself into her with an urgency
that caught Fran by surprise. She moaned and writhed beneath
him as he took her in several quick, sharp thrusts. As he achieved
his orgasm, he buried his face in her neck. ''Oh, Frannie,'' he
whispered breathlessly. ''Frannie . . .''

Fran stroked his hair and stared up at the ceiling. He was
good to her. He was gentle and affectionate and an exciting
lover. He said all of the right words and did all of the right
things. Many of her friends thought she had found the perfect
husband. And yet . . .

Fran began to weep.

. . .

Fran set up her easel on a grassy knoll overlooking the Sound. It had been a long time since she'd held a paintbrush in her hand, and she now felt the need to seek emotional release through her painting, which she had always regarded as inadequate, unsuitable for anyone's eyes but her own. She studied the peaceful, shimmering waters of the Sound, contemplating the seascape she wanted to paint. Peaceful . . . calm . . . tranquil. So unlike the wild, ambivalent emotions that churned through her soul like a great tidal wave.

She held the brush in her hand and stared at the canvas thoughtfully. Finally she began to paint, giving the work all of her thought, all of her concentration. She hoped that, by channeling her anger and frustration into her painting, as male artists did, she would be able to exorcise those feelings. She told herself she was being irrational and unreasonable, feeling as she did, but she had not been able to stop her emotions from tormenting her.

Fran was not sure when she had begun to feel so desperately unhappy; she knew only that she had awakened one morning to feelings that Jim was *not* a victim of his profession but that he was using his work to spend as much time as possible away from her. She began to suspect that he did not really love her, that he had lost interest in her shortly after their marriage. When she had not been able to talk herself out of her suspicions, she tried to discuss it with Kate, who dismissed her feelings as irrational and suggested she might want to speak to a psychiatrist about it. At first, Fran had been insulted by what her sister had implied. She did not need a psychiatrist—she was not crazy! She was just unhappy . . . unhappy because her husband was away most of the time, unhappy because she had not been able to have a child. Anyone in her predicament, she insisted indignantly, would feel exactly the same way.

She had tried to feel her father out, looking for a clue to Jim's real feelings about her, about their marriage. Her father had assured her that he was only doing his job, that he would be spending more time with her if he could. Her father was quite fond of Jim. He saw Jim as the son he'd always wanted but never had, the son who would one day inherit the family business. He did not think there were any grounds for her fears and suggested that if she were to become pregnant those feelings might change. She had not been able to make him understand that she wanted a baby more than anything right now, but that it took two to make a baby, and since Jim was away ninety percent of the time, her chances of becoming pregnant were practically nonexistent.

Thinking about it now, she realized that not only had Jim not been home on their anniversary since they'd been married, he had been with her only once on Christmas in the four years they'd been married. She'd received beautiful gifts on her birthdays—once from Paris, twice from Rome, and the last time from London. They had never enjoyed a romantic candlelight dinner to celebrate an anniversary or a birthday. They had never had an intimate celebration in the privacy of their bedroom to mark another year of marriage. He had always been away on those occasions. She got only phone calls from a hotel or an airport.

"How old are you, Mrs. Lynde?" the doctor asked as he listened to Fran's heartbeat and her lungs with his stethoscope.

"Twenty-eight." Fran wondered if anything could be seriously wrong with her. Her sixth anniversary was only a week away, and for the first time, Jim was going to be home. This was the last thing she needed right now. After all her careful plans for an intimate, romantic celebration . . . she just couldn't bear the thought of anything going wrong now. She had to make it up to him for being so suspicious of him, of his intentions as a husband . . .

"Your blood pressure's up a little," the doctor said as he removed the cuff, "but nothing to worry about. What's bothering you—specifically?"

Fran thought about it for a moment. She started to say that she didn't know, but she realized he was talking about physical symptoms. "I'm just so tired. It's all I can do to get out of bed in the morning," she said, looking discouraged.

"Do you feel worse in the mornings or evenings?" the doctor asked as he made notations on her chart.

"Mornings—most of the time."

He felt the sides of her neck, checking for any possible enlargement of her lymph nodes. "When was your last menstrual period?" he asked as he took out an ophthalmoscope and looked at her eyes.

Fran thought about it. "March sixth, I think."

"Is your cycle fairly regular?"

She shrugged. "My husband says I'm so regular that Greenwich should call me," she said blankly, recalling how frustrated Jim had been when he returned from one of his trips to find she was in the middle of her period and sex would have to be put off until the end of that week.

"I see." The doctor paused. "Is there any history of illness in your family?"

"I don't—which illnesses are you speaking of?" she asked.

"Heart disease?"

Fran paused. "My father had a heart attack—I think the doctor called it angina—a couple of years ago. He was hospitalized for a time," she recalled. "He's been on medication ever since, and I don't think he's had any more attacks."

"What about your husband's family?"

Fran hesitated, feeling slightly embarrassed. "I really don't know anything at all about my husband's family," she admitted finally. "He never talks about any of them. As a matter of fact, I've met only one of his relatives. His uncle Harry—he was at our wedding, and I haven't seen him since."

"I see." The doctor wrote something else on her chart. "Have you ever had measles, Mrs. Lynde?"

"Yes."

"How old were you at the time?"

"Nine, I think."

"Mumps?"

"No."

"Whooping cough?"

"No."

"Any surgery?"

"No—yes. An appendectomy. I was about twelve at the time. Twelve or thirteen, I don't remember which."

"And there were no complications?"

"None that I can recall."

"Nothing else?" he asked.

"No, not that I have any memory of."

"I see." He made some more notations. "I think I should do some tests," he told her.

"Tests?" Fran looked nervous.

"Relax, Mrs. Lynde," he told her. "Nothing to be alarmed about, I assure you. Just the usual routine lab tests that are done on everyone at one time or another—blood and urine tests. I just want to rule out a few possibilities."

Fran nodded. "What's wrong with me, Dr. Ellerman?" she asked anxiously. "I mean, what do you *think* is wrong with me? Surely you have some idea, some—"

The doctor smiled patiently. "I would prefer not to venture a guess without having something concrete to go on," he told her. "But if it will give you any comfort, I *am* fairly certain that it's not serious."

"How soon will you know anything?"

He wrote her a prescription. "Call me on Thursday afternoon. I should have the results by then. Until then, get this filled and take one whenever you feel nauseous. They should relieve it."

She nodded. "Thursday?"

"Thursday. If I get them back sooner, I'll call you. You have my word."

Fran drove along the Sound, heading back to Sound Beach. She was no more reassured now than she had been before she'd seen Dr. Ellerman. Why couldn't he at least have told her what he suspected might be wrong with her? This was infuriating. As if she didn't have enough on her mind!

She stopped at a local pharmacy and had the prescription filled. Bendectin. The name sounded vaguely familiar, and she wondered where she'd heard it before. She also bought a bottle of liquid antacid in case the pills didn't work. Remembering that there were no aspirin in the house, she selected a bottle of her usual brand and took the items up to the check-out counter in the front of the store. As she was paying the clerk, she noticed the ice cream parlor across the street and, on an impulse, decided to indulge her sweet tooth. She put the purchases in the car and crossed the busy street to the ice cream parlor.

She ordered a deluxe banana split piled high with nuts, cherries, and a mountain of whipped cream. As she sat alone at a small table near the window, she realized she had not indulged her cravings like this since she was a child. It had all been so wonderful then, growing up in Manhattan, the cherished and spoiled daughter of wealthy parents who in-dulged her every whim. She recalled now how her father would often take her and Kate to Macy's and buy them any-thing they wanted; then they would all go to Schrafft's and he would allow them to order anything they wished. Invariably, they both always chose the deluxe banana splits, eating as much as they could, until they felt as though their stomachs were going to burst. "Don't overdo it, girls," their father had told them. "If you eat too much, you'll get fat, and it will be hard for me to find a handsome prince for each of you." He had not been serious, of course, but Fran had felt as though all of her girlhood fantasies had come true when she met Jim. He was everything she had ever daydreamed about: he was handsome and charming and witty and roman-tic. He had literally swept her off her feet that night in the ballroom at the Lake Forest Country Club. She had fallen so totally in love that night that it had been impossible for her to imagine a life with him that would be less than perfect. In the beginning, it *had* been perfect, she recalled sadly.

She had never been certain what it was in his manner or behavior that had made her feel as though he did not really love her . . . until this morning, in Dr. Ellerman's office. Admitting to her gynecologist that she knew little about her husband's family made Fran realize that Jim had never really confided in her, had never been willing to share himself with her. He had never talked to her about his family or his child-hood or his hopes and dreams for the future. He had never given her even a glimpse into his soul. Fran felt the tears stinging her eyes as she scooped up the last of the ice cream and popped it into her mouth. That was it. He'd always been the perfect husband . . . on the surface. He had said all the words and gone through all the motions. He'd been attentive and considerate. He'd given her lavish gifts and expressed interest in anything she did—on the surface. It had all been on the surface.

Jim had given her everything she could want except the one thing that mattered most: he had given her nothing of himself.

Lynde phoned Fran on Wednesday evening. He was in Zürich. "I'll be home in a few days," he told her. "Things were a little more complicated than I expected."

They're always more complicated than he expected, she thought. "That's all right, darling," she said evenly. "I understand."

"Are you all right, Fran?" he asked. The connection was terrible, and she could barely understand his words.

"I'm fine," she said. "I went to see Dr. Ellerman the other day. He did some tests—just routine lab work, of course—and he said he'd know tomorrow what the problem is. It's probably just a virus."

"Well, you just take care of yourself, okay? If you're not up to making the drive to Idlewild, don't come in to pick me up. I can get a ride," he told her.

"Oh, I'm sure I'll be perfectly all right by then," she said confidently. "Don't worry about me."

"I can't help worrying about you, Frannie," he told her. "I want you to promise me you'll go to bed as soon as you hang up, okay? You don't sound like yourself at all."

"I'm just tired," she insisted. "And I think I will go to bed. I don't think I could stay awake tonight if I tried."

"Good. I'll see you on Monday. Take care, okay?"

"I will," she promised.

"I love you."

"I love you, too, Jim."

She replaced the receiver slowly and climbed the stairs to the master bedroom. As she sat at her dressing table, brush-

ing her hair, his words echoed through her mind. I love you
. . . I love you . . . I love you . . . How many times had he
said those words to her? How many times had he held her in
his arms and looked into her eyes and said those words? How
many times had he smiled at her and told her she meant
everything to him?

She looked at the picture on the corner of the dressing
table. Jim, as he had looked the day they were married . . .
smiling, happy. *What do you really want from me, Jim?* she
wondered now.

What is it you really see when you look at me?

Thursday passed so slowly that Fran thought the day would
never end. Finally, at two in the afternoon, she was so anxious that she could wait no longer. She phoned Dr. Ellerman's office. She was told to hold on and was kept waiting
for what seemed like an eternity. The young women who
worked for the doctor were so unsympathetic sometimes, she
thought crossly as she waited.

At last Dr. Ellerman came on the line. "Good afternoon,
Mrs. Lynde," he said cheerfully. "How are you feeling?"

"Terrible," she admitted. "Do you have the results of my
tests yet?"

"As a matter of fact, I have them right here in front of
me," he said. "As I assured you on Tuesday, there is nothing
seriously wrong with you."

"You said you thought it wasn't serious," she corrected
him.

"And I was right," he responded. "What is troubling you
is quite normal for a young, healthy woman such as yourself.
Mrs. Lynde, you are going to have a baby."

FIVE

New York City, May 1956. As he watched his daughter cross
the crowded restaurant to his table, Harrison Colby recalled
the last time Fran had asked to meet him for lunch. He hoped
she was not going to pressure him again to see to it that Jim
Lynde spent less time in Europe and more here in the States.
Fran knew the score, he thought resentfully. She had practically been raised to be a corporate wife. Her mother had been
a good influence on her—or so he had thought. But lately
Fran had seemed so unreasonable, so stubborn in her insis-
tence that he cut Jim's workload. In a way, Colby was worried
about his daughter, about her strange moods.

He stood up as she joined him at the table. She looked
more beautiful than he had seen her look in some time—
almost radiant. She was wearing a tailored white suit with a
wide-brimmed white summer hat, and the Burmese pearls
he'd given her years ago. She'd pulled her blond hair back
into a classic chignon, and her makeup was subdued, just
enough to enhance her natural beauty. She embraced him
gently before sitting down. "I'm glad you could make it on
such short notice, Daddy," she told him. "I know how busy
you are.".

He smiled and seated himself. "Never too busy to have

lunch with you, honey," he told her. "I think you know that."

"I got a letter from Kate last week," she told him.

"Oh?" He raised an eyebrow. "Is she still in Europe?"

Fran nodded. "She'll be coming home soon."

"I'm worried about her," Colby admitted.

His daughter looked surprised. "Why? Kate's a big girl," she reminded him. "She can take care of herself."

"I'd hoped she'd be married and settled down by now," Colby said, frowning. "Instead, she seems to be deliberately avoiding it."

"I think you're reading things into this that aren't there," Fran insisted.

"Maybe, but I'm not so sure."

"Have you heard from Jim?" she asked then.

"As a matter of fact, I have. He said he tried to phone you, but there was no answer," Colby told her. "Been out shopping?"

She shook her head. "I had a doctor's appointment."

"Aren't you feeling well?"

"I'm fine. As a matter of fact, I couldn't be better. I just had to have a checkup, that's all."

The waiter came to take their order. Colby asked for a second martini—he'd had one while waiting for Fran to arrive—but she declined to have anything. "No daiquiri?" her father asked, surprised.

"I don't think it's a good idea right now." Fran paused for a moment. "That's why I wanted to see you, Daddy. I'm going to have a baby."

Colby stared at her in disbelief. "You're really pregnant?" he asked. "Honey, that's the best news you could have given me! Does Jim know yet?"

She shook her head. "That's why I wanted to know if you'd heard from him. I was wondering if you knew when he's coming home." She hesitated for a moment. "I know he's been away for only four weeks, but it feels like months to me. First, he missed our anniversary—after all the plans I'd made to have a special celebration with him—then he had to go on to Paris from London. I know I'm supposed to understand these things, Daddy, but I just don't. Here he's going to be a father and he doesn't even know it yet. There are times I wonder if he'll see the baby before he graduates from college!''

"Frannie, we've been through this so many times before—''

"And you've always made the same excuses,'' Fran told him. "Daddy, I don't want to have this baby alone. I want Jim here with me. I want to know he's out in that waiting room, that he's going to be there when the nurse goes out to tell him if he has a son or a daughter. As busy as you've always been, you were there when Kate and I were born!''

"I know, honey,'' he agreed, "but this is different from politics. You know that.''

"I don't know what to think anymore, Daddy,'' she admitted. "Tell me something—does Jim really want to be home with me, or does he ask for all these overseas trips?''

"Frances! I think you know the answer to that without my having to tell you,'' he said, surprised by her question.

"Daddy, I'm scared,'' she admitted then. "I'm scared to have this baby alone. I'm scared, afraid that maybe Jim doesn't love me as much as he used to, that maybe I've let him down somehow as a wife. I try to tell myself that it's just a mood I'm in because I'm pregnant, but, to be honest, I felt this way long before I was pregnant.''

He reached across the table and patted her hand reassuringly. "Jim will be home in a couple of days. Wait and see. He'll be so thrilled about the baby that you won't be able to doubt his feelings for a minute. You know, women aren't the only ones who are affected emotionally by the birth of a child.''

"I hope you're right,'' she said, forcing a smile.

He looked at his daughter. "I know I am. You just wait and see, okay?''

Lynde had not been thrilled by the news of Fran's pregnancy, as Colby had predicted he would be. He had tried to sound enthusiastic when Fran broke her news to him, but she had sensed his ambivalence. "Don't you want a baby, Jim?'' she asked as they lay awake in the darkness that night.

"Sure, I do," he insisted. "Why would you ask a question like that?"

"I don't know. You just don't seem very happy about it, that's all," she said quietly.

"I'm just not very good at showing my feelings," he told her. "I've never been a father before. I don't know if I'll be any good with kids. It's a helluva big responsibility. But I'm happy about it, I really am."

"I know that. I just thought you'd be more pleased about it."

He leaned over in the darkness and kissed her. "I am happy about it," he said again. "Tell me . . . did the doctor say whether it would be okay to . . ." His voice trailed off as he slipped his hand under her nightgown and began stroking her breasts.

"He said it would be all right until about six to eight weeks before the baby is due—unless there are complications." Fran was not in the mood for sex—she was tired and deeply depressed by his reaction to her pregnancy—but she desperately needed to feel close to him in any way that she could. She lay back in the darkness, fighting the dark, unpleasant feelings that swept over her as he nuzzled her breasts. She felt his hand between her legs, touching her, and she tried to feel something, tried to get excited about his lovemaking. He was on top of her now, pulling her nightgown off, and she flinched as he launched himself into her. She tried to tell him that she was not ready, but he was inside her, taking her with an urgency that was completely unexpected.

She was glad he couldn't see her face in the darkness, couldn't see the tears in her eyes.

The baby was due in December, and the next six months seemed to be stretching on eternally for Fran Lynde. It seemed to her that Jim spent more time away from home than ever now, in spite of her pleading with him to stay, insisting that she needed him at home more than ever. Though he always brought gifts for the baby back with him from his trips, she was convinced that he did not really want this child, that he was only going through the motions, pretending something he did not really feel. *That's all right,* she told herself. *It doesn't matter anymore. I'll have my baby, and we will be happy together.*

She decorated the nursery in pink and blue, so that it would suit either a boy or a girl. She made several trips into Manhattan to select items for the layette, and on one of those trips, she purchased a silver spoon at Tiffany's. *Why not?* she thought as she paid for it. *I was born with that proverbial silver spoon—and now, so will my child.* She decided to have it engraved after the baby was born, with the child's name and birth date.

Lynde had shown no real interest in choosing a name for the baby, so Fran had made those choices without consulting him. The baby would be named James—after his father—if it were a boy, and Amanda if it were a girl. She had not chosen Amanda for any reason other than the fact that it was a lovely name and she had always liked it.

She wished she knew what names her husband preferred.

Lynde left for Rome on a Monday morning in July, promising to be home on Friday. He phoned Fran on Thursday. "Listen, honey, I really hate to disappoint you, but something's come up. I'm not going to be able to get away from here for at least another week."

"I understand, darling," she told him, fighting back tears. "We'll just make it an extra-special reunion when you do get home, all right?"

"It's a date."

He had phoned her from the Leonardo da Vinci Airport in Rome. Half an hour later, he boarded a commercial flight for Moscow.

He phoned her a week later. "I promise I'll be home tomorrow night without fail," he said apologetically. "Chill a bottle of Dom Perignon, and we'll have a real celebration—if you know what I mean."

He had called from Dulles Airport in Washington, where he had stopped over for a debriefing.

• • •

This was a pattern they were to follow for the duration of Fran's pregnancy. He was never home when she expected him. When he did come home, he was invariably gone again within a few days. *I feel like he's avoiding me,* Fran thought sullenly as she watched his plane take off for London, sitting in her car at the airport.

Fran's bouts of depression had worsened during her pregnancy. When she'd tried to discuss it with her doctor, he had informed her that there was really nothing he could give her, nothing he could prescribe to alleviate her symptoms. He explained that due to hormonal changes during pregnancy, childbearing women were often subject to moodiness and even severe depression. There was, he told her regretfully, nothing she could do but tolerate it until after her baby was born.

At a time that should have been the happiest of her life, Fran began to feel as though her whole world were crashing down around her. She felt alone and unloved, sure that her husband had abandoned her—at least emotionally, and physically to an extent—at a time when she needed him most. She was terrified that he would not return when the baby was due to arrive, that he would be off in some foreign country when she delivered their child. She was frightened at the prospect of having the baby alone, of not having her husband there to give her emotional support during what promised to be a most trying time in her life.

Fran often burst into tears without provocation, crying over what appeared to be nothing at all. She was given to outbursts of uncontrollable rage, often frightening her poor housekeeper, Sadie, to the point that Sadie had many times phoned Kate or Colleen Colby, asking that they drive out to Sound Beach to try to console Fran, to calm her down. Colleen was quick to blame Jim Lynde, though her husband insisted that Lynde was only doing his job when he was in Europe. It was not, Colby maintained, Jim Lynde's intention to desert his wife deliberately. He was merely doing what had to be done. Kate was concerned for her sister, suggesting again that it might be wise for Fran to consult a psychiatrist. She felt it might at least help Fran to come to grips with those irrational fears of hers, her suspicions that Jim was using his work to spend as much time as possible away from her.

They all would have been shocked if they had known what he was really doing in Europe.

Fran went into labor just after midnight on Thursday, December sixth. At first, she had been terrified. She called the only person she could think of who might be able to help her—her sister. "Katie, the pains have started," she said breathlessly into the telephone. "Jim's in Rome—I don't know what to do."

"Just take it easy," Kate told her. "I'm on my way. You call Dr. Ellerman—tell him I'll be bringing you to the hospital and that he can meet us there, okay?"

Fran nodded dumbly. "I'll call him," she said weakly.

Kate had arrived quickly. "I'm glad there were no police on the road between here and Shoreham," she said lightly as she carried Fran's suitcase downstairs. "I know I was going faster than the posted speed limit—much faster."

"Did you tell Mother and Daddy?" Fran wanted to know.

"Yes, I certainly did," Kate said, "and when I left, Daddy was on the phone trying to reach Jim in Rome."

"He's not due back until next week," Fran said darkly.

"Oh, I think he'll be back sooner than that—once he hears about the baby," Kate said confidently as she helped Fran into her car.

"I doubt it," Fran disagreed. "I don't think he wants this baby, Kate."

"Nonsense." Kate closed the door and hurried around to slide behind the steering wheel. "Even if he doesn't show much interest now, he's going to change the minute they put that baby in his arms. You'll see."

"Jim's not like other men," Fran insisted. "He's not quick to show what he feels."

"He always was with you—wasn't he?" Kate asked as she started the engine.

"I always thought so. But you know, I realized that he's never even talked to me about his family. He's never told me anything about them, how he feels about them, if any of them are still alive—''

''Maybe there's nothing to tell,'' Kate offered.

Fran gave her a puzzled look.

''Well, you said he doesn't get along with them. Except for that uncle who showed up at your wedding, of course. Maybe he just wants to forget about them.''

''Maybe,'' Fran said sullenly. ''I just wish I knew what he was really feeling.''

Fran was in labor almost fourteen hours. At one forty-five that afternoon, she gave birth to a seven-pound, three-ounce baby girl who entered the world screaming with rage and immediately tried to ram her tiny fist down her own throat. ''She's hungry,'' Kate told the nurse in the newborn nursery.

''Oh, no, that's not possible,'' the nurse insisted. ''Newborn infants are not hungry for at least six hours after birth.''

Kate grinned mischievously. ''Tell *her* that. My niece is hungry.''

Fran was allowed to hold her daughter for the first time late that evening. Though she had planned to name the baby Amanda, it had taken only one look at the baby to change her mind. ''She looks exactly like Jim,'' she said as she gazed into the tiny face.

''She certainly does,'' Kate agreed.

Fran stared at the infant for a long moment. ''I'm going to name her after Jim,'' she said finally.

Kate looked at her. ''Jimmy?'' she asked dumbly.

''No,'' Fran said, smiling. ''Jaime. Jaime Victoria Lynde.''

Harrison Colby met Lynde at the airport and drove him out to the hospital. ''I'm glad you could get an early flight, Jim,'' Colby told him. ''You know how jumpy Fran's been lately. She was convinced that you would not come back until next week, that you had no interest at all in the baby.''

''That's nonsense,'' Lynde snorted. ''I've tried to talk to her, tried to make her see that this is not something I want to do—especially at a time like this. I've talked with her doctor. He tells me that this is one of the hazards of pregnancy, that it happens more often than he would like. I just don't know what else I can do—unless I leave the firm and take a position that would enable me to keep regular hours and be home every night.''

"I don't think that's going to be necessary, Jim," Colby said confidently. "Now that the baby is here, Fran's going to be more content to stay at home and play the little mother. Take my word for it. Nobody could be less domestic than Colleen—but she was a real mother hen with both of the girls.''

"Maybe once she's back to normal—physically, I mean—her depression will vanish," Lynde thought aloud. "Dr. Ellerman said he thought it was hormone-related.''

"She's going to be fine, Jim. You'll see.''

Fran was resting when Lynde arrived at the hospital. He bent over and kissed her lightly on the forehead, and she opened her eyes. "Jim . . . I didn't think you'd be home until—"

He grinned. "And miss the birth of my first child?" he asked, forcing an enthusiasm into his voice that he didn't really feel. "Nothing could have kept me away." *Nothing short of the KGB,* he thought dismally.

"Have you seen her yet?" Fran wanted to know.

Lynde shook his head. " I just got here. Your father picked me up at the airport.''

"She looks just like you. In miniature. I hope you don't mind—I've decided to name her after you. Jaime Victoria. How does that sound?" she asked anxiously.

"It sounds wonderful," he told her. "I'm flattered.''

"She *is* your daughter, after all, and she *does* look like you," Fran said.

He stroked her hair lightly. "That bad, huh?''

"Worse," Fran said with a smile. "Kate says she was screaming her little lungs out the first time she saw her. And she was born hungry.''

He grinned. "That's my kid, all right.''

A nurse came to the door then. "Mrs. Lynde, they'll be

bringing the baby in to nurse soon.'' She looked at Lynde. ''This is your husband?''

Fran smiled. ''Yes.''

''Well, Mr. Lynde, if you want to stay, you'll have to put on a gown and a surgical mask. It's hospital regulations, I'm afraid,'' she told him almost apologetically.

''That's all right—I can wait outside until after—'' Lynde began.

''Oh, no—you'll do nothing of the kind!'' Fran said quickly. ''You might as well start getting to know your daughter right now.'' She turned to the nurse. ''Bring him the gown and mask.''

''Yes, ma'am.''

Lynde felt ridiculous in the surgical mask and baggy gown that tied in the back, but he was trying to keep Fran happy. He'd hold the baby, if that's what she wanted, anything to keep her happy right now. He just hoped he didn't drop the kid. Babies made him nervous.

Fifteen minutes later a nurse appeared, carrying a small bundle wrapped in a soft pink blanket. She placed the baby in Fran's arms, then turned to Lynde. ''I can see who she takes after,'' she said lightly.

Lynde grinned nervously. ''So I've been told.''

Fran beckoned him to her side. She pulled back the blanket so that he could see the baby's face. *By God,* he thought, *she really does look like me.* ''Can I hold her?'' he heard himself asking.

''Of course.'' Fran lifted the infant into his arms, showing him how to use his hands to support her neck and bottom. ''Don't worry,'' she told him. ''She's not going to break. She's a lot stronger than she looks—and remember, she's going to outlive both of us.''

Lynde was no longer listening. He was staring into that incredible, tiny face as it gazed up at him in absolute trust. She had his face, a strong, fine face. She had his eyes, those dark green eyes that looked like the darkest part of a pine forest. And the hair. Her small head was covered with dark red curls, the exact color of his own hair. Until now, until this very moment, James Lynde had never given a thought to his own mortality, to the notion of having someone to carry on the line. He had never cared about having a family, having children of his own. But now as he looked down at his new-born daughter, he was overcome by a tidal wave of emotion that threatened to engulf him. He was taken by surprise by the force of his own love, a love he had never known he was capable of feeling. Everything that had been locked up within his soul for so many years was released now, as he held his baby in his arms. For one moment, the rest of the world ceased to exist, Fran, the Colbys, the staff of the hospital, Harry Warner, the CIA, the KGB. Nothing existed for him but the tiny girl he held in his arms so gently. He wanted to never let her go.

Jaime, he thought, *how can I ever tell you how much I really do love you?*

SIX

Sound Beach, Long Island, June 1962. Lynde stood at the window in his study, watching Jaime playing with one of the neighborhood children out in the front yard. He smiled to himself. His daughter was a wonder. An absolute wonder. At five and a half she was tall for her age, a loud, boisterous child, tough and fearless. It was a damn good thing, too, he thought now as he watched her. She was pretty much an outcast among the little girls of her own age, much the same as he himself had been an outcast as a child. Since her mother showed little interest in instructing her in things of a feminine nature, she had no idea how little girls were supposed to act. Or the way society decreed they should act, anyway. Fran's growing indifference toward her own child—which had increased with the passing of each year—had caused Jaime to turn to him as a role model. She was a real tomboy, wearing her dark red hair in pigtails most of the time, and blue jeans and corduroy pants instead of the frilly dresses she dismissed as "silly stuff." She climbed trees and played softball and often carried a slingshot in her back pocket. The kid was a deadeye shot with that thing, Lynde thought, amused. He chuckled softly to himself. By the time she was in her teens, she'd probably be yelling her head off for her own gun. And he'd probably buy it for her.

Lynde shook his head and went back to his desk. It was funny, the unexpected way Jaime had so drastically changed his life in the few short years she'd been a part of it. He, who had never wanted children, never needed any assurance of his own immortality. He who had never thought himself capable of being the traditional family man was hopelessly in love with his own daughter. His child. That small, feminine replica of himself who could not possibly be more like him if she *had* been a boy. Bright, beautiful, fiercely stubborn Jaime, who'd stirred feelings deep within the wellspring of his soul—feelings he hadn't known he could have, prior to her birth.

He'd spent more and more time at home since Jaime's birth. When she was four months old, he'd demanded—and was granted—a considerable reduction in his workload for the Company, as it was called by insiders. He hadn't been home to see her take those first precious steps or speak her first words, but he *had* been able to spend quality time with her and to establish a close relationship. The bond between them was strong, stronger than that of most fathers and daughters. He and Jaime shared a special relationship that excluded family, friends—even Fran.

Lynde looked at the brass-framed photograph of his wife on the desk. Fran was still pretty, in a bland kind of way. She was physically attractive, but she lacked sparkle. He picked up the picture and stared at it for a long time. Her soft blond hair was cut in a bouffant style, her blue suit and pillbox hat an attempt at emulating First Lady Jackie Kennedy. She could have been beautiful. Trouble was, there was no life left in her. No spirit. None of the spunk their daughter had apparently inherited from him. He frowned. Fran had always complained that he'd been away too much, yet now that he was spending more time at home, she seemed more withdrawn than ever. She'd lost interest in her home, her painting, even in the daughter she'd wanted so passionately at first.

At first. He replaced the photograph on the corner of the

desk. When they brought Jaime home from the hospital, motherhood had been the only thing that mattered to Fran. For the first three years she'd been a doting mother. Nothing was too much where her daughter was concerned. The change in her had been so gradual that Lynde had not been aware of it at first. *I wasn't really paying attention,* he admitted. *I never did pay a hell of a lot of attention to Fran's moods.* But now it was impossible to ignore. Fran spent most of her time locked away in her bedroom, reading romantic novels like *Wuthering Heights* and *Gone With the Wind.* She daydreamed. And she became more and more depressed with each passing day.

How much of it is my fault? Lynde asked himself now. He'd married her not out of love, but out of necessity. He'd married her knowing how much *she* loved *him,* because it was necessary. Unfortunately, his feelings for his wife hadn't changed in the past six years, but he *had* mellowed somewhat. He'd learned compassion. He was no longer totally indifferent to her feelings and needs, but—

The sound of his daughter's voice raised in anger cut through his thoughts. Rising from his chair abruptly, he hurried to the window. Out in the yard, Jaime was fighting— physically assaulting—the boy she'd been playing with only an hour earlier. She had him down on the ground, straddling him as she pummeled him fiercely with her small fists. "Jaime!" Lynde called out to her. When she didn't respond, he half ran through the entrance hall and out onto the front steps. "Jaime!" he called out to her again, leaning over the balustrade. "Jaime—stop that this minute!"

Jaime looked up. When she saw her father, she scrambled to her feet quickly. The boy got up and scurried away. Realizing he was making his escape, Jaime whirled around and shook her fist at him angrily. "Show your face around here again and I'll kick you in the balls, you louse!" she screeched.

"Jaime!" her father called to her again, shocked by her language and violent behavior. "That's quite enough!"

She turned to face him again, shoving her hands down in the pockets of her torn, dirty overalls. Her green eyes were blazing with anger, but she kept it in check. Her left cheek was smudged with dirt, and one of the ribbons that normally was tied at the end of her pigtails was missing. The dark red hair spilled aimlessly down over her neck. "What did you do that for?" she asked as he came down the steps to get her. "I was beating him."

He smiled as he knelt down in front of her, taking his handkerchief from his pocket. "So you were," he chuckled, as he wiped her cheek gently. "You did give him a rough way to go, didn't you?" He was trying not to smile; it would only encourage such behavior on her part.

"I sure did," Jaime responded with an emphatic nod. "I would've won too, if you didn't scare him away!"

He laughed. "I don't doubt it for a minute, princess," he said as he scooped her up in his arms. "Still, you can't go on beating up every boy in the neighborhood."

Jaime drew back and looked at him, her small face dark with anger. "Why not?" she wanted to know. "I can fight any of them—and they all know it!"

"That's not what I meant," he said, rumpling her hair. "It's not very ladylike, you know."

She wrinkled her nose disdainfully. "You mean sissylike," she defined.

"Call it whatever you like," he said as he carried her up the steps easily in one arm and pushed the front door open. "You are *not* going to grow up to be a proper young lady at this rate."

"I don't want to be a lady," she said promptly. "I want to be like you." Her grin was mischievous.

"God forbid!" Lynde laughed aloud at the thought.

"That's what I want," she insisted.

"No, you *don't*," he assured her as he put her down on the floor in the entrance hall. "You're a girl—and I mean to see to it that you grow up right. And while we're on the subject, wherever did you pick up those words?"

"What words, Daddy?" she asked.

"You know perfectly well what words—what you said to Tommy about where you were going to kick him." He'd tried never to use vulgar language in front of his daughter, and now he was oddly uncomfortable discussing it with her.

"Oh, *that*."

"Yes, that." Lynde looked down at her disapprovingly.

She made a face. "I hear those words all the time," she confessed.

"Where?" he pursued.

She avoided his eyes, realizing he was angry. "Down at the stables," she finally admitted.

"They talk like that in front of you?" His first impulse was to immediately fire every stable boy in his employ.

Jaime shook her head. "Oh, no—but I hear them anyway, when they think I'm not around." She grinned. "I hear a lot of things when people think I'm not around."

"Like what?" her father wanted to know.

"Lots of things."

Lynde laughed. "I feel sorry for the man you marry, princess," he told her. "I have a feeling you're going to be a handful for any man."

Jaime giggled.

He straightened up. "Sadie!" he called out loudly. "Sadie!"

"Yes, sir?" The heavyset, gray-haired housekeeper appeared at the top of the stairs.

"Where's Mrs. Lynde?" he wanted to know.

The woman frowned. "I believe she's in her room, sir," she replied.

As usual, Lynde thought. *Why do I even bother to ask?* "Sadie, would you take Jaime upstairs and clean her up?" he asked. "I'm afraid she's had a little accident."

"Again, sir?" The older woman sniffed. "This is the fourth time today. I'm not sure she has anything clean left to wear."

"Well, look, will you?" he asked irritably, still annoyed at Fran for never being around for their daughter.

"Yes, sir," she said with a heavy sigh. "Come along, Jaime."

As he watched his daughter bound up the stairs, Lynde was filled with a growing concern for her welfare. Sadie did what she could, of course, but she was far too stern with the child. Too stiff and formal. *Dammit,* he thought resentfully. *The kid needs her mother!*

What the hell was wrong with Fran?

Fran Lynde sat at the dressing table in her bedroom brushing her hair, mentally counting the strokes. Her husband sat on the edge of the bed, taking off his shoes. "I think it would be a good idea if you spent more time with Jaime," he said. "She needs a woman's hand—a mother's influence."

"What would she need me for?" Fran asked coldly, not missing a stroke. "She's your daughter. Just ask her."

Lynde stopped what he was doing and turned to look at her, but she kept her back to him, still staring into the mirror. "Now what the hell is *that* supposed to mean?" he wanted to know, not bothering to conceal his annoyance with her.

"Exactly what I said." Fran's tone was indifferent. "She's your daughter. She's just like you. She doesn't need me—she doesn't need anyone."

"The hell she doesn't!" Lynde shot to his feet, tearing off his shirt. "Did you know she got into another fight today? Do you even care?"

"From what I hear, she's perfectly capable of taking care of herself." Having achieved the mandatory one hundred strokes, Fran put down the brush but still did not face him.

"She has to be—she certainly can't depend on you!" Lynde snapped, struggling to control his anger. He'd never struck a woman before, but at that moment he felt dangerously close to hitting his own wife. "Do you have any idea what you're doing to that child by turning your back on her the way you have? She always plays with boys—never girls her own age. She gets into fights just about every day. She's been hanging around the stables—you should hear the language she's using."

Fran shifted around on her rose-colored velvet stool, facing him at last. "She doesn't *want* my guidance or help, Jim," she said evenly. "She doesn't want any part of me. She wants you—and she resents anyone who intrudes on her time with you."

Lynde looked at her, unable to believe what he was hearing. "Good God, Fran, you sound as if you actually hate her! She's just a child—*your* child!" Disgusted with his wife's attitude, he shook his head angrily. Dismissing her with a wave of his hand, he stalked into the bathroom and slammed the door, a pointed reminder of his displeasure.

Fran drew in her breath and stared at her reflection in the mirror for a long moment. If there was anything that could arouse her husband's anger, it was the idea of *anyone* slighting his precious daughter. But, Fran thought, Jim had enough interest in Jaime for both of them. The child was his life—or at least it seemed that way to Fran now. Until Jaime was born, Jim had used any excuse to stay away from home. Away from her. She'd believed that giving him a baby would change that, and she'd been right. Now he hated to leave at all, but when he *was* home, every free moment was devoted to Jaime. He still didn't have time for anyone else. *Everything is always for Jaime,* Fran thought resentfully. *Jaime is all that matters to him.*

Good God, she thought as the realization hit her. *I'm jealous of my own daughter!*

Lynde looked across the dinner table at his wife as Jaime, too excited to eat, babbled on happily about her riding lesson that had taken place earlier that day. Fran did not look up from her plate, but she was not eating. She distractedly pushed the food around on the plate with her fork, as though her thoughts were somewhere else.

". . . And Hank says I can already ride better than any of the boys in the class," Jaime chirped, pausing just long enough to take a long swallow of her milk. "He's going to let me jump next week." She turned to Lynde, her green eyes aglow with excitement. "Can you come and watch, Daddy?"

He grinned. "I wouldn't miss it for the world, princess," he assured her. He glanced at Fran, who was still looking down at her plate. "Your first jump—that's quite an accomplishment!" he praised his daughter.

"Damned right it is!" Jaime agreed enthusiastically.

"Jaime!" Lynde looked at her disapprovingly.

She ducked her head slightly. "Sorry, Daddy."

"I think," he began as he rose from his chair, "that a girl's first jump is something of a milestone, don't you?" His eyes moved from Fran, who did not respond at all, to Jaime, who nodded emphatically. "I do believe an award is in order here."

"An award?" Jaime looked at him, her expression one of confusion. "But, Daddy—you didn't even know about the jump until just now!"

He laughed heartily. "You don't miss a move, do you, princess?" he asked as he picked up a large package wrapped in white tissue paper and tied with a wide red satin ribbon. He handed it to Jaime, who looked up at him questioningly.

"What is it, Daddy?"

"I suggest you open it and find out."

She tore at the delicate wrapping in the same enthusiastic manner with which she did everything, ripping it to shreds. When the paper was lying on the carpet at her feet in a mountain of torn fragments, she pulled the box open and let out a delighted gasp. Inside was a girl's riding habit, white breeches with a black jacket and cap. "I believe that's the one you admired the last time I took you into Manhattan," her father recalled with a smile.

"Oh, it *is*, Daddy, it is!" She jumped up and gave him a bear hug. "Can I try it on now, please?"

"May I," Lynde corrected.

"Yes, yes." Jaime nodded impatiently. "Can I?"

He smiled. "If it is all right with your mother," he said agreeably, attempting to draw Fran into the conversation.

Jaime looked at her mother, her expression eager. "Is it all right, Mother?" she asked.

Fran looked at the child dispassionately. "I would think that whatever you want to do is all right with your father," she said quietly.

"Goody!" Jaime moved away from the table with such force that she nearly knocked over her chair. She ran for the door, clutching the box in her arms, the riding habit half hanging out of it.

"Get Sadie to help you, princess," Lynde called after her.

"Okay, Daddy!" As she clomped up the stairs, she called out loudly, "Sadie! Get your ass up here on the double!"

"Jaime!" her father called out warningly.

"Sorry, Daddy!"

Lynde turned to his wife when he was sure Jaime was out of earshot. "That was uncalled for," he said angrily.

"What was, darling?" Fran asked pleasantly, avoiding his eyes. She picked up her glass of wine and sipped it slowly.

"The way you spoke to Jaime just now," he said tightly. "How can you be so goddamned cold and unfeeling?"

She looked at him blankly. "It's quite simple, my dear husband," she answered tonelessly. "I learned from a master—you."

His jaw tightened visibly. "Whatever beef you have against me, don't take it out on her, dammit!" he snapped.

Fran's blue eyes blazed with anger, the first show of emotion she'd displayed in a long time. "God forbid!" she shot back at him. "You've all but put that child on a pedestal! Nothing matters to you but Jaime! In all the years we've been married, you've done everything you could to keep from spending any time with me, but now that you have your precious daughter—" She began to sob openly. "God, you make me sick!" She threw down her napkin and jumped to her feet, glaring at him momentarily before she ran out of the room.

Lynde shook his head and drew in a deep breath. What was wrong with her? he asked himself, not for the first time. There were times he had the feeling she actually hated her own child! He frowned. He was going to have to have a talk with Harrison Colby, and do it soon. Fran most certainly needed professional counseling. Maybe a psychiatrist. . . .

"Daddy—how do I look?"

Lynde's head jerked up. Jaime stood in the doorway in her new riding habit. Her hair was pulled back and tied with an emerald-green ribbon at the nape of her neck. A few escaped curls framed her vibrant, excited face in a red glow beneath the black cap she wore. Around her neck was a green silk ascot matching the ribbon in her hair, secured with a small gold stickpin. Her black riding boots were polished to perfection, no doubt thanks to Sadie's meticulous care.

"You look real pretty," he told her. "Every inch the accomplished horsewoman."

She twirled around once so he could see from all angles. "Do you really think so, Daddy?"

"Would I lie to you?"

She smiled, buoyed by his compliment. "No, I guess not." She looked around. "Where's Mother?"

He hesitated for a moment. "She's not feeling well, princess," he said finally. "She went upstairs to lie down."

Jaime frowned. "Mother's sick a lot, isn't she?" she asked, her tone grave.

Lynde nodded. "Yeah, hon. She is." He extended his arms to her. She perched on his knee and hugged him tightly. "I'm sorry, baby," he whispered, holding her close.

I'm sorry Fran can't be the mother you need, he thought.

As the seasons melted into one another and summer turned into autumn, Fran Lynde slipped deeper and deeper into depression. She slept fitfully, ate barely enough to keep a small animal alive, and rarely emerged from her bedroom. When she did eat, she had Sadie bring a tray to her room, never joining her husband and daughter in the dining room. By the end of August, Lynde had moved out of the master bedroom and set up camp in one of the guest rooms. By early October, Fran had lost twenty pounds from her already thin frame. Her clothes hung on her body much the same way they hung on the wooden hangers in her closets. She drank too much and was dependent upon prescription drugs. Lynde had given up on her, on ever reconciling her with Jaime. He no longer questioned her lack of interest in their young daughter or even tried to make conversation with her. Fran's mother, father, and sister all tried to convince her to seek professional help, and they all failed.

Why couldn't they understand that she only wanted to be left alone? she wondered. A psychiatrist couldn't help her—no one could. Except perhaps Jim. But she'd given up on her husband a long time ago. He wasn't capable—or willing—to give her what she wanted, what she needed to be happy. Fran started to cry. All she'd ever wanted was his love. Hadn't she tried to be a good wife? Hadn't she given him what he wanted in a woman? Where had she failed?

Fran had realized too late that her husband had never really loved her. She was convinced now that he'd married her only to gain the favor of her father, to ensure his position within the Colby investment firm. In the beginning, he'd tried to put up a good front, to keep anyone from suspecting the truth about their marriage, but since Jaime was born, he no longer bothered.

Jaime. Jaime was all in the world that mattered to Jim. He adored her. Fran shook her head. And she'd been afraid he wouldn't *want* a child! The birth of their daughter had given Jim an incentive to spend more time at home, but it had done nothing for their marriage, as Fran had hoped it would. It had driven them even farther apart, if indeed that were possible. She didn't exist for Jim anymore. Only Jaime. *If I were to die tomorrow,* Fran thought dismally, *my own husband would not care. Nor would my daughter.*

If I were to die. Fran thought about it. She did wish she were dead. Surely death could not be worse than her present existence. It had to be better, in fact, than a loveless marriage and the realization that she was unable to love her own child. Jaime didn't need her. In fact, Fran had the feeling that her daughter would actually be happier without her. Jaime cared only for her father. She would be perfectly happy to have him all to herself. They would *both* be happier without me, Fran decided.

She looked at the antique mantle clock on the corner of her dressing table. Today was Sadie's day off. She was all alone in the house. Jim had taken Jaime to a horse show. Since Jaime's love affair with horses had begun, they were at horse shows just about every weekend. They both carried on about that pony Jim had bought for her as if the animal were Man O'War himself! They'd be gone all afternoon. She'd have plenty of time to do it. It was, she decided, the only way.

She went to her closets and selected her most stunning dress. *How long has it been since I cared how I looked?* she asked herself as she stared at the dress speculatively. *But then, I must look my best—after all, this is a special occasion, something that happens to a person just once.* She fingered the blue silk lovingly. Sebastian had designed it for her trousseau. How long had it been since she'd worn it? She couldn't remember. She put the dress on the bed and selected the right accessories—shoes, stockings, earrings, pearls—with the same care with which she'd chosen the dress. After she dressed, she did her hair and makeup carefully, as if she were going to a party. *In a way,* she thought, *I am. My going-away party.* She stared at the solemn face looking back at her from the mirror. *No wonder he doesn't love you,* she thought with disgust. *You're nothing more than a pale reflection of a woman.*

Taking her handbag, she descended the stairs purposefully and went out to the garage, where her blue Cadillac had been parked, untouched, for the past six months. She wondered if there was enough gas in the tank. Closing the garage door tightly, she got in the car and took out her keys. Slipping the car key into the ignition she listened for the low hum of the engine. *This shouldn't take long,* she thought.

Then she laid her head back and took a deep breath, praying it would all be over quickly.

"Oh, Daddy, I can't wait until I can jump Cristobal in competition!" Jaime said gaily as Lynde drove along Long Island Sound, headed for home. "It's going to be so much fun! You will be there, won't you—for all the shows, I mean?"

"I'll be there when I can, princess," her father promised. "You know I'm not always home when there's a show—"

"I know," Jaime acknowledged with a nod—and a touch of regret. "But when you're home—you'll be there when you're home, won't you?"

He smiled. "Absolutely." She was so keyed up she probably wouldn't sleep for a month, he thought with amusement. She looked like an angel one minute and a little devil the next, with her fiery red hair spilling about her small face and her wicked green eyes, bright with excitement as she clutched the blue ribbon she'd won that afternoon.

"What about Mother?" Jaime asked, interrupting his thoughts. "Do you think she'll come too?"

Lynde frowned. As bad as the situation had become, Jaime had never quite given up on Fran. She was still reaching out to her mother. "I don't think so, princess," he answered, refusing to hold out false hope. Why did Fran have to be so distant with her? he wondered bitterly. Jaime needed a mother—and Fran was like a total stranger to her. As Jaime grew older, she and Fran grew farther and farther apart. Their relationship was now virtually nonexistent, in spite of Jaime's overtures.

As he turned the car into the entrance to their property and headed up the long drive, he noticed the garage door was closed. He'd left it open that morning. Or had he? *Maybe I'm mistaken,* he thought, unconcerned. He parked in front of the house and took Jaime inside. "Run upstairs and change your clothes," he told her. "I'll take Cristobal down to the stables."

"Okay, Daddy." She kissed his cheek and dashed up the stairs, clutching the blue ribbon in her left hand. She'd probably try to show it to Fran, he thought as he turned to the door. *She'd be better off if she'd just give up on her mother.*

As he started down the steps to get back in the car, he thought he could hear a motor running in the garage. He paused to listen for a moment. It *was* a motor running. He ran the ten yards to the garage and forced the heavy door open. When he saw Fran's car, its engine running, when the fumes pouring from the garage threatened to overcome him, he was hit by the realization of what had happened—or, more accurately, what his deeply troubled wife had done. Pulling his handkerchief from his pocket, he clamped it over the lower half of his face and ran inside. The smoke from the Cadillac's exhaust was so thick he could barely see where he was going. He pulled Fran from the car and dragged her outside into the fresh air. Stretching her out on the grass, he slapped her face twice in an attempt to revive her, but there was no response. She didn't appear to be breathing. He checked her pulse and heartbeat. Nothing. *Good God,* he thought. *She's dead!*

"*Mommy!*"

Lynde's head jerked up. Jaime was standing only a few feet away, clutching the blue ribbon to her chest, her small face white with shock. "Go back to the house, Jaime—now!" he ordered sharply. *She shouldn't be here. She shouldn't see this.*

"What's wrong with Mother?" Jaime demanded, coming closer. Her lower lip trembled, and she was dangerously close to tears. "Why doesn't she wake up?"

Lynde didn't respond, because he couldn't. How could he tell her her mother was dead?

SEVEN

Washington, D.C., April 1966. "Look—I understand what you're saying, Harry. And I agree. One hundred percent. What I *don't* understand is why you seem to think *I'm* the only one who can get into Moscow." Lynde was leaning against the windowsill in Harry Warner's office, the unobstructed view of the Capitol Building providing a striking backdrop behind him. "What about Lew Baldwin or Allen Harris?"

Warner shook his head emphatically. "No one knows the city—or the people—like you do, Jim," he pointed out, pausing to light his pipe.

"Know it?" Lynde laughed aloud at the understatement. "It was my other home for the better part of five years."

"At your request," Warner reminded him.

"At my request," Lynde acknowledged with a nod.

Warner got to his feet. "As I recall, you preferred Moscow to spending time at home—with your wife." He poured two cups of coffee from the pot perched on a hot plate on the credenza behind his desk.

Lynde took the cup his colleague offered him. "A marriage made for the purpose of creating a cover," he said grimly. "What did you expect—hearts and flowers?"

"But the kid's a different story, right?" Warner concluded.

Lynde's jaw tightened visibly. "My daughter needs me more than ever, Harry," he said finally. "Fran's suicide was traumatic for her. She's a tough little kid—but I know she's hurting inside. Even while Fran was alive, Jaime didn't really have a mother in her life—but now that she's dead . . ." His voice trailed off.

"I understand your concern for your daughter," Warner said carefully, "but you *do* have a job to do."

Lynde rolled his eyes upward. "How well I know that," he said, his voice edged with sarcasm.

"You have a housekeeper, don't you?"

Lynde sipped the hot coffee, then put the cup aside. "Yeah," he said finally. "But Sadie's getting on in years— and Jaime would be a handful, even for a young, physically active woman."

"Hire a governess," Warner suggested. "Someone with references, someone who's good with kids—"

"She needs a father, Harry. She needs *me*," Lynde said sharply. "She needs to know she has at least one parent who cares! A nanny's not the same thing as a father or mother— believe me, I know!" He knew only too well. His own earliest memories were not of a mother who tucked him into bed at night and read him bedtime stories, or a father who taught him to play ball and carried him on his shoulders. No . . . *his* childhood memories were of a nanny who was good to him but hardly an acceptable replacement for a real mother, of the disembodied voices of his parents on the telephone, calling him from some exotic locale on all of those birthdays and holidays they missed while he was growing up. It wasn't the kind of life he wanted for his daughter.

"What about her grandparents—or your sister-in-law?" Warner pursued.

Lynde shook his head. "Colleen Colby still blames me for Fran's suicide. I'm not about to leave Jaime with her for any length of time, even though I still count her husband among the few people I consider friends. As for Kate, she's married now—to Senator Craig Pearson. She lives here in Washington and has a pretty busy life of her own."

"What about your family?"

Lynde frowned. "You know better than that." He paused, glancing at his watch. "You'll have to excuse me, Harry. I have a plane to catch and a daughter who's expecting me there by bedtime." He grabbed his coat and walked out, resolving nothing.

After Lynde was gone, Warner thought about it. He'd always respected Jim Lynde, even if he hadn't always liked the man. He was a tough nut to crack, cold, unemotional, a hard man to get close to. One never knew what he was thinking or feeling. There had been times over the years when Warner had wondered if he was capable of feeling anything for anyone. He always put his personal concerns aside, because in the end only one thing mattered. Lynde had been one of the best—if not *the* best—operatives to come out of the OSS training camps. He'd always done whatever had to be done without question. But now, fatherhood had changed him. Having a daughter had made him soft.

But as always, Harry Warner knew he would be able to deal with it.

Lynde thought about it on the plane flying back to New York that afternoon. In the three years since Fran's death, he'd become increasingly aware of the problems of raising a little girl without a mother. Though Fran had virtually ignored Jaime while she was alive, it *had* been different. She had been there, in body if not in spirit. By killing herself, Fran had dealt Jaime a blow from which the child was still reeling. Jaime had changed so much over the past few years. She was still a bright, active, and fiercely outspoken little girl, but she was emotionally isolated, as though she were afraid to let herself care for anyone or anything for fear of being rejected. Like father, like daughter, Lynde thought ruefully.

It brought back memories, memories he would have rather left buried. Memories of his own parents, world-renowned archaeologists who'd spent their lives trekking around the globe in search of those fabulous discoveries that got their names and photographs in newspapers and scientific journals all over the world. In fact, he'd seen his parents' faces more often in print than in person while he was growing up. He had a scrapbook full of photos, clippings, and postcards, a bundle of hastily written letters—usually apologies for not having made it home when promised; not once did they ask how he was or what he was doing in school—and an assortment of exotic gifts that had never interested the boy who had only wanted his parents to come home, even for a little while.

He remembered how disappointed he had been, waiting for them to return from one of their journeys, only to learn at the last minute that they wouldn't be coming after all. He remembered how, as he grew older, his loneliness and disappointment had turned to resentment and rebelliousness. He remembered the anger he'd felt when he was told they were dead, killed in a cave-in at an excavation site in Egypt. He remembered how he had hated them for dying, for not coming home as they'd promised they would. And he realized how his daughter must have felt when Fran took her own life.

But he'd always believed that he was as much to blame for Jaime's undisciplined rebelliousness as Fran had been. He was so seldom there for his daughter when she needed him, and now it looked as though he'd be spending more time than ever abroad. Even with a competent governess, he felt Jaime would be growing up without direction and, more important, without the emotional attachments she needed so badly at this point in her life. *Who am I trying to kid?* he asked himself. Try as he had in the past, he'd discovered he was not much of a disciplinarian when it came to Jaime. He'd tried to be firm with her because he knew she needed it, but in the end he'd never been able to deny her anything. Unfortunately, his weakness was doing Jaime more harm than good.

He knew Jaime was not deliberately mischievous; she was just spirited. She had an abundance of energy and a natural inquisitiveness that made it difficult for her to contain her inordinate curiosity about everything around her. Though he hadn't mentioned it to Harry Warner, the truth was that he had not been able to keep a governess in the past three years—though he'd certainly tried. Six of them had come and gone within eighteen months, and their parting tales were always the same: they adored Jaime, she was a delightful child, and he was not a difficult employer. The girl was simply too much for them. Even Sadie, who'd been a part of the Lynde household before Jaime was born, had lately begun to voice complaints. Not that he blamed her; Sadie was getting old, and Jaime was getting harder and harder to pin down.

"Thank you, no." He waved off the stewardess offering him a drink. Glancing through the window to his left, he could see the familiar skyscrapers of Manhattan below.

By the time his plane landed at La Guardia he'd come up with a solution to his problem.

"But *why*, Daddy?" Jaime looked up at him, her green eyes pleading. "Why?"

Lynde was determined to be firm with her this time. It was for her own good, he reminded himself as he felt himself begin to weaken. "Because this is what's best for you, princess," he told her. "You need to be with girls your own age. You need to learn to be a little lady."

"Bullshit!"

"That's exactly the kind of thing I'm talking about," he said, trying to sound stern. "The fighting and the language you use are deplorable."

"If I stop cursing and fighting, can we forget this?" She was trying to bargain with him now.

He forced himself not to smile. "I'm afraid not," he said, shaking his head. "You know I have to be away from you sometimes. This way you won't have to be alone."

"But a boarding school!" Jaime wailed. "They're so— yukky!"

"How do you know?" Lynde challenged. "To my knowledge, you've never even been inside one."

"And I don't want to be." Jaime shoved her hands down into the pockets of her jeans, as she always did when she was either frustrated or angry.

"It's not so bad," her father insisted.

"The hell it isn't!" Jamie snapped. "All those boring girls in their stupid sweater sets and plaid skirts and their prissy manners—"

"You could do with some of those prissy manners," Lynde pointed out.

"Shit!" Jaime snorted.

He looked at her disapprovingly. "That's something I'm hoping the ladies at Briar Ridge will change," he said evenly. "Your language, princess, is worse than any sailor's."

She looked up at him beseechingly. "I want to stay here, Daddy," she said softly. "I want to be with you—and Sadie, even if she is a pain sometimes."

"Sadie's too old to give you the kind of looking after you need, and you know perfectly well I'm only here half the time," he pointed out. "This, in my opinion, is what's best for you—and for once I'm not going to let you talk me out of it."

"But, Daddy—" She was near tears.

"No buts," he said with a shake of his head. "I want you to grow up properly, princess—no matter what."

The Briar Ridge School for Girls, located in a small, picturesque community near Greenwich, Connecticut, was considered one of the finest private schools in all of New England, and its alumnae had included the wives and daughters of prominent Social Register families, politicians, and entertainers. On the outside, it looked like a fine old Georgian mansion set back from the main road on five acres of rolling green lawns, but inside it was clearly a school despite the elegant trappings. The staff was housed on the first floor and had its offices there as well, while the second floor served as a dormitory for the students, with two or more girls between the ages of six and thirteen sharing each of the bedroom suites. One entire wing accommodated the classrooms. The gymnasium, dance studio, and stables occupied separate buildings on the grounds behind the main building. The instructors were polished, intelligent, well-bred women who all took a firm approach to teaching.

Jaime hated it instantly, but try as she might, for once she found her father unyielding. No matter how much she begged, pleaded, cried, or argued, he would not give an inch. The worst part was, he actually believed he was doing what was best for her!

She fought back tears as he accompanied her to her room and the school's administrator, Anita Raney, introduced her to her new roommate, Andrea Marler, a petite blond girl who appeared to be about Jaime's age. Andrea was small and well-mannered and neatly dressed in one of those tailored outfits Jaime loathed, and Jaime was prepared to hate her on sight. But Andrea was warm and friendly and greeted Jaime as if they'd known each other all their lives. "I hope we can be friends," the girl said with a perfect smile. "You can call me Andie. Everybody does."

Though a part of her wanted to lash out at anyone or anything connected with the school, she found herself shaking the other girl's hand. "Yeah, sure," she said. "I'm Jaime—and this is my Daddy."

Andrea looked up. "He's awfully tall," she commented.

Jaime shrugged. "Runs in the family, I guess."

"Andrea, perhaps you could show Jaime around once she gets settled," Miss Raney suggested.

"Sure," the girl said, still smiling.

How can she smile when she's trapped in a prison like this? Jamie wondered. *What must her home be like?*

Miss Raney returned to her office, and Andrea excused herself so Jaime could have a few minutes alone with her father before he left. "Chin up, princess," Lynde told Jaime, wiping away a tear that had escaped from the corner of one eye and rolled down her cheek. "It's not as if I'm going away for good, you know. When I'm home, we'll be together every weekend. I promise."

"Could I have that in writing, please?" she asked, forcing a smile.

"Signed in blood if you like," he agreed.

"No, thanks," she said, shaking her head. "Too messy."

He kissed her forehead. "I'll be here to pick you up Friday evening, right after your last class," he promised. "We'll do something special."

She hugged him tightly. "It's always special when we do it together."

• • •

Though Jaime never came to really enjoy life at Briar Ridge,
she learned to tolerate it. Her grades were good, and she
never skipped classes, for she knew that such actions meant
she would not be allowed to leave school for weekends with
her father at Sound Beach. She turned out to be a first-rate
dancer, with her slim build and long legs. She was a better
rider than any of her classmates and was wildly enthusiastic
about swimming. She and Andrea became close friends, the
first time in her life she'd ever had a girl for a friend. She got
along with the other girls at school, for the most part, but
chose to stay at school on those weekends when her father
was away rather than accept any of the other girls' invitations
to their homes, for that would have meant reciprocating when
she did go home. Jaime had no intention of sharing that precious time she had with her father with anyone.

When he wasn't abroad, Lynde came for her on Friday
evening and brought her back to Briar Ridge late Sunday
night. Though Miss Raney had tried to discourage him from
bringing the child back *too* late, her words had been ignored.
"Listen—she's all I've got, and we don't get to see much of
each other," Lynde had told the administrator more than
once. "As long as she's not falling asleep in her Monday-
morning classes, your concerns are groundless." And that,
he decided, was that.

At home at Sound Beach, they did all the things they'd
always enjoyed doing together: riding, archery, sailing their
seventeen-foot Daysailer on Long Island Sound, taking pictures of each other with the Instamatic camera Lynde had
given Jaime for her eighth birthday. Lynde was no photographer, but Jaime showed real promise for one so young. She
took hundreds of photographs, of Sadie, of her pony Cristobal, of birds on the Sound—but mostly of her father. Lynde
often found himself wondering which of them enjoyed those
weekends most.

He was frankly puzzled by the fact that Jaime never mentioned her mother. Not once since Fran had been buried had
Jaime brought up that terrible afternoon in the garage or discussed the few good memories she had of Fran. Lynde knew

she still felt the pain; even now, three years later, he knew his daughter still cried herself to sleep sometimes, knew she still thought about Fran. He did not ask her about it. Better to let her bring it up, he decided.

And one day she finally did. She was home from Briar Ridge for the weekend, and they had been walking barefoot in the surf on the beach along the Sound. "Why did Mother die, Daddy?" The question had come unexpectedly, taking Lynde by surprise.

Lynde looked at her, stunned. There it was. No preamble, no beating around the bush, just quick and to the point, like a bullet in the heart. How like his daughter to score a direct hit, to put all her cards on the table at once. "Why?" He repeated the question, stalling for time until he could gather his thoughts and give her a reasonable answer other than "Your mother was miserable, so she killed herself." He fumbled for the answer he'd rehearsed in his mind so many times over the past few years.

Jaime looked up at him, her small face serious. "Why was she so unhappy?"

He sighed. "Well, princess," he said, kneeling in the sand in front of her, "I guess your mother was unhappy because she wanted something she just couldn't seem to find."

"And that's why she died?"

Lynde nodded. "When people want things they can't ever have, it keeps eating away at them until one day they just stop living."

"That's what killed her?" Jaime asked.

"I'm afraid so, princess."

"Do you think she ever loved me, Daddy?" There was sorrow in her eyes.

He couldn't believe she'd actually verbalized her insecurities about her relationship with Fran. "Of course she did," he insisted. "Your mother never stopped loving you from the minute you were born." He wasn't sure this was true, but he couldn't tell her anything else. She was too young to understand. He didn't understand himself. "She was sick, that's all. She was so unhappy it turned into an illness. She couldn't show her love, even though she felt it."

Jaime looked him in the eye, her face a mirror image of his own when he set his mind to do something. "That's never going to happen to *me*, Daddy," she vowed, her voice filled with determination. "I won't let it. Whatever I want, I'm gonna get!"

He laughed and rumpled her hair. "I don't doubt it for a minute, princess."

"Why do you have to go to Paris *now*, Daddy?" Jaime asked her father as they drove up the long, tree-lined drive to Briar Ridge. "It's so close to Christmas—"

"I know, princess, but it can't be helped. It's part of my job," he reminded her.

"I hate your job," she said, and pouted.

"Sometimes I do, too," he admitted. He was torn, as always, between his love for his daughter and his desire to spend more time with her and the lure, the excitement of his work. He supposed it was in his blood, the need for travel, for excitement, for a real challenge. He'd been genetically programmed for it. In France, during the war, he'd lived, literally, on the very edge. Each day had been a new challenge as he matched wits with the enemy. After the war was over, he'd missed it. But now, traveling inside Russia—almost inside the Kremlin itself—the thrill he'd felt during his stint in Paris was back in his life again, and he discovered he needed it just as he needed food and water and oxygen. He needed to be active, to be doing what he did best, but at the same time he felt guilty about leaving Jaime. Especially now.

"Will you be home for Christmas?" Jaime wanted to know.

"I don't know, princess," he answered truthfully. "I'm sure going to try." He reached out and took her small hand in his and gave it a reassuring squeeze. "And I'll bring you something special, too."

"I just want you, Daddy. That's special enough."

He parked the car in front of the main building. Jaime watched in silence as he got out and strode around to open the door for her. He paused for a moment as he took her suitcase from the back seat, taking note of the gloomy expression on her face. "It's not as bad as it seems, princess," he told her.

"I need you, Daddy," she responded.

"And I need to be with you," he said quickly. "But I have to work. You know that. And you need friends your own age. Teachers. Women who can teach you all the girl things I can't."

"I can learn those things from Grandma or Aunt Kate," Jaime insisted.

"C'mon, princess—you haven't seen your grandmother in a long time, and you know your Aunt Kate's living in Washington with her new husband," Lynde reminded her.

Jaime made a face. "Why do I hate everything that's best for me?"

Her father laughed. "That, sweetheart, is one of the unwritten laws of nature."

Jaime sat at her desk in the room she and Andrea shared, staring out the window at the gray, gloomy December sky. She wondered idly if it would snow. The girls were all wishing for a white Christmas. *All of them but me,* she thought sullenly. *I want good weather so Daddy can fly home.* She didn't understand it. When her father was away, he always wrote to her at least once a week. He sent postcards and gifts. This time, she hadn't heard from him at all. Maybe he's planning a surprise, she told herself.

She wondered if she had passed her math exam. God, she hated math! Why did anyone need math to get by in the world? she asked herself. She looked down at the letter she'd received that morning from her Aunt Kate in Washington, inviting her to spend the holidays there if her father didn't make it home. As much as she loved her aunt, she hoped she would not be accepting the invitation. The only person she wanted to spend Christmas with was her father.

She picked up the framed snapshot of her father she always kept on her desk. She'd taken it herself. Everyone who saw her photographs thought she might have a future as a professional photographer. She'd never given it much thought. The photos she took were for her own pleasure. Nothing more.

Like this one . . . it had been taken on one of her cherished weekends at the beach.

"Jaime!" Andrea burst into the room breathlessly. "Godzilla Raney is looking for you—wants you in the office pronto!"

"Why?" Jaime asked with a heavy sigh as she stood up. "What have I done now?"

"Nothing, as far as I know," Andrea replied. "There's someone here to see you—your aunt and uncle, I think."

Jaime didn't hide her surprise. "My Aunt Kate's here?"

Andrea shrugged. "I guess that's the one."

"It would have to be—she's the only aunt I've got," Jaime told her as she stepped into her shoes.

As she walked down the deserted hallway, Jaime wondered why her Aunt Kate was here. Had she come to take her back to Washington for Christmas? Did Kate know her father might be home? Or had her father found out he wouldn't be home and written to Kate? Of course. That must be it. Jaime's heart sank. *I might as well make the best of it,* she resolved, pausing at the top of the stairs. She looked around to make sure no one was watching, then hopped up on the railing and slid down to the bottom of the staircase. Jumping down to the floor easily, she hurried down the hall to Anita Raney's office.

"Miss Raney, Andie said you wanted to see me—" She came to an abrupt halt in the doorway. The man and woman seated in front of Miss Raney's desk were *not* her aunt and uncle. She'd never seen either of them before. They looked to be in their fifties, conservatively dressed, both of them beginning to go gray at the temples. Jaime had heard all sorts of horror stories about people who kidnapped children from schools by posing as relatives. "I never saw them before, Miss Raney," she stammered. "They're not my aunt and uncle."

"Of course we are, dear." The woman got up and started toward her. Jaime took a step backward. "You don't know us because I haven't seen your father—my brother—since three years before you were even born. I'm your Aunt Alice, and this is your uncle, my husband Joseph Harcourt."

"Where's my father?" Jaime demanded, sure now that something was terribly wrong.

"We'll talk about it when we get home," the woman promised.

"Home?" Jaime stood ramrod-straight, suddenly galvanized by her anger. "I'm not going anywhere with you until you tell me where my father is and why I haven't heard from him!"

"Jaime, darling—"

"Don't touch me!" she cried, pushing the woman away.

"All right," Alice Harcourt said with a sigh of resignation. "I didn't want to break it to you this way, Jaime, but you leave me no choice. There's been an accident. Your father . . . your father was killed in a plane crash. He's dead, Jaime."

Jaime shook her head as the room began to spin wildly. Suddenly everything went black.

EIGHT

Jaime sat alone in the back of the station wagon as the man who claimed to be her uncle drove south on Interstate 95 through Westchester County. The woman glanced back at her occasionally, but said nothing. Jaime made no attempt at conversation either. She was still reeling from what they had told her back at school. Her father was dead. She couldn't accept it, and yet something inside her told her if he were not, he would have contacted her. She would have heard *something* from him. Was this why there had been no letter, none of the usual postcards? She wanted to cry, but the tears wouldn't come. She was numb with shock. Had she really fainted in Miss Raney's office? She couldn't remember. After they told her about her father, everything else was a blur in her memory.

She hadn't wanted to leave Briar Ridge with the Harcourts. She still wasn't sure she believed their story. Yet she felt she had to, because, with her father gone, where else could she go? To her grandparents? She hadn't seen them since her mother died. For all she knew, maybe they didn't *want* to see her. And what about her Aunt Kate? A visit was one thing, but would Kate's new husband want her living with them? She hadn't even met him yet. Maybe he didn't like children.

Maybe he wouldn't like her. Hadn't Sadie said more than once that she wasn't a "normal" little girl?

She looked down at the shoebox in her lap. Slowly, she lifted the lid. Inside was a bundle of letters and postcards she'd received from her father. Next to them was a music box he'd given her for her ninth birthday. A beautiful brass horse with a single horn on its head. A unicorn, he'd called it. She'd seen a picture of one in a book on mythology in the library at Briar Ridge. Lifting it from the box carefully, she pressed the tiny lever on one side of the thick, round base. The unicorn began to revolve slowly as the music box played "The Impossible Dream."

Jaime shut her eyes tightly as the melody brought back memories of the night her father had taken her to see *Man of La Mancha*. In her mind, she could see him sitting beside her in the darkened theater, holding her small hand in his large one. She recalled the restaurant before the show and his telling that nice waiter to bring "his girl" a dish of chocolate ice cream.

Can you really be gone, Daddy? she wondered. *Are you really dead?*

"You have to eat, Jaime," Alice Harcourt said as she entered Jaime's bedroom, carrying a tray on which Sadie had prepared the child's dinner. "I think we have all of your favorites here—pizza, cherry pie, and—"

"Daddy doesn't let me eat those things for dinner—only on special occasions." Jaime, curled up in the window seat overlooking the Sound, did not look at the woman.

"Well, I think we can make an exception just this once," Alice suggested pleasantly as she cleared off a corner of the white wicker table on the other side of the room and put the tray down.

"I don't think so. But thank you anyway, ma'am." Jaime still stared out the window.

Alice forced a smile. "You don't have to be so formal with me, honey," she said. "I'm your aunt. We're family."

"You may be my aunt, ma'am, but I still don't know you," Jaime said slowly. "You're a stranger to me. I never met you before you came to the school yesterday, and Daddy never mentioned you to me.''

"I'm not surprised," she responded. "We weren't very close, and—"

"Then why do you want to take care of me now?" Jaime wanted to know. "How do I even know for sure you are my aunt? How do I know Daddy's even dead?"

Alice straightened up and drew in a breath. "Jaime, we've been through all of this before," she said evenly. "Your father's not coming back. You have to accept it. We are now your legal guardians, your uncle and I."

"What does that mean?" Jaime asked without turning around.

"It means," Alice began, trying to put it into words a child could understand, "that when we learned of your father's death, your uncle Joseph and I went to court—before a judge, that is—and were appointed your legal guardians until you reach your majority."

"My—what?"

"Until your eighteenth birthday."

Jaime nodded slowly. "You did all of that awful fast, didn't you."

"We had to," Alice maintained. "You had no one and—"

"What about my Aunt Kate? At least I know her."

"Your aunt travels a great deal. You know that. She's away too much to provide a stable home life for you."

Jaime twisted around in the window seat, facing the woman for the first time. "Is my father really dead—or are you just telling me that?" she asked bluntly.

"I told you at school—" Alice began.

Jaime cut her off. "I know what you told me at school," she said crossly. "Is it true, or was that something you had to tell Godzilla—Miss Raney—so you could take me out of school?"

"Why would you question it?" Alice asked carefully. "What reason would we have to lie to you about such a thing?"

Jaime hopped down from the window seat and came forward. "I don't know," she said solemnly. "I just know that everything about Daddy's work was strange. He didn't have the kind of job my friends' fathers have. It was always different.''

''Different? How?'' Alice pursued.

Jaime shrugged. ''Just different.''

''Did he ever talk to you about his work?''

''Nope. Not much, anyway.'' The child paused next to the table on which Alice had placed the tray. ''How did he die?''

''I told you—a plane crash.'' The woman was visibly nervous.

''Where? How did it happen?''

Alice hesitated. ''In Rome—he was leaving Rome, about to fly home to spend Christmas with you, and—''

''My Daddy wasn't in Rome,'' Jaime said quickly. ''And he wasn't coming home. He was in Paris. He told me so before he left. He had business there, then he had to go to London, and he said he would call the school and let me know when he was coming—so if he couldn't be here for Christmas, I could spend it with one of my friends from school or with my Aunt Kate in Washington.''

Alice swallowed hard. ''Jaime, I hadn't wanted to get into any of this with you—you're really too young to be hearing any of it—but your father wasn't where he told you he would be,'' she said finally.

Jaime looked at her suspiciously. ''What do you mean?''

''Sit down, please.'' Alice patted a spot on the bed next to where she sat.

''If you don't mind, I'd rather stand, ma'am.'' Jaime fiddled with the fork on her tray.

Alice nodded with reluctance. ''All right.'' She paused. ''You know what kind of work your father did, don't you?''

Jaime frowned. ''He was a banker, wasn't he?''

''Something like that, yes,'' Alice said, nodding. ''He was with a large investment firm—he handled a great deal of business in other countries. He was responsible, at times, for very large sums of money.''

''So?''

''He was supposed to be putting together a deal in Rome— not Paris, as he told you,'' Alice said quietly.

"How do you know all this stuff?" Jaime challenged. "You said you and my Daddy weren't very close."

"We weren't," Alice said. "This was all told to me when we were contacted to get you at school."

"Who called you?" Jaime wanted to know. "Who told you to come for me?"

"It doesn't really matter now—"

"It matters to me," Jaime insisted stubbornly.

Alice ignored her demand to be told. "The point is, Jaime, your father took a great deal of money that didn't belong to him. He was trying to run away with it when his plane crashed," she told the child.

Jaime shook her head emphatically. "No. My Daddy wouldn't do anything like that," she argued. "He wouldn't. I don't care what you or anybody else says."

The woman's voice softened. "I'm sorry, Jaime. I never wanted you to know any of this," she said, almost apologetically. "Your father never intended to come home."

"Liar!" Jaime screamed, snatching up the glass of milk from the tray. She threw it in Alice's face furiously. "You're lying!" The glass shattered as it hit the floor. Before Alice could stop her, Jaime ran out of the room, slamming the door behind her.

Jaime sat on a large boulder on the beach, staring blankly into the placid darkness of Long Island Sound. Her eyes felt swollen and scratchy from crying, and her hair stuck to her damp, tear-streaked cheeks. The wind was cold and strong and she was freezing, but it didn't matter. Nothing mattered. Not anymore. She didn't care if she froze to death out here. She would never go back to that house. Never. Alice had lied to her about her father, and she never wanted to see that woman again.

"I thought I'd find you here."

Jaime looked up at the sound of a faintly familiar voice. Joseph Harcourt stood just a few feet away, bundled in a heavy coat. He looked down at her with a weary smile. "I'm not going back," she said stubbornly. "You can't make me."

"I could," he disagreed, "but I don't want to."

She stared at him, not sure she understood.

"I want you to come back on your own," he went on.

Jaime shook her head. "Not a chance," she said grimly. "I don't ever want to see that woman again."

Joseph smiled. "By 'that woman,' you must mean your aunt," he concluded.

She nodded, frowning. "She lied about Daddy. I know she did."

He hesitated momentarily. "No, Jaime, she didn't," he said as he sat down beside her. "Everything Alice told you is what we were told."

"Daddy wouldn't do the things she told me he did," Jaime said stubbornly.

He smiled patiently. "I know how much you love your father, Jaime, and I know how strongly you believe in him. And to tell you the truth, none of us may ever know what really took place over there," he said gently, putting one arm around her. He looked down at her. "You're freezing. Let me give you my jacket—"

"I'm okay," she said quickly.

"Maybe they were wrong."

"They *were* wrong," Jaime said. "I know they were wrong."

"I know he loved you, and if there were any way of coming back to you, he would have found it."

"You bet he would have." Jaime paused. "Is he really dead? I mean, will they send him back to us so we can bury him like we buried Mother?"

He frowned. "They can't."

She looked at him questioningly. "Why not?"

Joseph Harcourt took a deep breath. "The plane crashed, Jaime. It burned. There wasn't much left—"

She stiffened. "Then maybe my father isn't dead at all!" For the first time, she was smiling.

"His name was on the passenger list," Harcourt said solemnly.

"Daddy often made reservations and then didn't keep them," she recalled. "His work was so crazy that sometimes he didn't know until the last minute—"

"Jaime, I don't think you should get your hopes up—" Harcourt began.

She shook her head. "Don't you see? If Daddy is alive, he'll come back for me. I know he will!"

He held her close. "For your sake, I hope you're right, honey."

She had no idea how much he meant it.

As the days passed, Jaime's early hopes gradually diminished. There were times she would cry herself to sleep at night. She spent most of her days locked away in her bedroom or walking alone along the Sound. She rarely went near the stables anymore, leaving it to the stablehands to look after Cristobal and exercise him. She'd lost interest in everyone and everything that once mattered to her. She spoke little to anyone except Joseph Harcourt and used any excuse to avoid Alice.

Though Alice voiced strong objections at first, Jaime took all of her meals in her room. Evenings were also spent alone there, playing her music box or looking at the photo album her father had helped her put together. Sometimes Jaime would stare at the photograph of Fran in her wedding dress for long periods of time, as if trying to look into her mother's soul. She was trying to understand her mother, trying to figure out what had been so wrong with her that her own mother had been unable to love her. *You were pretty, Mother—and you looked so happy. I wish I had known you then,* she thought, tracing the photograph with her fingertips. *Why don't I remember you ever being happy? Why don't I have any good memories of you—of being loved by you?*

Then she would turn to the photo of her father—her favorite, one she'd taken herself. He was leaning against the fence down by the stables, wearing a blue plaid shirt and a gray jacket. He was smiling. Happy. All of her memories of her father were happy ones. She loved him more than anyone or anything in the world—and she knew with certainty that he loved her. He would never abandon her. Not if he could help it.

If you are alive, Daddy, you'll come for me, she thought. *I know you will.*

• • •

"I want to go back to Briar Ridge," Jaime announced over breakfast one Sunday morning. A month had passed since the Harcourts brought her back to Sound Beach, and this was the first time she'd joined them in the dining room for a meal.

Alice looked concerned as she passed a small basket filled with hot buttermilk biscuits to her husband. "Are you sure that's really what you want, Jaime?"

The child nodded. "I think I have to," she said simply. "I'm already so far behind in my classes, it'll take me weeks to catch up."

"That's not what I meant, dear," Alice said as Sadie poured Jaime another glass of orange juice. "I just thought you might want to stay here, attend a school closer to home."

Jaime shook her head, helping herself to a biscuit. "I don't think so." She reached for the small crock of butter near her plate and dug into it with her knife. "Daddy picked Briar Ridge, and I'm sure he felt it was the best place for me. I didn't like it much at first, but now that Daddy's gone, it's different. Briar Ridge is more like home than here. My friends are there." She paused. "No, I don't want to change schools. Too much has changed already."

"If that's what you want, Jaime, then it's perfectly all right," Joseph Harcourt said promptly, turning to his wife. "Isn't it, Alice?"

"Yes, of course," Alice agreed somewhat uneasily.

"Thank you." Jaime put down her fork and forced a smile. "May I be excused, please?"

"Of course," Harcourt said.

Jaime got to her feet and raced out of the room. Hearing the sound of her rapid steps as she hurried upstairs, Alice turned to her husband. "How could you just agree to let her go back to Briar Ridge without at least trying to talk her out of it?" she asked in a low but irritated voice.

"You heard her, Alice. It's the only place that's familiar to her now." He finished his coffee. "She's absolutely right. Her friends are there. That's all she has left to cling to."

Alice looked around to make sure Sadie was not within

earshot. "And what if he tries to contact her? What if he writes to her or calls—"

"You worry too much, pet," Harcourt said with a knowing smile. "If that should happen, Anita Raney will inform us immediately."

"I wish I could be sure of it."

"You can be," he insisted. "Besides, I can't believe Lynde would do anything so foolish."

"I'm glad you're back, Jaime," Andrea said as she helped Jaime unpack. "Things haven't been the same since you left."

Jaime forced a smile as she folded a sweater and put it in one of her bureau drawers. "You might not believe this, coming from me, but it's real good to be back," she said without much enthusiasm.

"What happened to your father?" Andrea asked. "Judy said Carol told her she overheard Miss Raney telling Mrs. Harrold he was in some kind of big trouble when his plane crashed—"

"I don't want to talk about it, Andie," Jaime said sharply.

The other girl looked at her for a moment. "Then it's true?"

"No, dammit, it's *not* true!" Jaime snapped, slamming the suitcase shut. She spun around to face her roommate. "My father was blamed for something he didn't do when he wasn't here to defend himself! You can tell *that* to Judy and Carol and Miss Raney and Mrs. Harrold and anybody else nosy enough to say anything about it!"

"I'm sorry," Andrea stammered. "I didn't mean—"

Jaime waved her off. "It's okay," she said with a sigh. "I didn't mean to bite your head off."

"That's okay," Andrea responded with a shrug. "I guess I'd feel the same way if it were *my* father they were saying bad things about." She paused. "Listen—want some cocoa? I can go see if there's any made—"

Jaime nodded. "Sure. Thanks." She didn't really care, one way or the other, but she really wanted Andrea to leave. She needed to be alone, if only for a few minutes. As Andrea dashed out, closing the door behind her, Jaime took the unicorn music box from its box and placed it on the nightstand between the twin beds. Perching herself on the edge of her mattress, she stared thoughtfully at the brass unicorn for a long moment before switching it on. As she watched it turn slowly, the familiar melody playing, tears came to her eyes.

Why, Daddy? she asked again. *Why did you leave me?*

Downstairs in her office, Anita Raney was on the telephone with Alice Harcourt. "You asked that I let you know if Jaime Lynde's father made any attempt to contact her," she said, looking down at the large package wrapped in plain brown wrapper on her desk. "A package just arrived. What? No, I'm not absolutely certain. There was no return address—but it *is* postmarked Paris."

NINE

Sound Beach, April 1978. Jaime walked barefoot in the surf along the Sound, her faded jeans rolled up to mid-calf and the sleeves of her off-white cotton shirt rolled to her elbows. Her long, dark red hair was blowing in the wind as she raised her Nikon, focused on a sailboat in the distance, then made an adjustment in the lens before snapping the picture. Making another adjustment, she took another picture, then lowered the camera. She stared at the boat for a long moment, then turned and headed for home. The beach was still her favorite spot, the place she always came when she needed to be alone, when she needed a quiet place to think. It was her favorite spot because her father always brought her here.

Daddy, she thought sadly. *You must be dead. They must have been telling the truth, because I know you would never have stayed away so long if you were alive. If you were able to come back . . . I know you wouldn't.*

Even now, almost twelve years later, the pain Jaime felt at having been abandoned by her father was as acute as it had been that awful morning at Briar Ridge when Alice and Joseph Harcourt had come for her. She would never forget that day as long as she lived.

. . .

"You're lying!" she screamed at them. "My daddy's not dead—he's not!"

The woman who claimed to be her aunt, the strange woman she'd never seen before, the woman her father had never told her about, reached for her, but Jaime jerked away.

"I know what a shock this must be for you, dear," the woman said patiently, "but it's true. Your father really is dead, much as I hate to have to be the one to tell you something so terrible—"

"No!" Jaime turned and ran out of the room before anyone could stop her. She didn't stop running until she reached the bathroom down the hall. She pushed her way past two of her schoolmates and ran into one of the stalls, dropping to her knees. She hugged the cold porcelain bowl as she vomited, spilling the contents of her stomach into the toilet until there was nothing left inside her to expel.

"Jaime—"

The voice coming from behind her sounded as if it were miles away. She felt Anita Raney's hand on her shoulder. "Go away," she sobbed. "Just leave me alone."

"I'm sorry, Jaime," Anita Raney said softly.

"He's not dead," Jaime said stubbornly. "I know he's not!"

"I know how you must feel—"

"No, you don't. You don't know how I feel." Jaime remained on her knees, holding onto the toilet bowl as if it were a security blanket.

"We have to go upstairs now, Jaime. You have to pack—"

She shook her head. "I'm not going with them."

"You have to. They're your aunt and uncle. They're your legal guardians now."

"I don't care who they are. I don't know them, and I'm not going with them."

But she *had* gone with them, because, in the end, she'd had no choice.

She remembered feeling lost and frightened and alone, more so than she'd ever felt in her life. Even the loss of her mother had not been so devastating. Though Fran's death had been painful, Jaime had felt she'd lost her mother long before she actually died. She realized much later that she'd always felt as if she didn't have a mother. Fran's rejection of her had made her feel unwanted and unloved, but her father had gone to great lengths to compensate for what her mother had been either unable or unwilling to give her. Losing him had been the final blow.

Jaime felt a tear escape from the corner of her eye and roll down her cheek. She kept walking, shaking her hair back off her face. The cold wind blowing in from the Sound stung her cheeks. She looked up at the dark clouds now crossing the sky. Rain. It had rained the day Alice told her about her father. . . .

"How are things at Princeton?" Joseph Harcourt asked over dinner that evening. When Jaime had arrived home for spring break, her uncle had been in Washington on another of his mysterious business trips. He'd just returned that afternoon.

"Same as usual." Jaime reached for a slice of bread. "Midterms were a royal pain, as always—but I think I can safely say I passed all of them."

Harcourt smiled. "You make it sound as though you passed by the proverbial skin of your teeth," he chided her gently, knowing full well that Jaime was an honor student who always made A's and B's.

She made a wry face. "Let's just say I lit a few candles to get me through the past couple of weeks." Though Jaime had turned her back on the Catholic upbringing of her early childhood—her father's one concession to the wishes of her maternal grandmother—she still made casual reference to the rituals of the Church whenever she found herself in a difficult situation.

"Come now, Jaime." This was Alice. "It can't have been that bad."

"Worse," Jaime insisted, attacking her plate as though it were the first good meal she'd had in weeks. "Calculus is definitely *not* my cup of tea. What use these colleges think anyone is going to have for it in everyday life still escapes me."

"You'd be surprised," Harcourt said, amused.

"I certainly would." Jaime took a bite and chewed thoughtfully.

"Have you thought about what you want to do after graduation?" Alice asked casually.

Jaime brightened. "I thought I'd try to get a job as a photojournalist with one of the news magazines in Manhattan," she said, dabbing the corners of her mouth with her napkin. "*Time, Newsweek*—I'll have a degree in journalism, and I've been told I'm a pretty good photographer. Whoever hires me will get two for the price of one."

"Maybe you should put that in your résumé," Harcourt suggested lightly.

Jaime grimaced. "What résumé? I haven't written one yet," she admitted. "Some journalist, huh?"

Harcourt put down his fork. "Maybe I can help," he offered. "I know a few people in publishing."

"That would be great, Joe!" Jaime declared enthusiastically. Though she'd stopped calling them aunt and uncle long ago, and had never quite warmed up to Alice, she genuinely liked Joseph Harcourt and welcomed his advice and help. She did find it unusual that a former career Army officer was so well connected in so many nonmilitary places, but she never questioned him about it. She got up from her chair and went around the table to give him an affectionate hug. "Thanks! You're a love!"

As Jaime dashed up the stairs, Alice gave her husband a knowing smile. "You've really gotten attached to her, haven't you?" It was more an observation than a question.

"She's like my own daughter," he admitted with fondness in his voice. "I think Jim would be proud if he could see her now."

Alice hesitated. "Do you regret not having children of our own?" she asked. She had never been able to conceive, and it had been a disappointment to both of them in the early years of their marriage.

He gave a heavy sigh. "Yes and no," he said finally. "I think we might have made good parents—if circumstances had been different."

"Circumstances?" his wife asked.

Harcourt shook his head. "Look at Jim and Jaime," he said simply.

The attic was dark and musty, cluttered with boxes and trunks and stacks of dusty old books that had been left there, forgotten, for many years. Knocking thick cobwebs out of her way, Jaime made her way through the maze of junk, in search of the old family photo albums she knew were there somewhere. In recent years, she'd become increasingly interested in her heritage, on both the Lyndes' and Colbys' sides. She told herself she was just curious, but in fact she was looking for something to cling to, something she could always carry with her, no matter what. Her parents were both gone. Her maternal grandmother had passed away several years ago. Her grandfather had suffered a series of strokes and did not even know her anymore. Kate was still living in Washington, where her husband was being groomed as a presidential hopeful. Jaime didn't know anyone from her father's side of the family—except Alice and Joseph, of course—but she was sure the albums must have something in them that would give her a clue. No one seemed willing to talk about it to her. She couldn't help wondering why.

She settled into a well-worn old armchair near the one window in the cramped room, a small, circular window that looked remarkably like a ship's porthole, and opened the nearest trunk. *As good a place to start as any,* she decided. The trunk was filled with letters and photographs that were so old they had turned yellow, their corners torn off and brittle with age. Jaime picked up a thick stack and placed them on her lap, handling them gingerly as she sorted through them. *God, they were old!* she thought, amused. Some of them dated back to the late '30s and early '40s. There were letters her mother had received from her grandmother and Kate while she was away at Vassar. Letters her mother had written to her father but never mailed while he was away on business. Photographs of her mother, aunt, and grandparents. A few of her father, too—yellowed snapshots of a tall, dashing man in military uniform, attractive but unsmiling. According to the dates on the back of the photos, they had been taken at the end of the war.

As she sorted through trunk after trunk, Jaime found it odd that her father had not kept any photographs or mementos of his family. No letters from home postmarked during the war years. Not even a snapshot. Nothing. But hadn't Alice told her their family had never been terribly close? *Still . . . it's as if he didn't even exist before 1942,* Jaime thought, puzzled.

There were photos of her father and mother together prior to their marriage. At the wedding. Aboard the *Queen Mary* on their honeymoon. In France, near the Eiffel Tower and the Arc de Triomphe. Her mother was smiling in all of them. She looked so happy, Jaime thought. Why don't I remember her being happy like that? Her mother was pretty—no raving beauty, but pretty in a well-bred kind of way. But her father— her father was handsome. Dashing. Jaime smiled to herself, recalling that day, years ago, when she'd told him she wanted to marry a man exactly like him one day. "I'd never allow it!" he had told her, obviously touched by the thought but making it clear it was out of the question as far as he was concerned. "You're still a child, princess. You love me and I love you, but you don't see me yet for what I really am. I have all kinds of faults, and the last thing I'd want is to see my only daughter married to somebody just like me."

That's my dad, she thought fondly. Painfully honest. How could a man that honest have done the things he was accused of doing? It didn't seem possible that he could have been the man Alice said he was at the time of his death. Alice. It always came back to Alice. Though Jaime was not quite sure why, she'd never really trusted the woman. There was something about Alice Harcourt that just didn't ring true. Jaime shook her head. Her father would have chalked it up to instinct. He was always big on relying on one's instincts, and so was she. After all, she *was* his daughter.

Having methodically searched each trunk and box in the attic, having collected a large bundle of old letters and photographs she wanted to examine more closely another time, she started to leave the attic. As she opened the door leading to the narrow stairway, the bright light coming from the other side knifed through the darkness, illuminating a large trunk in one corner of the cluttered room, almost totally concealed by a faded, tattered old chenille throw. Curiosity aroused once again, Jaime picked her way through the junk once more to check it out.

Upon closer inspection, she discovered it was actually a very old army footlocker. Prying the rusted lock with the large screwdriver she'd brought up with her, she forced it open. Inside, she found a number of packages of varying sizes, all of them addressed to her and all partially unwrapped. Jaime picked up the one on the top of the pile and opened it. Inside was a beautiful doll dressed in an elegantly detailed riding habit just like the one her father had bought for her years ago! The note with it was dated February 14, 1967: "Happy Valentine's Day to my best girl. Love, Daddy." Daddy! Jaime's heart almost stopped. February 1967—two months *after* he was supposed to have died in that plane crash! Hastily, and with trembling fingers, Jaime opened each package. They were Christmas and birthday gifts, sent to her each year! All of them were accompanied by either a short note or a long letter detailing the places he visited, telling her how much he missed her, but never hinting of any kind of problem.

Tears stung Jaime's eyes as she took all of the letters and closed the footlocker. They'd lied to her! All these years thinking he was dead—and all the time they'd been keeping this from her! Damn them both for putting her through hell like this! She slammed her fist against the wall. Was he alive now? Was he in some kind of terrible trouble? Had something happened to prevent him from coming home to her? Good God—something had to have happened to have kept him away all these years!

But what?

Alice was in the library when Jaime burst through the door, her face dark with rage, furiously waving the letters she held in her right hand. "Why did you lie to me?" she exploded, throwing the letters down on the desk in front of Alice.

"Lie to you about what, dear?" Alice inquired calmly, looking up from the household bills she'd been writing checks to pay.

"About my father!" Jaime shouted. "You told me he was killed in a plane crash!"

"He was, dear." Alice remained calm. "You know that—"

"You lying bitch!" Jaime snapped. "I just found these in the attic!"

Alice looked down at the letters in front of her. She did not have to open them to know what they were. One look at Jaime's angry face told her more than she wanted to know. "What were you doing in the attic?" she asked carefully.

"None of your goddamned business!" Jaime hissed. "All that matters is that I found my father's old footlocker—I know about the presents. And I'm willing to bet that my father is still alive somewhere! You kept this from me, Alice. What else have you been keeping from me?"

"If you'll just calm down—" Alice began as she stood up. She had to do something to smooth things over—and fast.

Jaime was having none of it. "Spare me any more of your lies," she said coldly. She felt dangerously close to physically assaulting the older woman. "I think you've done enough damage for one lifetime!" She snatched up the letters and started for the door.

"Jaime—please—wait!" Alice called after her.

Jaime stopped in her tracks but did not turn around. "What now?" she asked contemptuously.

"I—where are you going?" Alice asked nervously.

Jaime whirled around to face her. "First of all, I'm going upstairs to pack," she answered, her eyes blazing with anger. "Then I'm going back to Princeton. I have to know what really happened to my father. After that, I'm not sure. I just know I won't come back to this house while you're in it."

She stalked out of the room, leaving Alice Harcourt staring after her.

Jaime sat alone on the train, staring out the window absently as the train passed through Elizabeth en route to Princeton.

Her eyes were red and swollen, her cheeks mottled from crying. She had found herself unable to cry anymore. There
were no tears left in her to be shed. She'd cried—tears of
pain, tears of anger and betrayal—until her insides felt like a
great, vast desert, incapable of producing so much as a single
drop of moisture of any kind. For the first time in her life,
Jaime knew what it was like to actually want to kill someone.
She could have easily murdered Alice Harcourt with her bare
hands. She'd known she had to get out of that house before
she did just that. She had never known she could hate anyone
so much.

The past twelve years had all been a lie. Instinct told her
her father was still alive somewhere, that he was in some kind
of trouble and needed her. She drew her denim jacket around
herself, but it did nothing to ease the chill she felt deep within
her bones. He hadn't died in a plane crash. He hadn't embezzled all that money from her grandfather's firm. For all
she knew, Joseph and Alice Harcourt weren't even her aunt
and uncle. But if they weren't, who *were* they? And why had
they stayed with her and kept the truth from her all these
years? None of this made any sense. *But it will,* she promised
herself. *It will. I'll find the truth, somehow.*

No matter how long it takes.

Washington, D.C. Harry Warner was alone in his office, finishing a light lunch of tuna salad on toast and fruit cocktail
when his secretary buzzed him on the intercom. "They're
here," she announced cryptically.

He swallowed the last bite of his sandwich. "Send them
in, Terry," he instructed.

"Yes, sir."

A moment later the door opened, and Joseph and Alice
Harcourt entered. Warner looked at them for a moment.
"This had better be good," he said with unmasked anger in
his voice. "You were supposed to stay with the girl and make
sure Lynde didn't try to contact her. You were supposed to
find out how much—if anything—he might have told her about
his real line of work. Now, out of the blue, you call and tell
me it's all blown up in our faces, that she knows he's not

dead and is bent on finding him. How could either of you
allow this to happen?''

''She found all the packages and letters he sent her,''
Harcourt explained. ''They were in an old footlocker in the
attic—''

''What the hell were they doing there?'' Warner demanded.
''You were supposed to have destroyed everything!''

''It's too late to do anything about that now,'' Alice said
evenly, not telling Warner her husband had not been able to
destroy Jaime's last link with her father because he'd become
too emotionally involved with the girl over the years, not
telling him about the letter Joseph had received from Lynde
shortly after the Company had set them up, in a manner similar to the procedure used for participants in the government's
Witness Protection Program, where witnesses whose lives are
endangered by testifying are given new identities, as Jaime's
legal guardians. What had the letter said? *Jaime's all that's
ever mattered to me in this world. If I can't give her a father
in the physical sense, I can at least give her my love. At some
point I know you'll see to it that she gets all of this.* . . .
Somehow, he'd managed. Through his many contacts abroad,
he'd managed to get letters and packages to her on an amaz-
ingly regular basis. ''I think she could pose a real problem,''
she said aloud. ''I doubt she'll just put all of this behind her
and get on with her life, knowing what little she does know
now.''

''You think she'll start snooping around?'' Warner's eyes
moved from Harcourt to Alice and back again. It was Harcourt who finally responded.

''I'd bet on it.''

TEN

New York City, April 1984. Jaime bolted across Madison Avenue against the light, her fire-engine-red slicker flapping around her wildly in the brisk wind and rain. Bounding up onto the curb, she maneuvered quickly through the heavy Monday-morning pedestrian traffic and entered the Patterson Publications building on the southwest corner of Madison and Thirty-sixth. She made her way through the busy lobby to the bank of antiquated elevators and squeezed into one just as the doors started to close.

Jaime ignored the curious glances of the men and women in the elevator as it began its ascent with a sudden jerk. At five feet ten, she was as tall as most of the men sharing the crowded car and a good bit taller than most of the women. Unlike many tall women, Jaime didn't slouch, having always been comfortable with her height. Her bearing, combined with her striking looks and gleaming red hair, created an arresting image, whether she was dressed formally or running in Central Park in her emerald-green warm-up suit. At twenty-seven, Jaime Lynde was one of those women who turned heads wherever she went.

The elevator came to a grinding halt at the fifteenth floor. Jaime squeezed through the doors as they squeaked open and walked purposefully through the plate glass double doors on which "World Views Magazine" had been carefully painted in gold and black block letters. Though she'd been with the magazine for almost six years, it never failed to amaze her how modern their editorial offices were in contrast to the lobby and elevators. *Leave it to Patterson Publications to remodel only where it is absolutely necessary,* she mused wryly.

"Hi, Holly!" she greeted the attractive young receptionist as she sailed past the large, elliptical reception desk with its intercoms and multiple telephone consoles and made her way down a long corridor lined with framed covers from past issues. As she turned the corner leading to her own small office, she came to an abrupt halt in the doorway, her cheerful expression suddenly changing to anger at what she saw there. Mike Turner, the magazine's art director—and self-appointed office Romeo—was leaning back in her chair, arms folded behind his head, his feet propped up on one corner of the cluttered desk. Turner was, without a doubt, the most attractive man on staff—and the most insufferable, next to the editorial director, Terence Hillyer. Mike Turner was tall and well built, with strong, chiseled features, thick, blue-black hair, and mischievous blue eyes. Any of the women in the office would have been happy to find him waiting for her any day of the week—anyone except Jaime, who was clearly not interested in a relationship with him, casual or otherwise. For that reason alone, he took particular delight in pestering her on a regular basis.

"What the hell do you think you're doing?" she demanded hotly, pushing his feet off the desk with a decidedly forceful movement.

"Why, waiting for you, of course," he said with a grin. He took a slim, gold-plated cigarette case from his pocket as he got to his feet. "You missed the editorial meeting." Clucking with mock disapproval, he took out a cigarette, put it between his full lips, and lit it casually. "What's your excuse, woman?"

"None, as far as you're concerned." Jaime removed her wet slicker and hung it on a large metal hook on the back of the door. She wore a bulky forest-green sweater belted at the waist and camel-colored wool slacks tucked into high brown leather boots. Around her neck she wore a loosely tied print scarf in shades of ivory, green, and gold, and her only jewelry was a man's gold wristwatch that had belonged to her father and her mother's favorite antique gold ring.

"The executive committee selected the articles for next week's issue, if you're interested," Turner announced.

"Oh? Should I be?" Jaime asked, seating herself.

"I think so. They scrapped your layout on the protesters at Brown University."

"That bastard Hillyer's responsible, no doubt," Jaime said crossly. "That man's taste is all in his mouth."

"Ah—so we *do* agree on something!" Turner seemed amused by the discovery. "You know, that's what I like best about you, Red—you're so damned diplomatic." He took a drag on his cigarette. "Listen, if you need a shoulder to cry on—"

"What I need," she stated irritably, "is to be left alone long enough to come up with some new ideas."

"For Hillyer to veto, no doubt," Turner shot back.

She rubbed her forehead thoughtfully. "Would you please just get out of here?" she pleaded, one step away from throwing him out bodily.

"I'm out of here," he said, backing toward the door. "Never let it be said that Michael R. Turner can't take a hint."

"Sometimes I think a Mack truck has to run over you before you take a hint," Jaime said in a menacing tone.

He retreated, laughing. Jaime got up and closed the door, then sat down again. She was so furious with Hillyer she could have skewered the man and roasted him slowly over an open fire. *This is the third time in the past two months that son of a bitch has scrapped one of my articles.* Since becoming editorial director six months ago, the job had definitely gone to his head. *As the saying goes, power corrupts, and absolute power corrupts absolutely,* she thought.

She swung her chair around to face the window. Catching sight of one of the framed snapshots on the windowsill, she picked it up and stared at it thoughtfully. Herself and her father, taken when she was eight years old. Her mother had been dead almost a year. It brought back memories. . . .

"Why did you call Mr. Saunders a dumb son of a bitch, Daddy?"

She was standing in the doorway of the bathroom in a pink flannel nightgown, watching her father shave. Surprised, he put down his safety razor and turned to her. He was wearing jeans and a white cotton undershirt, a towel draped over one shoulder. The right side of his face was still covered with shaving cream. "Now where on earth did you hear that?" he wanted to know.

"From you, Daddy," she answered brightly, cocking her head to one side. "I heard you telling Grandpa—this afternoon, in the library."

Her father tried to hide his amusement. "Isn't there anything around here you don't hear?"

"Not too much," she responded with a mischievous grin.

"Jaime, sometimes I wonder what I'm ever going to do with you," he chuckled.

"Why don't you like Mr. Saunders?" she pursued.

He laughed. "I assure you, princess, the feeling's mutual." He picked up his razor again.

"Why?" Jaime tugged at her red curls impatiently.

He put down the razor again. "You know, princess, you'd make one terrific reporter," he told her.

"What's a reporter, Daddy?" she asked innocently.

"A reporter, my dear, is a professional snoop," he explained. "They go around poking their noses in where they don't belong and see and hear a lot of things they're not supposed to see or hear."

Jaime brightened. "I think I'd like that, Daddy," she said promptly.

Her father had laughed. "I'm sure you would, princess."

Everything at *World Views*, Jaime had decided long ago, was geared to meet the Monday night deadline for closing each issue. At that time, the mock-up was sent off via computer hookup to their printers in Philadelphia to ensure that the magazine would arrive at the various wholesalers' warehouses across the country by Friday and be on the newsstands by Monday. Each step taken was critical to every other step, and the pressure on the staff continued to build throughout each Monday afternoon until, by four o'clock, everyone was a candidate for a straitjacket. In her own six years with the magazine, Jaime had seen editors crawl under their desks for a catnap after working all night. "On Mondays, the closest you'll get to leaving the building is looking out the window," Ben Rollins, the managing editor, had told her on her first day on the job. It had not been far from the truth.

Jaime smiled at the memory. Not much had changed since then. She still felt as though she were being subjected to one continuous endurance test, as if her ability to function under pressure were being pushed to the limit. Not that she minded. There was nothing Jaime enjoyed more than a real challenge. *After all, you are your father's daughter,* she told herself.

The unexpected sound of an explosion of heated expletives punctuated by the slamming of a door down the hall cut through Jaime's thoughts. The loud, angry stream of profanity coming from that direction indicated that the latest story by Hannibal Crawford, the most vocal writer on the staff, had once again been completely rewritten. Jaime stifled a giggle. *Patterson should fire Hillyer before someone kills him,* she decided.

"They must've done a rewrite on Crawford again."

Jaime's head jerked up. Holly Christopher stood in the doorway. The young receptionist came forward, two of the familiar pink telephone message slips in her hand. Jaime took them and looked them over. Holly glanced at the sleeping bag rolled up in one corner of the office. "Planning on setting up camp again tonight?"

Jaime grinned. "My Monday night home away from home," she said. "I should be used to it by now."

"I thought things would get easier once we were computerized," Holly lamented. "I've thought about asking Mr. Hillyer to bring in a temp on Mondays, things get so crazy around here."

"Be careful what you ask for," Jaime warned, grinning.

"The last person who asked Terence Hillyer for a favor was found floating facedown in New York Harbor."

Holly looked skeptical. "Be serious!"

"I am," Jaime insisted. "When you ask him for special consideration, be prepared to pay the price. You'll owe him a big one for it—and if you don't pay up, forget it. He's got a guy working for him named Vito. You ask him for anything above and beyond, Vito pays you a visit and nails your knee-caps to the floor—with railroad spikes."

Holly laughed. "You make him sound like such an ogre!"

"This man makes an ogre look like Mother Teresa," Jaime responded.

"So—shall I order the pizzas?" Holly wanted to know.

Jaime nodded. "Might as well."

"Same as usual?"

"The works."

"Right." Holly started for the door.

"And tell them not to be so damned stingy with the good-ies this time," Jaime called after her.

After Holly was gone, Jaime picked up the telephone mes-sages again and studied them for a moment. One was from a contact in Washington. She'd call him later. She put it down and turned her attention to the other. It was from Alice Har-court.

Angrily crumpling the paper in her hand, she threw it in the wastepaper basket.

The Russian Tea Room on West Fifty-seventh Street is noted more for the dazzling decor than for its cuisine. With its impressive paintings, gleaming samovars, and chandeliers festooned with tinsel and Christmas balls, it is indeed stun-ning, but as any of the regular patrons know, lunch is not the best time to enjoy the restaurant's striking interior. Filled with big shots from the communications and entertainment industries, it is usually so busy that the only quiet place one can find to dine is upstairs, known to the regulars as Siberia.

"I only have an hour," Jaime announced as she ap-proached the table—ten minutes late for lunch—where An-drea Marler sat alone waiting for her. Jaime looked properly apologetic. "I'm doing a shoot at the French embassy this afternoon."

Andrea smiled. "You haven't changed a bit since Briar Ridge, do you know that?" she observed with amusement. "You're still always coming or going—never staying in one place."

"Well, you *have* changed—and quite spectacularly, at that," Jaime responded. At twenty-seven, Andrea Marler was, and had been for the past six years, one of the top photographic models in the business. Tall—though not as tall as Jaime—Andrea was a willowy blonde with a delicate, heart-shaped face, huge aquamarine eyes, and lush, wind-blown hair. "At Briar Ridge you were just another gawky kid with pigtails and braces."

"And Daddy's money to help the ugly duckling become a swan," Andrea chirped, recalling the old resentment she'd aroused among some of their classmates when the braces came off—along with the baby fat. "Jaime, the reason I wanted to see you—I'm getting married."

Jaime broke into a huge grin. "The stockbroker—what's his name?" She signaled the waiter as he passed their table.

"You sound like Daddy!" Andrea reprimanded her affectionately. "His name, as if you didn't remember, is Tom. Tom O'Halloran." There was a pause in their conversation while Jaime ordered a drink.

As the waiter disappeared, Jaime turned back to Andrea. "So when's the big day?"

"July fourteenth—at our place in Southampton. It was the earliest possible date Tom could get away from the office for a real honeymoon," Andrea explained. "We're going to France. Brittany."

"What do you want for a wedding gift?" Jaime asked with a wicked grin. "A toaster? A blender? The name of a good lawyer?"

"You."

Jaime raised an eyebrow questioningly.

"I want you to be my maid of honor," Andrea told her as the waiter returned with their drinks.

"I'd love to," Jaime responded without hesitation. "On one condition."

Andrea looked at her suspiciously. "And that is?"

"That I don't have to wear a pink dress—God, I hate pink!" Jaime moaned.

"No pink," Andrea promised with an emphatic shake of her head.

"In that case, I accept," Jaime said promptly. "Now that that's settled, could we please order? I'm starving—and the veal cutlets and strawberries Romanoff are to die for . . ."

Her Nike-clad feet hit the ground alternately and in a steady rhythm as Jaime ran alone in Central Park, bundled against the chilly April evening in her fleece-lined warm-up suit, a matching terry-cloth headband around her head. Her cheeks were flushed and her breath visible in the cold evening air, but she kept running. She ran for at least an hour every evening except Mondays, no matter what the weather, all year round. While still at Princeton, she'd discovered the physical and mental effects of running. Running faithfully every day not only kept her fit, it kept her sane as well. It helped her to relax. Her father had said—more than once, in fact—that she had the energy of ten people, and he had been right. Even as a child, she'd been perpetually in high gear. She'd never had the patience to keep up a yoga regimen and found herself unable to concentrate on nothing long enough to succeed at transcendental meditation. Going to a gym every day to work out was too much bother. But with running she'd found the ultimate mental high and a true "natural tranquilizer" at the same time.

Slowing to a walk, she turned and headed west, leaving the park at Seventy-second Street. As she passed the Dakota, she remembered the night she'd been there to cover the shooting of John Lennon. One of her biggest cover stories. She'd gained a great deal of professional recognition for that one. It gave her an eerie feeling just thinking about it. It was the first time she'd covered a murder, a young photojournalist out to prove herself. It made her think about her father, about what happened to him, whether he was dead or alive.

She walked on to her own building on West End Avenue. The doorman greeted her cheerfully as he held the door for her. "Don't think I could run like you do, Miss Lynde," he told her. "How do you do it in the winter?"

"Very carefully," Jaime laughed. "*Very* carefully."

She rode up to her floor alone in the elevator. Drawing a long neck chain out of the collar of her warm-up suit, she removed her key from it and unlocked the door. As she entered the apartment, she switched on the light in the small entrance hall and went into the kitchenette. Taking a can of orange-pineapple juice from a six-pack in the refrigerator—a ritual after every run to raise her blood sugar level—she popped the ring tab and threw it into the trash can, then paused at the window to look at the Hudson River and, beyond that, New Jersey. She smiled to herself, thinking about the day her father had taken her to the top of the Empire State Building.

"Can we see New Jersey from here, Daddy?" she asked as he lifted her up to one of those strange-looking telescopes on the eighty-sixth-floor observation platform.

"Sure we can, princess—but there's not a lot to see over there. New Jersey—that part of it, anyway—is not exactly scenic."

Jaime made a wry face. "Oh, Daddy!" she scolded him playfully.

It's certainly not scenic, Daddy—at least not from here it isn't, Jaime thought, returning to the present abruptly.

She walked into the living room and switched on her answering machine. *It's good to be home,* she thought. Home. Her first real home since she was nine years old. When she moved in, five years ago, she'd undertaken the task of decorating it herself in her own personal style. She had bought an antique brass bed and an old roll-top desk at an auction. She'd found some wonderful old Oriental rugs, woven with vivid colors and elaborate designs, and upholstered the overstuffed couch and chairs in tapestrylike materials. On the walls were the paintings her mother had painted at Sound Beach—cool, relaxing seascapes and sailboats, and horses in fields. On a large walnut table behind the couch were favorite family snapshots in an assortment of brass frames, along with the music box her father had given her the year before he left her. The unicorn still revolved, and it still played "The Impossible Dream" after all these years.

Her father's footlocker was in the bedroom. It sat at the foot of her bed, covered with a brightly colored patchwork quilt. Its contents had remained unchanged over the years—all of the cards, gifts, and letters were still locked inside. From time to time she would take them out and look at them. She would read the letters and remember happier times with her father.

It always made her cry.

Still, she continued to surround herself with the memories, to remind herself of the past, the good times *and* the bad. No matter how painful it was, Jaime put a great deal of effort into keeping her father's memory alive, surrounding herself with it.

It felt good, Jaime thought now, to know that no matter how much she traveled or where her profession sent her, there was a place she'd be coming back to, a place she could call home.

She switched off the answering machine after the last message was played and turned her attentions to the stack of mail she'd left unopened on the desk when she'd gone for her evening run. *Bills and junk mail,* she thought ruefully as she sorted it, placing the bills and other "significant correspondence" on the desk and tossing the junk mail into the wastepaper basket. Phone bill, doctor bill, credit card statements, bank statement, junk, junk, junk. Why, she wondered, did so many companies waste so much money on postage each year to send this stuff out? Surely they knew that a large part of it—most of it, in all likelihood—was thrown away unopened. Idly she wondered how many tons of junk mail were handled each year by the U.S. Postal Service. No wonder so much important mail was either lost or delayed—or never arrived at all. Maybe she'd suggest doing a story on it for the magazine. She made a mental note to talk to Ben Rollins about it. Terence Hillyer would probably shoot that one down, too. *He's probably the only person in the world who actually reads all his junk mail,* Jaime thought. *It's probably the only mail he gets.*

Travel confirmations, magazines—nothing new, except for a few personal letters from friends with whom she corresponded regularly. She stifled a yawn, stopping short as the return address on the envelope in her hand caught her eye. It was postmarked Sound Beach. From Alice Harcourt, no doubt, she thought as she stared at it momentarily.

"Junk mail," she proclaimed finally, tossing it into the wicker basket.

ELEVEN

Southampton, July 1984. "I admit it—I *am* nervous," Andrea confessed. "I keep having this vision of myself walking down the aisle, tripping, and falling flat on my face."

Jaime laughed as she reached up to adjust her friend's white silk and seed-pearl flower-petal headpiece. "Relax," she urged. "People get married every day."

Andrea looked at her anxiously. "But *I* don't," she wailed. "What if I make a complete fool of myself?"

Jaime grinned. "Look at it this way—if you make a *complete* fool of yourself, at least you'll have done it in a big way. And knowing your mother, no one will be permitted to notice, no matter what." Jaime straightened the long veil.

Andrea spun around to face her, the layers of white silk rustling with sudden movement. "Thanks a lot!"

"Stand still," Jaime ordered, attacking the headpiece with several large pins. "You'll lose your veil."

"If I don't lose my mind first."

Jaime smiled. "Maybe you and Tom should have eloped."

"*I* wanted to," Andrea told her. "My parents wouldn't hear of it—especially Mother. This three-ring circus was entirely her doing."

Jaime glanced down at her friend's bridal gown—twenty

thousand dollars' worth of silk, seed pearls, and antique lace.
The dress no one had seen, but which nonetheless had still
made the pages of that bible of the fashion industry, *Women's
Wear Daily. Leave it to Kitty Marler to make sure her only
daughter's wedding makes headlines,* Jaime thought with
amusement.

As Andrea crossed the room to her dressing table and put
on her three-strand pearl choker and earrings, Jaime stepped
in front of the full-length mirror to check her own dress.
Andie had kept her word—no pink. Her gown was deep apri-
cot silk, a simple, off the shoulder style with a wide ivory
lace ruffle. With her wide-brimmed straw hat banded in apri-
cot velvet, she decided she looked like a southern belle. *A
reject from the auditions for the role of Scarlett O'Hara,* Jaime
mused, suppressing a grin. Not her style—definitely not her
style—but perfect for a society wedding at Southampton in
the middle of summer.

Looking out the window, she could see the guests gather-
ing on the lawn. The garden, always picture perfect, was
bedecked with large white ribbons, and there were flowers—
mostly white—everywhere. A white carpet had been rolled
out to extend from the patio doors, where the bride and her
attendants would emerge on cue, to the altar where the minister and the groom would be waiting. On either side were
rows of chairs for the wedding guests. In her mind, Jaime
saw her parents' wedding portrait.

*"What's this, Daddy?" Jaime asked, pulling the thick white
leather book from the drawer. She had been only six years
old then and was barely able to lift it.*

*He'd looked at it for a moment, and a strange expression
crossed his face. "That's our wedding album, princess," he
told her. "Pictures taken when your mother and I were married."*

*"Were?" Jaime cocked her head to one side, looking
somewhat confused. "Aren't you still married?"*

*Her father laughed. "Of course we are, princess," he as-
sured her. "I only meant—"*

"Can I look at the pictures?" Jaime asked excitedly.

"If you want, we'll look together."

She nodded happily.

He lifted her up onto his lap and opened the book. It was filled with large photographs of the beautifully romantic outdoor wedding and reception. To Jaime, it was like looking at pictures of the beautiful princess and her dashing prince in a book of fairy tales.

"Mother looked so beautiful, didn't she?" Jaime observed, fascinated by the photos.

"She still is beautiful, honey," he said in a low, gentle voice.

"She's prettier when she smiles," Jaime decided, tracing one of the large photographs with the tip of her small finger. Then she looked up at her father and frowned. "She doesn't smile now."

Her father shook his head. "I know, princess," he said, stroking her tenderly. "Your mother's been ill. That's why she doesn't smile."

"Is Mother going to die, Daddy?" she asked then, her small face filled with concern.

He'd been stunned by her question. "No, sweetheart—of course not," he assured her.

But her father had been wrong. Her mother had died two weeks later.

It was almost dusk when Jaime slipped away from the festivities, changed into her jeans and a loose cotton shirt, and headed back to Manhattan in her Jeep Cherokee. As she drove west on the Long Island Expressway, she found herself thinking about the house at Sound Beach where she'd grown up. How long had it been since she'd left? Six years? In spite of all that had happened there to precipitate her abrupt departure, she still missed the big, rambling old house. The happiest times of her life had been spent there. She wondered if things had changed much since she'd been gone.

On impulse, she steered the Jeep off the Expressway at Route 21 and drove until she reached Sound Beach. Following the winding road along Long Island Sound that led to the Lynde house, she decided the area really hadn't changed too much in the years she'd been away. The houses hadn't changed much, even if some of the names on the mailboxes had. The families of some of the kids she'd grown up with had moved away, but she'd lost touch with most of them when she left to go to Princeton in 1974.

She brought the Jeep to a halt at the gates of the Lynde property and climbed out to have a look around. Climbing up on the white rail fence, she looked toward the house, several hundred yards away. It didn't look any different on the outside, but it was starting to get dark and she couldn't see it too clearly. The Harcourts were still living there. In *her* house. She should have thrown them out the day she discovered their deception, but somehow it hadn't mattered then. Nothing had mattered but the pain she'd felt that April day, the pain she *still* felt. Nothing had mattered but getting away from them, as far away as she could.

Why had they bothered to stay after she had gone? she wondered. They'd always told her they'd come there to look after her after her father's "death." *The only thing is, my father wasn't dead,* Jaime thought, the old anger building up inside her as she remembered that afternoon in the attic when she'd discovered the footlocker filled with all the letters and gifts her father had sent her. Gifts they'd never allowed her to see. He wasn't dead—so why did they want her to believe he was? And why on earth had they gone to so much trouble to prevent him from contacting her?

She had always been bothered by the unanswered questions, and by a nagging suspicion that Alice and Joseph Harcourt were not really her aunt and uncle. Why did she feel that way? In a way, she would regret it if they were not, because she had always liked Joe. He'd been good to her. Unlike Alice, he seemed to understand and, she suspected, to regret what they'd done to her. She'd never trusted Alice, however, and that afternoon in the attic she'd realized why. *She lied to me about everything else—why not about their relationship to me?* Jaime thought resentfully.

Thinking back, she realized there had been times Joseph Harcourt had been trying to tell her, without actually saying the words, not to give up on her father, to believe in what her heart was telling her. Was there some reason he couldn't tell her? she wondered now. Nothing made any sense. Everyone else had believed the stories, the lies, but Jaime knew her father. She knew there was no way her father would ever have left her behind if he had known he wouldn't be coming back. Never!

Up near the house, a car's headlights came on suddenly, and in the distance she could hear its engine start. A moment later, the car started down the long driveway toward the gates. Not wanting to be seen, Jaime hopped down from the fence and ran to the Jeep, driving away just seconds before the car reached the gates. *I'll come back—one day,* she promised herself.

After they're gone for good.

"Street gangs," Jaime said aloud.

"What about them?" Ben Rollins, a stocky man in his late fifties with sparse, graying hair and thick, horn-rimmed glasses, looked up from the yellow legal pad on which he'd been jotting a series of barely legible notes during the editorial meeting.

"I'd like to do a story on them," she told him, reaching for her coffee mug, which, since she never drank coffee, always contained either fruit juice or diet cola. "You know—photos, comments from police and some of the people they've victimized—"

"Who're the police victimizing now?" Mike Turner asked, joining the conversation without being invited.

"The police are not victimizing anyone," Jaime said crossly. "As usual, you weren't listening."

"Yes, I was," he insisted. "You said you wanted to interview the police and the people they were victimizing."

"Do us all a favor. Go research a story on going to the top of the Empire State Building—from the outside," Rollins told him. Then he turned back to Jaime. "You were saying?"

"It would make a great story, Ben," she said with enthusiasm. "Maybe I could even talk to gang members."

"That's a little risky, don't you think?" Rollins pointed out.

At the other end of the long conference table, Terence Hillyer gave a low chuckle. "You do have a death wish, don't you, Lynde?" he asked in his usual mocking tone. Hillyer was thirty-seven but looked forty-seven and often acted eighty-seven, as Mike Turner had so aptly put it on more than one occasion. He was a tall, exceedingly thin man with a prematurely receding hairline and a perpetually bad attitude. He did not object to a gamble as long as someone else was taking all the risks.

"Are you planning to shoot this one down, too, Terry?" Jaime asked, annoyed by his sarcasm.

"Not at all," he said quickly. "If you're willing to risk life and limb for a story, I'll certainly see that it's worth the risk." The animosity between them had started shortly after Jaime joined the magazine's staff—when she'd dared to challenge one of his editorial decisions—and had escalated into a full-blown war when Hillyer was promoted.

Karyn Barnes, Turner's assistant, spoke up. "I think Jaime's right," she said, shooting Hillyer a baleful glance. "It's a timely piece, one just about everybody will want to read."

"Maybe even a cover story," Ben Rollins agreed. "And with Jaime's talent for getting the kind of unexpected candid photographs she's been delivering over the years, it could be just the shot in the arm this magazine really needs." He turned to Jaime. "Okay—you've got the green light on this one."

Jaime smiled. "Thanks, Ben."

The meeting ended fifteen minutes later, following a discussion of stories in progress and ideas for the regular weekly features segments. As Jaime started to gather up her pencils, note pad, and mug, Mike Turner approached her again. "Nice going, Red," he said, grinning broadly.

"Thanks." She didn't look up.

"You surprised the hell out of everybody," he said in a low voice, oblivious of the fact that she was trying diligently to ignore him.

Now she looked up. "Oh? And why is that?"

Turner shoved his hands into his pockets. "Well, who would expect a woman to want to go after a story like that?"

Jaime calmly put down all the things she'd collected and faced him squarely. "Now what is that supposed to mean?"

"Come on—don't get defensive with me, Red," he said with a grin. "I'm just curious, that's all. Why would someone like you want to go chasing after street gangs in crummy neighborhoods?"

Jaime bit her tongue in an attempt to control her temper. "Someone like me?" she asked carefully.

"Well—yeah."

Her eyes narrowed in anger. "For your information, Mr. Hotshot Art Director, while you sit here in your nice air-conditioned office doing whatever it is they're paying you to do, I'm sticking my neck out to get my story. And for your further information, I was covering the heavy-duty stuff—airline hijackings, political protests, assassinations, and serial murders—long before you came here! So don't talk to me about what kind of story 'somebody like me' might or might not cover!"

"Now, wait a minute—I never said—" he started.

She glared at him. "Know what? I always thought most of your bullshit was a put-on," she said coldly as she picked up her things again. "But I was wrong. You really are a bastard." She walked out of the conference room, leaving him—and everyone else—staring after her.

It's not that they don't take woman photojournalists seriously—they just don't take me *seriously,* Jaime thought resentfully as she walked across West Thirty-fourth Street toward Penn Station, the large case containing her new Hasselblad and interchangeable lenses swinging from her left shoulder in rhythm with her quick, athletic stride. They still didn't see her as a serious journalist. To them—to most of them, anyway—she was a spoiled rich kid indulging in a hobby. Never mind the fact that she'd been orphaned—supposedly—at an early age and had learned to be independent out of necessity. She was the granddaughter of Harrison Colby, a man who was not only extremely rich but had, at one time, been a major power in Washington. She'd grown up with every advantage. *Or so they think,* Jaime thought grimly.

She'd had to work twice as hard as everybody else on the staff from day one just to prove herself. She knew she was good; her photographs had graced more covers of *World Views* than anyone else's. She'd won three important awards in the past five years. Recently, she had been approached by a gallery in Manhattan inviting her to exhibit the best of her work in a one-woman show. Yet there were still those among her colleagues—like Turner and Hillyer—who thought her success was either dumb luck or the result of the Colby name and influence. Jaime smiled to herself. Turner never took any woman seriously unless he was sleeping with her. *And probably not even then,* she thought, amused.

She descended the stairs at Penn Station at a run and headed for the subway. She reached the turnstiles just as the train came to a stop and the passengers disembarking came pouring through the gates like cattle being herded to slaughter. Pulling a token from her pocket, Jaime deposited it into the appropriate slot and boarded the still-crowded train. There were no empty seats and little available space to stand in the aisle. She positioned herself between a well-dressed blond man who looked to be in his late forties and carried a folded newspaper and a black leather physician's case, and a middle-aged woman with an overstuffed shopping bag from Macy's that was splitting down one side. She wore a tattered old hat that had to be at least twenty years old, judging from its style and present condition.

Winos, Jaime thought, glancing over her shoulder at the two dirty, unshaven, shabbily dressed men standing behind her. *Where the hell did winos get subway tokens?*

The train made its next stop at Times Square. Though several passengers disembarked, there were still no vacant seats. *Damn,* she thought, hanging on as the subway lurched forward. *Maybe at the next stop . . .*

She became vaguely aware of a hand groping along her backside as another body pressed against her from behind. The strong smell of body odor and cheap liquor sickened her. She looked over her shoulder at the seedy-looking man facing her from behind. "If you want to keep that hand, I strongly suggest you pull it back *now*," she said in a low, menacing tone. Intimidated, he withdrew abruptly and turned away from her.

Jaime took a deep breath, relieved. *Bet he hasn't had a bath since the crash of '29,* she thought, still not completely sure if he'd been trying to feel her up or pick her pocket.

She got off the subway at Seventy-second Street and walked the two blocks to her apartment. She hated taking the subway and used it only as a last resort. It *was* much easier than getting a taxi sometimes—and definitely easier than trying to find a parking space for her Jeep, she decided as she let herself into her apartment.

She put her things down on the couch and automatically checked for messages on the answering machine, then looked through her mail. Her thoughts, however, were still on the editorial meeting. Just thinking about Mike Turner and Terry Hillyer and their smug superiority made her burn. It had taken all of the self-control she could muster to keep herself from slapping those smug Cheshire-cat grins off their faces.

Maybe I will—eventually, she thought.

Jaime woke with a start. Pulling herself into an upright position, she looked around the darkened bedroom, at first not sure where she was. Had she been dreaming? Of course—she must have been! She'd been dreaming about her father. Dreaming he was here, that he was alive and in danger and trying to reach her.

Fumbling in the darkness for the switch, she turned on the lamp on the table beside her bed. The light seemed unusually bright, and she shielded her eyes with one arm. She was trembling. How many times in recent years had she had similar terrifying dreams? How many nights had she lain awake, thinking about him and wondering what had become of him that Christmas in Paris? Would she ever know the truth?

Would she ever see her father again?

TWELVE

New York City, August 1984. The taxi slowed to a stop behind one of the long black limousines parked in front of the Plaza Hotel at Fifth Avenue and East Fifty-ninth Street. Jaime emerged from the back seat and dashed up the steps to the brass-trimmed double doors. She nodded politely to the uniformed doorman who held the door for her as she whisked past him, crossed the busy lobby, and headed for the Edwardian Room with her large camera case swinging at her side. She stole a quick glance at her watch. Eleven-fifteen. She was already fifteen minutes late. *They've probably already started,* she thought dismally.

As she started for the door, in too much of a hurry to watch where she was going, she collided with someone else coming from the opposite direction. Raising her head, she found herself looking into the deepest indigo-blue eyes she'd ever seen. *And the rest of his face isn't bad either,* she decided in the less than a minute it took her to appraise the man standing in front of her. He was very tall—a good six inches taller than she, lean, almost too thin for his height, with sharply defined features and a dazzling smile beneath a thick but neatly trimmed mustache. His hair was medium brown, curly but not too curly, and just a bit too long. To his barber's

148

credit, it didn't look styled. *He looks even better in the flesh than he does on TV,* Jaime thought, recognizing him as Martin Cantrell, a newscaster for the TBC Evening News.

"I'm sorry—" she gasped.

"I'm sorry—" he started at exactly the same moment.

They both began to laugh. He motioned for her to move ahead of him, and she entered the already packed Edwardian Room. He followed her, with a cameraman and a technician trailing behind. "It's going to be hard to get a good tape from here, Marty," she heard the cameraman tell him.

"I think you're right," he agreed.

"That's what we get for being late," Jaime said in a half-joking tone.

"I was caught in traffic," he responded with a grin. "What's your excuse?"

"The same," Jaime admitted. "At least you came in a TBC van—I had to practically mow down two little old ladies to get a taxi! You wouldn't believe how hard it was to get a cab today."

"Yes, I would," he assured her. "I waited so long in front of my building this morning before one finally came along, I thought another strike had been called during the night."

"I played it safe," Jaime confided. "I took the subway. I probably would have made better time if I'd taken it here."

He raised an eyebrow. "The subway?" He smiled appreciatively. "I do admire a woman with courage."

Jaime looked around. "It appears we're not the only late arrivals," she observed. "The guest of honor isn't here either."

"The senator's been caught in traffic coming in from La Guardia," said the reporter standing to Jaime's right. "They keep telling us 'just a few more minutes,' but frankly I'm beginning to wonder."

"Terrific," Jaime said, rolling her eyes upward in frustration.

Martin Cantrell smiled. "I've never known Senator Marlowe to ever be on time, traffic or no traffic," he confided to Jaime. "In fact, during the last election, it was a joke. He

was referred to as 'the *late* Senator Marlowe.' Everyone made
jokes about whether or not he'd get to the polls on time.''

"Politicians always make it to the polls, even if they're late
for their own funerals," Jaime commented with a knowing
smile.

"You sound as if you're speaking from experience," he
noted with mild curiosity in his voice.

"In a way," she acknowledged with a nod. "My grandfather was a politician."

He looked at her, intrigued. "Oh?"

She nodded. "Harrison Colby."

The crowd hushed abruptly as one of Senator Marlowe's
aides stepped up to the podium and took the microphone.
"The senator has just arrived," he announced. "He'll be
joining us in just a moment."

"So they keep promising," one of the reporters in the
back of the room grumbled.

Jaime turned to Cantrell again. "Maybe the day won't be
a total loss after all."

"It hasn't been, as far as I'm concerned," he said, smiling. "At least it won't be—if you'll have dinner with me
tonight."

"Dinner—when we haven't been properly introduced?" she
asked, feigning shock.

"I can fix that," he said promptly, extending his hand.
"I'm Marty Cantrell, TBC News."

She laughed. "Do you always introduce yourself as if
you're signing off?"

"Only when I'm trying to impress someone," he admitted.

"Oh." She nodded slowly. "In that case, I have a confes-
sion to make. I already know who you are. I see you on TV
every night. I'm Jaime Lynde, *World Views* magazine."

He grinned. "Do *you* always identify yourself that way?"

She laughed. "Only when I want to impress someone.
Now, about dinner . . ."

Jaime seldom dated. Still carrying with her the emotional
scars of her childhood, she was reluctant to allow herself to

get close to anyone. She allowed herself few close friends and preferred to spend her evenings discussing the positives and negatives of her profession with colleagues. She told herself it didn't matter one way or the other if the colleague happened to be a handsome, successful man like Marty Cantrell—though she had to admit, if only to herself, that she did find him quite attractive.

"Tell me, Mr. Newsman—what's a big-time newscaster like yourself doing chasing small-time stories like Senator Marlowe's Operation Cleanup campaign?" Jaime asked, seated across from Marty on one of the exquisite tatami at Shinbashi on Park Avenue.

He grinned. "I guess it's just a throwback to my days as a small-time broadcaster for the hometown station," he answered, testing his Sapporo draft beer.

"Where are you from?"

"Brownsville, Texas—originally," he said. "Boca Raton, Florida, Miami, and Atlanta—in that order."

"A gypsy!" Jaime declared. "A man after my own heart."

His eyes met hers. "Definitely."

The waiter arrived with their sashimi and Jaime made a face. Unlike most native New Yorkers, she was not fond of sashimi. She didn't even like rare steak, let alone raw fish. *What has this man talked me into!* she wondered. Marty grinned as if he'd read her mind. "That's tuna," he said, pointing with his chopstick to the deep red slices on her plate. "Everything they serve here is fresh—and cool. Nothing jellied or ice-cold, as you might get elsewhere."

Jaime tasted the tuna and was pleasantly surprised. "What's this?" she asked, indicating a coral-colored blob surrounded by a seaweed collar.

"Sea urchin."

"And this one?"

"Octopus."

She wrinkled her nose, pushing it aside gingerly. "No, thanks."

Marty laughed. "Try it," he urged. "It's actually quite good."

Jaime shook her head emphatically. "I make it a point

never to eat anything that could possibly eat me," she maintained, feeling slightly nauseated at the thought.

"But it can't eat you," Marty pointed out with amusement. "It's dead."

She looked at him, resting her chin in one hand, her elbow propped on the table in a manner her mother would have found deplorable. "In the future," she began carefully, "I think I'll stick to the tonkatsu or the salmon teriyaki, thank you very much."

It was, she decided later, a pleasant evening in spite of the octopus. Marty insisted upon seeing her home, even though she insisted that it wasn't necessary. He in turn insisted upon taking her all the way to her door. "You'd better make it fast," she told him as she slipped her key into the lock and opened the door. "The meter's running, you know."

"I know." He took a step closer, following her inside. "Let it run."

"It'll cost you a small fortune." She felt mildly uncomfortable.

"No it won't." He pressed her back against the wall gently. "I'll put it on my expense account. Let the network pick up the tab." His lips sought hers in the darkness.

"You won't get away with that," she muttered against his mouth as he kissed her.

"Mmmm . . . sure I will." His tongue met hers, arousing her against her will. She felt his hands on her waist. To her horror, she felt her nipples harden beneath her silk blouse, and she was sure he was aware of it too. With one hand, he reached up under her blouse. His fingers undid the front of her bra hastily and his hand seized one breast. Jaime felt as though the walls were spinning around her as he teased her, pressing himself against her in a way that left no doubt in her mind what he was experiencing. His fingers played with her nipple. Taking a deep breath, she pushed him away abruptly. "Marty . . ." she whispered, making a helpless gesture with her hands.

He stared at her in the darkness. "I'm sorry," he breathed. "I didn't mean to rush you . . . I just thought . . ."

"I'm not ready for that," she said looking down at the floor.

He nodded, scratching the back of his head in a manner that indicated either frustration or irritation—or both. "I got carried away," he said finally.

She nodded.

"A lousy start." He smiled. "Think we could try it again—from go?"

She forced a smile. "Sure. Why not?"

"Tomorrow night?"

She nodded again.

"Where would you like to go?" he asked, clearly nervous.

"Italian or French, if I have the option." She smiled. "I've had enough octopus."

"No more octopus," he promised. "I know a great Italian place on the East Side."

"I love Italian."

"Pick you up at seven?"

She nodded. "I should be able to pull myself together by then."

It was not until he left the apartment and she heard the doors of the elevator closing that she sagged with relief. It had been a long time since she'd allowed herself even a casual sexual relationship with a man. It had been even longer since she'd been so intensely attracted to anyone. Especially someone she'd just met. The strength of her physical attraction to Marty Cantrell had taken her by surprise—even more so than his attraction to her. *As long as it's only physical, it's safe,* she told herself.

As long as it never goes any further.

Jaime saw Marty every day. When their hectic schedules permitted, they met for lunch. They went to favorite restaurants like the Manhattan Market, the Fonda la Paloma, or the Gloucester House. Sometimes they bought hot dogs from a sidewalk vendor or took a picnic basket to Central Park. They had dinner together almost every night and spent their weekends haunting art galleries, from Madison Avenue to SoHo. They rode the Circle Line around Manhattan. They took the ferry out to Liberty Island, even though the statue itself was closed for refurbishing and surrounded by scaffolding. They went to the ballet and to open-air concerts in the park. They thoroughly enjoyed each other's company, but Marty never made a move to get her into bed. "I'll wait until you're ready," he promised.

I am ready, she thought, looking at him thoughtfully as he spread out the blanket near the newly dedicated Strawberry Fields on the west side of Central Park. He looked as handsome in his yellow polo shirt and olive green pants as he had in his Italian suit the night he took her to the ballet. *Tom Selleck, watch out,* she thought.

"What, may I ask, are you thinking about?" Marty asked as he started removing items from the wicker picnic hamper. "From the look on your face, it must be something pretty good."

"It's not important," she insisted, still smiling.

"It doesn't look 'not important,' at least not from where I sit." He uncorked the wine. Taking two glasses from the hamper, he filled them and gave her one. "Well—are you going to confess or not?"

She laughed. "To what?"

"To all of those improper thoughts that must be dancing around that pretty head of yours," he said with a sly smile, tasting the wine.

She took a sip. "How would you know if my thoughts are improper or not?"

"By the look on your face. It's a dead giveaway." He stretched out on the blanket, supporting his weight on one elbow. "A good newsman knows how to read body language—and faces. Yours, my love, is an improper smile if I ever saw one."

"Thanks a lot!"

"I meant it as a compliment," he insisted. "I happen to like thoroughly wicked smiles—especially on such a beautiful face." He finished his wine, then put the empty glass aside and took hers. It was still half filled, and when he set it down, it spilled, staining one corner of the blanket. He paid no attention to it. "Come here, woman," he said huskily, pulling her down to him. He kissed her, a slow lingering kiss—yet unmistakably urgent. Jaime responded with equal enthusiasm, wrapping her arms around his neck. She did want him, she knew that—and now, so did he. It was not until she felt his hands moving down the length of her body that she returned sharply to reality.

"I think we'd better eat," she gasped, pulling away from him.

"Later." He reached for her again.

She withdrew abruptly, escaping his hands. "We're not exactly alone—in case you haven't noticed," she pointed out with an expansive gesture. "If we'd gone any further, you'd have been on the evening news—but *not* as a newscaster!"

"That's okay with me. I always did like to attract attention." He grinned devilishly.

"Well, I don't!" she told him, hastily removing whatever was still in the hamper. "You poor starving man—let's eat!"

"That was fun," Jaime told Marty as they entered her apartment. "We'll have to do it again soon."

He put the hamper down on the floor. "I'd like to make plans for the more immediate future," he said, closing the door.

"Oh?" She turned to look at him with a knowing smile. "And just what do you have in mind, Mr. Lecherous Newscaster?"

His eyes met hers, bright with desire. "I think you already know the answer to that," he said evenly.

She nodded slowly. "Yes—I think I do," she confessed in a barely audible voice.

"I've waited," he said slowly, taking a step forward. "I've tried not to rush you." He came closer. "It's been months, Jaime. I've kept my word . . ."

Jaime extended her arms to him. "Stop being such a damned perfect gentleman and make love to me, you big idiot."

In the next instant, they were in each other's arms. His mouth found hers in the darkness, hard and demanding, as he crushed her against the hardness of his own body. She could feel his heart beating wildly—or was it her own? She was filled with a strange inner excitement, one she'd never known before, as his large hands moved down her back, cupping her buttocks, pressing their loins together in a way that made his desire as clear to her as her own. He started to pick her up, but she stopped him. "I can still walk, thank you very much," she whispered as she turned and headed toward the bedroom, beckoning him to follow. Unbuttoning her purple cotton blouse as she crossed the room, she slipped it off and dropped it to the floor, leaving her naked to the waist. Casually, she pulled down the comforter on the bed, then the rest of her clothes as Marty struggled out of his impatiently.

As he opened the small condom packet with his teeth, he was intrigued by the uninhibited manner with which she'd disrobed in front of him. There was no false modesty about her, no coyness. He liked that. As she stood naked before him, he saw a woman with a magnificent body who was completely comfortable with her nudity, open in her desire for him. When they came together again, it was the urgency that came from weeks—months—of denying their needs and wants. He kissed her devouringly, and she responded with a hunger that belied her outward calm as she caressed his lean, hard-muscled back. They descended to the bed together, still locked in an embrace. They covered each other's faces with eager kisses, their arms and legs entangled as they began the process of exploring each other's bodies with their hands and their mouths.

"It's about time," Marty whispered, planting tiny kisses along her jawline. "I thought you'd never see the light . . ."

"I'm not as stubborn as everyone seems to think," she said softly, kissing his forehead between each word. "At any rate, love, I never deny myself anything I have a real need for. Like now." She threaded her fingers through his hair as he lowered his head to her breast. She gave an involuntary shiver of pleasure as he started teasing her nipples with the tip of his tongue, first one, then the other. She arched her back and pushed her breasts toward his face as if to urge him on. He began to suck at them, first gently, then with more desire. When she'd had enough, she pushed him away. He rolled over on his back, taking her with him. She kissed him again and again—first his forehead, then his nose, then his lips and chin, finally burrowing into the hollow of his neck. Then she bit him playfully. Surprised, he pulled away. "Hungry now, are you?" he asked with a wicked grin.

"Mmmm . . . famished," she breathed, shaking her long hair away from her face.

He gave a deep, throaty laugh. "I'll give you something to satisfy that voracious appetite of yours," he growled, guiding her head down to his swollen organ, rising high against his groin, throbbing with desire. "Something to satisfy both of us."

Smiling, Jaime bent her head to take it into her mouth. She licked it lazily, sucking at it from time to time, teasing it with her lips and her tongue until she knew he was ready. She pulled away suddenly, straddling him, guiding him up inside her. She rode him as his fingers probed through the darkness and found that spot at which they joined, stroking her until they both came to an explosive orgasm.

She collapsed on top of him, he still inside her. Their eyes met as they both struggled to catch their breath. "You're too fast, woman," Marty growled, tracing his fingertip across her lower lip. "I came here with every intention of making a night of it."

Jaime looked at him and smiled. "I'm counting on it."

Before she knew Marty, Jaime had enjoyed sex but never allowed herself to feel anything beyond physical desire for her partner. It was better that way, she reasoned, recalling too vividly the emotional pain of her mother's suicide and the rage and helplessness she felt at the unexplained disappearance of her father, the man she'd worshiped. She had always felt that if her mother ever really loved her or wanted her, she would not have taken her own life. Though she'd spent the last eighteen years convincing herself there had to be extenuating circumstances behind her father's abrupt departure from her life, a part of her had always felt abandoned. *The bottom line is that he left me,* she thought resentfully. *He did leave me.*

That belief had influenced all of her relationships all of her life. She dated occasionally, satisfied her sexual needs when it became necessary, but never allowed herself the luxury of forming any real emotional attachments. She had discouraged anyone who tried to get close, until Marty came into her life. Until Marty—bright, handsome, sexy Marty with his natural daring and his wonderful sense of humor—there had been no one who mattered. She'd fallen in love with the man without even realizing it, until it was too late, and there could be no turning back. She not only loved him, she trusted him as she'd never trusted any man before. She felt safe with him. *Safe—what a lovely feeling,* Jaime marveled. *I haven't felt really safe since I was six years old.*

She set the small table in her "dining room"—which was actually one corner of her living room—with a lace tablecloth that had belonged to her late grandmother and china and silver she'd picked up at an auction in Connecticut. Satisfied that it looked perfect, she went into the kitchen to check on the chicken. Normally, she and Marty ate out. They almost always spent the night together, either at her apartment or his. But tonight was going to be different, she decided. Tonight, she wanted to be alone with him. Completely alone. She was leaving for Chile on an assignment in less than twenty-four hours and was determined that tonight would be special.

She went into the bedroom to dress. She put on a forest-green silk smoking jacket with a shawl collar and black silk pants. She wore the same jewelry she always wore, adding a heavy gold nugget choker and a thick gold bracelet. She wore only the barest touch of makeup and combed her heavy curtain of red hair loosely over her shoulders. *Just the way Marty likes it,* she thought, pleased, as she checked herself in the mirror.

Marty arrived promptly at seven-thirty. "Am I late?" he asked, handing her a bottle of wine and a bouquet of flowers wrapped in green tissue paper.

Jaime kissed him. "Right on time, Mr. Newsman," she said cheerfully. "Twenty seconds to air time." She took his gifts off to the kitchen.

He raised an eyebrow questioningly. "You have a video camera in here?"

She returned, smiling wickedly. "In the bedroom," she said in a teasing voice.

He grinned. "You're shameless," he said, taking her in his arms. "But I've always been an exhibitionist at heart—did you know that?"

Her arms encircled his waist. "I've suspected it," she confessed.

"You mean that afternoon in the park?" His tongue traced the fullness of her lips.

"That, yes—and the day at the gallery." She kissed his chin. "And on the observation platform at the World Trade Center." And his lips. "At the Met." The tip of his nose. "On the Staten Island ferry." Her lips fluttered across his eyelids. "And how about that day on the escalator at Macy's? Mister, I think you'd make out on the anchor desk *during* the eleven o'clock news!"

He chuckled softly. "Now that you mention it, I think I would." He paused, sniffing the air. "Is something on fire?"

Jaime's eyes widened with horror as the reality hit her. "Oh, my God—the chicken!"

The bedroom was in darkness. Jaime and Marty, spent from a long night of lovemaking, lay locked in an embrace, their arms and legs tangled, their bodies flushed and moist with gratification. She traced his profile with the tip of her index finger. "Poor baby," she said, laughing softly. "You look exhausted."

He raised an eyebrow, the only part of his body he was capable of moving at that moment. "And I suppose you're not?"

"Not at all," she said brightly.

He gave an exasperated groan.

"What's the matter, Cantrell?" She was obviously in a teasing mood. "Can't hack it?"

"You know, woman, I came here tonight with every intention of asking you to marry me," he started with a weak voice. "But I think you'd make an old man of me in no time flat."

She sat up and looked at him. "Is that a proposal?"

"It was supposed to be, yes."

Her smile vanished abruptly. A marriage proposal was the one possibility she *hadn't* considered.

"You don't exactly look thrilled," Marty observed. "Is that a no?"

She shook her head. "I'm just surprised, that's all."

He pulled himself up on one elbow. "Don't tell me you're one of those militant career women who only wants a man from time to time to satisfy her—uh, urges." He ran one hand through his hair. "Talk abut role reversal!"

You don't know how close that is to the truth—or has been in the past few years, Jaime thought grimly. "No," she said evenly. "It's not that at all."

"Then it must be me," he said. Attempting to break the growing tension between them, he raised one arm and sniffed. "Maybe I'm using the wrong deodorant—or could it be the mouthwash?"

She didn't smile. "It's not you," she assured him.

He looked at her for a moment. "You just don't want to marry me," he decided promptly. "That's it, isn't it?"

"Oh, no!" she said quickly. "It's me, Marty. I've never been able to commit myself totally to a relationship." She gave a helpless shrug. "You wouldn't understand."

"Try me," he suggested.

She hesitated for a moment. "I'm afraid," she finally admitted, avoiding his eyes.

"Of what?" His voice was gentle.

"Of trusting, of caring too much," she said in a barely audible voice. "Of getting hurt again."

"Again?" He reached out and touched her face tenderly. "Who hurt you before?"

She shook her head. "I can't talk about it, Marty. Not yet."

He persisted. "I'd like to help—if you'll let me."

She wanted to talk about it. She wanted to share it with him, yet she held back. She'd never discussed it with anyone before. Revealing herself made her vulnerable, and she'd resolved never to be vulnerable again. Still. . . .

"My mother . . . and my father," she said finally, surprising herself with the sound of her own words.

"How did they hurt you?" he asked.

"They left me. They just left, no warning, nothing. They just left one day and didn't come back." Her voice was faltering. "My mother took her own life when I was six. My father traveled a great deal on business. One day he left, and I never saw him again." Unexpectedly, the words came pouring out, the emotions she'd kept pent up for so many years freed at last, and she told him all the things she'd never been able to tell anyone—her doubts about her mother's love for her, about what really became of her father, everything. Afterward, Marty held her close, stroking her hair and assuring her he loved her and would never leave her.

The next morning he suggested she look into the facts surrounding her father's sudden disappearance. "You say you don't think he's really dead," he pointed out. "Don't you think you should find out—one way or the other?"

She looked at him. "How?" she asked, uncertain.

He smiled patiently. "You're a journalist. Use your resources."

Jaime thought about it for a moment. "Do you think it's possible . . ."

Marty looked at her. "I think," he started, "the only thing the press *hasn't* uncovered to date is what really happened to Jimmy Hoffa."

THIRTEEN

New York City, April 1985. Jaime stood outside the O'Donnell-Colby building on Wall Street. Staring up at the twenty-seven-story, glass-and-steel structure, she saw it as a gleaming pillar rising from the row of much older, close-set buildings glowing in the late afternoon sun. Her father had not been with the firm when it was built, she realized as she read the plaque on the cornerstone: 1974. She wondered how many of the people he had worked with—if any—were still around.

She stepped into one of the revolving doors and entered the lobby. *Impressive,* she thought, casually taking in the huge potted plants and floor-to-ceiling windows. Sophisticated was the word that came to mind. She decided she was going to look like a fish out of water here, in her chocolate-brown pants and bulky ivory sweater, but she didn't really give a damn. *I'm not here to impress anyone,* she thought defiantly. *These are the people who accused my father of being an embezzler.* The heels of her tan leather boots clicked on the gray and black terrazzo floor as she made her way to the elevators. She paused long enough to check the directory on the far wall for a familiar name. Names of men or women who'd been here when her father was still with O'Donnell-Colby

Associates. *Three of them are still around,* she thought, jotting down the names on a small note pad. *Three possible chances to find the truth—or at least a clue to it.*

She took the elevator to the sixteenth floor. The first name on her list was John Matthews, who was now director of personnel. His secretary, a smartly dressed, gray-haired woman with a heavily lined face and the look of a hawk in pursuit of its prey, looked up from the memo she was typing as Jaime entered the personnel offices. *She looks like she's about to move in for the kill,* Jaime thought wryly. Upon closer inspection, Jaime decided the woman was wearing too much makeup—and that the instantaneous disapproval she felt was clearly mutual. "May I help you?" the other woman asked coolly.

"I'd like to see Mr. Matthews, please." Jaime was forcing herself to sound pleasant.

"Do you have an appointment?"

Ah—the sentry at the gates of Hell, Jaime thought. "Yes," she lied promptly.

"Your name?" The woman flipped through the appointment book on the desk in front of her.

Nothing gets past this one, Jaime decided. "Well—I don't actually have an appointment," she said quickly, "but Uncle John said if I was ever in town to give him a call, and I arrived rather unexpectedly, and—"

"You're his niece, then?"

Jaime nodded. *You catch on fast.*

At that moment, the door on the far side of the room opened and a tall, heavyset man with thinning gray hair and mustache emerged. He wore thick glasses and a suit Jaime guessed was probably very expensive. "Cora, I—" He stopped short when he saw Jaime, staring at her for a long moment. "Jaime?" he asked. "Jaime Lynde?"

She nodded.

"My God, you *do* look like your father," he declared.

She forced a smile. "So I've been told."

"It's been so many years. What brings you here?"

"I need to talk to you, Mr. Matthews—about my father," she said quietly. "It's important."

He hesitated for a moment, then nodded. "Come into my office."

Jaime glanced over her shoulder at the secretary, who looked thoroughly confused, as she walked into the office and Matthews shut the door. "Have a seat," he said, indicating a chair for her in front of his desk. Jaime sat down and took in her surroundings in one sweeping glance: Ultramodern . . . glass and chrome . . . abstract art on the walls . . . perfect for a man in his position. Stylish, but giving away nothing of the man himself.

"What can I do for you, Jaime?" Matthews asked.

Jaime's eyes met his. "You can tell me about my father, Mr. Matthews," she said promptly, skipping the amenities.

He knew without asking what she was talking about. "Are you sure you want to hear it?" he asked dubiously.

She nodded. "I'm a big girl. I can take it."

He drew in a deep breath, then nodded. "He had a spotless record—one of our best executives, and one of the most successful," he recalled, pursing his lips thoughtfully. "Then he had a run-in with Harrison—your grandfather—when Harrison caught him with one of his women."

"Women?" Jaime asked, surprised.

Matthews nodded. "Seems the Colbys got it in their heads that he'd only married their daughter for the money, for the Colby connections," he went on. "In the late forties your father had a lot of medals and a graduate degree but no job experience. By marrying one of Harrison Colby's daughters, he was assured of a place here. Rumor had it he had the hots for the younger daughter but married Frances because she'd be easier to handle, especially if he wanted a woman on the side once in a while—which, I've heard, he did."

Jaime's thoughts raced backward, trying to remember something, anything, that might make sense of what he was saying. There was nothing. Not a thing. She remembered things had been strained between her father and grandfather after her mother's death—but never before, not that she could recall. She supposed it was *possible* that there could have been another woman, but she didn't believe it. Still, her mother hadn't been much of a wife those last years of her life, locked away in her room all the time. . . .

"I was told he was accused of embezzlement," Jaime said, returning to the present abruptly, not wanting to hear any more about her father's alleged womanizing.

Matthews frowned. "I told you about that because it was— word had it around here at the time—the reason your father did what he did." He lit a fat cigar.

"I see. And just what did he do?"

Matthews paused momentarily. "He clashed with Harrison right after your mother's death. Everybody knew it was suicide, which just added fuel to the fire, so to speak," he remembered. "Harrison was ready to boot him out of the firm—and take legal action to gain custody of his only granddaughter, you. Jim Lynde knew he'd lose if it went to court, what with Colby's power and influence, but he was going to make Harrison pay for it. He had to fly to Paris. There was a big transaction taking place there in late December '66. He flew to Paris—but he never showed for the meeting. Nobody ever saw him again."

"And you know everything you've told me for a fact?" Jaime asked, unconvinced. She knew nothing of a clash between her father and grandfather. It was her grandmother who blamed him for her mother's suicide!

"Well—no. As I said, most of it was rumor, speculation. All anyone knows around here is that Jim Lynde disappeared one day with a lot of funds in his possession, and that nobody's seen him since," Matthews admitted.

Jaime got to her feet slowly. "For years, Mr. Matthews, I was told my father was dead," she said evenly. "I think I've been told every story in the book about what happened to him and why—but yours, I must say, should get the Pulitzer Prize for fiction!"

She turned on her heel and walked out without another word.

The other man she'd spoken to hadn't been any more pleasant, and the third had refused to speak to her at all. They obviously believed every vicious tale told about her father, from the embezzlement to the alleged infidelities, she decided in the taxi, heading back to her apartment that evening. They thought he was guilty as sin, no matter what the "extenuating circumstances" might be. No matter that no one seemed to have any concrete proof. *Screw all of them,* she thought angrily. *Daddy and Aunt Kate? Impossible! And as for that ridiculous tale about Grandfather accusing him of cheating on Mother and trying to take me away from him—bullshit!*

The taxi came to a stop at the curb in front of her building. Pausing to calculate the tip, she dug into her shoulder bag for her wallet. She paid the driver, climbed out of the car, and dashed into the building. She squeezed into a crowded elevator just before the doors closed and rode up to her floor in silence, deliberately avoiding conversation with anyone else in the car. She was not in the mood to talk. Not tonight.

When the elevator reached her floor, she stepped out into the hallway and fished through her bag for her keys. She dropped them twice, still trembling with anger. Her father had been tried, convicted, and executed as far as his former colleagues were concerned. They didn't give a damn if there were extenuating circumstances. They didn't care if something terrible had happened to her father. They cared only about the damned missing funds. *The hell with them,* she thought resentfully. *All of them.*

Letting herself into the apartment, she threw her bag down, not caring where it landed, and stalked into the kitchen angrily. She fought an overwhelming urge to punch the wall—or whatever else happened to get in her way. Rage and frustration surged through her like a great tidal wave, threatening to engulf her. She opened a can of juice and downed it quickly, suddenly wishing she had something stronger available. She squashed the empty can in one hand, tossed it into the trash can, then went into the bedroom. She took off her boots, seething with anger as she pointedly dropped them to the floor, one at a time. She was still thinking about Matthews and the others. Their responses to her questions had only fueled her determination to get to the bottom of the mystery, to uncover the real reason behind her father's disappearance.

Once and for all.

• • •

"They could have found him floating facedown in the Seine, and all they would have cared about is what happened to the goddamned money," Jaime told Marty over dinner at the Quilted Giraffe. "It was so infuriating."

Marty signaled the waiter for another drink. "Did you really expect anything more from them?" he wanted to know.

She put down her fork. "No—yes. Yes, I did," she admitted. "I expected to find at least one person who had doubts, who thought Daddy might have had a valid reason for what he did."

"Your anger's a waste of your energies," Marty pointed out. "You've got more important things to do than sit around swearing at all the narrow-minded bastards in the world."

"Like what, Mr. Newsman?" Her voice was touched with sarcasm.

He smiled. "You're a journalist. If this were a story you were covering, if you had no emotional involvement with it yourself, what would your next move be?"

She thought about it. "I'd talk to the family," she said finally, taking a bite. She chewed thoughtfully. "Except in this case I can't. There isn't any."

"None at all?"

"I never knew my father's family," she said, picking at the food on her plate absently. "Except for his so-called sister and brother-in-law."

"So-called?" Marty raised an eyebrow questioningly.

"They *said* they were my aunt and uncle," Jaime explained, her doubt clear in her voice. "They knew all kinds of things about my father, about me—but something just didn't feel right. Maybe because Daddy never told me he had a sister, I don't know. That shouldn't have surprised me. He never talked about them, only that they all came from Vermont, transplanted to Baltimore. All I know for sure is that I never really trusted them—especially her."

Marty studied her for a moment. "Did you ever really trust anyone after he left?"

She hesitated for a moment. "No—not really," she finally confessed.

Their conversation was interrupted by their waiter, who brought Marty's drink and asked if they were ready to order dessert. After he was gone, Jaime turned to Marty again. "Aside from Alice and Joe—who've lied to me so many times I've lost count—there's no one I can ask about it. Mother's dead, and so are my grandparents. My—" She stopped short.

Marty stared at her, waiting for her to go on.

"My mother's sister. My Aunt Kate," she said. "She lives in Washington now—in Maryland, actually. She's married to Senator Craig Pearson."

"Think she'll know anything?" Marty asked, reaching for his drink.

"Probably not much," Jaime said with a shrug. "But anything will be that much more than I know."

"So you call her. Then what?"

Jaime shook her head. "I *don't* call her," she said promptly. "I go talk to her. Face-to-face—in Washington."

The FASTEN SEAT BELT sign clicked on as the plane began its descent to Washington's National Airport. Jaime looked out the window to her left. As the clouds parted, she could see all the familiar landmarks below: the Capitol, the Mall, the Washington Monument, the Jefferson and Lincoln memorials, the White House. *How long has it been?* she asked herself. *Six months since I've seen Washington . . . over sixteen years since I've seen Kate.*

Air travel had long ago become routine for Jaime. Since joining the staff of *World Views*, she'd often quipped that she spent more time in the air than did most flight attendants. Even now, as the jet came to a bumpy landing on the runway, she was not fazed by it. In fact, she was not even thinking about it. Her mind was on the meeting that would soon take place. What would it be like, seeing Kate after so many years? They'd done their best to keep in touch, but their respective schedules hadn't always made it possible. It made her think about what John Matthews had said: *Rumor had it Jim Lynde had the hots for the younger daughter. . . .* Was it possible? she asked herself.

As the other passengers began to file out, Jaime unfastened

her seat belt and stood up, taking her tan leather carry-on bag from the overhead compartment. She squeezed into the aisle and made her way to the exit, still thinking about the telephone conversation she'd had with Kate the night before. Her aunt had seemed happy to hear from her—and eager to see her. *I wonder if she knows anything?* Jaime thought, looking around as she passed through the gates. *Will I even recognize her?*

"Jaime, darling! Over here!"

Her head jerked around in the direction of the vaguely familiar female voice calling her name. Kate Colby Pearson stood a little over thirty feet away, waving to her. Kate hadn't changed much in the past sixteen years, Jaime decided. She'd matured, of course. There were a few extra pounds, but in all the right places; the same style and sophistication Jaime remembered were still there, but altered to keep in with the current fashion trends. Her dark hair was cut fashionably short now, and she was wearing a blue Adolfo suit and a wide-brimmed hat.

"Kate!" Jaime cried happily as they flew into each other's arms, the years melting away with their embrace.

The older woman, shorter than her niece by a good six inches, drew back to have a better look at her sister's only daughter. "Kate?" she asked with a note of mild disapproval in her voice. "And what happened to *Aunt* Kate?"

"I grew up," Jaime said promptly. "Besides, 'aunt' makes me think of a dotty old woman rattling around a big mausoleum of a house with dozens of cats of all sizes and colors. You're much too youthful and attractive for that."

Kate laughed. "In that case," she began, putting one arm around Jaime as they headed for the baggage carousel, "you are not only forgiven, but you must promise never to call me 'aunt' again."

Jaime laughed. "It's a deal."

"I would have recognized you anywhere, even after all these years," Kate told Jaime as they walked together on the grounds of the Pearsons' Maryland home near Brookmont, overlooking the Potomac. "You, my dear, are every inch your father's daughter—the same hair, the same eyes, the same determined look on your face. You'd have to have been born a boy to look more like him.''

"You don't see anything of Mother in me?" Jaime picked up a twig, broke it in half, then cast it aside.

Kate shook her head. "You're very different from Frannie," she said quietly. "My sister was lovely, in her own way—but fragile, like a butterfly. Fragile-looking and fragile emotionally. She was, for most of her life, quite unhappy—though none of us ever knew why.''

"That's the way I remember her," Jaime said with a sigh. "Sad. I always wondered if Daddy and I were the reason for her unhappiness.''

Kate frowned. "Fran was always unhappy, dear," she said then. "Even when we were children, there was always something so melancholy about her. She spent a lot of time alone. I was the resident problem child, the rebel—always in trouble, sneaking out at night, running around with the undesirables, getting myself kicked out of school—''

"A typical teen-age girl," Jaime concluded.

"Or so I tried to convince Mother and Father," Kate agreed. "Fran didn't do any of those things. She did a lot of reading and painting—but mostly a lot of daydreaming. I always had the feeling she retreated into those imaginary worlds of hers because she couldn't deal with the real world. Until she met your father, that is." She brushed a leaf from her dark gray sweater.

Jaime looked at her, surprised. "My father made her happy?''

The memory brought a faint smile to Kate's lips. "Having the attentions of a man like Jim would have made almost any woman happy, I think," she said honestly.

Jaime was thinking about what Matthews had told her. "It sounds as if you were attracted to him too," she observed.

Kate hesitated for a moment. "I think I fell in love with him the first time I saw him," she admitted.

"You were in love with my father?''

"I fell in love with him before Fran did," Kate said, folding her arms across her chest as they continued to walk. "I always thought we would have been better suited to each other. There was a lawlessness in both of us that would have meshed perfectly. But he made it clear, right from the start, that he had eyes only for Frannie. They were worlds apart in every way, but they were in love, and that, apparently, was all that mattered.''

''Then the two of you were never—involved?'' Jaime asked carefully.

Kate looked surprised. ''No—of course not! Why would you ask?''

Jaime told her about her conversation with John Matthews.

Kate shook her head. ''Nothing ever happened between Jim and me,'' Kate insisted. ''Much as I wanted it to. Once he was engaged to Frannie, that was it as far as I was concerned, as far as both of us were concerned. To my knowledge, Jim never cheated on Fran in all the years they were married.''

''Do you think my father was an embezzler?'' Jaime asked.

Kate shook her head. ''Jim Lynde was a lot of things, but a criminal? No—no one would ever make me believe that.''

''What about Grandfather and Grandmother?'' Jaime pursued.

Kate sighed. ''Mother wanted to believe the worst because she held Frannie's death against him, but in his heart Father knew it wasn't true.''

''Did he think Daddy was cheating on Mother?''

''If he did, he never said anything, but you know how office gossip gets started,'' Kate pointed out.

''Then he never took legal action to take me away from Daddy?''

Kate looked surprised. ''No—of course not! Whatever else your father may or may not have been, he adored you. He was a good father, or he tried to be, and we all knew it. Even Mother.''

Jaime took a deep breath. ''Are you giving him the benefit of the doubt because you were once in love with him?''

''I'm giving him the benefit of the doubt because I've always been in love with him,'' Kate said softly. ''Don't get me wrong. I love Craig, and God knows he's been a wonderful husband. We have a good life together. But your father was always an adventurer—an Indiana Jones type, you know—and there was always something terribly romantic about the image. I suppose a part of me will always yearn for that, will always love him.''

"And that's all?'' Jaime asked. "Your faith in him is based solely on love?''

Kate was thoughtful for a long time. "Mostly—yes—but also because of the kind of man he was,'' she said finally. "Your father was a war hero, you know—much decorated and all that. It was rumored that he was involved in some sort of special service for the government that eventually led to the D-Day invasion. As a matter of fact, Lew, who brought him to the country club the night we met, served with him in the war. In France.''

"France!'' Jaime's mind raced at the mention of it. Her father had disappeared in Paris. Could there be some kind of connection? she wondered. "This man who introduced you—what was his name?''

"Lew. Lewis Baldwin.''

"Where is he now?''

"I have no idea,'' Kate replied, looking down at the ground as she walked. "I haven't seen him in years. Last I heard, he was living in Virginia, somewhere near Langley.'' She looked at Jaime suspiciously. "You had a specific reason for coming to see me, didn't you.''

Jaime hesitated for a moment, then nodded.

"Want to talk about it?''

Jaime stopped walking and turned to face her. "I want to know the truth, Kate,'' she said simply. "I've lived with the lies and the unanswered questions for so many years. I want to know where he went and why he never came back. I want to clear his name, if I can.''

Kate thought about it for a moment, as if trying to come up with something that might help. "Have you talked to Harry?''

"Harry who?''

"Your father's uncle, Harry Warner. I only met him once—

at the wedding—but he and Jim seemed to be very close,''
Kate recalled.

Jaime rolled her eyes upward in an exaggeratéd gesture.
''For a man with no family, my father's is getting bigger all
the time,'' she lamented. ''He didn't by any chance win the
lottery, did he?''

''The lottery?''

''Whenever someone comes into a lot of money, he suddenly has all kinds of friends and relatives he didn't know he
had before—'' She stopped short and shook her head emphatically. ''I don't believe the stories, Kate. Not for a moment. I *won't* believe them—unless someone can prove he
was guilty.''

Kate put an arm around her. ''I don't believe any of it
either,'' she said gently. ''Your father was, as I said, many
things—but an embezzler he was not.''

That night, Kate Colby Pearson didn't sleep. She was up all
night, curled up in a large armchair near the windows in her
bedroom, thinking, haunted by all the memories Jaime's visit
had stirred up. Memories of a young woman who'd always
been wildly but secretly in love with her sister's husband. She
remembered crying herself to sleep the night before the wedding. She remembered how much it had hurt, watching her
own sister marry the man she loved. She had been more
deeply in love with him than she could ever let anyone know—
especially Fran and her parents. Oh, they'd known something
was wrong, but they'd never known exactly what. She'd simply chalked it up to boredom with her life in general and
announced that she wanted to travel, intended to travel.

What good did it do? she asked herself now. It certainly
hadn't changed her feelings for her brother-in-law. It hadn't
made it any easier to deal with their marriage, once she did
return to the States. It hadn't made it any less painful. And
so she'd taken another trip. And another. Anything was better
than being home, having to spend time with the newlyweds.
God knew she loved her sister, and she loved Jim more than
she should have. But seeing them together . . . it had just
been too much.

And then she'd met Craig.

Craig Pearson had been a young junior senator from Virginia, hand-picked by her father. He was good-looking, educated, from an established political family much like the Kennedys. And like Jack Kennedy, Craig had the charisma to woo the voters, male as well as female. He'd actively pursued her, almost from the moment they met. She'd married him knowing in her heart he was only her second choice, because she'd come to the conclusion that it would be better than being alone. *Not the best reason in the world to get married,* she admitted to herself now, *but it seemed like a good idea at the time.*

To be fair, she did love her husband, not with the passionate intensity she'd felt for Jim Lynde, the passion she'd managed somehow to keep hidden all these years, but she loved Craig nevertheless. She didn't see much of him these days, though, with their schedules being what they were. She still traveled extensively, having involved herself with a number of charities and institutions. Craig was deeply involved with some Senate committee or other—he didn't talk much about it, even to her—and had spent a lot of time in the Middle East lately. That worried her, but she knew it would do no good to object. It was his duty, as he would say. Craig was big on duty. After each trip abroad, he would spend the better part of a day—sometimes more—in closed-door meetings over in Langley.

Langley, she thought. *CIA headquarters are in Langley. . . .*

Across the hall, Jaime was also having trouble sleeping. She was lying awake in the darkness, thinking about everything Kate had told her.

"Why didn't I end up living with you?" Jaime had asked over dinner. *"Didn't your husband approve—"*

"It wasn't that at all," Kate assured her. *"He—we—simply didn't feel it would be the best thing for you. You were so young, and we were away so much of the time. You would have been trading one boarding school for another."*

Jaime didn't believe it for a moment. She did know Kate

well enough to know Kate would have wanted her. No—she was sure it was Craig who had objected. Kate was just covering for him.

She thought about it. Craig Pearson was a U.S. senator. He was deeply involved in Middle Eastern affairs. *Maybe he knows something,* she thought. *Maybe someone got to him, too.*

Or maybe I'm just getting paranoid. . . .

At his office, Harry Warner was reading a National Security Council memo when his secretary buzzed him. "Call on line one, sir," she told him.

"Who is it?"

She told him.

"Put him on," Warner responded without hesitation.

There was a click, then a moment later a familiar male voice came on the line. "Harry, we've got a bit of a problem."

"In Syria?"

"A little closer to home, I'm afraid. Lynde's daughter's been snooping around, asking a lot of questions."

"About her father," Warner concluded.

"Mostly—but she's also asking about *you*—she's under the impression you're her father's uncle."

Warner thought about it for a moment. Then he remembered. "I'll take care of it," he said.

Your father was many things . . . an embezzler he was not. . . . Kate's words echoed through Jaime's mind as the Eastern shuttle taxied down the runway and became airborne. *At least two people believe he's innocent,* Jaime thought. *Never mind the fact that both of us love him.*

Kate was in love with her father; it was still so hard to believe. Had she not heard it from Kate herself, she wouldn't have believed it. She'd been sure Matthews and the others had been lying about their alleged affair. Or maybe lying was not the right word. They'd only told her what they themselves had been told. *You know how rumors get started.* All those

years, and no one knew—not her and certainly not her father.
Kate had wanted it that way, she said.

*"Why didn't you ever come to see me after Daddy left,
Kate?"*

*"I wanted to. I called several times. Mrs. Harcourt said
you were making a difficult adjustment and she felt that seeing
me would only make matters worse."*

"I'll just bet she did!"

*"Every time I called, there was always an excuse. I wrote,
but since I never heard from you, I was never sure you'd
received any of my letters."*

"I didn't. I never received a lot of things sent to me." She
had told Kate about the footlocker in the attic at Sound Beach.

Kate was going to help her.

Ten days later, Kate Colby Pearson drowned in the Potomac
River near her home. Her body was found washed up on the
bank by a man who was, it seemed, a longtime family friend.
He told police he'd stopped by to see her after receiving a
telephone call from her unexpectedly the day before.

The man's name was Lewis Baldwin.

"She was murdered, Marty," Jaime told him over lunch.

He gave her a quizzical look. "The coroner's report said
it was an accidental drowning, didn't it?"

"I don't give a damn what the coroner's report said," Jaime
said crossly. "Kate was a good swimmer. Even if she did fall
in accidentally, she would not have drowned—not in shallow
water!"

"Several supposedly good swimmers drown every year,
darling," he pointed out, taking a bite.

"I'm telling you, Marty, this was no accident," she pressed
on, ignoring the food in front of her. "Something about it
just isn't right. I can feel it."

"Like you felt the Harcourts were not really your aunt and
uncle?" he asked. "With nothing to go on but feelings?"

"Wait and see," she told him.

"All right—what, exactly, isn't right, other than the fact

that your aunt was a good swimmer and apparently drowned in shallow water?'' he asked, genuinely interested.

"Like the fact that it was Lewis Baldwin who found her body.'' Jaime picked up her fork.

"He *was* an old family friend,'' Marty reminded her.

"One she hadn't seen in years!''

"She called him. She asked to see him.''

"Because I asked her to locate him.'' Jaime picked at her lunch absently, pushing it around on the plate with her fork. "I asked her to find him—because he knew my father. They served together during the war—in France.''

"And you think your aunt was killed because of that?'' he asked, doubtful.

"I don't know why she was killed, Marty,'' she said, shaking her head. "I honestly don't know. All I know is that for a lot of years, a lot of people have gone to incredible lengths to cover up where my father went and why—and I have the feeling that it's something much bigger than embezzlement. Think about it. Kate talked to me, and now she's dead. Lewis Baldwin suddenly appeared out of nowhere—just in time to find her body. And Harry Warner, who's supposedly my father's uncle, seems to be something of a spook who just dropped off the face of the earth one day.''

"You're talking about a conspiracy of some kind?''

"I think it's very possible,'' she admitted. "What I *don't* know is why.''

Marty emerged from a taxi in front of his apartment building on Park Avenue, pausing just long enough to pay the driver. It was an unusually blustery evening, even for mid-April. His dark hair blew in the wind as he strode up to the entrance, nodding absently to the wizened old doorman who opened the brass-trimmed door for him. *They probably put the building up around him,* Marty thought with mild amusement. He walked on to the elevators across the lobby and rode up to his floor alone. He'd hoped Jaime would come back with him and spend the night, as she often did, but she had insisted he drop her at her apartment. She was upset over the unexpected death of her aunt and clearly wanted to be alone tonight. *Maybe tomorrow night,* he thought. *Or the next.*

As he stepped out of the elevator, he was approached by a man he'd never seen before, flashing an official-looking identification card and badge. "Martin Cantrell?" he asked in a low voice.

"Yes?"

"I'd like to have a word with you—privately."

Marty shook his head. "It's late," he said weakly. "Can't it wait until tomorrow, perhaps at my office—"

The man shook his head. "I must speak with you now," he pressured him. "In fact, I must *insist* . . ."

FOURTEEN

At four in the morning Jaime was still awake, curled up on the couch in her living room, absently sipping a cup of herb tea that had long ago grown cold. She stared into the darkness, trying to comprehend what appeared to be happening around her and why it was happening. She still found it hard to accept the reality of Kate's death—and even harder to accept the official explanation of that unexpected death. It was no accident; of that she was absolutely certain. Kate had been murdered—and Jaime was positive that it was somehow connected to her visit, to whatever her father had been involved in at the time of his disappearance. Jaime had no proof, of course, and without it she could hardly go to the authorities. No, she couldn't tell anyone—but she knew, just as surely as she knew her own name. The things Kate had told her, the things they'd talked about . . . and then her death, so soon afterward. Coincidence? No. Jaime had never believed in coincidences. Especially not now, not this time. Kate had kept her promise to track down her father's old army buddy. Kate had found Lewis Baldwin—and then she'd been killed. Baldwin—whom she hadn't seen in years—suddenly turned up just in time to find her body. In shallow water. *She probably did drown,* Jaime thought, *but it was no accident.*

How many times in the past few days had she picked up the telephone, determined to call Kate's husband, Craig Pearson, and talk to him about it, then changed her mind by the first ring? What, after all, would she tell him? And what could he do, even if he did believe her—which he probably would not? *Someone's done one hell of a mass snow job*, she thought bitterly.

She got up off the couch and crossed the room to the table where her most cherished photographs were arranged in their small brass frames. Picking up her favorite snapshot of her father, she stared at it for a long time in the dim light coming from her kitchen. *This is all connected to you, Daddy— somehow*, she thought. *I don't know how, but it is. And I have a feeling that if I can learn the truth, I can find you— or at least know why you left me.*

Maybe then we can both find peace.

Across town, Marty Cantrell had also endured a long, sleepless night. He sat on the terrace off his living room, staring blankly into the night, oblivious of the myriad twinkling lights that were so much a part of Manhattan at night, stretched out before him as far as the eye could see. Good God, to be in this position! If Jaime only knew just what she'd stumbled onto—if she had the faintest idea how big it really was! If only he could tell her she was in danger if she continued to pursue this thing.

If only he could tell her. She had been right all along. It *was* a conspiracy. But this was bigger, much bigger, than even she could have suspected. His visitor—who had intentionally remained nameless and tried to be just as vague about his reasons for wanting Jaime to back off her investigation— had made it quite clear that if Marty failed to stop her, he and his people would be forced to stop her themselves. The unspoken message had been, *the same way Mrs. Pearson was stopped.* The important thing was to protect Jaime. No matter what, he had to protect her. Whatever her father had gotten himself involved in, it must have been something big. Really big.

And the newsman in him smelled a story, a big story.

Possibly the biggest of his career. Maybe . . . just maybe, if he were to lay low for a while, to play it their way for now. . . . Sure. He could keep Jaime out of danger and still find out exactly what had happened to her father. And in the process, he'd get the scoop of the year! Jaime would forgive him when it was all over. He tried to justify what he was about to do by telling himself she'd realize he'd done it to protect her, just as much as he was doing it for himself. It would all work itself out, in the end. He'd get his exclusive— and no doubt an anchor position on the network's evening news. Maybe even a deal as sweet as CBS had given Dan Rather to fill Walter Cronkite's shoes when Cronkite retired. He and Jaime would get married. They'd have a good life together, once she was able to put the past behind her.

By morning, he'd convinced himself he was doing it all for love. For Jaime.

"It's done," the voice on the phone reported.

"Can we count on Cantrell to do it right?" Warner wanted to know.

There was a low chuckle on the other end of the line. "We're fortunate that she managed to fall for a man with lofty ambitions."

"Then you anticipate no problems?"

"None whatsoever."

"I thought we had a date for lunch."

Marty looked up from the notes he was reviewing. "I'm sorry, sweetheart," he said apologetically. "Things got pretty crazy around here this morning. I'm not going to be able to get away."

"Aren't the telephones working?" she wanted to know.

He frowned. "I thought you'd be out of the office."

"You could have left a message, you know." Jaime settled into a chair in front of his desk, dropping her shoulder bag and camera case on the floor at her feet. "You look like hell," she observed. "What's her name?"

"What's whose name?" He was too preoccupied to catch the joke.

"The woman who kept you up all night," Jaime said with a grin. "Who is she?"

Marty didn't laugh, as he normally would have. "You know there's no one but you," he said irritably.

She stared at him for a moment. "I'm beginning to wonder." She was also beginning to get quite annoyed with him. *What's gotten into him?* she wondered.

He looked up at her again. "I'm sorry," he said again. "It's work, that's all. I'll make it up to you tonight, I swear."

"I don't know if I'm free tonight," she said, standing up abruptly. She did not bother to conceal her displeasure. "Call me later." She collected her things and started for the door, then turned to him again. "If we do go out this evening, kindly leave that chip on your shoulder at home. It'll ruin the evening for both of us." She walked out.

Marty watched her leave but made no attempt to stop her. After she was gone, he took a large brown envelope from his attaché case and stared at it for a long time. The "information" his visitor had left with him last night. Everything he would need to convince Jaime—or so he'd been told. He removed its contents and looked everything over carefully. How much of it was fact and how much fiction? Would he ever really know for sure? Did it really matter?

It was, after all, only the end result that mattered.

I wonder what's gotten into him? Jaime asked herself as she walked along Central Park West. She'd seen him under pressure before. He had been tense, distracted, even short-tempered at times, but this was different. He said it was work-related, but Jaime had the feeling there was more to it than that. It was obvious that he did not want to talk about it. *Must be serious,* she thought, stopping at Seventy-second Street, waiting for the traffic light to change. She'd been annoyed with him at the time, but now that she'd had time to think about it, she felt she should try to understand. After all, she'd had bad days herself. *Maybe later. We'll talk about it later.*

As she crossed the busy intersection, heading for her apartment building, she glanced over her shoulder briefly at the man behind her. She was brushed by a faint sense of unease.

He *was* following her . . . and had been since she left her office. She'd noticed him in the lobby, watching as she was leaving. She'd also seen him when she stopped to buy a newspaper from a vendor on Madison Avenue but hadn't given it a second thought—then. At the time, she just assumed they were headed in the same direction. She'd taken the crosstown bus to Central Park West and hadn't noticed him following her—again—until she reached Seventy-second Street. It was not her imagination, although that's how Marty would have explained the incident. This man was following her . . . at a discreet distance, of course, but following nonetheless.

The light at the intersection of Broadway and Seventy-second was red. She waited impatiently for it to change, and the moment it did, she hurried across Broadway and headed for West End Avenue. She never looked over her shoulder again, but she knew he was still there. *End of the line, friend,* she thought as she entered her building and strode across the lobby to the elevators.

Better luck next time.

"Maybe you should give this up, Jaime. Stop driving yourself crazy and get on with your life." Marty stood in the middle of his living room, clearly nervous.

"Just because I saw someone following me?" Jaime asked. "I'm telling you, Marty, he *was* following me. He followed me all the way from the office!"

"It's getting to you, sweetheart," he said in a concerned tone. "I just don't think it's worth all the pain it's causing you."

She stared at him incredulously. "I can't believe this is really coming from you," she said, irritated. "*You* were the one who encouraged me to pursue this whole matter to begin with! *You* were the one who told me I'd have to find answers for my questions before I could put the past behind me and get on with my—"

Marty cut her off. "I was wrong, okay?" he snapped crossly. "Everyone's entitled to be wrong once in a while, aren't they?"

"Yes," Jaime said as she faced him squarely. "Yes, they are. Even me."

His eyes met hers. "Exactly what are you saying?" he asked carefully.

"I thought you had *guts*, dammit!" she snapped. "I thought you, of all people, understood! I *have* to do this—for my father *and* for myself! Now, just because the situation's getting risky, you—"

"Your father was a spy, Jaime." There. It was out in the open.

"What did you say?"

"You father was a spy," he repeated quietly. "He worked for the government all along."

"I don't believe you," she said angrily.

"I have proof," he insisted.

"*You* have proof?" She shook her head in disbelief. "And just how did you happen to come by this proof when I've been searching for months and come up with zip?"

"I have connections in Washington. I didn't want to tell you anything until I was certain, but—" He turned, walked over to the desk, and picked up a large brown envelope. He offered it to her. "I hoped you'd never have to see this," he said regretfully.

She looked at it apprehensively, as if it were a snake about to strike. She took it and opened it slowly, removing its contents with trembling fingers. There were photographs—photos that meant nothing to her, photos of her father in Paris, in London, in Moscow, in Beirut. There were also documents—official-looking memos detailing her father's activities on behalf of the U.S. government. She sank down onto the couch. "This is impossible," she said in a barely audible voice, shaking her head.

"He wasn't allowed to discuss his work with anyone—not even his family. I'd hoped you'd give this up without ever having to know," Marty said quietly.

She looked up at him as if seeing him for the first time. "This is why Kate was murdered," she gasped.

"We don't know for certain that she was murdered," Marty reminded her.

"I know, Marty," she insisted. "I've known all along. This just proves it. All along, it's all been a cover-up—the embezzlement charges, the stories of his death, all of it. Whatever my father is—was—doing, it was important enough to go to incredible lengths to keep it all quiet. God, Marty, he wasn't a criminal at all! Whatever he's done, he's done it for his country—"

"Your father's dead, Jaime," Marty said gravely.

Her mouth flew open. She was trying to scream, but no sound would come. She shook her head violently. Marty reached out to comfort her, but she pushed him away. "No," she gasped, as if strangling on the word. "No!"

"It's true," he said softly. "It's all there, in the reports—"

"*No!*" She jumped to her feet, her face contorted with pain. "No—it can't be! Not after all this time, after all the searching and hoping, thinking he was dead, then finding out he wasn't, and now this—" She began to sob uncontrollably.

He took her in his arms and held her close, hating himself for what he'd done to her, yet continuously telling himself he was doing the right thing for both of them. "It's okay, sweetheart," he whispered, stroking her hair. "Go ahead and cry . . ."

"How did he die, Marty?"

They were lying together in the darkness in his bedroom, both fully clothed. Marty held Jaime in his arms as if she were a lost, frightened child. *That's what she is right now,* he thought, stroking her hair. He'd insisted she stay because he knew she did not want to be alone, because he knew she *shouldn't* be alone at a time like this.

"Marty?"

The sound of her voice brought him sharply back to the present. "What?" he asked.

She repeated the question. "How did my father die?"

"He was killed in France—where, I'm not absolutely certain—in 1975," he told her. "I don't have all the details, but apparently his cover was blown, and he was eliminated by a hostile agent. He was buried in a cemetery in Nice." He paused. "I know this is hard for you, sweetheart, but there's

nothing you can do about it now. You've got to put it all
behind you and—'' He stopped short.

Jaime, lying against his chest, could feel his sharp intake
of breath. ''And get on with my life,'' she finished the sen-
tence for him.

''Yes.''

''I can't,'' she said quietly. ''Not yet.''

Jaime opened her eyes slowly and blinked, temporarily
blinded by the brilliant morning sunlight streaming through
the windows. She drew one arm across her face to block it
out, and it was at that moment that she realized Marty was
not in bed. She sat up abruptly, trying to remember what had
happened last night. It all came rushing back to her like a
terrible, destructive tidal wave . . . Marty's unexpected rev-
elations, the documents that linked her father to the government's covert operations abroad, the news of his death. *It was
a bad dream, just a bad dream,* she told herself. *It didn't
really happen. It couldn't have happened.*

She pushed her hair back off her face with one hand and
looked at the clock on the nightstand. Ten forty-five. Marty
had probably already gone. She started to get up, then sank
back down onto the bed. Her head was pounding. *Like war
drums,* she thought miserably. She sat there for a long moment, her head cradled in her hands, trying to block out the
pain. The pain of truth.

She got to her feet slowly and crossed the room to the
door. God, it felt as though someone were using a jackham-
mer inside her head! She rubbed the back of her neck gingerly
as she stumbled into the living room. No sign of Marty. She
wasn't surprised. His workday normally began very early—
he was almost always at the station before sunrise.

What did surprise her, though, was that he didn't wake her
before he left. All right, so he probably figured she wouldn't
be up to going in to the office today—that was a textbook
understatement if there ever was one. The truth was, she
didn't know if she could face anyone right now. She certainly
didn't want to try. But she did have to call in. She did have

to let someone know she wasn't going to be there. Marty knew that. He should have awakened her.

I'd better call now, she thought, taking a deep breath. Knowing Ben Rollins, he was probably having a coronary right about now. As she seated herself at the desk, she noticed the red light on the answering machine was flashing. She didn't remember hearing the phone ring—but then, she'd been pretty well out of it. Whoever called had probably done so after Marty left—or he would have taken the message himself.

She thought about it for a moment, debating whether or not to play back the tape. It could be important. She could take the message and call Marty at the station. She wanted to talk to him anyway. Just hearing his voice right now would comfort her.

Maybe it was Marty who had called. It wouldn't be the first time he'd called to leave her a message after they'd spent the night together. And last night, painful as it had been, had brought them even closer than they'd been before. *At least one good thing came out of last night*, she thought glumly as she pressed the button to play back the incoming message.

There was only one, and it wasn't from Marty. Jaime didn't recognize the voice. The caller was a man, but it sounded muffled, as if he were trying to keep his voice down—or maybe disguise it. "Cantrell, you were supposed to get back to me yesterday, you sonofabitch. You'd better not be playing games with me, dammit. You don't know what you're up against here. You get back to me today, got it? I have to know if you sold her on—"

Jaime shut the machine off and stared at it, confused. What did it mean? she wondered. The message almost sounded like a threat. Was Marty in some kind of trouble? And who was the "her" the man was referring to? Sold her on what? What could be so urgent that he had to call this person back immediately?

And why didn't the caller leave his name?

By the time she returned to her own apartment later that day, she'd managed to put the incident out of her mind. She was so sensitive about everything right now, she'd probably been making too much of it anyway. It probably didn't mean anything at all. Or at least not anything as terrible as she'd imagined. She was almost relieved Marty hadn't been available when she called the station to tell him about it. She would have ended up feeling like a fool, though she was sure he would have understood. After all, in his profession, it wasn't exactly unusual to get strange calls at all hours of the day and night from all kinds of odd people. That man on the tape—he was probably calling with a lead on a story or something.

I'm really getting paranoid, she thought as she glanced absently through her mail. But after last night, after everything Marty had told her about her father, she wasn't sure who or what could be believed anymore. It all seemed so unreal, so impossible. How, she asked herself now, could her father, to whom she'd been closer than anyone on the face of the earth, have led such an incredible double life without anyone around him being even remotely aware of it?

A tear escaped from the corner of her left eye and slid down her cheek as she thought about her father, about how he'd just disappeared from her life one day without a trace, without any kind of warning.

Daddy . . . why? she asked again.

She hadn't wanted to go out that evening, but Marty had talked her into it. "It'll do you good," he'd insisted when he called. Then he'd turned up at her door an hour ago, not having even stopped by his own place before coming over—and clearly not willing to take no for an answer. "You can't just shut out the rest of the world indefinitely."

"I can try," she'd responded.

"Come on—trust me, it'll be okay," he'd pressed.

He'd finally talked her into it. But now, alone in the shower with the warm water beating down on her neck and shoulders, she found herself having second thoughts. She knew Marty was only thinking of her, but she also knew she wasn't going to be very good company. All she really wanted to do was crawl into bed—alone, this time—and hide under the blankets until the pain went away. If it ever went away.

She turned the water off and opened the door, grabbing a towel from the rack. She wrapped it around her head like a turban, tucking all of her wet hair under it, then used a second towel to dry herself off. Slipping into her robe, she considered the alternatives. They could order a pizza, eat here. Marty could spend the night if he liked. It would be much better that way, she decided as she walked barefoot across the bedroom.

She paused at the door, hearing the sound of Marty's voice coming from the other side. Opening the door, she could see him standing by the desk, his back to her, talking on the phone. "I showed her everything, just as you told me to." He spoke in a low, irritated tone. "Yes! No . . . she's not about to give up. She wants to know everything, and she won't stop until she does. What? Yes, I know we had a deal. I know that. All right, dammit! I'll keep talking to her. Yeah. Sure." He slammed the receiver down on its cradle and turned just as Jaime came into the room.

He frowned. "I thought you were still in the shower."

"I was—until just a few minutes ago." She gestured toward the telephone. "What was that all about?"

"Business," he lied.

"It didn't sound like business to me." She took a step forward.

"It was," he insisted. "A story I've been working on—I got a lead, but she didn't want to talk."

"The truth, Marty. Please, don't lie to me—not you, too."

He hesitated for a moment, knowing he should stick to his story but unable to go on lying to her. "The fellow who gave me the dope on your father—that was him on the phone," he said finally.

"He called you here?"

Marty shook his head. "I called him. I got a message—"

Then it hit her. The voice on the answering machine. "He was the one who called," she said aloud.

Marty looked at her. "You heard it?"

She nodded. "Who is he?"

"I have no idea."

"You've accepted information from him as truth, you know

how to reach him, but you don't know who he is?'' Jaime was suspicious now. ''Marty, you're a newsman. You know better than this!''

''The documentation—it was straight out of government files,'' he defended himself.

''It could have been faked.''

''It could have been, I suppose—but who's going to verify it?'' he asked. ''The guys at the CIA certainly aren't going to talk.''

''And what were you expected to do in return?''

''What do you mean?''

''I heard you say, and I quote, 'We had a deal.' What kind of a deal?''

He frowned. ''I was supposed to talk you out of this.''

''Out of searching for information about my father?''

He nodded, avoiding her eyes.

''You bastard,'' she said in a low, menacing tone, her eyes narrowed in anger. ''You goddamned—you're in on this too!''

''No, sweetheart—you don't understand—'' Still recovering from the shock of having been discovered, he took a step forward. ''If you'll just let me explain—''

''Explain *what*, you son of a bitch?'' she asked contemptuously. ''Explain how you sold out to the highest bidder? Do you really think I'd believe anything you tell me now?''

''It's not like that at all,'' he insisted, reaching out for her.

''Don't touch me!'' she exploded, backing away from him. ''Damn you—I trusted you! Worse—I loved you! God, you are the last person I thought would ever betray me! You know, you could have at least given me the opportunity to top their offer.'' Tears streamed down her cheeks as she fought for what little remained of her self-control. ''Get out, Marty. Get out of my sight—and don't ever come near me again!''

''You don't mean that,'' he said calmly.

''I've never meant anything more in my life,'' she told him. ''I don't ever want to see you or hear from you again.''

He looked at her for a moment, then nodded. ''All right. I can't say that I really blame you.'' He picked up his jacket and walked to the door, then turned to face her again. ''I love you,'' he said quietly. ''No matter how it looks to you now, I've always loved you. I did this for us.''

''I'll just bet you did,'' Jaime said acidly.

''This whole business is making you crazy. You've become obsessed with it,'' he told her. ''That's why I suggested you try to uncover the truth to start with.''

''And that's why you made this—this deal?'' She looked skeptical.

He nodded.

''Forgive me for not seeing the point immediately, but exactly how is this for *us*?'' she asked coldly.

''It was a way for you to put the past behind you, for us to get on with our lives—together.'' He paused. ''I thought once you knew what happened to your father—''

''I had to know what *really* happened!'' she snapped.

''Don't you think I *know* that?'' he wanted to know. ''I did everything I could to unearth the truth for you! I followed every lead I could—I kept running into dead ends. Then this guy contacted me—he said he'd heard I'd been asking around, looking for information. He told me his story. I thought it was pretty incredible at the time, but he said he had proof. He said he'd give it to me if I could guarantee you'd give up your search. He said the people he worked for were getting uneasy about it—they felt you were getting too close.''

''To what?'' she asked carefully.

He shrugged. ''He wouldn't say. The CIA, I suspect. I looked into it, but again I hit a lot of dead ends. They were covering their tracks very well, but that doesn't come as any great surprise.''

''So you made a deal with them.'' There was cold fury in her voice.

''With him.''

''Without any regard for what you might be doing to me.''

''I was doing this *for* you!''

''Sure you were!'' she snapped. ''Get out, Marty.''

''Jaime—''

Her eyes blazed with unmasked hatred. ''I said get out!''

He hesitated momentarily, then started for the door. With one hand on the doorknob, he turned to face her again. ''I *do* love you, no matter what you think,'' he said quietly. Then he walked out.

Her expression never changed. She stood immobile, watching him leave, dismissing him from her life once and for all. It was not until she heard the sound of the elevator door closing out in the hall that her lower lip began to tremble. She sank down onto the couch, crumbling in pain, sobbing openly at having suffered yet another loss.

Once again, she was alone.

FIFTEEN

Washington, D.C., September 1985. Jaime walked alone through the busy terminal at Dulles International Airport, dressed casually in her favorite "uniform"—a loose top belted at the waist and tight jeans tucked into high boots. She strode through the crowd purposefully, her heavy carry-on bag hanging from her left shoulder. Making her way to the baggage claim carousel, she took her claim check tickets from her pocket and scanned the bags on the carousel in search of her own. Where the hell were her bags? she wondered as case after case, all in varying sizes and colors, appeared and were claimed, none of them remotely resembling hers. *Ah—there it is!* she thought as a tan leather suitcase appeared on the belt. She reached out to take it at the same moment a tall, painfully thin man who looked to be in his mid-forties, balding and bespectacled, dressed in an impeccable blue Brooks Brothers suit, grasped the handle.

"I believe this one's mine," he said quickly, comparing the ticket in his hand to the one on the suitcase.

She released it abruptly and withdrew. "Sorry," she apologized. *Damn!* she was thinking.

After finally collecting her own luggage, the next stop was the car rental desk. The only cars available, much to her dismay, were either compacts or subcompacts. She was given a candy-apple-red Toyota. She adjusted the seat as best she could, but found it slightly uncomfortable in comparison with the ample room in her own Jeep. *Obviously, neither the airlines nor the automobile manufacturers have any mercy for the tall,* she thought wryly.

As she drove along the Dulles Airport Access Road, headed into Washington, she found herself thinking about Marty. Try as she had to exorcise him from her thoughts—and from her heart—she hadn't yet succeeded. She felt like such an idiot. She had loved the man, loved him enough to have seriously contemplated marrying him. It had *not* been just another casual affair—far from it. And he had sold her out! For what? she wondered now. What had they offered him? How much did he stand to gain? She wondered if she would ever know. Unbidden tears stung her eyes and streamed down her cheeks. She'd promised herself after her father left that no one was ever going to hurt her again, but with Marty she'd let down her defenses, allowed herself to fall in love with him. *Damn him,* she thought. *It's never going to happen again—never!*

Once again, she wondered how much of the past six months had been a wild-goose chase. How much of the information she'd uncovered regarding the real reason behind her father's last trip to Paris had been lies? How much of it had been specifically contrived to throw her off the track? Was her father an embezzler—or had Marty been telling the truth when he said her father had been working undercover for the government? As incredible as it had sounded at the time he told her, the spy story was the only one that really made any sense. Someone had gone to a great deal of trouble to make damn sure she *didn't* learn the truth. Who would bother to try to cover the tracks of an alleged embezzler unless, of course, he'd had an accomplice, which didn't seem likely.

She caught sight of a blue Ford Escort in her rearview mirror, the same car she'd noticed following her off the airport parking lot. The same car she'd seen on the expressway earlier. *Is he following me?* she wondered. *God, I'm becoming paranoid!* She took a deep breath. She had to get hold of herself. She couldn't lose it now. The road ahead of her, she suspected, was going to be long—and rocky.

Like an obstacle course.

"Treason?" Jaime shook her head emphatically. "No—I can't believe that. I *won't*!"

Congressman William Blackwell looked at her sympathetically. He and Harrison Colby had been close friends for many years, and he'd dreaded having to be the one to tell Harrison's granddaughter the truth about her father, but when he agreed to help her, he'd had no idea he would turn up anything quite so sensational. He resigned himself to being as honest as possible with her, suspecting that—under the circumstances—she'd probably heard enough lies over the past years to last a lifetime. He drew in a deep breath and frowned. "I know how you must feel, Jaime, but—"

She shook her head again. "No, Congressman Blackwell," she said evenly. "No, you *don't*. You can't. He was my *father*, for God's sake! How am I ever supposed to believe—" She stopped short and made a helpless gesture with her hands.

"It really shouldn't come as a surprise," Blackwell pointed out, lighting his pipe. The smell of cherry tobacco filled the air almost instantly. It made Jaime mildly queasy, but she said nothing. "That," Blackwell went on, "was the way it was supposed to be. Because of the nature of his work, he had to keep quiet. No one—not even his family—could be told."

"How long—" Jaime was unable to finish the question, choking on her words.

"Many years," Blackwell told her. "He was recalled to active duty shortly after the war. The OSS had been dissolved, but a new agency took its place, a forerunner of the CIA as we know it today."

"And the treason charges?" Jaime wasn't sure at that moment that she really wanted to know.

Blackwell looked away from her. "Apparently, he sold out to the Soviets."

Sold out, Jaime thought bitterly. *There's been a lot of that going on lately*. She looked up at Blackwell with disbelief in her eyes. "Not my father," she said with conviction in her voice. "It's simply not possible."

"There's more," Blackwell said grimly. "He was taken into custody in Nice and brought back here for trial. From there, he was sent to a federal prison."

Jaime's head jerked up. "Here?" she asked, suddenly hopeful. Marty had said he'd been killed in France—maybe he *was* still alive! "Which prison?"

"Fort Leavenworth—Kansas." Blackwell paused. "That's where he died."

Her hand flew to her mouth; for a moment, she was too stunned to speak. "When?" she asked when she finally found her voice. "I mean, how long has he been—" She couldn't bring herself to say it.

"About ten years—if my sources are correct," Blackwell answered gently.

Jaime felt the tears welling up in her eyes and willed herself not to cry. "Why didn't he ever try to contact me?" she wondered aloud. "All that time, and he never called, never even wrote to me! If I'd known he was there, I would have gone to see him—"

"My guess is that that's exactly what he *didn't* want," Blackwell told her. "I know if I were in prison, if I'd been convicted of treason, I wouldn't want my daughter to know—if I could prevent it."

Jaime was dangerously close to breaking down. "All those years . . . so damned many lies." She got to her feet slowly. "I don't know who—or what—to believe anymore."

Blackwell frowned. "For what it's worth, Jaime, I believe my sources are reliable," he said quietly, putting the file back in the drawer.

She managed a slight smile. "It's not much of a comfort, no—but thank you for your time." She extended her hand.

He gave it a gentle squeeze. "Be careful, Jaime," he told her. "You're playing with fire if you pursue this further."

She nodded. "I know. But I have to do it."

That night, she flew to Kansas City.

• • •

"What did she find out from Blackwell?" Warner wanted to know.

"Only what's in the official reports."

"Good."

"Bad," the voice on the phone retorted. "She's on her way to Leavenworth right now."

"You know what to do, then."

Fort Leavenworth, Kansas. The federal prison is located approximately twenty-nine miles northwest of Kansas City. Jaime telephoned the warden as soon as she'd checked into her room at the Hyatt Regency. He seemed reluctant to talk to her at first but finally agreed to meet with her when he realized she wasn't going to give up and go home, as he'd so bluntly suggested. He made it all too clear that he was a busy man and that the time he'd be able to give her would be quite limited. Touring the prison and speaking with inmates would be out of the question. *What's he hiding?* Jaime wondered as she drove north on Highway 73, bound for Leavenworth. She was now suspicious of everyone she spoke with. *But not without good reason,* she told herself.

She brought her rental car to a stop at the prison gates. The main building, still a good distance away, was much larger than she'd imagined, gray and gloomy and foreboding. *Just like Castle Dracula,* she thought grimly. There was a large prison yard surrounded by a series of fences topped with barbed wire. She found it hard to believe, even now, that her father had ever been here. *Not my father,* she thought.

She followed the directions the guard at the gate gave her and drove up to the building where she was told she would be met by someone who would take her to the warden's office. The uniformed guard waiting for her there took her inside the building and instructed her to wait. Then he disappeared into a small office. *He's going to get Bela Lugosi,* Jaime thought, feeling a sudden chill.

He returned a few moments later. "The warden's expecting you," he told her. "Come this way."

As they crossed the prison yard, Jaime was greeted with

wolf whistles, catcalls, and lewd remarks from some of the prisoners. "Try to ignore them," the guard advised.

"I am," she told him. *But it's not easy.*

Fifteen minutes later she was sitting in the warden's office. The man seated across from her turned out to be the *acting* warden, a short, stocky man in his mid-fifties with a porcine face and a spare tire that would have done Goodyear proud. The warden, it seemed, had been called away quite unexpectedly the day before she arrived. *Why?* she wondered. Coincidence? She didn't believe it for a minute.

"According to the records," he said, "your father was a prisoner here from March 1968 until his death in May 1975."

"What did he die of?" Jaime asked, her face expressionless.

The warden leafed through the file folder on the desk in front of him. "The files are not complete, you understand— there was a fire in our file department a few years back and a good deal of paperwork was destroyed."

Of course, Jaime thought. *Why am I not surprised to hear that?* "But you do have *something—*"

"Yeah, sure. Here it is," he said with a forced smile. "Cancer. Lung cancer. Initially diagnosed by a prison physician in August 1974."

Jaime couldn't hide her surprise. "But he did have chemotherapy, didn't he?" she wanted to know.

"I'm sure he did," the warden replied. "I can't find any record—but I'm sure he did."

"Of course," Jaime said coolly. "Tell me—where is he buried?"

The man looked flustered. "The bodies are always turned over to the families for burial," he told her.

"I'm his only living relative," Jaime pressed on. "Why wasn't I notified?"

"I—I don't know," the man stammered nervously. "I'm sure someone must have attempted to contact you—"

"I was never contacted," Jaime said evenly, but with malice. "And you're telling me you have no idea what was done with his body?"

"The fire," he reminded her. "I have no record—"

"I don't believe any of this. Not for a moment." Her eyes met his. "My father spent most of his life serving his country. He was, I've been told, one of the first operatives recruited by the OSS during World War Two—a hero, as far as the French Resistance was concerned. No one will ever convince me he betrayed his government. I'm not even absolutely certain he's really dead." She stood up, her eyes dark with rage. "Good day—for now." She turned and walked out, slamming the door in her wake.

After she left, the warden snatched up the telephone on his desk and dialed hastily. "This is Baker at Leavenworth," he said in a low, hushed tone. "We've got a problem . . ."

"You Jim Lynde's daughter?"

Jaime looked up as she was getting into her car. The man who'd addressed her was large and quite tall. He had a reddened, windburned face and curly gray hair and was wearing a guard's uniform. "Yes, I am," she said quietly, still struggling to curb her anger.

"I knew your father—when he was here, I mean."

Digging into her bag for the car keys, Jaime stopped what she was doing and looked at him again. "My father?" she asked. "Are you sure?"

"You look an awful lot like him," the man said with a grin. "Kinda cynical like him, too."

The product of years of conditioning, Jaime thought ruefully. "Why are you so willing to talk to me when no one else is?" she asked suspiciously.

"I figured nobody up there would tell you anything," he said, nodding toward the warden's office. "Probably because they were told not to, it's my guess."

"And why would that be?" Jaime asked coldly.

"He *was* a spy, wasn't he? A turncoat?"

"He was an agent, yes," Jaime said slowly, biting off each word in an attempt to curb her swiftly mounting anger. "He was not a turncoat."

"To tell you the truth, little lady, I never believed that one myself," he admitted with a conspiratorial grin. He pulled a fat cigar from his pocket, unwrapped it, then bit off the end and spit it out. Taking a disposable lighter from his pocket, he lit it and got it going.

Jaime studied him for a long moment, trying to decide if he were legitimate or not. *These days, it's hard to tell the players even with a scorecard,* she thought. "Just how well did you know my father, Mr.—" She stopped short, realizing she didn't know the man's name.

"Bearden. Hank Bearden." He took another few puffs of the cigar. "I met him right after he come here. I was probably the only one around here he talked to very much. Jim was a real loner—stayed to himself most of the time. When he did talk, it was usually about you. He talked about you a lot."

"What did he tell you?"

"That he missed you, that he wished he could see you—but not here. He said you was a real hell-raiser," Bearden added with a chuckle. "He told me you was real good with a pony."

"He told you that?" Jaime was surprised. Maybe he did know her father, after all.

He nodded. "He talked about your mama, too—but not too often. Guess it wasn't easy to talk about that."

"It's never been easy for me, either," Jaime admitted with a frown.

"I'm sorry, ma'am. I didn't mean to—"

"It's all right," she insisted, shaking her head.

"I was with him when he died, you know," Bearden said then.

"You were?" His last statement took her by surprise.

He nodded. "I tried to tell him—guess he figured I was just the pot callin' the kettle black, y'know?"

Jaime gave him a quizzical look. "What do you mean?" she asked.

"Smoking." The cigar hung from one corner of his mouth now. "He liked his cigarettes—two packs a day, sometimes three. I told him it was gonna be his undoing, but he wouldn't listen. Calmed his nerves, I s'pose."

"I see." Jaime was thoughtful for a moment. "He was a heavy smoker, I take it?"

Bearden nodded. "Said he'd been smokin' since he was a kid—that old habits are hard to break," he recalled. "I guess that's true 'cause I've never been able to kick the habit myself."

"I don't recall my father ever smoking," Jaime said, puzzled.

"Maybe he took it up in here," Bearden offered. "A lot of the inmates do. Not many pleasures left for the guys who are doin' life."

Jaime nodded. "How is it that you were with him when he died?"

He gave a low chuckle, obviously amused that she even had to ask. "I'm a prison guard, ma'am. That's my job. Your father was an inmate. Somebody had to be with him at all times, even at the end. I was it."

"I see."

Jaime paused. "I have to go now, Mr. Bearden—I have a plane to catch—but could I call you later?"

"Oh, sure." He stared at her for a moment, then, realizing she didn't know how to reach him, pulled a ballpoint pen and a small note pad from his pocket and scribbled his address and phone number on the top sheet. He tore it off and gave it to her. "I'm usually here days—except Tuesdays and Wednesdays. My days off. The wife's always after me to get Sundays off so's I can go to church with her, but you know how that is."

Jaime nodded, smiling. "Thank you, Mr. Bearden," she told him. "You've been a big help."

That night, she flew back to New York.

Jaime leaned back in the back seat of the taxi and took a deep breath. Looming ahead of her, the familiar sight of the Manhattan skyline at dusk indicated she was home, but she paid no attention to it. Her thoughts were on the events of the past week. She thought about what she'd found—or rather, what she hadn't found—at the Hall of Records. She recalled her conversations with William Blackwell and the warden at Leavenworth and Hank Bearden, the prison guard who'd claimed to have known her father so well. She'd almost believed him, too—until he started talking about her father's smoking habits. *Guess it calmed his nerves.* That was what he'd told her, but it made no sense to Jaime. Her father was not—nor had he, to her knowledge, ever been—a nervous man. Of course, prison could make anyone nervous, and she'd accepted that possibility, until he started telling her how her father had told him he'd started smoking when he was still quite young. Her father had *never* smoked, but she saw no reason to tell him that. *Play dumb,* she thought. *Let them do the talking.*

What are they all trying to hide?

SIXTEEN

"I told you I don't want to see you. Not today, not next week, not ever. I don't want to talk to you. I don't even want to hear your voice on my answering machine. I'm really surprised you have the nerve to show your face around me."

Jaime kept walking down Madison Avenue, her tartan-plaid shawl flying in the wake of her brisk pace. Marty was at her side, determined not to be dismissed before he'd had the opportunity to plead his case. He reached out and grabbed her arm. "If you'd just give me the chance to explain—"

She shook herself free with a quick, furious movement. "I'm not interested in your goddamned explanations!" she snapped, her face taut with rage. "I'm not interested in *anything* you have to say!"

He stopped in his tracks. "Jaime—I love you!" He blurted it out as she walked away.

She came to an abrupt halt and turned on him in anger. "More lies, Marty? God, you must be desperate to keep stringing me along! What's in it for you, anyway? What did they offer you? Money? A big story? Maybe an exclusive?"

"I didn't want to do it—"

"Sure," she said acidly. "They held a gun to your head and made you do it, right? Come on, Mr. Hotshot Newsman, you can do better than that! Save your breath—I'm not buying any of it!''

He took a step forward, dropping his voice to a whisper. ''They told me you were in danger if you didn't give it up,'' he admitted. ''I made a mistake—I realize that now!''

''So did I,'' she said evenly. ''I trusted you—and that was *my* big mistake!'' She started walking again, and this time she didn't look back.

How could he have the nerve to face me after what he did? Jaime thought angrily as she stalked into her office and slammed the door. *Did he really expect me to forgive and forget and act as if nothing happened? Damn him, anyway!*

She collapsed into her chair and swung around to face the window. She rubbed her brow gingerly, feeling the beginning of a monumental headache. How could she have been so stupid? How had she allowed him to fool her so completely? He had managed to melt all of her defenses, make her fall in love with him—and she'd never suspected for a moment that she was being used.

She recalled the day they met at the Plaza. Why hadn't she realized then that his interest seemed to be sparked *after* he discovered she was Harrison Colby's granddaughter? Why hadn't she suspected then that his interest lay in who she was—or, more accurately, who her family was? Had he known about her father all along? she wondered now. Was he one of them? Had he been sent to keep tabs on her, to make sure she didn't find out too much? *I* am *getting paranoid!* she thought.

She turned back to her desk and opened one of the drawers. She took out a large framed photograph of Marty and stared at it for a long time. She'd put it away the day after she threw him out of her apartment. *I should have thrown it away,* she thought bitterly. *God only knows why I've kept it around this long.* Staring into his handsome, smiling face, she felt an uncontrollable rage building up inside her. Never would she let herself be taken in like that again. Never would any man make a fool of her again.

Finally, unable to contain her rage any longer, she hurled

the photograph across the room. It hit the wall, the glass in the frame shattering on impact. Jaime looked down at the broken frame and bits of glass on the floor but did not move from her chair. She was still staring at it when Holly Christopher ran into the office. "I heard glass breaking," she said, sounding as if she'd run all the way and was out of breath. She looked down at the broken frame. "What happened?"

"An error in judgment on my part," Jaime said dispassionately. "Could you send someone in to clean it up?"

Holly looked at her oddly. "Sure. Right away," she said slowly, bending to pick up the photograph. She handed it to Jaime. "You can always buy a new frame."

Jaime nodded. "Of course."

After Holly was gone, Jaime looked down at the photograph in her hand. It hadn't been damaged. *Unfortunately,* she thought. Slowly, methodically, she tore it into several small pieces, then dropped it into the wastepaper basket.

Washington, D.C. Harry Warner was alone in his office when the telephone rang. His private line, the number that had been given only to a select few. He snatched up the receiver on the second ring. "Warner," he said sharply.

"It's Baldwin," said the male voice on the other end.

"You still in New York?"

"For what it's worth, yes."

"Did Cantrell deliver?"

"He did as he was told. Trouble is, Lynde's not buying it. She's one stubborn woman."

Warner's laugh was mirthless. "Too much like her father."

"What do I do about Cantrell?"

"Keep him quiet, of course—until we find a way to throw Lynde off the track. You know what to do."

"Right."

"What do we do about Lynde?"

"Let me worry about that."

"I think she's going to be a real problem."

"I said I'll handle it," Warner snapped crossly. He thought about it as he replaced the receiver. He had to do something.

Nothing could be allowed to jeopardize the operations in the Middle East.

Not now, when they were so close.

Jaime didn't know who or what to believe anymore. Now, sitting atop the highest hill in Central Park, watching the sun setting on the western horizon, she thought about all that had happened in the past few months. She was no closer to finding the truth than she'd been when she first began her search for answers six months earlier. She'd talked to half a dozen people and heard half a dozen stories—and still had no idea which of them, if any, were to be believed.

She did believe her father had been a government operative. She believed it was the only explanation that made any sense at all, the only possible reason anyone could have for wanting to keep his activities—whatever they had been—under wraps for so many years. She remembered the day Joseph and Alice Harcourt came to Briar Ridge to take her away . . . the talk she'd had with Joseph on the beach the afternoon she'd discovered the footlocker in the attic. They'd told her he was dead—but he wasn't, not at that time. She thought about Marty and his lies and the things he'd revealed to her that day at her apartment. He'd told her her father had been killed in France, that his cover had been blown. She thought of the elusive Harry Warner, the man who had apparently ceased to exist—yet another relative her father had never told her about. The man she'd searched for but had been unable to locate. She thought about William Blackwell, who'd told her about his alleged treason and subsequent imprisonment . . . about her journey to Leavenworth and the warden who hadn't wanted to talk to her . . . about the records that had been conveniently destroyed in a fire . . . about the guard who'd claimed to have known her father so well, the man who'd gotten it all right and had almost fooled her until he told her about her father's smoking habits. They'd all had a different story to tell—but had any of them been telling the truth?

She thought about the things Kate had told her. Kate, who'd been eliminated because she knew too much. Kate, who had loved her father all those years. Her father had been a hero during the war. He'd fought with the French Resistance. France. Her father had mysteriously disappeared in Paris. It always came back to that. Jaime had the feeling that if she were ever going to know the truth, her journey would have to begin there, where her father's journey had begun—and ended. Whatever he'd been doing, it must have been important, important enough to make a lot of people do a lot of things to keep it all quiet. Jaime did not believe for a moment that he'd been guilty of treason—not only because he was her father, but because he was the man he was. It was not possible. She remembered what a wonderful father he'd been, even when he had to leave her.

"Are you leaving again, Daddy?"

Jaime was seven years old, standing in the doorway of her father's bedroom watching him pack. It had been just over a year since her mother's death. She'd been playing outdoors and looked as though she'd just participated in a wrestling match. Her yellow cotton shirt had grass stains and was pulled partially out of the waistband of her jeans, and her red braids were loosened, strands of hair trailing down her back.

Her father stopped what he was doing and turned to look at her. He tried not to smile, but she could tell the sight of her amused him. "Have you been fighting again, princess?" he asked suspiciously.

"No, Daddy," she said with a perfectly angelic smile. "Tommy and me were after the ball—"

"Tommy and I," he corrected her.

"Yeah, I guess," she said with a nod. "Anyway, we were both running after the ball. We just sort of ran into each other."

"You look like you 'just sort of' ran into the back of a truck," he chuckled. "What does Tommy look like?"

"He looks like hell," Jaime said promptly.

"Jaime!" He looked at her disapprovingly. "This was no accident now, was it?"

She grinned sheepishly. "No," she finally confessed.

He picked her up easily in one arm. "Ah, Jaime—what am I going to do with you?"

She looked down at the open suitcase. "You could take me with you," she suggested innocently.

"Sorry, princess." He shook his head. "Not this time."

"You always say that." She wrinkled her nose disdainfully. "You never take me with you."

"It's business," he told her. "No place for a little girl to be . . ."

No place for a little girl. The words echoed through Jaime's mind now, over twenty years later, as she sat on a hill in Central Park. She'd been too young to realize it at the time, but he'd been telling her it would not be safe for her to go with him. It was his job, and he'd been telling the truth about that. It was no place for a child.

As dusk fell over the city, enveloping it in a blanket of darkness, Jaime got up to leave and tried to recall all the times he'd left her to go off on those "business trips." He was often gone for weeks at a time. She vaguely remembered her mother lamenting that he was away more than he was home. She recalled Kate saying her mother had been deeply in love with her father. It must have been hard on her, his being away so much. Had that been the reason for her unhappiness, the reason she eventually took her own life?

My entire life's been one long series of unanswered questions, Jaime thought dismally, plucking leaves from a branch without even realizing she was doing it. The soft evening breeze gently ruffled her long hair around her face. She took no notice of it. She was still thinking about her father. Unless she could uncover the truth, there would always be a void in her life, an emptiness she'd never be able to fill. Her father would always be labeled a criminal and a traitor. Unfortunately, he was the only one who could give her the answers to her questions. If by some miracle he was still alive.

At that moment, unconsciously, her decision was made.

"You're resigning?" Ben Rollins asked, surprised, looking up from the letter she'd given him.

She nodded.

"It's Terence Hillyer, isn't it?" It was more a statement than a question. "The straw that finally broke the camel's back?"

"No," she insisted, shaking her head. Hillyer was certainly a perfectly good reason for resigning, but she'd never have given him that satisfaction. "Terry's a pain in the ass, yes, but he has nothing to do with my decision. Actually, my reasons are more personal than professional."

"What do you plan to do?" Rollins asked.

"Free-lance," Jaime answered. "I'm going to be traveling a great deal in the future—in Europe—and thought this might be a good time to test my wings professionally as well. Maybe I'll even submit projects to you."

"You'd better," he warned in an affectionate tone. He hesitated for a moment. "If this doesn't pan out, then what?"

She forced a smile she didn't really feel. "Then I hope there will still be a place for me here," she responded.

He smiled back. "I'll *make* a place," he promised.

"Thanks, Ben."

It's done, she thought as she left his office. *As the saying goes, every journey begins with a single step.*

For her, that crucial first step had just been taken.

Jaime thought she would never finish packing. She had no idea how long she would be away, and while she'd started out with the intention of taking along only the essentials, she now felt as though she was taking every piece of clothing she owned. *So much for traveling light*, she thought, surveying the four suitcases lying open on the bed.

She had made all the necessary arrangements and was confident that nothing had been overlooked in her haste to get to Paris. She had considered subletting her apartment but ultimately decided against it. *I could be back next week—or next year*, she thought. It would be comforting to know that no matter what she found—or didn't find—in France, she would still have a place to call home, a place she could come back to when it was all over. Now, more than ever, she needed that.

Though Jaime had done a great deal of traveling and had
placed herself in jeopardy over the past years in search of a
story, she knew even as she packed that this was going to be
different. She'd always been self-sufficient, able to take care
of herself. She'd taken responsibility for her own safety in
her professional pursuits. On a personal level, she'd felt an
even stronger need for independence. She couldn't let herself
be vulnerable—especially after Marty's betrayal. But now she
was uneasy. This was not just another story. It was her own
past, and possibly her future as well, she was pursuing. What
she might discover in the course of her quest was more frightening to her than the element of physical danger could ever
be.

It could take time, a great deal of time. She knew that.
Fortunately, she had the resources to stick it out. Her grandparents had left her a large trust fund—she was, after all,
their only grandchild—and her mother's share of their estate
had also gone to her. There was also the money that had
supposedly been left to her by her father.

Supposedly.

As she walked back into the living room, a familiar face
on the TV screen caught her eye. It was Marty, but on a rival
network and appearing to be part of the story rather than
covering it. Jaime snatched up the remote control device and
turned up the volume.

". . . And the TBC newscaster was arrested this morning
on charges of possession and sale of narcotics by an undercover agent who was part of the federal government's task
force against drugs," the anchorman said. "He has been released on bond tonight, and . . ."

Jaime didn't hear the rest. She sank down onto the couch,
unable to believe it. Marty arrested on drug charges? It wasn't
possible—God, he'd even been working on a story on the war
against drugs—but once upon a time she would not have
thought it possible that he could ever betray her love for him,
either. The Marty Cantrell she'd loved would not have done
any of those things. Still, she found all of this so hard to
believe.

What she *didn't* find hard to believe was that Marty could have been framed.

Washington, D.C. The office was in darkness. Harry Warner sat at his desk, looking out the window, contemplating the magnificent dome of the Capitol, illuminated by gigantic spotlights at night. When the phone rang, he snatched it up. The private line again. "You were supposed to call three hours ago," he snapped. "Where the hell have you been?"

"Right now I'm at Kennedy Airport," said the voice on the other end. "Jaime Lynde's here, too—catching a flight for Paris, in case you're interested."

"Follow her," Warner ordered.

As the 747 lifted off the runway and began its steady climb upward, Jaime leaned back in her seat and tried to relax. It was going to be a long flight, seemingly even longer because she had no idea what lay ahead of her in Paris. If she did find her father—or even the answers to her questions—would she end up regretting not having left the past buried? Only one thing was certain now: if she didn't find out, one way or the other, she would never find peace. There would always be blank spaces in her life.

She looked down at the folded newspaper in her lap. She'd bought it in the terminal at Kennedy Airport while she was waiting for her flight to be called but hadn't had a chance to look at it yet. *Maybe there will be more details on Marty's arrest,* she thought idly as she unfolded it and scanned the front page. Not that it mattered to her, of course; Marty was no longer a part of her life. Still, it was hard, no matter what, to simply stop caring for someone who had been so important once, someone who'd almost been her husband. She had loved him once, and those feelings did not die easily. *They didn't die at all,* she thought bitterly. *They were murdered—and Marty was the murderer.*

She found what she was looking for, and something she never expected to find, on the fourth page. Accompanied by a photograph of Marty was a brief article with a headline that made Jaime's heart stop for a brief moment: *Newsman ar-*

rested on drug charges dies of overdose. Marty—dead? Her
heart pounded furiously in her throat as she read on. He'd
been released the night before on bond—she knew that—and
had been found at his apartment that morning by an unnamed
colleague, shot full of heroin. The newspaper account hinted
that it had been suicide, pointing out that, while the network
denied rumors of professional problems, he had experienced
recent personal difficulties. Personal difficulties. *That's putting it mildly,* Jaime thought, remembering the last time she
saw him. Even so, she did not believe for a moment that he
could have taken his own life. Not Marty. He was too ambitious. He wanted too much. Nothing meant more to him
than his career. She knew that better than anyone else possibly could. He'd sold her out, turned his back on what they'd
had together. For what, she might never know.

She dropped the newspaper and closed her eyes as tears
streamed down her cheeks. She was trembling violently, unable to stop. She was crying, though she wasn't sure if she
was crying for Marty or for herself, for the realization his
death had made her face. Her father might be dead. He was
apparently the key to something very big, very important.
Kate had been murdered. Kate knew too much and was therefore considered a threat to the shroud of secrecy that surrounded her father and his activities abroad. And now it
appeared that Marty had also been eliminated. He'd served
his purpose, and now that they—whoever "they" were—no
longer needed him, they had decided to get him out of the
way. Who, she wondered now, had enough at stake to resort
to murder to keep it all under wraps?

And how far would they go to stop her?

SEVENTEEN

Paris. Jaime stood at the Empire reception desk in the lobby of the Hotel George V, conspicuous in her bulky sweater and corduroy pants tucked into boots as she waited for the desk clerk to locate her reservation. She'd considered less expensive options but decided she *had* to stay at the George V. It was necessary. Her father had been staying here when he disappeared. His trail ended here—and it was here that her own journey would begin. With that in mind, she picked up the pen and signed the register the same way her father had always signed everything: *J. V. Lynde.* She reasoned that if her father had been involved in some sort of espionage operation, his contacts could very well have been made here. And since the boys in Langley, Virginia, hadn't lost interest in him, it was a safe bet that the other team—whoever they were—hadn't either. The more she did to draw attention to herself, the more likely she was to make contact.

I feel like I'm trying to touch base with UFOs, she thought wryly as she was escorted to her room. *And it'll probably be just as likely.*

The room was even more luxurious than she'd expected: eighteenth-century furnishings, paintings she guessed to be well over one hundred years old, a Flemish tapestry—even a beautiful old Regency clock. As Jaime looked around, she found herself thinking about the days when her father had stayed here. Who'd picked up the tab then—O'Donnell-Colby Associates or the CIA?

She gave the bellman a generous tip. After he was gone, she went on about the business of unpacking and settling in. *Might as well—this could take a while,* she thought, resigning herself to the possibility. If circumstances had been different, she would have enjoyed her luxurious surroundings, enjoyed being in Paris. She would have seen all of the things she'd heard so much about, things her father had once told her about: the little cafés and bistros not frequented by tourists; the lesser-known galleries and theaters; the artist's Paris. *Maybe some other time,* she told herself as she opened the drapes. Paris was such a beautiful city— She stopped short. Down below, across the street, she saw a man leaning against a lamppost, looking up as if he were looking right at her. She'd seen him before—in New York. The man who'd followed her home from *World Views* offices that night, months ago. She was sure it was the same man. Absolutely sure. Quickly she drew the drapes again and collapsed onto the bed.

So they *were* still keeping tabs on her.

She slept fitfully. She was unusually restless and woke three times during the night. Each time, she got out of bed and went to the window. The man was never there. *But he's here somewhere,* she thought with certainty. *He's still here . . . watching.*

Though she'd never experienced jet lag to any degree of severity, she experienced it now at its worst. She was nauseated, her head was pounding like a thousand war drums, and it took a monumental effort just to get out of bed. *If this is what morning sickness is like, I'm glad I decided never to have children,* she thought ruefully as she stumbled into the bathroom.

She took a warm shower and washed her hair, but felt no better afterward. The thought of food made her feel even more queasy—if that were possible—but she knew she'd have to eat something. She rang room service and ordered a light breakfast. As she nibbled, she thought about her physical distress. It wasn't jet lag at all. It was the prospect of facing the unknown, of having been followed here by an unidentified assailant who might be willing to do anything to stop her from uncovering the truth about her father.

As she dressed in tan wool slacks and a cream blouse, she thought about Marty. They—whoever "they" really were—had used him, and when they no longer needed him, when he didn't deliver what they wanted, had eliminated him. Eliminated. It sounded so cold. But they were apparently just that: very cold, inhuman killing machines.

What could her father have done that it was so important someone would be willing to kill to keep it quiet? Kate had discovered something—something involving her father and a man named Lewis Baldwin—and she'd been silenced. Permanently silenced. Marty had been nothing more than a pawn. He'd been enlisted to distract her, to keep her from her search. He'd paid for his failure with his life.

Would they kill her, too?

Jaime climbed out of the red Renault taxi in front of the American embassy on the Avenue Gabriel, just off the Place de la Concorde. She paid the driver, then paused at the entrance for a moment. What was she going to say to the ambassador? She couldn't just march into his office and say, "Hi, I'm Jaime Lynde. My father's a spy, and I need your help in finding him." She couldn't tell him her father was a spy at all. Still, she couldn't see herself posing as a concerned daughter looking for a missing father—a father who just happened to have been missing for almost twenty years. *Well, you see, sir, I just noticed he was gone, and. . . .* She frowned. It wasn't even funny.

She could, however, meet with the ambassador as exactly what she was: a professional, a photojournalist interested in the whereabouts of a man who'd disappeared in Paris in 1966, a man who just happened to have been her father. *But the ambassador is government,* she reminded herself. *What if he's one of them?* Then he'd know who she was and what she was after. And so would they. As if they didn't already. Even if the ambassador himself weren't involved, someone else at the embassy might be. Stories about leaks were popping up in newspapers all the time—secretaries, Marine guards, even diplomatic staffers.

This is ridiculous, she thought. *Suddenly I'm suspicious of everyone—even the U.S. ambassador to France! But it's not as if it's without good reason.*

She was admitted to the embassy and directed to the press office. She was told a press attaché would speak to her before scheduling a meeting with the ambassador himself, that perhaps the press office could help her themselves. As she started down the corridor to the office to which she'd been directed, she felt another wave of nausea sweep over her. She paused momentarily. *I didn't drink any water. It couldn't be Montezuma's Revenge—who gets Montezuma's Revenge in France? I knew I should have skipped breakfast.*

Then she collapsed.

When she opened her eyes, she was in strange surroundings, lying on a couch in what appeared to be someone's office. A man who appeared to be in his mid to late thirties, a very attractive man with dark hair and blue eyes and strong, angular features, was hovering over her. He was also unbuttoning her shirt.

"Just what the hell do you think you're doing?" she demanded hotly as she pulled herself upright, pushing his hand away.

"Take it easy," he said quickly, withdrawing his hands without protest. "I wasn't trying to take advantage of you, if that's what you're thinking—and it obviously is. You fainted. I'm told loosening clothing is the first step in treating that sort of thing."

She caught her breath. "I fainted?"

He smiled. "You made one beautiful swan dive—right into my arms, mademoiselle," he told her.

She looked at him suspiciously. "Nobody does a swan dive when they faint," she pointed out.

"Can I help it if I prefer to make it sound more poetic?"

He showed her a damp washcloth. "Lie back—you shouldn't jump up too quickly. I'll put this on your forehead—unless you intend to break my arm for doing so, that is."

She lay back. "Truce," she assured him.

"That's better." He put the damp cloth in place. "I'll bet you're the world's worst patient."

"I presume you're a doctor?"

"You presume wrong. I'm a press attaché. Nicholas Kendall's the name," he introduced himself. "And you are—"

"Jaime Lynde. *World Views* magazine," she said. She studied him closely. He really was quite handsome, from the deep cobalt blue of his eyes to the way his dark hair teased the collar of his shirt, to the beautiful smile with which he regarded her. *I should have kept my mouth shut,* she told herself. *I've died and gone to heaven—always knew angels would look like this.*

"What brings you to Paris, Jaime Lynde?" he wanted to know.

"A manhunt," she said sullenly, without thinking.

He grinned. "You've certainly come to the right place," he said pleasantly. "Your first impression could use a little polishing, though."

"What?"

"You'll hardly find a man if you go around making threats on their lives," he pointed out.

"That's not the kind of manhunt I had in mind," she said pointedly.

He raised an eyebrow. "There's another?"

"For your information, I'm looking for a missing person," she said, pressing the cold cloth to her forehead. "He's been missing a long time, so it won't be easy."

"How long?" he asked.

"Almost twenty years." She tried to sit up but fell back abruptly, dizzy again. He came to her assistance.

"There's no hurry. Just lie there until it passes," he insisted. He offered her a drink of water. "Does this sort of thing happen often?"

"Never," she answered without hesitation. "I'm as healthy as a horse."

He hesitated momentarily. "Could you be pregnant?" he asked carefully.

She laughed for the first time. "If I am, I'd better start looking for three guys on camels and a bright star in the east."

Nicholas smiled. He had a nice smile, Jaime decided. Very nice indeed. "About this man you're looking for," he said. "What else can you tell me about him?"

Jaime paused. "He's my father."

Washington, D.C. Harry Warner was in his office unusually early, before five o'clock. He was alone, waiting for the call from Paris to come through. When his private line rang, he snatched it up immediately. "Warner here."

"Jaime Lynde's paying a visit to the American embassy right now."

"Has she talked to anyone yet?"

"A press attaché. Nicholas Kendall."

"He's not one of ours," Warner commented. "Keep following her."

"What about Kendall?"

"What about him?"

"She may have told him—"

"I doubt that." Warner was confident. "After all, she just met him. She's very distrustful of strangers—even of friends—at this point. She won't be too quick to open up to anybody, not after Cantrell and the others."

"Are you sure about that?"

"It's one of the few things I *am* sure of."

"My father was a spy."

Jaime still wasn't sure she should be telling this to this man she'd just met. She'd been betrayed by those she trusted, used by the man she loved. All around her, people were dying to preserve the veil of secrecy surrounding her father and his questionable activities. *She* was beginning to feel like a moving target herself. How could she let herself trust anyone, let alone a perfect stranger?

Nicholas stared at her for a moment. "An intelligence agent?"

She nodded. "I believe he was on an assignment—under the guise of a business trip—when he disappeared."

Nicholas rubbed his chin thoughtfully. "That certainly complicates matters further," he said finally.

She looked at him, puzzled. "In what way?"

"If your father had been an American tourist or a businessman, someone who'd disappeared, say, a week or even a month ago, then there might be something we could do," he said, pacing the carpet in front of his desk as he spoke. "But a government agent who dropped out of sight during a mission almost twenty years ago—"

"He was an American citizen, dammit!" Jaime snapped. "He vanished right here in Paris while in the service of the United States government! *That's* the bottom line!"

"Almost twenty years ago," he reminded her calmly.

She stared at him incredulously. "Are you telling me Uncle Sam washes his hands of our own men if they're caught or killed? Why is it any different from the seizing of the embassy in Teheran or the hijacking of the TWA flight back in June or any of the other attacks on U.S. citizens?"

He sat down beside her again. "It's different," he began, drawing in his breath, "because your father was involved in covert operations. There are certain disadvantages the spy accepts when he joins the ranks."

"What disadvantages?" Jaime asked, biting off each syllable.

"The life of the spy isn't really much different from the days of the old OSS, back during World War Two," he explained. "The spy's life is essentially a lonely one—alone and unwanted in an alien society, he faces grave danger almost every day with no real protection but his wits. He knows one wrong move can be fatal. He also knows that, if he's captured, his own government will deny his existence. Facing life imprisonment or execution, he has only one other option open to him: he can become a turncoat and work for his captors."

"Not much of a choice," Jaime said grimly.

Nicholas shook his head.

"How can they just wash their hands of a man just because he's gotten himself captured?" she asked.

He shook his head. "Secrecy. That's the name of the game. Nobody is willing to admit they've been looking through key-holes at the other guy—so if he gets caught, the spy's on his own. Always."

"You seem to know an awful lot about it," Jaime observed.

He frowned. "Before Paris, I was at the embassy in Te-heran," he told her. "I was transferred two months before it was taken by the Iranians. In some countries, covert contacts are made through the embassies, usually those countries like Iran and Lebanon, potential hotbeds of trouble."

"But not here," she concluded.

"France is one of our allies," he said simply.

"If nothing was going on, why was my father here?"

He thought about it for a moment. "Maybe he wasn't. Maybe it was just a cover. An American businessman in Paris on business. Checks into his hotel, then goes on to wherever it is he's really supposed to be."

Jaime nodded slowly. "That's possible, I suppose." She'd never thought about it before. "Then there's nothing you can do?"

"Diplomatically, no," he admitted.

He watched her leave. He'd never been one to allow his personal feelings to get in the way of duty. He wasn't influenced by his own attraction to a woman, any woman.

So why had Jaime Lynde gotten to him now?

Was it a mistake to trust him? Jaime wondered as the taxi came to a stop in front of the George V. *He seemed so sincere, but so did all the others. They all wanted to help. Marty, Bearden, all of them. And none of them could be trusted.*

She paid the driver as she got out of the car, then entered the hotel. Striding purposefully across the lobby to the front desk, she checked to see if there were any messages for her. There was only one: *Nicholas Kendall. 296.12.02.* The embassy number. He wanted her to call. *He certainly doesn't waste any time,* Jaime thought, not sure if it was a good sign or not.

She called him as soon as she reached her room. "I take it you've spoken with the ambassador."

"No," he admitted, "but I think I may have come up with something."

"And that is?"

"Not over the phone," he said quickly. Almost too quickly. Jaime was brushed by a faint sense of unease. "Are you free for dinner tonight?"

She hesitated. *Another wild-goose chase?* she wondered. "Yes," she said aloud. "I'm free."

"Are you familiar with Paris at all?"

"Vaguely."

"Have you ever been to La Closerie des Lilas?"

"Never."

"It's in Montparnasse." There was a pause on the other end. "I'll pick you up at your hotel around seven-thirty, all right?"

"Fine."

But was it? she wondered.

La Closerie des Lilas, on the Boulevard du Montparnasse, is known more for its literary patrons than for its cuisine: Hemingway, Trotsky, and Verlaine were all regulars in their time. Outside, a lovely green terrace provides a backdrop for the statue of Marshall Ney, while inside it boasts the most typically Parisian bar in all of Paris, tended by two innovative bartenders who are constantly coming up with creative new cocktails. The real atmosphere of the brasserie is provided by Ivan Meyer, an incredibly gifted old-time piano player.

"There are some real characters who hang around here," Nicholas told Jaime as they were escorted to a table. "It's not at all unusual for any of the regulars to drop in for a drink at one in the morning."

"Oh?" Jaime raised an eyebrow. "You've been here that late?"

He grinned. "Once or twice."

He ordered for both of them from the bar in impeccable French. Jaime studied him as he conversed with their waiter. She liked him. She wasn't quite sure why, but she did. Trouble was, she wasn't convinced she could trust him. She wasn't sure she could trust anyone.

"You said you were with *World Views*," Nicholas recalled as the waiter departed. "What are you doing now—aside from taking on Uncle Sam?"

"Same thing, only now it's free-lance."

He smiled. "I admire anyone with the guts to make a move like that."

"There was never any choice as far as I'm concerned," Jaime said simply. "I have to find my father—or at least find out what happened to him."

Nicholas paused. "I've been thinking about what we discussed this morning," he began. "As I said then, there are CIA people on staff at embassies in Eastern bloc and Middle Eastern nations. I suppose it's possible there might be some in friendly countries as well, though to my knowledge there are none here in Paris."

"You already told me that."

"I said, 'to my knowledge,' " he pointed out. "I'm sure I wouldn't be told about it, even if there were."

The waiter returned with their drinks. When he asked if they were ready to order, Jaime realized she hadn't even looked at her menu. "Mind making a recommendation?" she asked Nicholas.

"Best bets are the haddock and the steak tartare," he responded without hesitation. "I usually have the steak."

"I think I'll have the haddock," she told him.

He grinned. "I take it you don't like your steak rare."

She shook her head rapidly.

Nicholas turned to the waiter again, ordering in French with the ease of someone who'd spoken the language all of his life. As the waiter retreated with their order, he turned back to Jaime. "There are a number of staffers at the embassy who've been around for years," he said, reaching for his drink. "Some of them were here twenty years ago."

"And?"

"And maybe they know something. Anything." His gaze met hers. "It's worth a try, isn't it?"

She forced a smile. "Right now, I'm willing to try anything."

EIGHTEEN

The sound of the telephone ringing roused Jaime from a sound sleep. She sat up in bed and, still slightly disoriented, picked up the receiver and pressed it to her ear. "Hullo?"

"Jaime?"

"Yes," she acknowledged sleepily.

"It's Nicholas. Did I wake you?"

"Yes, but that's okay," she assured him, pushing a heavy curtain of red hair back off her face with one hand. "What time is it?"

"Ten-fifteen." There was a pause. "You're probably still on New York time."

"You're probably right," she conceded. Then, realizing why he must have called: "You've found out something? Already?"

He hesitated. "Can you make lunch today?"

"Of course. Where and when?"

"There's a great little sidewalk café on the Champs-Élysées," he said. "The food's good and the view is even better. Is twelve-fifteen convenient?"

"Sure."

"I'll meet you in your lobby, all right?"

"Fine. See you then." She replaced the receiver slowly.

How had he managed to come up with anything so quickly—
or had he? Was he really trying to help her—or just keep tabs
on her?

She swung her long legs off the side of the bed and shook
her hair back over her shoulders. She wished she could trust
him, really trust him. She *wanted* to trust him. She wanted
to know there was someone she could turn to, confide in. She
wanted that person to be Nicholas Kendall. Yet a part of her
couldn't help being suspicious. She was suspicious of everyone she met these days.

But not without good reason.

"You were right," Jaime told Nicholas over lunch. "The
food *and* the view are *magnifique*."

They were having lunch at a small sidewalk café on the
Champs-Élysées, at a table from which they had an almost
unobstructed view of the Arc de Triomphe. Pedestrian traffic
along the front of the restaurant was heavy. "I suspect you
prefer the view to the meal," Nicholas observed, eyeing her
plate. "You've barely touched your food."

"It's just me," she insisted, taking a token bite of her
sandwich. "I haven't had much of an appetite since I've been
in Paris."

"Which, may I point out, could account for your fainting
the other day at the embassy," he said, his eyes meeting hers.
They were as deep and as blue as the ocean. Had circumstances been different, she was sure allowing herself to drown
in their depths would have been a pleasure.

"Better make an effort," he was saying. "You're going to
need all the strength you can muster."

She perked up immediately. "You've found something,"
she concluded.

"Hold on!" he said quickly, raising one hand. "I *did* come
up with something, but nothing earth-shattering, I assure
you."

"Whatever it is, it's a start," she said promptly.

He nodded, reaching for his coffee. "A woman—a secretary at the embassy. She's been there almost twenty-three
years," he explained. "She's American, of course, but she

studied at the Sorbonne. Her father's money ran out before she could finish her education, but she loved Paris so much she wanted to stay here, and—''

''She was here at the time my father disappeared,'' Jaime interjected impatiently.

Nicholas nodded. ''I talked to her this morning,'' he said, finishing his coffee. ''I showed her the photograph you left with me. She recognized him.''

Jaime's heart skipped two beats. ''And?''

He frowned. ''There's not much more,'' he said regretfully. ''He was at the embassy twice. Both times he spoke privately with the ambassador—that is, the man who served as ambassador at that time. Barbara says she was told he was an American businessman in Paris on behalf of his firm.''

''That apparently was his cover,'' Jaime said darkly. ''He was with my grandfather's firm in New York.'' She continued to pick at the food on her plate absently. ''Until last year, I didn't know about his real profession myself.''

''The current ambassador was here at that time as well,'' Nicholas said then. ''He was serving as the deputy chief of mission.''

Jaime looked at him hopefully. ''Then he would have been the person closest to the ambassador himself,'' she deduced. ''He might know the truth!''

''If he does, he's not talking,'' Nicholas said tightly. ''I tried, Jaime, believe me. I tried to get him to talk to me. He insisted there was nothing to tell, that James Lynde was simply a businessman in Paris who came to the embassy because of some minor problem.''

''Minor, my ass!'' Jaime snorted.

''I'll keep checking around. Surely there's someone—''

She cut him off. ''Why are you so willing to help me when everyone else treats me as if I'm carrying the Black Plague?''

He looked at her and asked himself the same question. He knew he was playing with fire. He knew poking around the skeletons in Uncle Sam's closets could only get him into trouble. He knew he was walking through a political mine field and one wrong move could spell the end of his diplomatic career. One wrong move and he'd be out on his ass. Yet looking at Jaime Lynde, sensing her anguish and frustration, made him forget about things like caution and responsibility and duty. He forced a smile as his eyes met hers.

"Beats the hell out of me," he told her.

Washington, D.C. "She's still in Paris?" Harry Warner asked.

"And apparently not all that anxious to leave," said the disembodied voice on the other end of the telephone. "She's been spending a great deal of time with Kendall for the past two weeks."

"Kendall," Warner said thoughtfully. "He's been asking questions around the embassy, from what I hear."

"Unfortunately. Nosing around where he doesn't belong. I think he should be transferred."

"Possibly." Warner paused. "Has he uncovered anything?"

"Nothing to be concerned about—yet."

"Better keep tabs on him, too," Warner decided. "For now, that is."

"Yeah. I'll put somebody on it."

"Keep me informed."

"Where are you from?" Jaime asked.

She was having dinner with Nicholas at the Relais Plaza on the Avenue Montaigne, amid the elegant 1930s ocean liner decor. Between bites of salmon with a light dill sauce, she'd managed to tell him the story of her life all within an hour and a half.

"Maine," he said, reaching for his wineglass. "A place called Tenants Harbor. Ever heard of it?"

Jaime shook her head. "Can't say that I have," she admitted. "How did you end up here—in diplomatic service, I mean?"

He smiled wearily. "It was a compromise."

She gave him a puzzled look. "A compromise?"

He nodded. "I majored in communications in college," he explained. "I wanted to get into television—figured I'd have my own station one day. My father, it turned out, had other plans. He'd always had political aspirations, but it never quite panned out, so he decided one of his sons would have to enter politics.''

Jaime raised an eyebrow quizzically. ''*One* of his sons?''

''There were three of us,'' Nicholas told her. ''Daniel became a neurosurgeon and Thomas a stockbroker. As the youngest, I became Dad's last hope.''

''You're doing this for your father, then,'' Jaime concluded.

''In a sense, yes.''

''Don't you think you should be doing whatever it is *you* want to do?'' She hoped she sounded civil.

His eyes met hers. ''Don't you?''

She forced a smile. ''I guess I deserved that.''

''You did,'' he agreed. ''Anyway, I will do what I want, eventually.'' He didn't seem overly concerned about it. ''What about you? When are you going to let the past go and start thinking about the future?''

''When I exorcise all the ghosts,'' she said quietly.

If only it were so simple.

Nicholas Kendall lived in an apartment building on the Rue de Marignon, not far from the embassy. From the windows of his bedroom, he could see the Eiffel Tower, but having lived in Paris for almost five years, the sight of it no longer impressed him—any more than any native New Yorker was moved by the Empire State Building or the Chrysler Building or the twin towers of the World Trade Center. But now, as he dressed for work, he found himself pondering that sight he'd come to take for granted. He'd never seen Paris from the Tower's observation platform, nor had he eaten in its restaurant. He'd never even thought about it until now. Now he wanted to go to the top. He wanted to take Jaime there.

He'd been physically attracted to her the moment he saw her that day at the embassy. He'd used every excuse he could think of to spend time with her in the past two months, though he suspected his luck would run out soon, when she decided he was not much help to her and moved on to another city and another source of information. He dreaded that day, though he wasn't quite sure why. It wasn't as if they were lovers; they could barely be called friends. Yet the more he was with her, the more drawn to her he was. She'd gotten under his skin as no other woman ever had—without even trying. He smiled to himself. She probably didn't even realize how strongly attracted to her he was. All she could think about was her father.

God knows I'd like to help her, he thought. Still, a part of him wondered what she'd do once she had the information she was looking for. She'd leave Paris, no doubt. It was the last thing he wanted to happen. He wanted more time with her. He wanted to get to know her better. He wanted to know her in the most intimate way possible. He did feel guilty that he was using her obsession with finding that long-lost father of hers as a means of getting close to her. *I have been trying to help her,* he reminded himself. *I have been trying to track down information for her.*

He turned to the mirror over his bureau as he knotted his tie. In the five years he'd been in Paris, there had been a number of women in his life. He'd developed a definite preference for French women. Older French women. While several of them had been intimate relationships in the physical sense, none of them had ever reached the "serious" stage emotionally. In the beginning, his mother's correspondence had invariably included gentle reminders that it was time to start thinking about "settling down." Lately, her letters were more desperate. She felt it was a disgrace to still be single— and not even thinking of marriage, at that—at the ripe old age of thirty-five. His brothers, she never failed to point out, had both married in their twenties and now had children of their own.

Nicholas had never been in any great hurry. He liked women, genuinely *liked* them—not only as sex partners, but as people. Sex, he'd discovered early on, was invariably better with a woman he liked and respected, someone with whom he had more in common than an overactive libido. Still, none of the women with whom he'd enjoyed satisfying relationships—in and out of bed—had turned out to be *the* woman he was looking for, the one who could make him give up the freedom he'd come to enjoy. Until Jaime Lynde. Right from the beginning, he'd had the feeling she was going to be different.

Ah, Jaime, he thought. *I do have it bad for you!*

"Microfilm. Old newspapers. Nineteen-sixty-six." Jaime fumbled for the correct French words to tell the library clerk what she was looking for, but he seemed distracted by her jeans, rust-colored pullover sweater, and boots. *"Journaux. Vieux."* She gestured impatiently.

"Oui, mademoiselle. Vieux." The man's face brightened with sudden comprehension. Speaking in rapid French, he directed her to the library's microfilm room. Though Jaime had been able to translate only half of what he'd said, she was sure she'd understood enough to find it.

"Merci," she acknowledged with a nod. *"Merci beaucoup."*

It was eerily quiet in the basement of the old library on the Left Bank. The only sound to be heard was that of her own heels clicking on the concrete floor as she walked down a long corridor to the microfilm room. *It's like a mausoleum,* she thought. *The burial ground for old periodicals.*

After a moderately successful attempt at bridging the language barrier with yet another librarian, she was given boxed spools of microfilm copies of all the Paris newspapers for the months of November and December 1966. She spent most of the day scanning the film, stopping just long enough to phone Nicholas from an antiquated pay telephone in the corridor to cancel their plans to meet for lunch.

"I can't leave now," she told him. "There may be something in one of these old newspapers . . . and it's been hell trying to communicate with the library staff. I don't want to do it again if I don't have to."

"I understand," he said carefully, but she was still able to detect the annoyance in his voice. "Shall we make it dinner, then?"

"Sure." She figured it was the least she could do after canceling lunch. After all, he *was* trying to be of help to her. The only person in the world who was. She was reluctant to lose any time on her search but had to admit she did enjoy his company. "You pick the restaurant."

He laughed then. "Don't you have any preferences?"

"Well," she began hesitantly, "I do—but if I were to tell you, you'd probably laugh."

"I would not!" he insisted. "Name it."

"McDonald's. I'm having a Big Mac attack," she confessed.

He roared with laughter.

"You promised you wouldn't," she reminded him.

"Okay, I'm sorry—I couldn't help it," he insisted. "McDonald's it is."

"Not very original, is it," she chuckled.

"In Paris it is," he told her.

"I'm at your mercy," she said wearily. "Just pick someplace with good food and no dress code, okay? I think after the day I've been having, I'm going to need to relax more than anything."

"You've got it," he promised. "I'll pick you up at seven—and you can wear jeans and sneakers if you like."

"Uh-oh—sounds ominous," she laughed. "Listen, I'd better get back to my microfilm. The clerk's giving me the French equivalent of the evil eye."

"Sure. See you tonight."

Jaime hung up slowly. *Careful now,* she warned herself. *You've started to like him just a little bit too much.*

Haven't you learned your lesson yet?

"I was only kidding when I suggested McDonald's, Kendall," Jaime laughed as Nicholas steered her through the busy arcade on the Champs-Élysées. "Jesus, it doesn't even *look* like a real McDonald's—no golden arches!" she exclaimed at the sight of the small sign that looked more appropriate for a dentist's office than a fast-food restaurant.

"This is Paris," he reminded her. "They'd never stand for anything so commercial."

"You mean they wouldn't want anything so tacky," she responded, pretending to be insulted.

"You said it, not I." He held the door for her. "After you, mademoiselle."

"Ah—chivalry isn't dead," she proclaimed. "Just a little comatose."

"Move it, sweetheart," he growled. "We have to stand in line here, you know."

She paused to look at the menu over the counter. "The *filet de poisson*—has to be the fish sandwich," she deduced. "Why, pray tell, is the cheeseburger in English?"

"Apparently it's untranslatable," he commented. "What's your pleasure?"

"A Big Mac—with everything on it but pickles."

"Why no pickles?" he asked.

"I heard stories back in the States about what some of the fellas working in fast-food restaurants do to the pickles, but believe me, you don't want to hear it before you eat," she laughed.

"Depends. Are the stories true?" he asked cautiously.

She winked. "That's anybody's guess."

"You're terrible," he told her. "How about a *bière*?"

"A what?"

"A beer. They do serve them here," he pointed out. "Though the French wouldn't dream of having coffee *with* their meal—not even a fast-food meal—a beer's not out of the question."

She grimaced. "Just a Diet Coke, thank you," she said. "The Big Mac's my unpardonable sin for the day."

He arched an eyebrow. "A compromising woman?" he asked, obviously enjoying this. "I'd never have thought it!"

"Only when it's absolutely necessary," she assured him.

Jaime was beginning to feel the need to put some distance between herself and Nicholas. It was clear to her now that his interest in her went beyond that of a member of the embassy staff coming to the assistance of an American citizen in Paris. Not that she couldn't handle that. What troubled Jaime most was *her* growing attraction to *him*. In spite of her doubts, in spite of her reluctance, she was attracted to him. Maybe in more ways than one. She enjoyed being with him.

She was even beginning to trust him a little—and placing her trust in another human being was something she'd told herself she must never, *ever* do again. For someone in her uncertain position, no one would ever really be "above suspicion."

Yet she needed to trust someone. *Wanted* to trust Nicholas Kendall.

Nicholas stared thoughtfully at the file lying on his desk. Someone had been careless. Or had they? It made him uneasy. While he knew little about the government's covert operations, he was certain they *didn't* tolerate bumbling idiots within their ranks. Their operatives would never have left such obviously important documents lying around where anyone might find them. But what if it *hadn't* been a mistake? Could it have been left there, where it was certain to be seen, deliberately?

According to Jaime, anything was possible. *My own fiancé was one of them, Nicholas—a man I loved and planned to marry. He sold out to them.* That was why she was so hard to get close to. Suspicion—and fear. *They killed him. When he was no longer of any use to them, they eliminated him.*

Was it possible? Nicholas wondered. Could Jaime be right? Could her father have been involved in something so big that someone had been willing to kill—and might very well kill again—to keep it all quiet? *My aunt was on to something. A man who served with my father during the war. She drowned—in shallow water. But she was a good swimmer.*

He opened the file and leafed through it slowly. It didn't make sense. What were all these papers doing at the embassy, anyway? And who did they belong to? Someone had been unpardonably sloppy. *I went to the prison. Leavenworth. I talked to the acting warden. God only knows what they did with the real warden while I was there. They had no records—conveniently lost in a fire. And no decent explanation why, if he died there, I was never notified.*

A father who'd been a bit of a Houdini, pulling his big disappearing act when she was just ten years old. A government operative who was apparently working on something so vitally important that some people were willing to kill to protect the secret. A smoke screen with more holes in it than a slice of Swiss cheese. It just didn't add up. And Nicholas wasn't altogether sure he should tell Jaime anything at all about the file or its contents. Still. . . .

He picked up the phone and dialed the George V and asked for her room. "You're becoming predictable, Kendall," Jaime warned when she came on the line. "You call at the same time every day, you know that?"

"Can't have that." He forced a cheerfulness into his voice that he didn't really feel. "How about a change of pace?"

"What have you got in mind?" she asked.

"Dinner—at my place. I'll cook."

"Now that *is* a change of pace," she laughed. "I'll bring the wine. What time do you want me there?"

He wanted to say "Sunset to sunrise," but resisted the temptation. "I'll pick you up at six-thirty," he said.

"Don't be silly," she scoffed. "I can take a cab."

He fingered the file as he spoke. "I don't think that's such a good idea—"

"No arguments," she insisted firmly. "Give me the address." He did. "See you tonight," she told him.

"Yeah."

He replaced the receiver slowly. He didn't want her to know how concerned he was for her safety, but was he that good an actor? If what he'd begun to suspect was true, she could be in a great deal of danger.

When he left the embassy that evening, he had the uneasy feeling he was being followed.

NINETEEN

"I've been going over all the letters my father sent me over the years—when I was at boarding school," Jaime told Nicholas as they walked together along the Seine at sunset. "He always wrote to me, no matter where we were, even if it was only for a week. He'd send a postcard at the very least." She stared off into the distance at something only she could see. Her lips pursed thoughtfully. "I keep thinking there must be something in those letters that could lead me to him."

Nicholas frowned, pulling up the collar of his trench coat against the brisk November wind. "Jaime, are you absolutely sure you really *want* to know the truth?" he asked hesitantly.

She turned to look at him, genuinely surprised by his question. "Of course I want to know. I *have* to know," she insisted. The wind whipped her long hair about her face like a magnificent red banner, the individual strands catching the pale sunlight that seemed to turn it into a hundred different shades, ranging from red to rust to orange to the pale gold of wheat. The colors of autumn, her father had often said. "My father was accused of everything from embezzlement to treason, Nicholas. I've got to find him—or at least clear his name."

He hesitated again, moved by the quiet determination in

her eyes. "What if it's true? What if he was a double agent—or a traitor? You could be opening a Pandora's box here, you know."

Her face grew instantaneously dark with anger. "I don't believe that for a minute," she said harshly. "I *won't*—no matter what they say."

Nicholas touched her arm. "You believe in him because he was your father," he pointed out. "You can't be objective. I don't expect you to be."

"Not *was* my father," she said crossly. "*Is* my father. As far as I'm concerned, he's still alive—until I have proof otherwise. And for the record, I believe in him because I know what kind of man he was."

"He was the kind of man who abandoned his own daughter without warning."

Reacting without thinking, Jaime's hand lashed out across his face. "You didn't know him, so don't sit in judgment, dammit!" she snapped.

He pressed his hand to his cheek, silent for a long moment. "I'm sorry," he said finally. "I guess I deserved that."

"You sure as hell did." She leaned on the railing, refusing to look at him.

He debated with himself about the information he had, then decided to tell her about the file. "I found a file at the embassy yesterday," he started carefully. "Some personal notes, apparently, made by the ambassador—that is, the ambassador when your father was supposed to have been here."

Now she looked at him. "And?"

"It was incriminating, to say the least."

"Incriminating against my father, you mean."

He nodded.

"And you believe it."

"I'm wary of it," he admitted. "It doesn't feel right. I get the feeling there's something very wrong here."

She looked back at the water again. "The same feeling I've had for the past twenty years," she said quietly.

"Yeah."

"You think it's fishy, too?"

"You could wrap it in newspaper and serve it with chips,"

he said grimly. "It's all too pat. Too easy. The file was just sitting there, waiting to be found." He paused. "These people are professionals, Jaime. They don't make stupid mistakes—and this definitely qualifies as a stupid mistake, unless it *was* deliberate. My guess is that they figure you'll back off if they can convince you your father really was a turncoat." The wind ruffled his dark hair as he spoke.

"They're wrong on both counts," Jaime said stubbornly. "I don't believe their lies, and I'm not about to give up."

He stared at her for a moment. "Are you willing to put your own life on the line, Jaime?" he asked. "That's exactly what you're doing, you know. You told me yourself they'd already killed to keep this all hush-hush. Don't you realize they'll kill you, too?"

"They might," she conceded, her green eyes blazing with anger, "but they'll damn well know they've done something when they do. Besides, Nicholas, it's already gone too far."

He looked at her questioningly.

"It wouldn't matter if I gave it all up today. They'd never stop keeping tabs on me, wondering when I'd pick up on it again. I can't live like that." She looked out across the river. "There's no turning back now," she said with finality.

It wasn't possible.

They'd never make her believe her father had betrayed her *or* his country. Never. Whatever else he was—and she knew only too well that he was no saint—he would never sell out his own people. He would never abandon her, as Nicholas had put it, if he'd had a choice. He just wasn't capable of that. She was sure of it. Yet someone had gone to a great deal of trouble to make it look that way. Why?

She reread her father's letters over breakfast, looking for a name, a place, any clue that might lead her to him. After so many years, after having read those letters so many times they were each permanently etched in her memory, she was still convinced she could have missed something—and so she read them each again. There was nothing. Not a hint. *Daddy, you must've been a genius at covering your tracks,* she thought, annoyed. *Too damn good.*

She turned her attentions to those letters he had written to her mother during their courtship, in the six months prior to their marriage. Letters that were generally more informative than those intended for a small child. Letters artfully crafted, she decided, to make her mother and anyone else who might happen to read them believe without a doubt that he was deeply in love with their recipient. *I'd believe it if I didn't know better,* she thought. Those letters bore postmarks from Paris and London and Amsterdam and Antwerp and Rome— and Moscow. They included names of men with whom he'd supposedly done business. Jaime wrote down each name and each city on a steno pad. Anything was worth looking into at this point.

By eleven-fifteen, she was ready to give up. She was meeting Nicholas for lunch and getting nowhere fast. As she was returning the bundle of letters to her suitcase, one envelope fell out. Bending to pick it up, she noticed the postmark: Lyon. On an impulse, she opened it. Inside was a brief letter—in French—from a man named Julien Armand. Also enclosed was an old, yellowed photograph of two men. One was her father. The other was not familiar at all. On the back were two names, her father's and that of Julien Armand, and a date: June 19, 1947. Julien Armand. She searched her memory for some recollection of his having been mentioned to her. . . .

"I should go with you, Daddy."

She was eight years old. Dressed in pink cotton shorts and a white T-shirt, she sat cross-legged in the middle of her father's bed, watching him pack his suitcase. "I'd love to take you with me, princess, but a business trip's no place for a little girl," he told her.

She pushed her lower lip out, pouting. "Would you take me if I were a little boy?" she wanted to know.

He stopped what he was doing, taken by surprise by her question. "You know better than that," he said, his tone mildly scolding.

"Don't most daddies want little boys to do things with them?" she pursued, not about to let it go.

"Maybe," he said as he lifted her into his arms, "but this

daddy is quite happy with his little redheaded girl and wouldn't trade her for a dozen boys." He rumpled her hair playfully. *"Boy or girl, princess, you'll always have what it takes to do whatever you want to do. You just have to believe in yourself. Got it?"*

She grinned, saluting smartly. "Got it," she giggled as she snuggled close to him. She loved being close to him. She liked the smell of him, so strikingly different from that of herself or her mother or even Sadie. She liked the feel of him, so much harder and stronger than any woman. His skin was rougher, but it was a nice kind of rough. The stubble on his cheeks when he didn't shave tickled her when he kissed her. She told herself she'd never love any other man the way she loved him. "I still wish I could go," she said wistfully. "I wish you didn't have to be away so much. I miss you so much."

He shook his head, smiling. "You're not alone. You have Sadie," he pointed out.

"It's not the same," she insisted. "Besides, you're alone. You need somebody to keep you company."

"To tell you the truth, princess, I'm almost never alone," he admitted. "I have friends over there, too, you know. Like Julien."

She wrinkled her nose disdainfully. "A lady?"

He laughed, that deep, husky laugh she knew so well. "Julien, princess—not Julie," he told her. "A man. A Frenchman. We've been friends for a very long time. Long before you were born. We fought together during the war, against the Nazis."

She gave him a quizzical look. "What're Nazis, Daddy?"

He grinned at the question. "Nazis," he started, amused, "were a bunch of soldiers led by a psychopath who wanted to rule the world."

"What's a psy-cho-path?"

He considered that one for a moment. "A person who's not quite normal up here." He tapped his temple a few times. "Somebody who can't see reality."

"Like Tommy?" Jaime asked. "He can't see reality either. When we play games, he's always changing the rules."

Her father laughed. "Something like that," he said with a nod. "Only I think Hitler was a lot more dangerous."

"Hitler?"

"The man who led the Nazis during the war," he explained.

"What's war?"

He shook his head, chuckling softly. "War," he began, "is when one person or country tries to take away the rights of another—you know, like when Tommy or Carrie or one of your friends at the riding school tries to take your turn at the hurdles." He'd been trying to explain a concept she couldn't possibly understand in terms she might understand.

She nodded. "I get it," she said promptly.

"I'm sure you do." He grinned.

She hugged him tightly. "I'm going to miss you, Daddy," she told him.

He kissed her. "I'll miss you, too, princess."

"I think this may be it, Nicholas," Jaime told him over lunch, taking the envelope from her bag. "This man, Julien Armand—my father knew him for years. Since the war, in fact."

He read the letter carefully, then examined the photograph. "This is almost forty years old," he pointed out as he turned the photograph over and checked the date. "This man may not even still be living—and even if he is, he may not be in Lyon."

"But there's just as good a chance that he *is*," Jaime said stubbornly.

Nicholas thought about it for a moment. "All right. You have the address right here," he said promptly. "Write to him. Find out if he is—and if he'll talk to you."

She shook her head emphatically. "That takes too long," she said, reaching for her glass. "I'm going to Lyon."

He looked surprised. "It could be a waste of time."

"Maybe. But I'm still going."

He stared at the photograph again. "All right," he said finally. "But wait until the weekend. I'll go with you."

She shook her head. "I think it's better if I go alone."

"Why?"

She put the glass down again. "If my father *is* involved in something top secret—which apparently he is—this man's probably not going to want to talk to *me*. He certainly won't feel comfortable with both of us," she reasoned.

"It's not safe," Nicholas argued. Realizing that the other diners around them had begun to stare, he lowered his voice. "This is a dangerous business, Jaime. You said it yourself. People have been killed because of this."

She avoided his eyes, busily tracing her own initials on her napkin with her fingernail. "Do you really think you could stop them if they decide to come after me?" she asked, moved by his concern but unwilling to let him know it.

"I think there's safety in numbers."

Finally she met his gaze. "Look . . . people *have* been killed over this, whatever it is my father's been involved with," she acknowledged, keeping her voice low, controlled. "And yes, maybe I am putting myself right in their line of fire—but I'll be damned if I'll let one more innocent person die because of me if I can prevent it!"

"Bullshit!" Nicholas hissed. "Stop trying to play it tough, will you? Stop acting like you don't need anybody and give me a chance to help you!"

"I thought that's what you'd already been doing," she stated evenly, picking up her fork.

"You know damn well what I'm talking about," he said crossly.

She nodded. "I know what you're talking about," she admitted finally. "But I still have to go alone. I *need* to go alone."

"Why, for God's sake?"

"I just need some time alone, that's all. I need to do some thinking. The drive will be good for me." She didn't want to tell him that she really needed to put some distance between *them*, that she was feeling confused about her feelings for him and needed to sort things out in her own head.

"Just what is it you have to think about?"

She shrugged. "A lot of things."

Nicholas looked unconvinced.

"I'll be all right," she assured him.

"I can't help worrying," he said. "You do know you're playing with fire—"

She frowned. "I know."

In more ways than one, she thought.

Washington, D.C. The office was in darkness. Except for Harry Warner, everyone had gone home for the day. He sat at his desk, leaning back in his high-backed executive chair, staring at the telephone expectantly. When it finally rang, he snatched it up immediately. "Warner," he identified himself tersely.

"She's going to Lyon," said the voice on the other end. "She knows about Armand."

"Is he still living there?"

"He's there, all right."

"Maybe you should have a talk with him first," Warner suggested.

"For what it would be worth." There was a pause. "He's been more than a little disenchanted with us for a lot of years, you know."

"Talk to him anyway."

"I'll give it my best shot."

"You do that."

Warner replaced the receiver carefully. Something had to be done, and soon, he realized.

She was getting too close.

"I wish I could talk you out of this."

Nicholas was leaning against the bumper of Jaime's rental car, looking on as she rummaged through her shoulder bag, making sure she hadn't forgotten anything. "I'm sure," she said quietly. "But you can't, so don't try. Please."

"Will you do something for me?" he asked then.

"Depends." She looked up at him, her expression wary.

"Call me every night—just so I'll know you're all right," he said.

She hesitated for a moment, then nodded. "Sure," she

said, raking her hair back off her face with one hand. "I think I can swing that."

"And be careful," he added.

She forced a smile. "I certainly intend to try."

He smiled back. "Good."

"Try not to get too many gray hairs while I'm gone, okay?" she said with a wink. "I don't think you'd look good prematurely gray."

"If I do, I'll dye it before you get back," he said lightly.

"Thank you."

"You're making me old before my time, do you know that?" he asked, closing the door for her.

"You're not the first, I assure you." She reached up and touched his cheek, the first time she'd allowed herself any kind of physical contact with him at all since that morning at the embassy. "I'll call you when I get to Lyon."

"Yeah." Impulsively, he bent down and kissed her cheek gently. "I'm going to miss you. You broke up the monotony around here."

"You make it sound as if I'm leaving the country," she said with a halfhearted laugh. "I'll be back in a few days, you know."

"You'd better be."

Neither of them realized that when Jaime left Paris, she was being followed.

Nicholas closed the file folder lying in his lap and rubbed his eyes. He had a stiff neck, and his back was killing him. He looked at his watch, the Rolex his father had given him as a graduation present years ago. It was well past midnight. He put the file aside and got to his feet, stretching in an attempt to relieve the tension in his knotted muscles.

Jaime hadn't called yet, and he was concerned. She should have been in Lyon hours ago. He told himself he should never have let her go off alone like that, but how could he stop her? He didn't have the right to try to stop her. She hadn't given him that right and probably never would. He smiled to himself at the thought. He had the feeling that no man would ever have any "rights" where Jaime Lynde was concerned. She was, he realized now, a law unto herself. Every inch her father's daughter, according to the things she'd told him about the mysterious James Victor Lynde. The man must have been a maverick of sorts, considering the life he'd lived and the daughter he'd produced. The daughter Nicholas was beginning to care deeply for.

He took a deep breath and ran his fingers through his hair. Until two months ago, his life had been quiet and organized and—or so he thought—satisfying. There had been women, even if none of them had been "the" woman. He'd enjoyed his work, enjoyed living in Paris, enjoyed being a free agent. Then—without warning and very much like a violent storm— along came that beautiful, unpredictable, hot-tempered, and infuriatingly stubborn redhead who'd managed to turn his neat, orderly world upside down, drag him into her cloak-and-dagger world—a world he hadn't been sure he wanted to be dragged into—and made him suddenly question not only his desire to remain single for a few more years, but his career choices as well. He'd become a willing accomplice in this madness because of her, because—and this came as a complete surprise to him—there was little, if anything, he *wouldn't* do for her.

Heaven help me, he thought, suddenly amused. *Am I falling in love with that crazy woman?*

I'm living proof of the validity of Murphy's law, Jaime thought, too exhausted to be either upset or angry. After a flat tire she'd found nearly impossible to change and a violent thunderstorm that had made her stop in a small town whose name she couldn't recall now, she was beginning to wonder if she'd ever get to Lyon. *If the bad guys don't get me, the elements will,* she decided.

She looked at her watch. One-fifteen. She smiled to herself. Nicholas was probably pacing the floor at his place right about now, wondering why she hadn't checked in. He worried about her. Sometimes—no, most of the time—she wished he wouldn't. She wished he'd make it easier for her to maintain an emotional distance between them. *I don't want to care,* she thought stubbornly. *Caring would only complicate things.*

She finally decided to find a telephone and let him know she was all right, though not yet in Lyon. She stopped at a gas station and called from a pay telephone that rejected her coins twice and cut her off from the operator on the third attempt. When she finally got through to Paris, Nicholas answered on the first ring. "Hello?" Anxiously.

"I thought you'd be asleep," she said, keeping her voice light.

"Jaime!" She could almost hear his sigh of relief. "How the hell do you think I could sleep not knowing if you were all right or not?"

"If I weren't, you'd have heard about it on the evening news."

"I doubt that. The crowd you play ball with doesn't publicize its triumphs," he said sarcastically.

"Tell me about it," she said crossly.

"Where are you? Are you all right?"

"Where I am is a long story, and I don't have that much change," she told him. "As for how I am, the jury's still out on that one."

"Something's happened—"

"Yes, but not what you think," she said quickly. "Between Mother Nature and my less than adequate French, I've managed to have quite an evening down here."

"Yeah." He didn't seem convinced.

"What's the matter?" she asked.

"Nothing," he insisted. "Just be careful, all right?"

"I promise to be very careful," she said. "I'll call you in the morning, okay?"

"Okay." Reluctantly.

As she was walking back to her car, she noticed a dark green Renault parked across the street. She studied it for a moment, sure it was the same car—and driver—she'd seen as she was leaving the restaurant in Ferrières where she'd stopped for lunch. And again in Auxerre where she'd had dinner. She was sure, absolutely sure, it was the same car. The same man. Was she being followed, after all? *Nicholas's paranoia must be contagious,* she told herself as she got into her own car, determined not to let it frighten her.

But the headlights behind her as she drove away still made her nervous.

TWENTY

Lyon, November 1985. Jaime walked alone along the narrow streets of the Croix-Rousse, which for centuries had been the city's renowned silk-weaving district. She tried to imagine what it had been like during the war, when members of the French Resistance used their knowledge of the maze of alleys and stairways to their advantage in evading the Germans. *World War II. The French Resistance,* Jaime thought. *Were you ever here, Daddy?*

Julien Armand, she discovered, lived just beyond the Croix-Rousse in an old, steep-roofed house with a tall chimney, much like any other of the houses on the Grand-Côte. He lived alone, having been a widower for over ten years. He was a tall, painfully thin man for one with his large frame. He appeared to be in his late sixties, with sparse, thinning gray hair and a well-kept beard of the salt-and-pepper variety. Though softened by the passage of time, the strong lines of his face were still very much in evidence in his bone structure. His eyes were blue—actually more the color of aquamarines—and his gaze penetrating. Still, in spite of the differences the years had made, she recognized him instantly as the man in the photograph, the man her father had counted as a friend. And, she hoped the man who would lead her to her father now.

"I would have known you even if I had met you only by chance on the street, mademoiselle," he told her upon her arrival. "You are every inch James's daughter—you look so very much like him."

Jaime settled into a well-worn chair in the small living room. "Thank you, Monsieur Armand," she said, glancing around the room momentarily.

He smiled wearily, realizing what she was thinking. "The Armands were quite wealthy once," he offered in explanation. "The war left us with little to show for it—and what we did have was given to the Resistance to enable us to keep fighting."

She nodded, slightly embarrassed that she'd been so obvious. "When did you last see my father?" she asked then.

He frowned. "It has been many years," he told her. "Why do you ask?"

"I haven't seen my father in almost twenty years, Monsieur Armand," she said gravely. She went on to explain how her father had left her at Briar Ridge one day and never returned. She told him about the letters the Harcourts had kept from her all those years, about all the things she'd been told in the course of her search. "I can't believe any of it. I don't know who to trust anymore," she confided. "I *have* to find my father—or at least know what did become of him."

Armand shook his head, frowning. "Whatever James's mission is, it must be very important," he commented.

She looked at him. "Mission?"

"Of course. Your father *is* an intelligence agent, mademoiselle," he pointed out.

"Then you believe he's still alive?"

"I am sure of it," the Frenchman said with conviction. "Your father was one of his country's best operatives during the war, you see. I am quite certain that he would be kept active for as long as possible—especially now, with so much turmoil and anti-American activity in the Middle East."

"But what makes you think he's still alive?" Jaime pursued.

"He has been in touch," he said simply. "He has told me nothing of his whereabouts or what he is doing, but he has been in touch."

"But why—" Jaime began, confused, unable to find the right words.

He gave her a tired smile. "In your father's, shall we say, line of work, being covered is vitally important," he pointed out. "Unfortunately, there are leaks in every intelligence organization, and operatives' identities are discovered. For their own protection, it often becomes necessary to arrange their own 'deaths' or make them appear to have betrayed their own governments."

"Or in my father's case, both," Jaime said grimly, drawing in a deep breath.

The Frenchman nodded. "Unicorn was almost always involved in matters involving national security," he recalled aloud.

Jaime gave him a quizzical look. "Unicorn?"

"Your father's code name," Armand explained. "We all had such names during the war. It was necessary for the purpose of communications and transmitting messages. James was Unicorn. Jack Forrester—another American and your father's partner in many missions—was Minotaur. I was Centaur, and Lawrence Kendrick—an Englishman with MI6—was Pagan. We were the links between the French Resistance, British MI6, and the American OSS."

"Do you believe it's even remotely possible that my father could have been guilty of treason?" Jaime asked then.

"Absolutely not!" He reacted indignantly and without the slightest hesitation. "I fought with James Lynde during the war, mademoiselle. When two people face death together and for the same cause, each comes to know the other's soul. Your father and I, we received and relayed information that directly contributed to the success of the Normandy invasion. We saved many lives during the Occupation—the Nazis were brutal, merciless. They raped, tortured, and murdered, all without conscience. Right here in Lyon, mademoiselle, many bear the scars of monsters such as Klaus Barbie. It was made easy for those who were willing to betray their own to the Third

Reich, but your father never took the easy way out. He was a brave man. He did much to drive the Nazis out of France."

Jaime forced a smile. "Your story is very different from any other I've heard," she said with a sigh.

"I am sure it is," he said. "But mine, mademoiselle, is also the truth."

Jaime thought for a moment. "Did you know a man named Lewis Baldwin?"

"Baldwin?" He paused momentarily. "No. I did not. But I knew those who did. He was in Provence while we were in Normandy. Those who did know him knew little about him."

"What do you mean?"

"He was a very private man, very quiet," Armand explained. "He did his job but made no friends while he was here, no ties to bring him back."

"Then he wasn't my father's partner?"

"No," Armand said with a shake of his head. "This is important, I take it?"

Jaime nodded slowly. "He introduced my father to my mother after the war. I was told they fought together during the war."

"Not to my knowledge," he said, "and I was with Unicorn most of that time."

"Why would they tell everyone that, then?" she wondered aloud. "What difference would it make?"

"I wish I could tell you, mademoiselle." He paused. "Your parents were evidently introduced for the wrong reasons, and there were more lies than either of us could know."

She looked at him. "Why would you say that?"

"It is nothing," he said with a shrug. "I should not have brought it up."

"But you *did*, and I'd like to know why," she said, not about to let it go.

He sucked in a deep breath. "Your parents did not meet by chance," he told her reluctantly. "They were introduced because Frances Colby's father, the senator, could provide an ideal cover for your father's travels abroad. Because it was decided that he needed a wife as part of that cover."

She stared at him in disbelief. She was aware that her

mother's great love for her father was not reciprocated but this was still hard to digest. "Who told you this?"

His eyes met hers. "Your father told me himself," he said quietly.

He's telling the truth, Jaime thought. *He has to be.*

"Find Jack Forrester," Armand said then, his expression grave. "Find him, and you will find your father."

The room was dark. Jaime lay on her back on the bed, her arms folded behind her head. She was still trying to absorb everything Julien Armand had told her. It was hard for her to think of her father as the man she'd been led to believe he was—an embezzler, a traitor, a double agent—but it was equally hard to reconcile her memory of him with that of Armand: a swashbuckling adventurer known as Unicorn, a man in whose capable hands national security had been placed more than once. A man who'd married not for love, but for convenience, for the cover she and her family could provide.

It was so hard to accept, and yet she'd seen all the signs: her mother, so unbearably unhappy that she'd taken her own life; her father, spending most of his time away, and what little time he was home with his young daughter. She couldn't recall now any outward show of affection between them. She couldn't remember them ever being happy.

"I see you're off to Europe again," Fran observed icily as she watched her husband pack—again.

"It's business, Fran," Lynde answered tightly. *"Your father's business, I might add. You, of all people, should be accustomed to it by now."*

"I'm accustomed to many things," she said acidly as she settled onto the corner of the bed. *"Most of all to a husband who will use any excuse to spend time away from me."*

"I told you, it's business," he said crossly, folding a shirt and placing it in the open suitcase. Neither of them saw Jaime, then four years old, peeking around the corner.

"It's always business!" she snapped. *"You wouldn't come home at all if it weren't for Jaime!"*

"I think you're getting paranoid, Fran," he said with ir-

ritation in his voice. "Have you talked to your therapist this week?"

"Trying to have me committed again, Jim?" she asked sarcastically. "You'd like that, wouldn't you? You'd like to be rid of me so your women friends could come and go—"

"Come off it, Fran!" he exploded. "What women? If I went near a woman, the way news travels around here, you'd know about it by sundown. Anyway—I wouldn't carry on like that in front of Jaime, even though sometimes I'd like to. What with being married to a cold fish like you—"

"Jaime—it's always Jaime, isn't it?" Fran demanded. "Jaime is all you really care about."

He stared at her in disbelief. "Will you listen to yourself, Fran?" he asked incredulously. "You sound as if you resent your own daughter!"

"Has it ever occurred to you that I might resent knowing that you care more for Jaime than you've ever cared for me?" she shot back at him.

"Don't be absurd!"

"Am I absurd, Jim?" she asked coldly. "Am I wrong in assuming Jaime is far more important to you than I've ever been? I don't think so! You know, Jim, now that I think about it, I wonder why you ever married me . . ."

The loud wail of sirens cut through Jaime's thoughts. She sat up in bed, trying to determine which direction they were coming from. From the window, she could see the flickering of their lights. It had to be close. She got to her feet and went to the window for a better look.

She could see the flames in the darkness, bright orange flames licking the midnight sky, smoke filling the night. A fire consumed one of the tall buildings of the Grand-Côte, beyond the old silk-weaving district. Jaime's heart began to pound furiously as the realization hit her.

Julien Armand's house. . . .

"They killed him, Nicholas," Jaime cried into the telephone as she gripped the receiver with trembling fingers, having just come from the site of the fire. "Those bastards murdered him just like they murdered Kate and Marty and God only knows how many others!''

"Calm down, Jaime." Nicholas's voice was firm. "Look . . . I think you should come back to Paris. Today. Right now. Leave the car. Just get on a plane and get back here— I'll pick you up at the airport."

She shook her head emphatically, too upset to realize that he couldn't see her. "I can't," she insisted. "I can't drop it now. My father's alive, Nicholas. I know that now. I have to find him."

"You mean if you live that long," Nicholas said irritably. "Tell me, Jaime, is it worth your life?"

She took a deep breath. "I believe it is, yes," she said finally.

"And I believe you're *nuts*!" he snapped. "You talk about your father as if he were the Second Coming! Do you think if he knew about this, he'd want you to put your life on the line like this?"

"I think," she began carefully, "that my father would want me to do whatever I feel is right, regardless of the consequences."

"So what does that mean *now*?" Nicholas wanted to know.

"It means I'm going to Nice," she answered.

"Nice?"

"The last thing Julien Armand said to me was 'find Forrester, and you will find your father.' A man named Jack Forrester—he was my father's partner. They went back a long way. And a man named Lawrence Kendrick who was with MI6. He lives in Nice now," she explained.

"And this Forrester?"

"Julien Armand said he believed Forrester had gone to Switzerland. He said Kendrick would know."

"And of course you have to track down both of them."

She took another deep breath. "I have to," she maintained. "Kendrick may be able to tell me where I can find Forrester—and whatever it was that Julien Armand never lived to tell."

• • •

Paris. Nicholas wasn't sure which he wanted to do more—hold Jaime in his arms and do whatever he could to protect her and make things right for her again, or strangle her for being so headstrong and stubborn and totally disrupting his once orderly life as she had. She infuriated him, and yet there were times he was certain he was falling in love with her.

In love with Jaime! He almost laughed aloud at the thought. Only an idiot would fall in love with Jaime Lynde. The man who ended up with her would be asking for trouble—and would most likely get more of it than he bargained for. He knew from his own experience that this was no woman for a less than secure man. In the short time he'd known her, she'd managed to disrupt his life, undermine his sexual confidence, and make him paranoid as he'd never been before. All that, and still she intrigued him, this woman who kept the world at arm's length and fought her private wars with a passion that threatened to be contagious. She infuriated him, yes— she drove him to sleepless nights. But she also inspired his admiration. He didn't know many women—any other women, in fact—who would be willing to do what she had done, go through all that she'd been through, to find a father who'd walked out on her as a child.

Nicholas had never really defined his ideal woman, even to himself. He'd only known that he'd recognize her when he found her. He had never figured his so-called "ideal woman" would be a headstrong redhead with a hot temper, an unreasonable nature and a penchant for getting into trouble. In fact, that kind of woman would definitely *not* have been at the top of his list. And yet now, having met her, having gotten to know her. . . .

God help me, he thought. *I have found her.*

Nicholas cared about her. Jaime was sure of that. In fact, it was one of the few things she *was* sure of these days. He cared more for her than she would have liked at this point in her life. The trouble was, she wasn't sure how *she* felt about *him.* She knew she cared for him. She'd come to confide in him, even trust him, when she knew she should not let herself trust anyone. And from that trust her need had grown, a need for him, for someone she could turn to. She also felt a strong physical attraction she'd persistently denied from the day they met. She wanted him, yes—she wanted him sexually. But love? She wasn't yet ready to admit to love, even if a part of her was beginning to feel it. Love was a luxury she'd denied herself after Marty's betrayal. Everyone she'd ever loved, she reminded herself, had either left her or betrayed her.

She thought about it now as she drove east along the Côte d'Azur, bound for Nice. After two brief stops—in Orange and again in Aix-en-Provence—since leaving Lyon, she was on her way. She was exhausted but determined not to stop again until she reached Nice. Lawrence Kendrick, and a grave in the American Cemetery in Nice that was supposedly her father's, were there. Waiting for her. Possibly the answers to all of her questions awaited her there as well.

The view was spectacular from every direction, and Jaime was sure she would have enjoyed it tremendously had circumstances been different. But now she found it hard to think about anything but her father and what he must have done—or was doing at this moment. What, she asked herself once again, could be so important that it could be worth people's lives? Kate, Marty, Armand—and how many others? How many had died—or would die—to keep the Unicorn's secrets?

Upon her arrival in Nice, she checked into the Hotel Windsor on the Rue Dalpazzo, a less expensive and more idiosyncratic hotel in terms of decor than its elegant neighbor, the Negresco. From the lobby, with its Oriental touches, to the bar that bore a strong resemblance to a traditional English pub, to the rather bizarre blue tropical mural near the pool, it was what Jaime liked to call a "duke's mixture." In some ways, she found it charming.

She spent less than an hour at the hotel, staying no longer than it took to check in and unpack. With that done, she headed for the American Cemetery. Finding it had been no problem. Finding the grave in question, however, had been another matter entirely. She eventually managed to locate the caretaker who directed her to it. It was at the south end of the cemetery, overlooking the azure Mediterranean, in the shade of a huge tree. The scent of freshly cut grass and the strong smell of the ocean filled the air. It was a beautiful setting, too beautiful for a cemetery, she decided. Someone had obviously seen to its upkeep, Jaime decided as she approached. The lawn surrounding the large marble headstone was immaculate. Fresh flowers, expensive monument, someone had gone to a great deal of trouble. *Too much trouble for an alleged traitor,* she thought, bothered by this inconsistency. In the back of her mind, she couldn't help wondering if a traitor could indeed be buried in an American cemetery— even if that cemetery wasn't on U.S. soil.

She knelt down, staring at the headstone thoughtfully. It was creepy, looking at it, seeing her father's name on it, and yet knowing he wasn't below it. But if he wasn't, who was? And who wanted the world to believe he was not only a turncoat, but a dead turncoat?

Where are you, Daddy? she wondered once again.

The Kendricks' home was located in that part of Nice known as the Old City. It was accessible from the seaside via the Quai des États-Unis, a picturesque little village characterized by very old houses painted in soft pastel shades. Fragrant flower and fruit and vegetable markets, filling the air with the scents of fresh-cut roses, citrus, and other agreeable odors, populated the town square, along with an assortment of pizza stalls, cafés, and bistros. The morning Jaime went to see Lawrence Kendrick, the fish market on the Place Saint-François was bustling with activity. Though considerably less aromatic than the flower market and less colorful than the fruit and vegetable market, Jaime decided that the fish market, with its strong odor of red mullet, sea bass, squid, and octopus and the raucous, resounding shouts of the merchants, had a character all its own.

The Kendrick home was smaller than Jaime had expected, painted a pale shade of yellow, and looked to be at least two hundred years old. She was met at the door by a small, dark woman Jaime guessed to be in her early sixties. She had a very serious look about her and spoke English with a heavy French accent.

"I am Solange Kendrick, Lawrence's wife," she told Jaime

in the pleasant living room after hearing the reason for her visit. "Unfortunately, it will be impossible for you to speak with my husband, mademoiselle."

Jaime looked at her, confused. "May I ask why, Madame Kendrick?" she asked.

"My husband is dead, mademoiselle."

Jaime's heart skipped a beat. She stared at Solange Kendrick, hoping she hadn't heard correctly but knowing in her heart that she had. "Dead? But—"

"A boating accident. Two weeks ago," the Frenchwoman went on. "He drowned."

"But I saw Julien Armand a few days ago," Jaime told her. "He didn't know—"

"He didn't know because I did not contact him," she said quietly. "I did not feel it wise. There were reasons. Very good reasons."

Had they gotten to him, too? Jaime wondered, immediately suspicious.

"Monsieur Armand is also dead," Jaime said then.

Solange Kendrick looked stunned. "Julien? How?" she asked, barely able to mouth the words.

"There was a fire. They say it was an accident, but—" She shrugged helplessly.

"But it was not," Solange Kendrick finished.

Jaime looked at her. "Why would you say that?"

The woman looked flustered. "I was only making an assumption from what you just told me," she insisted. "I should not have said anything at all."

"But you did," Jaime responded.

"Please, mademoiselle, this has been a difficult time for me. Do not make matters worse," she pleaded. "Just let it be. There is nothing we can do, you and I, but accept it."

Jaime looked at her for a moment, tempted to pursue it further, then changed her mind. The woman was right. She'd been through enough—for now. Jaime would come back later. "I'm very sorry," she said, rising from her chair. "Thank you for telling me." She started for the front door.

"Mademoiselle Lynde—wait!" the woman called after her suddenly.

Jaime stopped and turned.

"Your father—his name?"

"I told you—James Lynde."

"No—his *other* name."

Jaime gave her a puzzled look. Then she realized what the woman wanted to know. "Unicorn," she said slowly. "And your husband was Pagan."

Madame Kendrick nodded. "Stay," she said, smiling for the first time. "We will talk."

"My husband kept everything up here," Solange Kendrick told Jaime as they climbed the narrow stairs to the dark, musty attic over the old house. It was full of old furniture and dressmakers' forms and boxes and trunks. "This is where he kept all of his important correspondence." She pointed out a large, battered old steamer trunk in one corner of the chaos. Pulling a large ring full of keys in assorted sizes, she selected one and unlocked the trunk. "Lawrence was always so very careful to keep such things from prying eyes. He was convinced no one would ever think to look here."

"You seem to know a great deal about his other life," Jaime observed as Solange Kendrick took a large stack of old, yellowed letters from the trunk and gave Jaime half.

"I knew because I was a part of that life, mademoiselle," the Frenchwoman said with dignity. She gestured toward the letters. "Look through them. There may be something there that will help you."

"You were part of it?" Jaime asked.

The woman nodded. "I am French, mademoiselle, and I fought for France wherever the Resistance needed me," she said simply. "That is how I met Lawrence. We were married after the war was over. We had a wonderful life together—until we lost our daughter."

Jaime looked at her. "You had a daughter?"

Madame Kendrick nodded, avoiding Jaime's eyes. "She would be about your age now, had she lived," she said quietly. "But Lilliane was born imperfect—a hole in her heart, the doctors told us. She lived only three days. After that, Lawrence was never the same. It was as if he stopped living at the same moment as Lilliane—at least in all the ways that mattered.''

Jaime didn't know what to say after that, so she turned her attentions to the letters in her lap. As much as she wanted to ask Solange Kendrick about her husband's accident, she couldn't bring herself to do it. She concentrated on the letters, checking return addresses and postmarks on envelopes. There were several from Julien Armand and a few from her father, but they were all dated prior to December 1966. None of them told Jaime what she needed to know.

After several hours of searching, she was ready to give up. It was always the same. Everywhere she turned, she hit a roadblock. *These guys are really good,* she thought miserably. *Always one step ahead of me.*

"I believe this may be what you are looking for.'' Solange Kendrick passed her an envelope.

Taking it, Jaime stared at it for a long moment, unable to believe what she was seeing. It was from Jack Forrester.

It was postmarked Brussels.

Beaune. "Forrester's in Belgium,'' Jaime told Nicholas over the phone. "He's still alive, still an active agent.''

"Even if he is, what makes you think he's going to tell you anything?'' The telephone connection was terrible, but his annoyance came through with crystal clarity.

"What makes you think he won't?'' Jaime countered.

"He's one of them, remember?''

"Okay, maybe he won't talk to me,'' she conceded. "But Julien Armand and Solange Kendrick did, so maybe I'm on a roll and he will. There's only one way I'm going to find out, isn't there?''

There was a moment of silence. "When are you coming back?''

"Tomorrow,'' she told him. "I'm stuck in Beaune for the night. The wind's so damned strong I can't even steer the car.''

"The mistral,'' he said.

"I have another name for it,'' she said. "I'll see you tomorrow—unless the car gets blown away tonight.''

• • •

Jaime wasn't looking forward to the idea of venturing outdoors. She was, however, looking forward to having a quiet dinner alone at the Relais de Saulx on the Rue Louis-Véry, a narrow street behind the Hôtel-Dieu. Its reputation as one of the most beautiful dining rooms in town was well deserved, she decided as she was escorted to her table. Crossed with heavy timbers and decorated with yards of warm velvet and good paintings, it was indeed quite beautiful.

Over a dinner of trout with a cream sauce heavily laced with wine, she found herself thinking about how much her life had changed since she'd decided to investigate her father's double life. *It is like opening Pandora's box,* she thought, remembering what Nicholas had said more than once. *I've unleashed all the evil in the world. My father's life was shrouded in evils. A life he preferred to being with his own family.*

She thought about Nicholas. He was worried about her. She knew only too well that he had good reason to worry. This was riskier than playing Russian roulette with a full chamber. If she had any common sense at all, she'd get herself as far from this madness as possible. *But I don't have that kind of sense,* she thought. *I'm my father's daughter.*

Walking back to the hotel in the darkness, fighting against the fierce winds of the mistral with every step, she had the vague feeling she was being followed. *By the time this is over,* she decided, breathing a sigh of relief as she entered the hotel lobby, *I'll be a candidate for a rubber room.*

She knew something was wrong the minute she opened the door and entered her room. It was dark and she couldn't really see anything, but she could feel it. Switching on the light, her suspicions were immediately confirmed.

Someone had trashed her room.

TWENTY-ONE

"Do you realize what could have happened if you had walked in on whoever broke into your room?" Nicholas was angry and not bothering to hide it. "You could have been killed!"

They were in Paris, driving from the railway station to the George V. When Jaime had called him from Beaune to tell him what had happened, he'd insisted she leave her rental car and get the next train.

"I'm not totally stupid," Jaime said crossly. "I know perfectly well what could have happened—and I don't want to even think about it, much less discuss it."

Nicholas wasn't about to drop it. "You're a minor leaguer playing in the big leagues, Jaime," he told her. "You don't stand a chance against them."

"That's what they told David about Goliath," she said sullenly.

He took his eyes off the road for an instant and glared at her. "You're not a kid fighting some monster with a slingshot," he said. "You happen to be one person up against something much bigger and much more dangerous than you can possibly imagine."

She looked at him, her anger rising. "And you can?"

He sucked in his breath so sharply that she could hear it. "Yes, dammit, I *can*!" he snapped.

She paused for a moment. "Why does it matter to you?" she asked finally. "Why should you care what happens to me, anyway?"

"Because I love you."

She stiffened. "What?" she asked, not sure she'd heard him correctly.

He didn't divert his eyes from the road. "I said I love you," he repeated quietly.

She looked away from him. "I wish you wouldn't."

"Wouldn't what?"

"Love me."

"Why?"

"You'd be better off. I'd be better off."

Now he turned to look at her again. "Not exactly the response I was hoping for," he admitted, keeping his voice light.

"I can't love you," she said, rubbing her temples. "How can I even think about the future—much less *do* anything about it—until the past is settled and behind me?"

"Maybe if you were thinking more about the future, the past wouldn't be so important," he suggested, negotiating the heavy traffic almost automatically.

She shook her head emphatically. "I can't just pretend none of it ever happened," she maintained.

He turned, just for a moment. "Tell me, Jaime—how *do* you feel? About me, I mean? About us?"

She shook her head. "I don't know," she answered honestly. "I care. Maybe more than I really want to."

"Why more than you want to?" he pursued.

"Several reasons," she said tightly. "Mostly, I just don't want to get burned again."

Frustrated, he smacked the flat of his hand against the steering wheel—hard. "Dammit, Jaime, I'm not your father—and I'm not Marty Cantrell!" he snapped. "I love you and I have no intention of ducking out on you!" He paused, pursing his lips thoughtfully. "I only wish I could say the same for you."

• • •

They had dropped the subject after that. Both of them were unusually quiet over dinner that evening, except for a brief discussion of her "fact-finding mission," as Nicholas called it. When he left her at the hotel afterward, he'd seemed somewhat petulant. Now, lying awake in the darkness, she found herself less at peace than ever. Torn between her past and her present—and possibly her future as well. Wanting to love, *needing* to love, yet not wanting to make herself vulnerable again. Not wanting to be hurt again.

Nicholas is different, she thought. *But then, I thought Marty was different, too. I thought he could be trusted—once.*

But Nicholas wasn't like Marty. He'd never been like Marty. Right from the start, he'd made it clear that he did understand, that he did want to help, yet he'd expressed a genuine concern for her safety. There had never been any secrets, any lies. His biggest fault was in trying to be too protective of her. She hadn't made it easy for him. Or for herself.

She did love him, as much as she was capable of loving anyone after all she'd been through. A part of her wanted to love him more. Wanted to love him completely, as he deserved. She wished she could do what he wanted her to do and put the past behind her, but she couldn't. Not until she knew what had really become of her father and why.

Until then, she could have no peace.

"I promise—no heavy discussions," Nicholas swore when he called the next day. "Just dinner. That's all. I think we both need a little R and R. My place, all right? I'll cook."

Jaime laughed, relieved. "I think you're right about that," she agreed. "All right. What time do you want me?"

"All the time."

There was a pause. "You promised," she said accusingly.

"All right." He backed off promptly. "I take it all back, okay?"

"Don't take it back," she responded without thinking. "Just don't push it. Not yet."

There was a momentary pause. "I'll try not to, but it won't be easy," he said honestly. "How's seven-thirty?"

"For what?"

"For dinner." He laughed. "Have you forgotten already?"

"Almost," she confessed. "Seven-thirty will be fine."

"See you then."

Jaime hung up slowly. What would it be like, she found herself wondering now, to have a normal life, a truly normal life? How would it feel to be married to a man like Nicholas Kendall and maybe even have a couple of kids, a house in the suburbs and all that went with it? What would it be like to be free of secrets, the lies, the unanswered questions? What would it be like to be free of her father's double life, to not constantly be looking over her shoulder? To not live every second in danger? She decided she'd probably never know.

After all, she *was* the Unicorn's daughter.

"You really are a wonderful cook," Jaime said, settling down onto the couch after a wonderful, all-American, New England-style dinner. "You'd make someone a great wife."

He gave her a suggestive look. "Are you making an offer?"

She stiffened. "You promised," she reminded him.

"And you brought it up," he pointed out.

"I want you to help me locate Jack Forrester, Nicholas," she said then, changing the subject. "I have to find him. Julien Armand said he'll know how to reach my father."

"If your father is still alive."

"Armand said he is."

"And Julien Armand had not seen him in years. And Armand believed Kendrick was alive. Speculation—with a dash of wishful thinking," he insisted.

"They know these things," Jaime insisted.

He smiled wearily. "They only *call* them spooks—that doesn't mean they really are, you know."

"My father *is* alive," she said stubbornly. "I knew it before Armand said anything. I could feel it."

He sat down beside her. "Jaime, I know how you must feel, but . . ."

She faced him squarely. "Are you going to help me or not?"

"You might as well ask me to go find a cure for cancer," he told her. "We don't even know where to begin! It would be like looking for the proverbial needle in the haystack—no, I think finding that needle would be a hell of a lot easier!"

"He's in Brussels," she said calmly.

"He *was* in Brussels," Nicholas corrected.

"He may still be there. It's worth looking into."

He shook his head. "Even if he is there, Brussels is a big place," he maintained. "What do you expect me to do? Check the Brussels Yellow Pages under 'Spies'?"

"Don't be absurd!" she said crossly.

"This whole business is absurd," he snorted. "Even if we do find this man—assuming he's still an active agent—what makes you think he'll even talk to you, much less tell you anything of any importance?"

"There's only one way I'm going to find out," Jaime said promptly.

"Even if he does, he may not even know where your father is—if he's still alive," Nicholas went on.

"He was my father's partner."

"*Was*—that's the key word."

"If anyone will know, he will," she insisted.

His voice softened. "Look, I understand how you feel," he assured her. "I really do. But these people mean business, sweetheart. You know damn well they'll kill you if you get too close to whatever it is they've been hiding all these years."

"They might," she conceded.

"And if they don't? Suppose you do manage to uncover the truth—and live to tell about it," he said. "What if the stories turn out to be true? What if your father *was* a traitor? What then?"

Her eyes flashed angrily. "I don't believe that—I won't believe it!"

"Of course you don't," he said with a nod. "But it *could* be true."

She looked at him. "Then it's a chance I'm going to have to take," she decided promptly.

He took a deep breath. "You are one stubborn woman, do you know that?" It was more of a statement than a question.

"It's hereditary," she said sullenly.

"Apparently."

"I've come this far," Jaime began carefully. "I can't just forget it now. Wherever my father is, whatever he may or may not have done, *I have to know*. I won't be able to find any real peace of mind until I do."

He regarded her with concern. That was the bottom line. She couldn't put the past behind her without the missing pieces to the puzzle. She couldn't have a future with him or with anyone else—or even just for herself—until she was able to accept the loss of her father. He held her close, stroking her hair. "I wish I could make this easier for you," he said softly. "I wish there was something I could do." He suddenly realized she was kissing his neck. "Jaime—"

She nibbled lightly at his earlobe. "Let's discuss this later," she purred, slipping her arm around his neck.

For a moment, he was tempted to respond, to make love to her as he'd wanted to right from the beginning. But as strong as his desire was, the realist in him knew there was more to her attempted seduction than simple sexual desire. He wanted her, but not like this. Gently, reluctantly, he pried himself free. "That's enough, Jaime," he told her, his voice low but firm.

She looked at him. "Don't you want me?" she asked, smiling.

"You know damn well that I do," he said irritably, backing off. "What I don't want is a woman—even you—crawling into my bed because she wants something else from me. I don't play those games—not even with you."

She pulled back abruptly. "That's a hell of a thing to say!"

"But it's true, isn't it?" He got to his feet. "Just this afternoon, you asked me not to rush you. You said you needed space. Now all at once you're ready to hop into bed with me. I wonder why."

"Just because I said I needed time doesn't mean I don't have other needs."

"Come off it!" he snapped. "We both know what you want! You want me to use embassy resources to track down Jack Forrester. I've told you it would be damned near impossible to do."

She stood up, trembling with rage. "You sure as hell don't sugar-coat anything, do you?" she asked coldly, collecting her coat and bag. "Thanks a hell of a lot for letting me know where I stand!"

"Wait a minute!" he called after her as she started for the door. "Where are you going?"

"Back to the hotel—where I should have stayed!" Before he could stop her, she walked out, slamming the door behind her.

Jaime was absolutely certain she was being followed this time.

When she left Nicholas's apartment, there wasn't a taxi in sight. She'd walked to the Champs-Élysées to catch the bus and had noticed a man walking several yards behind her. At first, she hadn't given it a thought. Then he boarded the same bus. She was mildly suspicious but told herself it was only coincidence. When he got off the bus behind her, that was another story. And when he followed her all the way to the entrance of the George V, she was convinced.

She felt an overwhelming sense of relief when he didn't follow her into the lobby. Alone in the elevator, she leaned back against the wall and drew in a deep breath. Nicholas was right. They'd kill her before they'd let her get too close to the truth. They'd killed Kate. And Marty. Julien Armand. Possibly Lawrence Kendrick as well. Why, she wondered now, hadn't they already tried to kill her?

Unless someone expected her to lead them to her father.

Nicholas was worried.

He'd tried to reach Jaime at her hotel three times between eight-thirty and ten. Each time, he was told she wasn't answering her calls. Was she just letting him know how angry she was by not picking up the phone? Or had something happened to her? She'd been so angry when she left. Jaime would never, under ordinary circumstances, even consider walking back to the hotel, particularly at night. But tonight . . . tonight, she might have. She'd been furious with him. She might have wanted to walk off some of that rage.

"If I had my hands on you right now, Jaime Lynde, I'd—" He stopped short, realizing that he was talking to himself. And he cared too much about her.

On impulse, he picked up the phone and dialed the George V. When the switchboard rang her room, he drummed his fingers on the desk impatiently at the empty, repetitious ring. "Come *on*, Jaime—answer the goddamned phone . . ."

Washington, D.C. "She's back in Paris?" Harry Warner asked.

"I think the mess I left in her hotel room in Beaune scared her away," said the voice on the other end of the line.

"You idiot!" Warner snapped. "I told you she's not to know she's being followed!"

"It couldn't be helped. I had to do it fast—never knew when someone might walk in."

"I don't give a damn what your reason was," Warner told him. "You had your instructions, didn't you?"

"Yeah," the other man said tightly. "I had my orders."

"Good," Warner said. "Keep me posted."

It was against his better judgment, but Nicholas was going to help Jaime find Jack Forrester, or he was going to try, anyway. Using all the available resources via diplomatic channels—computer data, contacts with the U.S. embassy in Brussels, and even such primitive methods as referring to the Belgian telephone directories—he spent the better part of an afternoon holed up in his office at the embassy, trying to track down the elusive Minotaur. Finally, late that evening, he received a call from one of his contacts in Brussels.

A man—an American citizen—named Jonathan Forbes Forrester was living in Leuven, just east of Brussels. He fit Jaime's description from the photograph given to her by Solange Kendrick.

Twice, Nicholas picked up the phone to call Jaime, then changed his mind. She hadn't returned any of his calls—and he'd left a dozen messages for her. *Damn her and that stubborn streak of hers,* he thought angrily. *What good would it do to call her? She probably wouldn't even take the call!*

The shrill ring of the telephone startled him. His hand still on the receiver, he snatched it up. "Kendall," he said tightly.

"Nicholas, it's Jaime," said the familiar voice on the other end. "About last night—"

"It's all right," he said quickly. "I understand." *So much for giving her hell,* he thought.

"No, it's not all right," she disagreed. "You were right, you know."

"It doesn't matter." It did, but he'd never admit it—not even to her.

"Someone followed me back to the hotel last night," she said.

He wasn't sure he'd heard her correctly. "What?"

"I was followed—from your apartment building, on the bus, right to my door, you might say." Jaime paused. "I must be getting too close."

Nicholas debated whether or not to tell her what he'd found out. It could only make matters worse. "Are you sure?" he asked, stalling for time.

"I'd swear it on a stack of Bibles."

He thought about it for a moment. "Give up this madness, Jaime," he urged, "before it's too late."

"I can't. You know that."

He hesitated. "If you did know where this Forrester is—if you could talk to him, if he would tell you what you want to know—then would you give it up?"

There was a pause. "You've found him," she guessed.

TWENTY-TWO

"Are you nuts?"

"You've asked me that question before. You already know the answer." Jaime strode across the lobby of the George V, briefcase in hand. Nicholas followed, carrying her suitcase.

"If you'd just wait until the weekend, I'd go with you," he told her.

She shook her head. "I've waited long enough," she said as the uniformed doorman held the door for her. As she stepped out into the cold November wind, her red hair whipped about her face. "Even waiting another day could enable them to get to him before I do—if they haven't already. I'm not about to give them the chance if I can help it."

He put the suitcase in the back seat of his car. "They've probably known where he is all along—if he's still one of them," he pointed out, opening the front door on the passenger side for her. "And even if they didn't and you do happen to get to him first, he may not want to talk to you anyway."

"We've been through this before," Jaime said sullenly, pulling the door shut.

"So we have." He gave the door a push even though it was already closed and strode around to the driver's side. "I don't know why I don't just give up," he grumbled as he slid behind the wheel.

"Neither do I."

He looked at her. "I don't want to argue with you, but—"

She cut him off. "Then don't, okay?"

Nicholas drew in a deep breath as he turned the key in the ignition and the car's engine immediately came to life. "Okay, okay—I know this is all pointless," he conceded, steering the car into the street. "You're going to go ahead with this no matter what I say."

She nodded. "Right."

"All right," he surrendered. "Do it. But for God's sake, don't make me sit here in Paris worrying about you and wondering if you're all right," he said crossly. "Will you at least call me every night—just so I know you're all right?"

She nodded, trying to keep from smiling. He *was* worried about her, and she was oddly pleased that he was. "That I can handle," she said aloud.

"Thank heaven for small favors," he responded with a hint of sarcasm in his voice.

"As you yourself said, we've been through all of this before, and I for one have always hated reruns," she told him. "When I asked for your help, I didn't expect you to become my keeper."

"Sometimes I think you need one."

"I don't recall asking for an opinion," she said sharply, annoyed by his remark.

"Excuse me for giving a damn!" he snapped, maneuvering through the heavy traffic out of Paris. "I didn't know it was a goddamned crime to want to keep someone I love from putting her life on the line!"

Jaime slumped back against the seat. "We agreed—"

"I agreed not to pressure you," he said tightly. "I did *not* agree not to love you—because I can't just turn my feelings on and off like a goddamned faucet!" He brought the car to a stop at a traffic light.

Jaime frowned but said nothing. If only she could turn off *her* feelings.

• • •

Brussels. Jaime piled her luggage into the trunk of the car
she'd rented at Zaventem Airport and slammed it shut. She
was still angry with Nicholas—and with herself. Mostly with
herself. She knew his heart was in the right place where she
was concerned. No doubts there. Nor did she doubt that he
loved her. No . . . the trouble lay in his determination to
protect her. And in her determination not to acknowledge *her*
feelings for *him*.

She'd promised herself that once this was all over, once
she'd found her father—or at least knew what had become of
him—things could be different. That once she was able to put
the past behind her, really put it all behind her, she could
have a future. Maybe even a future that included a husband
and children. Now, she wasn't so sure. She wasn't convinced
at this moment that she'd ever really be able to put all the
pain and betrayal in the past, or that her life would ever be
what anyone might consider "normal." After all, she hadn't
come from "normal" parents. Her father was a spy, a man
as elusive as the mythical unicorn for which he'd been code-
named. Her mother had been deeply disturbed, a mother in
name only for as long as she was able to remember. Jaime
had never had a normal life. *Why start now?* she thought
ruefully.

It was a short drive, no more than twenty minutes, from
the airport to the Hotel de la Madeleine, near the Grand'-
Place. As soon as she'd checked in, she made good on her
promise to Nicholas and placed a call to Paris.

"Were you followed?" he wanted to know.

She almost laughed at the question. "Not that I noticed."

"You weren't paying attention?"

"I didn't exactly have a bumper sticker reading 'Honk if
you're following this car,' " she said lightly.

"Jaime, for God's sake—"

"Listen—do you want the number here, or do you just
want to argue with me?" she asked irritably.

"Yes, I want the number. Let me get a pen." There was
a pause on the other end of the line. "All right—what is it?"

"I'm at the Hotel de la Madeleine and the number is 513-
73-92.

There was another pause. "I've been thinking, and I'm going to take a leave of absence from the embassy," he told her. "I think I should be there with you."

Jaime sucked in her breath. "I told you, Kendall, I don't need a baby-sitter—" she began.

"Quit trying to be tough, Jaime," he growled. "You've got a lot of guts—but Rambo you ain't, sweetheart. You can't do this alone, so don't even try. Let somebody help you. Let me help you."

She dropped into a nearby chair. "Do you really want to help me?" she asked in a controlled voice.

"You know I do."

"I don't know anything of the kind. And what I'm wondering right now is if you're trying to get in my way, like everyone else," she admitted.

"That's a hell of a thing to say!" he exploded. "You're so damned suspicious of everyone and everything that you just can't accept the fact that someone might actually care about you and your bloody search!"

She shook her head. "Okay, okay—I didn't mean that," she said wearily. "It's just that you seem to be trying to smother me, and that's the last thing I need with everybody else getting in my way now. I'm always looking over my shoulder, if you want the truth. And you know what? I'm starting to feel a lot like my father must have felt."

"Not without good reason," he said darkly.

"Tell me about it."

"Would you kick me out if I came up for the weekend?" he asked.

"Nicholas—" she began.

"I only want to help," he insisted. "Two heads *are* better than one, aren't they?"

"Only if they're cooperating."

"I'll cooperate if you will."

"Nicholas, this is my war, not yours—"

"You made it my war when you dragged me into this cloak-and-dagger world of yours, lady," he reminded her.

"I just can't see both of us having to give up our jobs when I'm the one who needs the answers."

"I never said I was giving up my job," he pointed out. "Anyway, I have a stake in this too."

"Once you're involved with me and my problems, getting out is no longer a matter of choice," she said gravely.

"Too late," he told her. "I'm already involved."

"Nicholas—"

"It's no longer open for discussion," he said firmly. "I'll see you on Friday."

Jaime lay awake in the darkness that night, unable to sleep. From her room she could hear the traffic on the Grand'Place, but it wasn't the sounds of the city that kept her awake. It was, as always, her father. Even in his absence—or perhaps especially in his absence—he dominated every aspect of her life.

"Why do you have to go away again, Daddy?"

Jaime was five years old. She sat on the steps in front of the house at Sound Beach, her face cupped in her hands, elbows balanced on her knees, pouting. Her father stood over her, smiling down at her.

"We've been through this before, princess," he reminded her. "It's part of my job."

"Tommy's father has a job," she stated. "He works in a bank. He's not away all the time—he doesn't go away very much at all. Tommy says his mother wishes he would, most of the time."

He gave a low chuckle. "My job is different."

She twisted around and looked up at him. "What is your job, Daddy?"

"I'm an investment banker."

"Like Tommy's father?"

"Not exactly." He sat down on the steps beside her. "Tommy's father's a loan officer. That means he works in the same place all the time. I work for an investment bank that handles big loans all over the world. That's why I have to spend so much time in those places."

"Couldn't they send someone else sometimes?" she asked, confused.

He shook his head. "I'm afraid not, princess," he said regretfully.

"Not even half of the time?"

"Not even half the time. At least not yet . . ."

He had never told her about his "real" line of work. He'd never told her anything at all. But then, how could he? He'd left her without ever telling her. Now, as she thought about it, she wondered if he ever would have.

Would he have left her, had the choice been his to make?

"Mr. Forrester? Mr. Jack Forrester?"

"Yes." The deep masculine voice on the other end of the telephone line sounded mildly uncomfortable, even though he didn't know who she was or what she wanted. "My name is Jack Forrester."

"My name is Jaime Lynde," she introduced herself. "I believe you may know my father."

"Your father?" Still a strange note in his voice, one Jaime couldn't quite identify.

"James Lynde." She paused. "Unicorn."

There was a long silence on the other end. "I don't know what you're talking about," he said finally, hesitantly.

"I think you do," Jaime pressured him. "I think you not only knew my father—and worked with him—I believe you know where he is right now." She was bluffing, but it was the only way she could think of to get him to talk.

"You're mistaken," he insisted.

"I don't think so."

"You must have me confused with someone else, Miss—"

"Cut the crap!" Jaime exploded. "You're my father's partner. You know it, and I know it. Why won't you just admit it, dammit?"

"James Lynde is dead! I—" He stopped short.

"So—you *do* know him!"

There was another long pause. "James Lynde was a traitor to his country," he said evenly. "He sold out to the highest bidder. Where he is today, if indeed he is still alive, I have no idea."

"I don't believe you!" Jaime snapped. "And I don't believe you think he was a traitor any more than I do!"

"Believe what you wish," he said carefully.

"You know he wasn't a turncoat," she pursued.

"And how would you know that?" he asked with a stone-like coldness in his voice.

"Simple. I've talked with Julien Armand and the widow of Lawrence Kendrick," she said. "Surely you remember them—Centaur and Pagan."

"I remember. But how do I know you have really been in contact with them?"

"Easy enough. You can ask them." She paused, remembering that Julien Armand was dead. "You can contact Madame Kendrick, that is." She told him about the fire in Lyon.

"I'm sorry to hear that." There was a strange note in his voice.

"I'm at the Hotel de la Madeleine in Brussels, Mr. Forrester," she told him. "If you change your mind, give me a call. I'll be here at least until the weekend."

Washington, D.C. "She's in Brussels," Warner's contact reported. "She arrived yesterday—checked into the Hotel de la Madeleine."

"Has she seen Forrester yet?" Warner asked.

"No. She did talk to him over the phone, though."

"Dammit, you had better get to him first!" Warner snapped crossly.

"Listen, Harry—she's not an easy one to outsmart," the other man complained. "She's too damn much like her father for her own good—or ours, for that matter! She's wise to us—and doing a damn good job of covering her backside!"

"Well for *your* own good, you'd better make damn sure Forrester doesn't tell her anything!" Warner issued an unmistakable warning.

"Don't worry. He's still not convinced that she really is Lynde's daughter," he said. "I'll pay him a visit tonight, and after I do, he won't tell her anything."

"See that he doesn't."

• • •

Paris. Nicholas threw down his pen in frustration and got up from the desk. He'd been in his office at the embassy early but had not been able to concentrate on his work all day. He was thinking about Jaime, about what could be happening in Brussels. About what she might be getting herself into. *Damn,* he thought. *Even when she's not around, she's still getting to me.*

From the moment he'd met her, he'd known Jaime Lynde had gotten in way over her head. She'd been outnumbered, playing out of her league. She was playing a game she couldn't hope to win, and yet she refused to give up. She was determined to find her father, and the more curves they threw her, the more determined she became. She knew the odds were against her, yet she kept fighting for what she believed in. He admired her for that, even though he suspected she was going to make him an old man before his time.

Of all the women in the world I could have fallen in love with, I had to fall for Joan of Arc, he thought, more annoyed with himself than with her. *Me—with a goddamned crusader! The folks back home would never believe it.*

He'd always figured he'd end up with a "traditional" wife like his mother, a lovely woman who would be a good wife, lover, companion, and mother. Someone who would be there when he came home every night, travel with him when he was required to travel, be the perfect hostess when he entertained, give him the children he'd always assumed he'd have. But that woman paled in comparison with Jaime, hardheaded, hot-tempered Jaime who had burst into the embassy—and into his life—as unexpectedly as a flash flood. Jaime, who was at the center of some sort of puzzling conspiracy that had turned her life, and now his as well, upside down.

"I don't believe it. Nick Kendall goofing off? Now *there's* one for the tabloids!"

Nicholas's head jerked up. Roger Milford, a close friend and the embassy's chargé d'affaires, stood in the doorway, a look of mock disapproval on his face. His gray eyes twinkled with amusement as he raked his fingers through his wayward brown hair. "Not goofing off," Nicholas insisted. "Just don't seem to be able to keep my mind on my work today."

Roger grinned. "Wouldn't have anything to do with that redhead you've been seeing, would it?"

"It's not what you think," Nicholas said wearily. *Believe me, it's not at all what you're thinking, Roger.*

"Then I take it she's *not* keeping you awake all night?" Roger asked in a disbelieving tone as he crossed the room and took a seat. He and Nicholas were almost the same age, and, having arrived in Paris about the same time, had quickly become fast friends.

"Oh, she's keeping me up nights, all right," Nicholas admitted. "Trouble is, she's not there with me while she's keeping me up."

Roger still looked unconvinced. "You are joking, right?" he asked, folding his arms behind his head as he leaned back in the chair.

Nicholas shook his head. "Unfortunately, no," he said. "Just my luck—the first time I meet a woman I really want, she's got other things on her mind."

"What's the problem?"

"It's a long story," Nicholas said dismally. "I can't get into it just now."

Who'd ever believe it? he thought.

Brussels. "What do you mean, you can't talk to me?" Jaime, dressed in jeans and a bulky, Aztec-patterned sweater, rocked back on the bed in her room at the Hotel de la Madeleine, clutching the telephone receiver as she spoke. "Didn't you contact Madame Kendrick?"

"Yes, I did," Forrester said flatly.

"And she told you?"

"She told me James Lynde's daughter came to see her. How do I know you *are* that same person—or that she wasn't taken in by an imposter?"

"But—"

"They—Julien Armand and the Kendricks—haven't seen James Lynde in many years," he pointed out. "They didn't know he had betrayed his government in later years. They didn't question you because they had no real reason to."

"And you do?"

"Miss—"

"You know, Mr. Forrester, you and your colleagues are going to a great deal of trouble to protect an alleged traitor," she said carefully. "I can't help but wonder why."

"There are reasons."

"Oh, I'm sure there are, Mr. Forrester," she said agreeably. "But if you think for a moment I'm just going to accept it because that's what I've been told, forget it!" She slammed down the phone with such force that the bell rang sharply.

Damn you, she thought, furious. *Damn all of you!*

Leuven. Jack Forrester, a tall, barrel-chested man in his late sixties with a strong, craggy face and thinning gray hair, hung up the telephone slowly. He was frowning.

"Well? Did she believe you?" asked the man standing behind him.

Forrester shook his head. "Not for a moment," he said quietly, turning to face the other man. "She has faith in her father. No one's going to make her believe he's a traitor."

"That's too bad—for her, that is."

Forrester nodded, disapproval plain in his expression.

"Is she still set on coming here?"

"I seriously doubt it," Forrester said grimly, walking past the other man and into the next room.

He smiled evilly. "Good."

Brussels. Jaime climbed into her rental car and deposited her briefcase containing all of her father's letters, his photographs, and her important papers—birth certificate and passport—on the seat beside her. *Nicholas was right,* she thought, still angry, as she turned the key in the ignition and listened absently to the low hum of the engine. *I should never have come here. I should have expected resistance. I should have expected to have doors slammed in my face.*

She was still thinking about it as she headed for Zaventem Airport. Right from the beginning, she'd met with fierce opposition in her search for answers. One obstacle after another had been thrown in her path. Few had wanted to help her at all, and many had pretended to help, only to attempt to throw her off the track. Most treated her like a leper, avoiding her at all costs. *Why,* she asked herself now, filled with a mixture of bitterness and frustration, *should Forrester be any different?*

Forrester *should* be different, she concluded. He was her father's partner. He knew her father, possibly better than anyone else ever could. *After all, when two people face death together, fighting for the same cause, they see each other's souls.* Hadn't that been the way Julien Armand had put it? Forrester had to know her father wasn't a traitor.

He had to know a lot of things.

Abruptly, Jaime swung the car over to the shoulder of the road and braked it to a stop. Forrester *knew*—of course! He was her father's partner. He not only knew her father, he knew all about his covert activities as well. He had to! He probably knew where her father was right now . . . and she was damned if she'd just walk away without at least trying to pry it out of him. Or, at the very least, giving it her best shot.

She turned the car around and headed east on Route 3 toward Leuven.

Leuven. "I know it's a long shot," Jaime told Nicholas on the phone that afternoon, "but I can't leave without at least trying to get him to talk to me."

"You did try. He turned you down," Nicholas pointed out.

"I have to try again," she insisted. "This Forrester was my father's partner. They worked together for years, according to Julien Armand."

"And he says your father was a traitor," Nicholas reminded her.

"He wasn't a very convincing liar," she maintained.

"Did it ever occur to you that maybe he was uncomfortable at having to tell you those things about your own father?"

"No, it didn't—and I don't think it occurred to him, either," Jaime snapped.

"Come on, Jaime, listen to reason—"

"I've got to talk to him," she insisted. "One way or another, I have to talk to him. Maybe I can change his mind.

At any rate, I am going to see him. I'm driving out there just as soon as I hang up.''

There was a pause. ''Be careful,'' he cautioned, knowing she would promise to do so, then turn around and do whatever she damn well pleased.

''I intend to,'' she responded predictably.

''Wait!'' he said quickly as she was about to hang up. ''Where are you staying?''

''La Royale. The number is 221252,'' she told him. ''Got to run. I'll call you tonight, okay?''

''All right,'' he said, with a hint of reluctance in his voice. ''I'll talk to you tonight, then.''

''Right.''

The moment she hung up, she left the hotel and, after obtaining directions from the desk clerk, headed for Jack Forrester's home, fifteen kilometers southwest of the city. As she drove, oblivious of the beautiful Belgian countryside, she was filled with a renewed determination to confront Forrester and make him listen to her—and she hoped—talk to her as well.

The roads outside the city were narrow and winding, punctuated with sharp, dangerous curves. *Looks like the highway department followed a snake through the hills*, Jaime decided. *When Forrester decided to go into hiding, he really went into hiding.*

Approaching a steep grade downward, she pressed on the brake pedal. When the car showed no response, she pressed harder. Nothing.

She had no brakes!

It didn't register immediately. She pumped the pedal furiously. Her heart was pounding as the car raced down the long, steep hill. It was picking up speed. She clutched the steering wheel, fighting for control of the careening car. As it reached the bottom of the hill and took the wide curve below, it gained momentum. She floored the brake with every ounce of strength she could summon up, but to no avail. The brakes were useless.

She stole a quick glance at the speedometer. She was going too fast, and the needle was racing upward. She looked around wildly, searching for a place to run the car off the road and slow it down, if not bring it to a complete stop. Everything around her was a blur, images moving in fast forward. Then she caught a glimpse of a heavy wooden fence, several yards ahead and to her right. It was risky, but when she considered the alternative, she decided it was a risk worth taking. In that split second, she made her decision. She fought the wheel, steering the speeding car off the road. She thrashed about in the seat as it rolled over the bumpy surface of the land. Aiming it straight for the fence, she closed her eyes tightly and braced herself for the impact. There was a sudden jolt that threw her from the car, followed by a deafening roar.

And after that, darkness.

TWENTY-THREE

When Jaime opened her eyes, she wasn't sure where she was. It appeared to be a hospital. Her vision was blurred, but what she could see looked white. It smelled like a hospital, unless her sense of smell had failed her too. She tried to move but discovered something was holding her down. There was a sharp pain in her left wrist that intensified with any degree of movement. The throbbing sensation in the back of her head felt like a continuous series of hammerblows pounding into her skull. She tried to speak, but the words wouldn't come. She attempted to move her hand again, but the pain that shot through it was excruciating. *Oh, God—where am I?* she wondered, suddenly alarmed. *What happened?*

"Jaime?"

The voice sounded familiar. Yes, of course . . . Nicholas's voice. But where was he? His voice sounded strange, as if he were calling to her from the other end of a long tunnel. She tried to respond but still couldn't find her voice.

"Jaime? Can you hear me?"

Yes . . . it was Nicholas! *Yes, Nicholas, I can hear you. Why can't you hear me?*

"Blink twice if you hear me, Jaime."

I am blinking, Nicholas. At least I think I am.

"Doctor! She's awake! She understands me!"

Of course I understand, Nicholas. You're the one who can't understand me.

Her eyes were beginning to focus now. She could distinguish his face, looking down at her. She wanted to reach out to him but couldn't. *Nicholas. . . .*

"Can you talk, Jaime?"

What do you think I'm trying to do? Why wasn't her mouth moving? Why wouldn't the words come? She tried harder now to move her lips. "Where—am—I—"

"She's trying to talk, Doctor!"

"Nicholas . . ."

"I'm here, Jaime." He was clutching her hand. Leaning close. "I'm here."

"Why—why can't I move?" she asked, her words faltering.

"The tubes," he told her. "You're hooked up to machines. There's an IV in your wrist." He touched her face. "It's okay. You're going to be okay."

Okay? she wondered. *I'm wired up like Frankenstein's monster, and you're telling me everything is okay?*

There was another man standing over her now. He was wearing a white coat. That much was clear to her. The doctor, no doubt. He leaned close, examining her eyes with an ophthalmoscope. The stethoscope felt cold against her chest as he listened to her heart. "You were very fortunate, mademoiselle," he told her in French.

"Fortunate?"

"Fortunate to be alive," he explained. "It was a very bad accident."

Accident? Now it was all coming back to her . . . the car, racing down that steep grade . . . taking the sharp curves at dangerous speeds . . . crashing into that high fence. . . .

I am lucky to be alive, she thought.

"How long have I been here?"

"Four days." The doctor looked at her eyes again. "You've been unconscious most of that time."

"What happened?" she asked carefully, not able to remember everything.

"You were in an automobile accident, mademoiselle," he said gravely. "By some miracle known only to God, you were thrown from the car before it exploded."

"Exploded?"

He nodded. "You were found by a passing motorist, who summoned the authorities." He paused. "When you were brought here, you were unconscious. You had suffered a concussion and, we believed at first, a skull fracture as well."

"Four days . . ." she began, confused.

"There was edema. Swelling of the brain tissue," he told her.

She looked over at Nicholas. "You've been here all the time?"

"Almost," he said with a nod. "When I didn't hear from you, I started to worry. I flew up here and learned you'd never returned to the hotel that day. I called the police, and they helped me track you down."

"You're going to lose your job," she said.

He shook his head. "Don't worry about it."

She turned to the doctor again. "When can I leave?"

"We will discuss that later, mademoiselle."

The tubes and IV were disconnected the next morning. Nicholas was there. He was always there. "Don't you ever sleep?" Jaime asked as he attempted to feed her from a breakfast tray heaped with food that had no trace of flavor whatsoever.

"I sleep," he assured her, pushing a forkful of something she didn't recognize at her face. "Eat."

She tasted it, then made a face. "Is there some kind of unwritten universal law that says hospital food in any language has to be bad?"

He smiled. "When you're up to it, I'll take you to the best restaurant in town," he promised. "But for now, you're stuck with this stuff. Now—open!"

"If I have to keep eating this crap, I'll never have the strength to go anywhere," Jaime maintained. "But if you're going to insist . . .'' She took a bite, but without much enthusiasm.

"The sooner you regain your strength, the sooner we can return to Paris."

She looked at him. "Do you have anything to return to?" she asked skeptically.

"I hope not." He paused. "I've put in a request to the State Department. I'm getting out of diplomatic service."

"Are you sure you really want to do that?" she asked.

He smiled. "You've been a bad influence on me," he told her. "I've seen you chasing all over Europe, risking your neck for what you believe in, and I've asked myself how I could ever have settled for less than what *I* really want from my life."

"And?"

"I think the time has come to make that move we talked about awhile back," he said simply.

She was silent for a moment. "Nicholas, I've been thinking about the accident," she said finally.

"There's no point in rehashing—"

"It wasn't an accident," she stated flatly.

He looked at her.

"There were no brakes." She lay back against the pillow. "The car was fine until I reached Leuven. When I left the hotel, they were okay—"

"Then how do you figure?"

"The brake line must have been cut. By the time I hit the hills, the brake fluid had all drained out," she reasoned.

He whistled softly. "I think you're getting too close to something important," he said grimly. "They're playing a lot rougher."

"The stakes are a lot higher."

"Where are you going?" Jaime asked as Nicholas put on his coat. It was almost dusk, and there was little he could do at this late hour.

"I want to talk to the mechanic who checked your car after the accident."

"Think it'll do any good?"

"Can't hurt." There was an odd note to his voice.

"I'm beginning to wonder."

He turned to look at her. "I won't be long," he promised, fiddling with his buttons.

"Nicholas—" she called after him as he started for the door.

"Yes?"

"Ask them about my briefcase."

"Briefcase?"

"The one with all the letters in it. No one seems to know where it is."

He frowned. Why did that not come as a surprise?

"There was little left to examine, as you can see, monsieur," the mechanic told Nicholas.

In a garage in Leuven, they stood by the charred remains of Jaime's rental car. "If indeed the brakes were tampered with, would you be able to tell—even under the circumstances?" Nicholas asked.

"Yes—that is, I believe I would." The man looked somewhat nervous.

"Then you wouldn't mind if I were to bring in an expert to have a look at it?" Nicholas asked as he studied the wreckage thoughtfully.

"*I* am an expert, monsieur!" the mechanic snorted indignantly. "I have examined this vehicle—or what is now left of it, I should say—and I find no evidence of tampering, with the brakes or anything else!"

Nicholas nodded slowly, suspicious. He was still staring at the wreckage. Then he turned to look at the other man again. "You went to the scene of the accident, didn't you?" he asked carefully.

"I did," the mechanic answered.

"Tell me—was there a briefcase in the car?"

"A briefcase?"

He nodded.

"If it *was* in the car, monsieur, it is most certain that there is nothing left of it now." He gave a shrug. "I saw nothing outside the car, but perhaps if you were to check with the police—''

''I've already talked to them. Thank you anyway.'' Nicholas drew in a deep breath as he walked away.

What was he going to tell Jaime?

''It was destroyed in the explosion.''

''Everything?'' Jaime asked, clearly upset. ''There wasn't *anything* left?''

Nicholas shook his head. ''I'm afraid not,'' he said. ''I'm sorry.''

She looked as if she were going to cry. ''My whole life was in that briefcase,'' she said, her voice barely above a whisper. ''My father's letters, the photographs, my birth certificate and passport—''

''The passport I can take care of,'' he assured her. ''I wish the rest could be so simple.''

She nodded, biting her trembling lower lip. ''What about the brakes?'' she asked finally.

Nicholas shook his head. ''He claims he found no evidence of tampering.''

''He's lying or he's just wrong,'' Jaime said flatly. ''*I* was driving that car, and it had no brakes. None at all.''

''You don't have to convince me,'' he told her. ''I believe you. Actually, I had the feeling he was hiding something the minute we started talking.''

''Then you don't believe his story?''

He looked at her. ''I think someone else got to him before I did.''

''When can she go home, Doctor?'' Nicholas asked.

''I would be willing to release her tomorrow,'' the doctor told him, ''but she tells me she's been living alone in a hotel in Paris. I do not think she should be alone at this time. She is still experiencing the aftereffects of her injury and will for some time to come.''

''Don't worry about that,'' he said finally. ''She won't be alone. She'll be staying with me.''

• • •

Paris. "Don't argue with me," Nicholas growled as he steered Jaime through his apartment to the bedroom. As she watched, still somewhat dazed, he turned down the sheets and patted the bed gently, indicating that she was expected to lie down.

"I don't think this is such a good idea," she said.

"You don't really have a choice," he pointed out. "The doctor said you couldn't be alone yet. It was the only way he'd agree to release you from the hospital."

"Where are you going to sleep?" she asked.

"On the couch."

"I couldn't let you do that."

"Well, there *is* one other alternative," he suggested.

She raised a hand to silence him. "Never mind."

"Then this is the only way. Doctor's orders," he reminded her.

"I don't need a goddamned nursemaid," she said irritably.

"And I don't have any intentions of becoming one, so I guess we're even," he said promptly. "But I'll be damned if I'll let you go off by yourself—under the circumstances."

"You're not my keeper, Kendall."

He stopped what he was doing and straightened up. "You know what? I liked you a hell of a lot better when you were in the hospital," he told her. "You were certainly less difficult."

"I wasn't capable of objecting to too much of anything," she reminded him.

"So you weren't." He grinned. "Now—are you going to lie down willingly, or do I have to come and get you?"

"All right," she surrendered. She lay down on the bed fully clothed, legs crossed and her arms folded across her chest. "I never realized you were such a tyrant."

"And you're a prize pain in the ass, but I'm still not going to leave you alone at a time like this." He bent down and pulled off her boots.

She laughed for the first time. "Still trying to get my clothes off, Kendall?"

He laughed too. "Can't blame a man for trying."

• • •

"I was so close," Jaime told Nicholas over dinner. "If I could only have seen Forrester, talked to him . . . I'm sure he could have answered most of my questions—if not all of them."

"He refused to talk to you," Nicholas reminded her, reaching for his napkin. "What makes you think you could have changed his mind?"

"I wouldn't have left him alone until he did," Jaime said flatly.

"That's what I figured."

They had a traditional Thanksgiving dinner together. Nicholas prepared the entire meal himself, refusing to let Jaime near the kitchen until afterward, when she insisted upon doing the dishes.

"Are you sure you want to harbor a known political enemy?" she asked, washing while he dried.

He stacked the finished dishes to one side of the counter. "Is that what you are?" he asked, mildly amused by her description of herself.

"I'm a target." She reached for a towel. "That's worse."

What *was* worse, he realized, was that she was right. She really was a target.

That had become painfully obvious to him in Leuven.

"Where are you off to so early?" Jaime asked sleepily as she stumbled out of the bedroom.

Nicholas was on his way out the door. "I've got to run over to the embassy," he told her. "It appears the State Department's decided to accept my resignation."

"No questions asked?"

"Apparently not."

"Are you sure this is what you want to do, Nicholas?" she asked dubiously.

He winked. "Absolutely."

"What will you do now?" she asked, concerned—and feeling somewhat guilty at having prompted his decision.

"Return to the States—eventually."

"And now?"

He grinned. "I'm playing it by ear—for the moment."

"What are we celebrating, Kendall?" Jaime asked over dinner at the Tour d'Argent, once known as the best restaurant in Paris. Though it has lost its distinction, it is still one of the finest, and the cuisine is matched by an opulent dining room that could have been decorated by Louis XIV himself. From their table, Jaime could see Notre Dame and the barges in the Seine below. "Doesn't seem to me there's a hell of a lot for either of us to celebrate right now. You're out of a job and I still don't know what happened to my father."

"I may be out of a job, but I feel like I've been set free," he told her, sampling his sliced duck breast. "This is something I should have done a long time ago."

"None of us is ever *really* free," Jaime said cynically, toying with her wineglass. "We are *all*, I've discovered, prisoners of fate."

"Where'd you get all that faith and trust?" he asked, his eyes meeting hers.

"It was my father's legacy."

If Nicholas thought he was in love with Jaime before, he was sure of it now. She'd been living with him—or perhaps sharing his apartment was a better summation of their living arrangements—for almost a month now, and the more time they spent together, the more convinced he was that they were absolutely right for each other. He knew now, without a shadow of a doubt, that she was the woman he wanted.

Of course, Jaime seemed perfectly satisfied with the present state of their relationship. She was, it appeared to Nicholas, content to be living here with him platonically. For him, it was both heaven and hell, having her here with him, knowing she was sleeping in his bed and yet not being able to touch her.

"I don't know what a good relationship is," she confided to him one night while they watched TV together. "I have no basis for comparison. Every one I've seen is unquestionably lousy."

"What about your parents?"

"Especially theirs," she said with contempt in her voice. "Hardly what I'd call a good example for their only daughter."

"Want to talk about it?" he asked.

She shook her head. "Not really."

He studied her for a moment. "Tell me about it anyway," he pressured her, sensing that she needed to talk about it.

She hesitated for a moment. "My parents got off to a bad start," she said finally. "My father only married my mother because he needed a cover. He needed a job and a nice, passive wife who wouldn't rock the boat too much when he had to spend most of his time away. As it turned out, my mother fit the bill perfectly."

"In what way?"

"She was not only the kind of woman they were looking for, she was one with all the right connections," Jaime said coldly. "Her father was a senator, soon to retire to take over the family business, which just happened to be a large international investment banking firm. A firm where my father could find a place and travel under the guise of handling their business. The icing on the cake was that my mother happened to be wildly in love with him." She drew her knees up to her chest and hugged them tightly.

"But your father loved *you*, didn't he?" Nicholas asked.

Jaime smiled wearily. "I never doubted that," she said quietly. "He was the only person in the world who *did* love me—but unfortunately, not enough to keep him from leaving me."

"You're nothing at all like your mother, are you?" Nicholas asked later.

Jaime shook her head. "It's ironic. She always said she felt as if she'd had nothing at all to do with my creation," she said sadly.

"And how do you feel about that?" Nicholas wanted to know.

She looked away. "Like I never had a mother."

• • •

They had an old-fashioned American Christmas. Nicholas came home one cold December afternoon with a tree that was lacking in height but lush in all the ways that counted, according to Jaime. They decorated it, then popped popcorn and strung it on the tree as well, Jaime eating it as they went along. "It's not exactly 'Jingle Bells' and 'Silent Night,' but it'll do," she declared as they admired their handiwork, arms around each other under the mistletoe.

He kissed her gently. "We've only got each other now, sweetheart," he told her.

Jamie slept fitfully that night. She was dreaming of her father. They were at opposite ends of a long, dark tunnel, and he was calling to her. She was running through the darkness, trying to get to him, but it seemed that the harder she ran, the further away he was and the longer the tunnel became. She could hear his voice, but she couldn't see him. She called out to him. There were demons in the tunnel, ferocious spirits she could hear but not see. They were laughing at her, taunting her, daring her to go on. Loud, malicious laughter . . . evil laughter. Then she saw her father—he was hanging from the gallows! They had executed him! "Daddy—No!" she screamed. *"No!"*

She jerked upright in bed, still trembling, still screaming. *"No . . . !"*

Nicholas woke with a start, roused from a sound sleep by the sound of Jaime's tormented screams. Leaping off the couch, ignoring the fact that he was wearing nothing but his underwear, he raced into the bedroom and practically fell onto the bed as he gathered her in his arms. "My God," he whispered as he held her close. She was shaking violently. "What happened?"

"It was horrible," she gasped. "It seemed so real . . ."

"You were dreaming," he said softly, stroking her hair. "That's all it was—just a dream."

"Don't leave me," she whispered, clinging to him. "Just hold me . . ."

He could feel her tears, damp against his skin. He felt the

softness of her, so close . . . the warm swells of her breasts, pressing against his chest through the thin nightgown she wore. He took in the woodsy scent of her perfume. And though he tried to fight it, he found himself aroused by it all. *Not now,* he told himself. *Not now.* . . . She was so vulnerable, and he had never wanted her so much, yet. . . .

"Stay with me," she whispered as she looked into his eyes. "Make love to me."

He looked down at her. "Sssh," he said, pressing a finger to her lips. "You're upset. You don't know what you're saying."

"Yes, I do," she insisted. "I want you to make love to me. I *need* you to make love to me."

He told himself that this was not the right time, that she was just frightened and wanted him there with her, that he could sleep with her without making love to her, but in the end his need for her was stronger than his common sense. Easing back slightly, he lifted her face to his and kissed her deeply as he reached under her nightgown. Cupping one of her breasts in his hand, he stroked the nipple with his thumb until he felt it grow hard. Unable to wait any longer, he lifted the gown over her head in one swift movement and cast it aside. His breath caught in his throat. She was so beautiful, even more so than he'd imagined. He kissed her hungrily as he lowered her to the bed again, still caressing her with one eager hand. She put her arms around his neck and held him tightly, returning his kisses with an eagerness that matched his. She reached down to help him as he tugged at her underpants, finally pulling them off. Her hand slipped inside his briefs, stroking him as he lowered his head to her breast and sucked at her nipples, sending shock waves through her entire body. He tore off his briefs and entered her, taking her with an urgency that had come from having waited much too long for this moment. All he could think about was how much he'd wanted her, how long he'd waited. And now, at last, she was his.

"I love you, crazy lady," he whispered hoarsely as he held her close afterward.

"I love you, too," she admitted at last—to him and to herself.

"I want you," he told her. "Not just for tonight, not just now . . ."

"I can't make any promises," she told him reluctantly.

Only for tonight.

TWENTY-FOUR

Nicholas was humming cheerfully as he walked into the bathroom, and turned on the shower. Last night, making love with Jaime, had exceeded his wildest erotic fantasies. Even in her state of mind, she had been as fiery and passionate in her lovemaking as she was in everything else she did. Just as he'd known she would be. But it wasn't the intensity of their lovemaking that made it so special, it was the emotions that each of them evoked in the other, like a white-hot current that connected them. He had never been in love before and had no idea it would be like this. That he could feel so strongly about anyone or anything. *You're contagious, sweetheart,* he thought.

Stepping into the shower, he was immediately invigorated by the force of the warm water pounding against his flesh . . . or was it the thought of last night, of the way they'd come together so eagerly, that exhilarated him? She'd told him she loved him. He believed she'd meant it. He knew he loved her. He was ready to make a commitment to her, right here and now. If only she were as willing. Even as she'd told him she loved him, she kept saying "no promises." Why? Why did it all have to be so complicated? He didn't have any answers. He only knew he couldn't give up on her now if he tried.

She was in his blood.

Jaime lay in bed, the sheet pulled up to her waist, staring up at the ceiling. She had mixed feelings about last night. She wasn't sorry about what had happened, not at all. Yet she wasn't sure she should have let it happen.

She knew Nicholas loved her. *God knows he's told me often enough,* she thought, confused. She also knew now that she loved him, and she wasn't at all sure she was happy about it. Love was a luxury, one she couldn't afford. Not now, maybe not ever. Love, she'd discovered, came with a hefty price tag, one she wasn't sure she was willing to pay again. She didn't want to hurt him.

And she didn't want to be hurt herself.

"Let's get married," Nicholas suggested.

"Let's not push it, okay?" Jaime said firmly, pulling on her boots.

He put on his shirt. "Still determined to hold on to your independence?" he asked, keeping his voice light as he buttoned the cuffs.

"You know I can't make any plans right now," she pointed out, pushing her long hair back off her shoulders.

"Until you find your father," he concluded, struggling to keep the bitterness out of his voice.

She nodded, avoiding his eyes.

"Maybe it's a mistake," he said, turning to face her. "Maybe there are some skeletons in his closet, even if he wasn't a traitor. Maybe you'd be better off not knowing."

"No, I wouldn't," she disagreed with certainty. "I'd spend the rest of my life wondering, and eventually it would make me crazy. At least if I know—good or bad—I can deal with it."

"Are you sure about that?"

"It's a chance I have to take."

Nicholas studied her for a long moment, realizing that he would never be able to talk her out of it. She was never going to give up her quest for the truth. If he expected to have any kind of future with her, he'd have to accept that. Not only accept it, but aid her wholeheartedly in her search.

Only then could they get on with their lives.

On January 9, 1986, a bar in Glyfada, Greece, frequented by U.S. servicemen, was the target of a terrorist's bomb. When Jaime read about it in the Paris newspapers, she wondered if what Julien Armand had told her was true. Was her father involved in counterterrorism?

And if so, could he be in Greece right now?

Washington, D.C. "She's out of the hospital?" Harry Warner asked.

"And back in Paris," the disembodied voice on the telephone told him. "She's moved in with Kendall."

"Interesting," Warner said thoughtfully. "He left the embassy staff recently."

"Not before he managed to raise a lot of questions."

"That was unfortunate," Warner said tightly. "What about Forrester?"

"Dissatisfied . . . but off on an extended vacation when last seen."

"No second thoughts about talking to Lynde's daughter?"

"If he had, he never said anything."

"Good. Keep me posted."

Jaime stood on the Pont Alexandre III, staring into the Seine as if she could see something in the river's depths. In truth, she was not looking into the water at all. She was looking into the past.

"What's a unicorn, Daddy?"

"It's a mythical creature, a horse with a single horn sprouting from its head," he told her.

Jaime was seven years old, only months away from her eighth birthday. She and her father had spent an entire day in Manhattan. They'd had lunch at a small Italian restaurant on the Upper East Side and spotted a painting on display in the window of a gallery as they were walking along Madison Avenue. It was a large painting of a beautiful white unicorn with a golden horn, surrounded by moonlight and rainbows and mist.

Jaime looked up at him, her small face serious. He seemed so big to her at the time, almost like a giant. "What's myth-ical?" she wanted to know.

"A fable. A story, like a fairy tale. Something some people believe in but nobody can prove exists," he told her.

"Like God?" she asked.

He gave a low chuckle. "Not exactly, princess."

"Then what?"

"It's sort of like 'Jack and the Beanstalk.' "

"You mean it's something that's not really true," she promptly concluded.

"Something like that, yes."

"Then there is no such thing as a unicorn?"

He smiled down at her. "No, though I suspect some people will argue with that."

She gave him a quizzical look.

"Some people believe," he explained. "There are people who will tell you that the unicorn is real and that it has certain magical powers."

"What kind of magical powers?" she asked.

He shrugged. "Depends on where you hear the legend, princess."

"Do you believe in unicorns, Daddy?"

He looked at her with a sly smile and winked. "Me? No way."

"I believe in unicorns," she told him.

I believe in unicorns, she thought, still staring into the water. *I believe they're magical and elusive and valuable . . . valu-able enough to kill for.*

"Okay. You win."

Jaime looked up as Nicholas came into the bedroom. "Great," she responded. "What did I win?"

"I've decided if you can't beat 'em, join 'em."

She smiled. "Meaning what?"

"Meaning," he began wearily, "if you're so damned determined to put your own head on the chopping block in order to find your father, I can't stop you."

"I'm glad you finally realize that," she said as she put down her hairbrush.

"Let me finish," he said, pulling off his tie as he turned to look at her again. "*We* will do whatever's necessary to find him."

She looked at him questioningly. "We?"

"You're playing a dangerous game, Jaime," he told her. "I'm not about to let you go on playing it alone if I can help it."

She managed a smile. "I didn't think you had been," she said.

He drew in his breath. "I'm not fighting the inevitable anymore."

"Could I have that in writing, please?" Jaime asked, unconvinced.

"I'm serious." He leaned against the bureau, arms folded across his chest. "I love you, lady. If this is what it takes to satisfy you, to make you forget about the past and start thinking about the future—our future—then I'm willing to take the risks with you."

She stood up, smiling. "Kendall, you may be worth my time after all," she stated, extending her arms to him. "I think it's time I showed my appreciation . . ."

"You know what I was just thinking about?" Jaime asked.

"No. What were you thinking about?" In the darkness, Nicholas lay on top of Jaime on the bed, supporting his weight on his elbows as he kissed her neck.

"The day we met. Do you remember that?"

"Mmmmm . . . how could I forget?" His lips moved lower.

"When I came to in your office and you were unbuttoning my shirt, I thought you were some lech trying to undress me." She stroked his hair.

He started nuzzling her breasts. "I gave it serious consideration.'' He teased her nipple with the tip of his tongue. She arched her back, offering herself to him. He took the hardened nipple between his lips and sucked it greedily.

''You're a sex maniac, Kendall,'' she whispered as her hand slid down his back. ''A blue-chip, card-carrying sex maniac.''

He raised his head and smiled lazily. ''Would you want it any other way?''

''Can't say that I would.'' Taking his face in her hands, she kissed him deeply. ''Some of my favorite people are sex maniacs.''

''Oh?'' He arched an eyebrow. ''And just how many do you know personally?''

''Several,'' she teased. ''In fact, I've lost count.''

''I'll bet.'' He pressed himself against her, making his intentions known. ''I would have thought you always had too many other things on your mind.''

''Come on, Kendall—I am human, you know,'' she giggled, wrapping her arms around him.

He kissed her shoulder. ''There have been times I've wondered.''

She ran her fingers through his hair. ''Are you wondering right now?''

''Now?'' With one hand he caressed her breast. ''Not at all. I know only too well how human you are, my love.''

She reached downward between them, stroking his hardness with eager fingers as they kissed again and again. His body quivered with excitement as her hand worked its magic. Finally, unable to stand it any longer, he pulled her hand away abruptly. Her whole body shuddered pleasurably as he entered her, moving his hips in a slow, circular motion. He kissed her, quick, hard kisses as he took her swiftly. Jaime held on to him tightly, savoring the moment—the force of his thrusts, the smoothness of the taut skin over the well-defined muscles of his back, the unmistakably male scent of him. But most of all, she wanted to savor the love she saw in his eyes.

She loved him. She wanted to love him—and wanted him to love her. She wanted all of the things she'd never had before: love, trust, stability. She wanted all of those things and more. She wanted them with this man.

If only she could let go of the past.

When Jaime woke the next morning, Nicholas was gone. There was a note taped to the bathroom mirror:

CAME UP WITH A COUPLE OF POSSIBILITIES I
THOUGHT SHOULD BE CHECKED OUT. BE
BACK AS SOON AS I CAN. WILL CALL IF I'M
GOING TO BE LATE. LOVE, NICHOLAS. XXX

Jaime smiled to herself. He'd meant what he had told her last night. How many people in the course of her twenty-nine years had made all kinds of promises, only to betray her in the end? *At last,* she thought, *I'm not alone.*

The sound of the doorbell cut through her thoughts. She glanced at the clock on the nightstand. Ten-fifteen. It had to be the fellow who delivered their dry cleaning twice weekly. She put on her robe and went to let him in. "You're early," she said as she opened the door. "You're—you're not the delivery man."

The man standing in the doorway was definitely not the delivery man from the dry cleaners. He was tall, well dressed, and appeared to be in his late sixties. He had a strong, craggy face and thinning gray hair. Something about him seemed vaguely familiar, though she was sure they'd never met before.

"You do look like him," he observed. "No mistake about who you are now."

"Who? What are you talking about?" Jaime asked, somewhat confused and not yet fully awake. "Do I know you?"

"Indirectly," he said with a tired smile. "My name's Forrester. Jack Forrester."

TWENTY-FIVE

"Your father was always perfectly suited to our way of life. He was an adventurer at heart," Jack Forrester remembered. "In the days of the old OSS, we worked with the French Resistance, and there was nothing he would not do. Once he conducted his radio transmissions to our people in England right under the Gestapo's collective noses. He was inside a huge wine cask with the radio, and I was pushing the cart through the streets of Le Havre. Another time, he donned a German general's uniform and waltzed right into Gestapo headquarters in Paris." He paused. "After the war, it was never quite the same for him. He missed the challenge, missed living by his wits."

"So he went back to it," Jaime concluded as she poured him a cup of coffee.

Forrester nodded. "No one was more enthusiastic than your father when the intelligence department was revived," he went on. "During the cold war era, he went in and out of Russia with great regularity—on the pretense of business, of course."

"Of course," Jaime said dismally.

"In 1961, what with all the trouble brewing in Cuba, he

was sent to Havana to keep tabs on Castro and all those missiles the Russians were hauling into Cuba.''

''And now?'' Jaime asked.

Forrester gave her a wary look but responded anyway. ''Your father is a specialist in counterterrorism.''

''Meaning exactly what?''

''He was involved for a time in training counterterrorists for the American Delta Force and the British SAS teams,'' Forrester told her, pausing to sip his coffee. ''Right now, he's working undercover in a terrorist training camp in Libya.''

''Libya!'' Jaime looked at him, stunned.

He nodded. ''He's been there for some time now.''

''Why all the lies?'' Jaime wanted to know. ''Why did you tell me he was a traitor? Why have I been led to believe he betrayed his country?''

''It was necessary to ensure his safety,'' he said simply.

''He's in Libya,'' Jaime told Nicholas in bed that night. ''He was first sent there in 1969 when the CIA supported Qaddafi's bid to overthrow King Idris. They had to make him look like a traitor so he'd be accepted into Libya as one of theirs.''

Nicholas looked relieved. ''So now you know,'' he said as he held her close. ''Your father's alive, just as you always said he was. He's not a turncoat, he's not a double agent.'' He kissed her. ''Now can we please give up this madness and get on with our lives?''

She looked up at him, surprised. ''Not by a long shot.''

''You've got the answers you wanted,'' he pointed out, afraid he already knew what she was leading up to. ''You know he didn't do any of the terrible things he was accused of doing, but you sure as hell can't tell anyone what you know, so what's left?''

''I have to see him.''

''He's in Libya, Jaime. They have Americans for breakfast there, remember?''

''I still have to see him.''

He slapped his forehead in frustration. ''Jesus—you can't be serious!''

"Oh, but I am," she insisted.

"You can't go into Libya looking for your father," he argued. "Especially under the circumstances."

"The hell I can't!"

Even in the darkness, he could see that familiar flash of determination in her dark green eyes. And he could see just as clearly that she had every intention of going to Libya to find her father.

And he knew, with just as much certainty, that he would be going with her.

Washington, D.C. Harry Warner was having breakfast at his home in Georgetown when the telephone rang. His wife, Myrna, answered it, spoke briefly, then passed the receiver to him and discreetly left the room, almost as if on cue.

Warner put the phone to his ear. "Hello?"

"It's me."

"Dammit, I told you never to call me at home!" Warner snapped irritably.

"It's important."

Warner sucked in his breath. "What's important?"

"Forrester double-crossed us."

"What?" Warner almost came up out of his chair.

"He's paying Lynde's daughter a visit this morning."

"Is he telling her anything?"

"What do you think?" There was a pause. "It's a damned good thing I planted those bugs."

Warner's jaw tightened nervously. "I want you to stick to them like glue."

"What do you think I've been doing?"

Warner brushed the last comment aside as if he hadn't heard it. "Don't let them out of your sight."

"What do I do about Forrester?"

"Don't worry about Forrester," Warner said crossly. "I'll take care of it."

"You think Jaime Lynde would be foolish enough to go to Libya?"

"I think she'll try."

• • •

"In 1969, the CIA supported Qaddafi in his bid to overthrow King Idris I, who was old and in poor health—and supposedly staunchly anti-American," Forrester told Jaime. "Qaddafi was twenty-seven at the time and backed up by some sixty young officers from Libya's Signal Corps—none of whom was more than thirty years old. With U.S. aid, they took Tripoli and Benghazi, occupied the palace, and seized military installations and communications centers. Again, with CIA support, he—Qaddafi—recruited some seven thousand soldiers to join his ranks."

"And my father was involved in his rise to power," Jaime concluded thoughtfully.

He hesitated for a moment, then nodded. "Yes. Yes, he was," he said finally. "He had reservations about Qaddafi himself, right from the word go, but he was doing his job."

"And now he's there to undermine that power." Jaime pulled at the bottom of the apricot-colored sweater she wore as she sat ramrod straight in her chair, her face expressionless, her voice carefully controlled.

"He actually left Tripoli shortly after Qaddafi's people thwarted an attempted countercoup. He was in Syria for a time," Forrester recalled. "We—the Company, that is—were conducting an investigation into terrorist activities there. That was the beginning of your father's work in counterterrorism."

"Why didn't he ever return home?" Jaime asked. "Why didn't he at least try to contact me?"

"He couldn't. It wouldn't have been safe—for you or for him," Forrester told her. "Remember, he was supposed to be a traitor, a man who could never go home. Had his cover been blown, it would have placed both of you in jeopardy."

Jaime blinked back a tear. "When did he return to Libya?" she asked in a tremulous voice.

Forrester thought about it for a moment. "He's been in and out of Libya since Qaddafi's takeover. That maniac's been nothing but trouble from the beginning. The Company ended up with egg on its collective face. Qaddafi's more anti-Western than old King Idris could ever have been, and he's proterrorist to boot."

"Isn't he some sort of religious fanatic?" Jaime asked, recalling some of the things she'd read.

"You could call it that, yes," he said. "His police, acting on his orders, strictly enforce Brother Colonel's own interpretation of the Shari'a morality. Young women are detained on the streets of the larger cities if their skirts are deemed too short and their legs marked with a red dye that's damned near impossible to remove. But the truth of the matter is, the cops are usually more interested in fondling the offender's legs than in enforcing morality."

He paused. "Of course, the laws don't apply only to women," he went on. "Men are not allowed to have their hair long or to wear tight pants. Qaddafi considers both effeminate and a sign of unwholesome Western influence. When your father first returned to Tripoli in 1970—when Qaddafi shut down Wheelus Air Force Base and the British air bases at Tobruk and El Adem—he dyed his hair black so as not to call attention to himself. With that red hair of his, he would certainly have stood out among the Arabs."

Jaime thought about it, unable to imagine her father with black hair.

"It has since turned completely white," Forrester added, almost as an afterthought.

"Under the circumstances, I'm not at all surprised," Jaime remarked.

"Brother Colonel turned out to be a full-time job for the Unicorn. Your father was one of a handful of specialists who kept tabs on the Libyan terrorist training camps in general and on Qaddafi in particular." He finished his coffee. "When it became evident that the 'mad dog of the Middle East' posed a real threat, it was decided that he would have to be under constant surveillance and the U.S. would have to use extreme caution in its dealings with him. In 1970, the State Department denied export licenses to two U.S. companies proposing to sell nuclear reactors and fuel to Libya, which only served to further incense Qaddafi."

"And my father?"

"James sent warnings that Libya's terrorist activities posed a threat not only to Western countries but to a number of

Libya's Arab allies as well. He was reported to be behind the PLO's attempted assassination of Jordan's King Hussein in Amman that same year. He also backed attempts on the lives of Nimeiry of the Sudan, Morocco's Hassan, and Bourguiba of Tunisia. He forged alliances with Malta, Uganda, and Syria—nations with known terrorist connections. His connections with organizations such as Black September and Italy's Red Brigade were strong. The more the tension in the Middle East escalated, the more important it became that your father remain there—and under cover.''

''There's one thing I still don't understand,'' Jaime began carefully. ''Why did my father have to pretend to be a traitor?''

''To catch the real traitor,'' Forrester answered quietly.

''You are nuts.''

''I have to see my father,'' she stated, indicating it was not open for discussion.

''Look, I know how you feel,'' Nicholas insisted. ''I know how much this means to you. I know I promised to be behind you all the way. But this is Libya we're talking about. This is not just dangerous, it's suicide!''

''You don't have to go with me,'' she maintained.

Nicholas sat up and stared at her in disbelief. ''What does Forrester say about this?''

''He feels the same way you do. He thinks it's too risky.''

''Listen to the man. He knows what he's doing.'' He lay back down again.

''But he's going with me,'' she added, turning out the light.

''There has been a growing suspicion for some time now that there is a traitor among our people in Libya,'' Forrester told Jaime the next day.

''Edwin Wilson,'' she guessed. She remembered reading about the Wilson case. He was, according to all published reports, a renegade CIA agent who'd been involved in selling arms to the Libyans. There had never been any such reports concerning her father in any of the newspapers. Just a lot of conflicting rumors and speculation. Now, at least, she understood why.

Forrester nodded. "Your father suspected others as well," he revealed.

"Wilson didn't act alone," Jaime recalled.

"No, he didn't," Forrester conceded. "But James was convinced there were other renegade agents operating in Libya independent of Wilson and his people."

"And if his cover is blown?"

Forrester looked Jaime in the eye. "They'll kill him."

Washington, D.C. Harry Warner was brushed by a faint sense of unease as he studied the memos on his desk. James Lynde's cover—his alleged betrayal of his own government and his self-imposed exile in Libya—had been so carefully planned, right from the beginning. The few people aware of what they were doing had all been in agreement that there could be no discrepancies or the Libyans would become suspicious.

Yet someone had deliberately fed Jaime Lynde a series of conflicting stories about her father's disappearance. Someone within their own ranks. Why? he asked himself. Why would someone within the Company try to arouse suspicion concerning Lynde and his status within the U.S. government?

Unless they wanted to blow his cover.

"I was told so many different stories," Jaime confided to Forrester, recounting the obstacles that had been thrown in her path in the course of the journey that brought her to Paris. She recalled to him her conversations with the Harcourts, with her father's former colleagues at O'Donnell-Colby, with Kate, with Marty, with William Blackwell, and with the acting warden at Fort Leavenworth and the guard, Hank Bearden. "Everyone had a different tale to tell. I finally decided I had to keep going until I found my father—or at least the truth about what happened to him after his disappearance."

Forrester looked at her with alarm in his eyes. "Something is very wrong," he said uneasily.

"Tell me about it," she said sullenly.

"No—I mean that there was to be no variation from the

official story,'' he said thoughtfully. ''It was agreed that it must appear to be entirely legitimate.''

''Meaning what?''

''Meaning that someone has been using you, dear girl, to track down your father—someone who wants to find him just as badly as you do.'' He paused. ''If my suspicions are correct, we haven't a moment to lose. I'll have to leave for Tripoli tonight.''

''*We'll* have to leave tonight,'' she corrected him.

''No,'' he said, shaking his head. ''It's too dangerous. I must go alone.''

''I'm going,'' she insisted stubbornly. ''With you or on my own. Which is it going to be?''

He hesitated, not sure which posed the greater risk. ''Very well. You will go with me.''

''Shouldn't you contact someone? I mean, if my father's in danger—'' she started.

He shook his head. ''We can contact no one.''

''Why—''

''We don't know who the leak is,'' he pointed out gravely. ''For now, we can tell no one.''

''This is insane!'' Nicholas exploded. ''You can't just go racing off to Libya like it's Club Med or something! Do you have any idea how tense the situation is there right now?''

Jaime glared at him. ''Yes! I do know!'' she shot back at him. ''I do read the newspapers, you know!''

''Then you just don't give a damn about your own life—is that it?'' he demanded hotly. ''Maybe you have some kind of death wish?''

She jerked around to face him. ''What happened to all that love and understanding?'' she wanted to know. ''What happened to that promise you made to support me in this, no matter what?''

''I prefer you alive—if you don't mind!''

''There are lots of Americans in Libya right now,'' she reminded him.

''And they're all there against the orders of the State Department," he pointed out. "You're not exactly going to blend into the crowd there, you know."

She shot him a murderous look. "Who the hell do you think you are, anyway—my keeper?"

"Not at all," he fumed. "I'm just the brainless idiot who happens to be in love with you!"

Jaime stared at him for a moment. "I'm sorry," she said quietly. "I didn't mean any of that. I love you. I know you love me. I know you're worried. But you know how I feel, too—you know I have to find my father. I have to see him, talk to him. Even if it turns out to be the last time."

He took her in his arms. "I know," he said, stroking her hair. "Or I'm trying to, anyway. I just can't deal with the idea of you making yourself a sitting duck in Qaddafi's shooting gallery." He kissed her forehead. "God, it's like knowingly going for a swim in shark-infested waters!"

She snuggled against him. "For what it's worth, I'm scared too," she admitted. "I have been ever since I started this thing. Every morning I wake up and ask myself, 'Am I doing the right thing?' and no matter how I wrestle with it, the answer is always yes. This is something I need to do—no, have to do—for myself."

He held her for a moment longer. "Then I guess we'd better pack," he said finally.

She looked up at him. "We?"

He forced a smile. "I'm sure as hell not letting you go without me."

TWENTY-SIX

On March twenty-fourth, the day Jaime and Nicholas left Paris with Jack Forrester, a U.S. armada consisting of thirty warships and two hundred planes crossed Qaddafi's "Line of Death" and began military maneuvers in the Gulf of Sidra. Qaddafi, predictably, made good on his threat to fire on any and all non-Libyan craft crossing that line and ordered the firing of Libya's Soviet-made surface-to-air missiles. The confrontation lasted less than twenty-four hours, and in that time, the American ordnance, with its shells, bombs, and missiles, sank two Libyan patrol boats, severely damaged three more, and bombed a radar installation on the mainland.

The three waited out the conflict across the Libyan border in Algeria. Forrester took them to a small hotel near Edjeleh, a border town, and despite Jaime's impatience, he insisted they remain there until the military maneuvers were over. "Right now, they'll shoot anything that even looks American," he told her, "and there's no way on earth you're going to pass for an Arab woman."

"Don't bet on it," Jaime responded, rising to the challenge.

"What have you got in mind this time?" Nicholas asked suspiciously when they were alone in their room.

Jaime only smiled. "You'll see."

When they met Forrester downstairs for dinner, he was unable to hide his surprise at her changed appearance. She wore the long, flowing cotton caftan typically favored by Arab women of North Africa, mostly white but accented in muted tones of green and brown. Her red hair was completely covered by the large square of fabric she'd tied over her head. Her eyes were outlined in kohl. On her feet she wore *babouches*, pointy-toed leather slippers.

"I have to admit I wouldn't have recognized you if you hadn't been with Kendall here," Forrester admitted with definite approval in his voice.

Nicholas looked at him questioningly.

"I have a contact here," Forrester went on. "He'll provide us with clothing and supplies and take us across the border to Tripoli—it's some five hundred kilometers from here. Looking as much like the locals as possible will go a long way toward a safe journey."

"In that case, I'm all for it," Nicholas said promptly.

The hotel's café looked like something straight out of *Casablanca*: small tables crowded together in a smoke-filled room, ceiling fans overhead squeaking as they rotated slowly; men in traditional *galabiyya*, loose cotton gowns in white or stripes, some wearing turbans, much like those Forrester and Nicholas wore, were seated at a number of the tables, conversing in Arabic and French. In one corner of the room, three Arab men in olive-drab military garb, unkempt and unshaven, their knives sheathed in snapped leather scabbards, talked with a fourth man, a civilian, in hushed tones. The man looked as nervous as Jaime felt.

They found a table on the other side of the room. A waiter came promptly, and Forrester ordered for all three of them in fluent Arabic.

"Would either of you like something to drink?" Forrester asked Jaime and Nicholas, translating the waiter's question.

"Make mine a double," Jaime said sullenly.

Nicholas nudged her under the table. "Alcohol's taboo here," he whispered.

"Make it mint tea all around," Forrester instructed their waiter.

The young man nodded. "*Shukran*," he said in a low voice. "Thank you." He disappeared into the kitchen with their order.

"I'll do the talking from here on out," Forrester told them after he had gone. "If we're to be convincing, we have to speak the language."

Nicholas looked concerned. "Do we have to play deaf-mutes, then?"

Forrester shook his head. "Just let me talk for all of us whenever possible," he said in a low voice. "I'll teach you enough Arabic words to get by."

"I'm not even going to ask what you ordered for us," Jaime said. She was starving and concerned that the food might not be edible.

"Whatever he brings out, you'd *better* eat it," Nicholas told her. "We're supposed to be Arabs, remember?"

She made a face. "How could I possibly forget?"

What the waiter brought them turned out to be quite tasty: grilled lamb seasoned with a blend of savory spices, a mixed salad, and *briouats*, small pillows of paper-thin pastry stuffed with honey and almonds for dessert.

"Are you sure my father's still in Tripoli?" Jaime asked when the waiter was beyond earshot.

Forrester nodded. "He was as of last night."

Both Jaime and Nicholas looked at him, neither of them able to hide their surprise.

Forrester shrugged. "I told you—I have contacts here," he said simply.

Washington, D.C. It was almost noon. Harry Warner was holed up in his office, venting his anger and frustration by pacing a path in the carpet in front of his desk. His man in Paris had not contacted him in more than thirty-six hours. Had something gone wrong? What had Forrester told Lynde's daughter? Was she going to go through with that craziness and try to get into Libya?

Good God, she doesn't know what she's doing, he thought

angrily. *She might as well put a loaded gun to his head and pull the trigger! If she blows his cover, he's as good as dead!*

He stared at the phone on the desk and sucked in a deep breath. He wanted to place a call to Lynde himself in Tripoli, but he knew it was out of the question. It would be too risky. Especially now. They were so close . . . and Libya was a powder keg about to blow. In just a matter of days. . . .

You're on your own now, old friend, he thought, staring out the window absently at the gleaming white dome of the Capitol building in the distance. *Where had they gone wrong?* he asked himself. *They'd taken so many precautions. Only four people knew the truth. How had they been discovered? Who was the leak?*

Who had betrayed Unicorn?

Edjeleh. While Nicholas slept, Jaime, curled up in an armchair in one corner of the room, read by the light of a small oil lamp. In her lap was a large manila envelope containing newspaper clippings from all over the world. Clippings reporting terrorist activities in Europe and in the Middle East.

March 1983: bombings in England targeting anti-Qaddafi Libyan exiles. April 16, 1984: two dissident students hanged in Tripoli on the orders of Qaddafi himself in retaliation following the attempted assassination of his cousin and most trusted aide, Ahmed Qadafadam. June 13, 1985: the hijacking of TWA flight 847, en route to Beirut from Athens, by Lebanese Shiite Moslems. July 22, 1985: the Islamic Jihad bombing of the U.S. airline offices in Copenhagen. July 16, 1985: a grenade attack on the Café de Paris in Rome.

Jaime felt an involuntary shiver course through her body as she read on. Terrorists were like animals—cold-blooded killers with no regard for human life. And this was the world in which her father had existed for so many years. The world in which he operated to combat terrorism.

She got to her feet slowly and stood at the window, taking in the incredible calm of the desert at night. She hugged herself, suddenly cold inside.

She felt as though she were about to descend into hell.

• • •

"How do I look?" Nicholas asked.

He was wearing one of the *galabiyya* Forrester had provided, a lightweight cotton gown slit at the neckline, white
with vertical gray stripes that hung to his ankles, and a turban. Jaime couldn't resist laughing. "Like you're ready for
bed," she told him.

"Bed?" He made a wry face.

"It looks an awful lot like a nightshirt," she indicated,
still laughing.

"Very funny," he grumbled.

"You should look in the mirror," she advised.

"This is supposed to be a disguise," he reminded her.
"You know, when in Rome and all that."

She nodded. "Oh, it's a hell of a disguise, all right,"
she assured him.

"Did I laugh at you when you donned that caftan?" he
asked.

"No, but I look better in a nightshirt than you do," she
responded.

"Thanks." His tone was less than enthusiastic.

Their conversation was interrupted at that point by an urgent knock at the door. "Who is it?" Jaime asked, suddenly
cautious.

"Forrester."

She unlocked the door and let him in. He, too, wore a
galabiyya and turban. "Trick or treat," Jaime greeted him
cheerfully.

Forrester didn't smile. He gestured to her to close the door,
then placed his portable radio on the table and switched it
on. The transmission was in Arabic.

"What're they saying?" Nicholas asked, concerned.

"There's been an explosion aboard a TWA airliner over
Greece. Four passengers—all Americans—were killed,"
Forrester translated tersely. "Qaddafi's taking bows for it."

Jaime looked from Forrester to Nicholas and back again.
"Does this mean—" she began, unable to finish.

Forrester shook his head. "It means we're not going anywhere—yet."

• • •

The explosion aboard TWA flight 840 on April 2 occurred when the plane was flying at 15,000 feet. Had it reached a higher altitude, the craft would surely have been completely destroyed. Below, a construction worker in Argos, Greece, saw the bodies of the four passengers falling from the sky: a woman, her daughter and infant granddaughter, and a man who was still strapped to his seat when it crashed to earth in a bloody tangle of metal and flesh.

A Lebanese woman, a known terrorist with ties to the Lebanese Armed Revolutionary Faction, had been on the Cairo-to-Athens leg of the flight. She was considered the prime suspect in the bombing, not only because she had been aboard the 727, but because she had occupied the seat under which the bomb had been placed. Arab revolutionary cells claimed the explosion aboard flight 840 had been in retaliation for U.S. action in the Gulf of Sidra.

The tension in Libya escalated further.

On April 5, an explosion leveled the La Belle disco in West Berlin, killing two people—a Turkish woman and an American serviceman—and injured some two hundred thirty others, many of whom suffered third-degree burns over ninety percent of their bodies. Burned and injured bodies were strewn all over the street in the rubble.

U.S. intelligence reported intercepting a message en route to Tripoli from the Libyan People's Bureau in West Berlin: "Mission successfully accomplished. Our hand not detected."

The tension continued to build. . . .

On the morning of April 11, Forrester came to the room Jaime and Nicholas shared at the hotel and roused them from a sound sleep at four-thirty. "What's going on?" Nicholas asked sleepily as he opened the door. "Has something happened?"

"Get dressed," Forrester ordered. "We're leaving for Tripoli."

"Now?"

"Now," he said gruffly. "You've got thirty minutes. Meet me downstairs."

Jaime sat up in bed. "I thought we were waiting until the situation in Libya improved."

"It's not going to get any better." Forrester's expression, even in the shadows, was unmistakably grim. "In fact, it's going to get a hell of a lot worse."

"Worse? But—" Nicholas began.

"Thirty minutes," Forrester repeated. "If we're going at all, it has to be now."

"Do you think he knows more than he's telling us?" Jaime asked as they dressed hastily.

"I'd stake my life on it." Nicholas stopped halfway into his clothes. "In fact, I have a feeling that's exactly what we're about to do."

Jaime sighed. "I'm sorry I dragged you into this," she said finally, avoiding his eyes.

He turned to look at her. "You didn't drag me into anything," he insisted. "I dragged myself into it."

"Sure you did," she said darkly.

"You didn't exactly take me out of Paris at gunpoint, you know," he reminded her.

Her eyes met his now. "You know what I mean."

He nodded. "I know. But just for the record, I'm here because I want to be here."

"Only a certifiable lunatic would want to be here."

"You know what I mean," he said, throwing her own words back at her.

"Um-hmmm."

He grabbed her by the shoulders. "Promise me something, will you?"

She forced a smile. "If I can."

"If we get out of this alive," he began carefully, his gaze meeting hers in the darkness, "promise me we'll get married and have that normal life we talked about back in Paris. You know—a couple of kids and a house in Connecticut, a membership at the nearest country club and winters in Palm Beach and vacations in the Orient."

She bit her lower lip as she wrapped her arms around his waist. "Kids, no kids, a house in Connecticut or an igloo in the Yukon," she said, pausing to kiss him. "It doesn't matter. You're stuck with me now."

He looked at her. "Is that a yes?"

She nodded, kissing him again. "That's affirmative, partner."

Forrester was waiting for them in the hotel lobby with his contact, a young Arab man who looked to be in his mid-thirties, thin and of average height with thick, unruly black hair, a thick mustache, and a black patch worn over his left eye. He was dressed in familiar camouflage garb and had a red bandanna tied around his chest, a machete strapped into his scabbard, and a gun in a shoulder holster.

"This is Rashid," Forrester told Jaime and Nicholas as they walked outside. "His English is not too good, so don't be offended if he doesn't answer when spoken to, okay?"

"Swell," Jaime grumbled.

Their transportation turned out to be an old military truck that could have been left over from World War II, a vehicle of dubious stability that—according to Forrester—was guaranteed to fit in anywhere in the desert.

"That's probably where it's been for the past forty years," Nicholas whispered to Jaime.

"Are you sure about the safety of this thing?" Jaime asked as they climbed into the back of the truck.

Forrester nodded. "It's old, but we won't be conspicuous," he promised. "The only thing that would draw less attention would be a camel. If you'd prefer—"

Jaime shook her head. "No camels, thank you very much."

She huddled next to Nicholas as Rashid started the engine and the old truck lurched forward, beginning its bumpy journey out of the city and into the desert. *This is it,* she thought. Everything else that had happened to her, everything else they'd been through had been nothing compared to what they were about to do now.

No turning back now, she told herself.

TWENTY-SEVEN

The Libyan border. Friday, April 11, 1986. 5:36 A.M.

"Keep down and keep quiet," Forrester instructed Jaime and Nicholas as they approached the border. "I'll do the talking."

"You're more than welcome to it," said Nicholas, ducking his head as Rashid brought the truck to a stop. Grabbing Jaime's arm, he pulled her down with him.

From their hiding place in the back of the vehicle, Jaime could see the three men in military fatigues approaching. One of them spoke to Rashid in Arabic. He responded, then Forrester addressed them. Again, he spoke in fluent Arabic. *He speaks the language so well,* she thought, reminded that someone had betrayed her father and was out to kill him now. Someone who wanted her to lead them to him. How could she be sure it wasn't Forrester himself? But even as the first glimmer of suspicion rose in the back of her mind, she hastily dismissed it. *This man's been trying to help us. He's brought us here to find Daddy.* And yet how many others had professed to want to help? Who could *really* be trusted?

She saw two more men, similarly attired, coming up from behind. Both were carrying M-1 rifles. She held her breath, but she could feel her heart beating wildly in her throat. She instinctively leaned a little closer to Nicholas, who put his arms around her. ''I'm sorry,'' she whispered.

''I'm not,'' he told her, and she knew that he meant it.

They could hear the men talking, and it was frustrating because neither of them understood a word of Arabic and had no idea what they were saying. Finally, one of the Libyans waved to Rashid to go on, and Jaime breathed a sigh of relief. She leaned against Nicholas's shoulder as the truck's engine sputtered to life again and they started on their way.

They were both acutely aware that they were now in hostile territory.

Washington, D.C. Friday, April 11. Noon.

Members of the National Security Council converged in the Oval Office to meet with President Reagan. Vice President Bush and Secretary of Defense Weinberger were conspicuously absent from that meeting, both traveling outside the country at the time. One council member expressed concern at the possibility of taking military action against Libya. CIA director William Casey was openly concerned about getting his agents out of Libya before any such action was taken. But everyone present was in agreement with Secretary of State George Shultz, who maintained that the U.S. had taken enough, that the time for action had come.

The President had, in fact, approved a tentative plan for an air strike against Libya two days earlier. All involved had agreed that the attack should be a surprise one, launched by carrier planes as soon as the flattops were in position. President Reagan directed that every precaution be taken to minimize casualties among Libyan civilians.

Unfortunately, when the news blackout came down, there was enough speculation in the absence of any hard facts to give the President and the NSC cause to doubt their chances of a surprise attack. As their doubts and worries grew, they all agreed that a postponement was necessary.

For the moment.

The Libyan desert. Saturday, April 12. 6:42 A.M.

The old truck rumbled across the desert, leaving an enormous cloud of dust and sand in its wake. Rashid floored the accelerator until the rattletrap vehicle began to vibrate wildly. "What does he think he's doing—time trials for the Indy 500?" Jaime asked irritably as she dusted sand from her caftan.

"He's trying to make up for the time we've lost already," Forrester told her as he opened one of the leather carryalls he'd brought along from the Algerian hotel and took out two long loaves of homemade bread and four canteens. After having been delayed by a dust storm and two mechanical mishaps in the course of their journey, they were already more than twenty-four hours behind schedule.

"How long before we get to Tripoli?" Nicholas wanted to know.

"Hard to tell." Forrester broke one of the loaves and handed half up to Rashid, along with a canteen. "We should have been there yesterday."

He looks worried, Jaime observed. *What isn't he telling us?*

He broke another loaf and gave each of them half. Then he opened one of the canteens and filled two tin cups with what appeared to be milk. Jaime, parched and desperate for a cold drink, eagerly took a long swallow. She made a face as it went down. "What *is* this stuff, anyway?"

"Camel's milk," Forrester told her.

"I had to ask."

"At this point I'd drink anything—even motor oil, if it was the only thing available," Nicholas said, downing his quickly. "What's on the bread?"

"Nothing."

"Nothing? Just bread?"

"It's a Qaddafi sandwich," Jaime told him. "Nothing but hot air."

Forrester didn't smile. "Best we could do on short notice," he said, taking a bite of his and chewing thoroughly.

Jaime studied him for a long moment. "Want to let us in on it?" she asked finally.

"Let you in on what?" he asked absently, taking a long swallow of the milk.

''What's really worrying you.''

He looked at her. ''In case you haven't noticed, we're about to walk through the flames of hell, dear girl,'' he pointed out. ''If that realization alone doesn't worry you, then there's something wrong with you.'' He took another bite of bread and chewed with some difficulty.

I'm worried, all right, Jaime thought.

Washington, D.C. Saturday, April 12. 11:15 P.M.

Harry Warner's offices were eerily quiet. He sat at his desk, alone in the darkness, staring at the telephone. His private line. Why didn't the goddamned thing ring? His frustration grew as the minutes ticked away. He had to reach Lynde . . . somehow. Vice President Bush had just returned from Saudi Arabia. Weinberger was en route to Washington from the Philippines. The U. S. ambassador to the United Nations was in London meeting with British Prime Minister Margaret Thatcher. Earlier that day, it was announced that the Italian prime minister would receive a U.S. presidential envoy on Monday. *Time's running out,* Warner thought grimly.

For him, the most difficult thing to accept was the realization that he'd made one critical error, that he'd unwittingly sent the real traitor to find Lynde and his daughter.

If only he could warn them that a killer was on their trail.

Tripoli. Sunday, April 13. 8:52 A.M.

After a series of frustrating delays, Rashid drove through the streets of the Libyan capital early on Sunday morning. In the back of the truck, Jaime slept soundly in Nicholas's arms, blissfully unaware that they had finally reached their destination.

''Rashid will go find Unicorn,'' Forrester told Nicholas. ''All we can do is wait until he comes to us.''

Nicholas looked at him for a moment. ''Jaime's right, isn't she?''

Forrester avoided his gaze. ''About what?''

''There *is* more to this than just the political situation here, isn't there?'' he wanted to know.

Forrester hesitated momentarily. "Yes," he said finally. "A lot more."

"Don't you think you should let us in on it?"

"There are some things you—or more precisely, *she*—would be better off not knowing," Forrester said tightly, peering out from under the thick canvas covering over the back of the truck.

"You've said yourself that this is a life-or-death situation," Nicholas reminded him, breathing deeply. "I, for one, like to know all the facts when I'm putting my life on the line."

Forrester was thoughtful for a long moment. "I suppose you do have the right," he said finally. He glanced at Jaime, who was still sleeping. "From the day she began the search for her father, someone's been deliberately feeding her all kinds of misinformation, counting on fueling her determination to dig for the truth. Someone's been pushing her here, toward Lynde, so he himself could locate Unicorn and eliminate him before he blows his operations here."

"And you know who that person is?"

Forrester nodded.

"Will you tell her?" Nicholas asked carefully.

Forrester shook his head. "Not if I can avoid it."

The Gulf of Sidra. Sunday, April 13. 11:57 A.M.

The U.S. Sixth Fleet moved into position off the coast of Libya. The aircraft carriers *America* and *Coral Sea*, with one hundred sixty fighters and bombers on board, were accompanied by fourteen escort warships and two additional support vessels. Among them was the U.S.S. *Ticonderoga*, with its sophisticated Aegis air defense system. Their crews were on standby, awaiting word from Washington.

Waiting. . . .

Tripoli. Sunday, April 13. 4:25 P.M.

"What do we do now?" Jaime wanted to know.

"We wait," Forrester said tersely. "Rashid will find your father. We can't go to him. It would be far too dangerous. We can only wait until he comes to us." He had decided the safest place to wait would be at the British consulate in down-town Tripoli.

"I can't believe I've really made it," Jaime told Nicholas when they were finally alone in an upstairs room at the con-sulate. "I'm really going to see my father after all these years."

"We're not out of the woods yet, sweetheart," he re-minded her, holding her close.

"But it's going to happen. It's finally going to happen," she insisted.

He looked at her suspiciously. "Are you nervous?"

She nodded, somewhat embarrassed to admit it. "A little. It's been a long time," she said quietly. "I've changed—surely he has as well."

"Most likely," Nicholas acknowledged, wishing he could somehow make this easier for her but too concerned with what was happening all around them to concentrate on Jaime's reunion with her father.

She looked up at him. "What am I going to say to him?"

He stroked her hair. "What would you have said to him nineteen years ago?"

Jaime smiled. "I would have asked him if he had brought me anything."

London. Monday, April 14. 2:54 P.M.

British Prime Minister Thatcher officially gave her coun-try's support to U.S. plans for a surprise air strike against Libya, stating that it would be "unthinkable" that Britain would not back the United States in defending itself.

That same day, eighteen F-111 bombers from the Third Air Force departed from three Royal Air Force bases in England and began a 2,800-nautical-mile journey—having been de-nied permission to cross French airspace—around the conti-nent to join the Sixth Fleet in the Gulf of Sidra.

Time was running out. . . .

Tripoli. Monday, April 14. 8:30 P.M.

"He's here," Forrester announced.

Jaime looked at Nicholas, and he gave her the thumbs-up

signal. She flashed him a smile. "Want to meet your future father-in-law?" she asked, trying to keep her voice light.

He grinned. "I don't know. If he doesn't like me, he may turn me over to a Libyan firing squad for target practice."

"No, he wouldn't," she insisted. "He'd do the job himself."

"That's what I was afraid you'd say."

"Do I look all right?" she asked.

He smiled. "Just like an Arab princess," he told her, scrutinizing her brightly colored caftan.

She took a deep breath. "Let's go, then."

Hand in hand they descended the stairs to the office of the British consul. Jaime's heart was pounding wildly as Forrester pushed open the door and she saw her father for the first time in almost twenty years.

He wasn't as tall as she remembered him, but, she thought, she was a good deal taller than she'd been in 1966. He looked a bit heavier. His hair had gone completely white. His face was lined with age, and yet looking at him now, she realized she would have known him anywhere. She stepped forward cautiously. "Daddy?" she addressed him in a faltering voice.

He broke into a broad grin. "It's me, princess." He opened his arms to her. "God, I've waited so long for this!"

"Oh, Daddy!" Bursting into tears, she flew into his arms. As he enveloped her in a bear hug, they both sobbed openly.

The past twenty years had evaporated in a matter of seconds.

The Gulf of Sidra. Tuesday, April 15. 1:45 A.M.

All was calm for the moment. The Sixth Fleet, now in position, was still on standby. In exactly fifteen minutes, they would make their move. Up until 1:59 A.M., the President of the United States could still call off the strike.

As of 1:45, he had not.

Washington, D.C. Monday, April 14. 6:58 P.M.

In his office, Harry Warner was staring at the digital clock on his credenza. It was Tuesday morning in Libya now. There had been no word from the White House, which could only mean the strike was still on.

Harry Warner had never been a particularly religious man, but tonight he prayed.

Tripoli. Tuesday, April 15. 1:58 A.M.

"I hate to break up the reunion," Forrester apologized halfheartedly as he ushered everyone out of the British consulate and into the streets of Tripoli. "But we've got to get out of here. Rashid will be along any minute."

"Where are we going?" Nicholas wanted to know.

"Tunisia's our best bet at this late stage in the game. We can be across the border in no more than a couple of hours."

"If we have that much time," Lynde said thoughtfully, staring up at the eerily calm, dark sky.

Forrester looked both ways down the darkened streets. "Damn!" he muttered impatiently. "Where the hell is Rashid now?"

Lynde looked at his watch. "If he doesn't get here fast, we won't be going anywhere," he muttered.

"They're talking as if we're on the verge of Armageddon," Jaime commented to Nicholas.

Her father turned to look at her, his face deathly serious. "Close," he said grimly. "Very close."

"Hello, Jim—it's been a long time," said a voice from behind them.

They all turned at once. The man standing in the shadows looked to be Lynde's age, and definitely American. Only Lynde recognized him on sight. "Hello, Lew," he said calmly. "Even at your age, you still look like a goddamned Ivy Leaguer."

"And you still haven't lost your dry wit," he observed.

"Got to keep a sense of humor in our business, don't you think?" Lynde asked, not moving. "It's all that's between us and those padded cells sometimes."

Lew? Jaime froze. "This is Lewis Baldwin?" she asked, turning to her father. And to herself: *This is the man who destroyed so many lives?*

"In the flesh," he responded quietly.

"The real traitor," Forrester put in, stepping forward slowly.

"I wouldn't try anything if I were you, Mr. Forrester," Baldwin advised as he emerged from the shadows and the gun in his hand became visible. "Surprised that I recognize you? You shouldn't be. I've known all about all of you, almost from the beginning, thanks to your little girl's determination to find you, Jim."

Jaime looked at him and then at her father, her eyes wide with shock. "He's the one—"

Lynde nodded. "He's been selling arms to Qaddafi since 1982," he revealed. "MAC-10s, Redeye missiles, M-1s, Colt Cobra .38s, M-16s, AK-47s, RPG mini-bazookas; you name it, he's traded it. He just delivered a large shipment of Primacord with C-4 to the Libyans this week."

"Sorry I had to use your daughter to flush you out, old friend," Baldwin said with an evil smile, "but you left me no alternative, what with all the secrecy surrounding your work here. When Jaime started getting nosy and Harry decided to put Harris on her trail, he didn't realize he was sticking your neck in the noose."

"Allan Harris? He works for you?" Lynde asked. Harris had been one of his few confidants during the days of training for the OSS.

"He did," Baldwin said with an offhand shrug. "I had to get rid of him, once he'd served his purpose. I couldn't risk the possibility that he might eventually talk." He paused. "Just like I have to eliminate all of you now—much as I hate to, of course."

"Of course." Lynde was acutely aware of the revolver inside his jacket—and of the reality that Baldwin could kill all of them in the seconds it would take him to reach for it.

"I hate long good-byes," Baldwin started, "so—"

He was interrupted by a loud squeal of the brakes of the old truck as it came to a sudden stop only yards away. Before Baldwin could react, Rashid bounded from the driver's seat and opened fire with his M-16. Reacting instinctively, Nicholas shoved Jaime to the ground and threw himself over her. As Lynde and Forrester drew their guns, they saw Baldwin's body lurch crazily, falling to the ground in a bloody heap. It was over before it had begun.

"Come on!" Forrester yelled, running for the truck. "We've got to get the hell out of here!"

"Right behind you," Lynde called back to him as he and Nicholas pulled Jaime to her feet. At that moment, the darkness was punctuated by a blinding flash of light, and the earth shook beneath their feet as above them the sky exploded.

It was already too late.

TWENTY-EIGHT

Tripoli. Tuesday, April 15. 2:05 A.M.

The loud roar of bombs detonating all around them sent terrified Libyans pouring into the streets on foot and in automobiles. There were traffic jams and horns honking everywhere. High above the city, A-6 Intruder jets and A-7 Corsairs discharged 500- and 2,000-pound laser-guided bombs. In the distance, heavy antiaircraft artillery could be heard as tracer fire lit the sky. Smoke from the attack drifted across the city. Qaddafi's Revolutionary Guards were suddenly everywhere.

As the old truck rumbled through the least congested side streets, Forrester surveyed the activity to the west of the city via his high-powered binoculars. "Wheelus has been hit," he observed. "There's a hell of a lot of smoke."

The truck lurched crazily as the earth beneath it felt the impact of each explosion. Rashid maneuvered around the rubble expertly as he headed out of the city. In the back of the truck, Jaime, wrapped in a heavy blanket, looked on as Nicholas loaded ammunition into every gun they had. Her father fiddled with the portable radio, on which he seemed able to get nothing but static. "Why do we always end up with this antiquated shit?" he muttered irritably.

Finally, the old radio came to life. There was still a great deal of static, but they could hear a man's voice, speaking in rapid Arabic.

Nicholas put down the revolver he was loading and leaned forward to listen. "What's he saying?" he asked.

Lynde shook his head. "Not much damage to the city itself," he translated. "Their main military airport was hit—and the naval training base and the Azizyah barracks." He paused to listen further. "There was also a strike at the missile base at Benghazi."

"What about Qaddafi?" Forrester called out to him. "Did they get that son of a bitch or not?"

"No word yet," Lynde told him. "His residence was hit, but they don't know if there were any casualties."

"Somebody should blow that bastard away," Forrester grumbled angrily.

Rashid fought for control of the truck as he pushed it as hard as it would go, applying all of his strength to the steering wheel. Forrester hung onto his seat, while in the back of the truck Lynde, Jaime, and Nicholas braced themselves as best they could.

Lynde looked at his daughter in the darkness and smiled wearily. "What the hell ever possessed you to come here?"

"Once I knew you were still alive, I had to see you," she answered without hesitation.

"Wouldn't it have been easier to let Jack come in after me and see me on the outside?"

Now Jaime smiled too. "And miss all the fun?"

Her father laughed for the first time. "You're my daughter, all right," he declared. "God help you!"

The Libyan desert. Tuesday, April 15. 3:25 A.M.

The air strike lasted twenty minutes. For another fifteen minutes afterward, artillery fire could be heard in the distance. As the truck continued eastward across the desert, Lynde continued to pick up sporadic transmissions over the radio. Damage to military installations in Tripoli and Benghazi was reported as extensive. Several members of Qaddafi's family were injured in the assault on the Libyan leader's residence, and his infant daughter was among the casualties.

Libyans throughout the country demanded swift retaliation against the "savage American intruders."

"How can they stand behind that maniac?" Jaime wondered aloud.

Rashid laughed. "They think of the Brother Colonel as a big zero," he answered in stilted English.

"I think you mean 'hero,' Rashid," Nicholas corrected him.

"I think he was right the first time," Jaime put in.

"They're reporting that three U.S. planes were shot down and their pilots executed by Libyan civilians," Lynde said as yet another broken transmission came over the radio.

"Do you believe that?" Nicholas asked.

Lynde's smile was forced. "About as much as I'd believe anything else coming out of the Qaddafi regime," he said grimly. "Still, we can't take any chances. We've got to get into Tunisia as fast as this old jalopy will take us."

"Which, unfortunately, isn't very fast at all," Jaime remarked, leaning her head against Nicholas's shoulder.

"Don't knock it," Nicholas told her. "It's all we've got, you know."

Lynde looked at him as he settled back to relax for a few moments. "So—you want to marry my daughter, do you?" he asked, a sly smile on his face.

Nicholas nodded. "As soon as we get out of this hell-hole," he answered.

Lynde raised an eyebrow. "Think you can handle her?"

Nicholas laughed. "The jury's still out on that one," he admitted.

All conversation ceased when the truck came to an abrupt halt in the middle of the desert. "Quiet!" Forrester issued the order sharply from his position next to Rashid in the front seat. Lynde pulled on his turban. Jaime stuffed an errant lock of red hair underneath her head scarf. Nicholas, whose dark coloring—save his blue eyes—made it possible for him to pass as an Arab, made no move.

Suddenly they were surrounded. There were Libyan Revolutionary Guards everywhere, brandishing weapons. Lynde drew his revolver and waited. Jaime shrank back into the shadows, her hand under the folds of her robes touching the smooth, cold metal of the gun her father had given her, not certain that, should the need arise, she would be able to use it. They listened as Forrester and Rashid conversed with the guards in Arabic. Jaime couldn't understand the words, but she could tell by the tone of their voices that it was not a pleasant conversation. She started to open her mouth and say something, but Nicholas pressed a finger to his lips to silence her. Then he looked at Lynde, who gave him a nod. He drew his gun and moved all the way to the back of the truck.

Outside, voices were raised in anger. Lynde moved swiftly, silently, to a spot from which he could see what was going on at the rear. Jaime was surprised he was still so agile at his age. Nicholas positioned himself as a backup. Jaime was still touching the handle of her gun, still wondering if she would be able to use it. She could hear Rashid, arguing with one of the men in what she was certain had to be gutter Arabic. She drew her gun slowly.

The first shot was fired.

It set off a chain reaction. Rashid and Forrester opened fire with their M-16s as the Libyans attacked. Her father and Nicholas fired on the men advancing to the rear. Suddenly her father fell backward, clutching the upper part of his right arm. Jaime scrambled to her feet and went to him while Nicholas covered both of them.

"I'm okay, princess," he told her as she ripped the fabric of his *galabiyya* away from the wound.

"Oh, God—Daddy—" she gasped.

"It's just a flesh wound," he assured her. "God knows it's not the first time."

"There's so much blood—" It was pouring out of him, soaking both of them in a blaze of scarlet.

"Damn!" Nicholas muttered, scrambling to the floor.

She jerked around to look at him. "What's wrong?"

"Out of ammo," he breathed, feeling in the darkness for another weapon.

"Take mine." As she raised her head, she found herself looking down the barrel of a Libyan rifle. Reacting instinctively, she squeezed the trigger of the gun in her hand and felt the jolt as it discharged. The Libyan rocked backward, then slumped to the ground.

At that moment, the truck once again exploded to life and rolled forward with surprising speed for its condition. Jaime, caught off-balance, fell backward onto the floor.

"Cover us from the back!" Forrester shouted back to Nicholas.

"You've got it!" Nicholas fired two more shots as the truck sped away.

Jaime half crawled to her father's side again. He'd lost a great deal of blood and was now only semiconscious. Thinking quickly, she ripped a length of fabric from the bottom of her caftan and made a tourniquet to slow down the bleeding.

Oh, God, Daddy, she thought as she struggled to stop the bleeding. *Please—not now, not after it's taken me so long to find you.*

Washington, D.C. Tuesday, April 15. 10:56 A.M.

Harry Warner hadn't left his office all night. Now, as he stared at the small screen of the portable TV he kept there, he wondered if they had gotten out in time. If only they'd make contact.

According to the newspapers, radio, and TV, damage to the civilian areas was minimal. The target areas had been Libyan military installations and suspected terrorist training camps, and they were the areas suffering the most extensive damage. There were conflicting reports as to the amount of damage to the French diplomatic mission in downtown Tripoli. There were also conflicting reports concerning the number of casualties, and whether or not Qaddafi himself had been among them. He had not been seen since the attack, some sixteen hours earlier, and rumors of his death dominated the airwaves. Libya still claimed to have downed three American aircraft and executed the pilots, but according to the Pentagon, only one F-111 was still unaccounted for.

Where the hell are they? Warner wondered.

The Libyan border. Tuesday, April 15. 11:15 P.M.

"He needs to get to a hospital," Jaime told Nicholas as

she checked her father's vital signs again. He had only a thready pulse, he was feverish, and he appeared to be in shock.

"We're almost home free," Nicholas tried to reassure her. "It won't be long now."

Jaime looked at him in the darkness, her eyes reflecting her fear. "I don't think he can wait much longer."

They could hear voices as the old truck came to a grinding halt. For a moment, Jaime felt as if her breath had caught in her throat. *Not again,* she thought, her heart racing. *Please—not again!*

Two men—both armed—came around to the back of the truck and peered inside. Jaime froze for an instant as she stared into their faces, wondering what they wanted, what they were going to do to them. With trembling fingers she groped about in the darkness for her gun.

"Jaime—uncover your head!" Nicholas ordered her.

She was confused. "What—"

"Uncover your head—prove you're American!"

When she didn't respond, he reached up and yanked off her kerchief, allowing her long red hair to fall freely over her shoulders. The two men looked at each other. There was a brief exchange between them in Arabic, then they backed off.

"They're Tunisian," Nicholas whispered.

Jaime sagged with relief as Rashid started up the engine again and the truck crossed the border into Tunisia.

They were safe at last!

TWENTY-NINE

Wiesbaden, West Germany. Saturday, April 19. 3:35 P.M.

"He's going to be fine," the doctor at the U.S. military base hospital told Jaime. "He did lose a lot of blood, but with the transfusions we gave him and plenty of rest, he'll be as good as new."

"When can he leave the hospital?" she asked, taking Nicholas's hand as she spoke.

"Tomorrow," the doctor answered without hesitation. "I'll sign his release first thing in the morning."

"Could we see him now?" Nicholas asked.

"Of course." The doctor stepped aside so they could enter.

When they went into the room, Lynde appeared to be asleep. Jaime took a chair beside the bed, and Nicholas stood behind her, his hands on her shoulders. She studied her father for a long moment. Only now, with their ordeal in Libya behind them, did the reality of having found him—alive—fully sink in.

"Where's Jack?"

Jaime looked surprised. "Daddy—I thought you were—that is, you're awake!"

"I've been awake since you came in," he said in a tired voice. "Where's Jack?"

"He left this morning," Nicholas told him. "He went back to Belgium. He said we were too dull, that he had to go find a little excitement."

Lynde managed a smile. "Jack always was a wet blanket." He paused. "When am I going to be sprung from this god-damned maximum security institution?"

"Tomorrow," Jaime promised. "The doctor says he'll sign you out in the morning."

"Can't be soon enough for me."

"Or for me," Jaime agreed with a nod. "When we get back to New York—"

He raised a hand to silence her. "I'm not going back to New York, princess," he said quietly.

She looked at him quizzically. "But I thought—" she began.

He reached out and took her hand. "I know what you thought, princess," he said. "I should have told you before now, I know."

"After all these years, Daddy, after waiting so long," she began in a faltering voice. "I just assumed you'd go home with us—"

He nodded. "I know, and I let you believe it. That was my mistake." He paused thoughtfully. "Listen, princess— I've had nothing to do these past few days but lie here and think. I've spent most of that time thinking about you, and what I've done to you."

She shook her head emphatically. "You haven't done any-thing—"

"Let me finish," he said firmly. "I did you a disservice by leaving you the way I did, I know. I left you with an image of me that no man could ever live up to."

"Daddy, I—"

"You've always thought of me as some kind of big hero, haven't you?"

She hesitated for a moment, then nodded. "I guess I did, yes."

"Well, I'm not," he told her frankly. "I was a lousy father

and an even worse husband. I loved you, but I sure as hell didn't stick around to watch you grow up." A pause. "A part of me was always afraid to let myself care too much—'til you came along. Even then, it scared the hell out of me. While I've been out there playing cloak-and-dagger, I've actually been running away."

"Running away?" Jaime looked up at Nicholas, then at her father again.

"Yes . . . running away from you and from myself, if that makes any sense." He sighed. "Why do you think your mother killed herself?"

Jaime shook her head. "I know why Mother killed herself," she said quietly. "She thought you didn't love her."

"She *knew* I didn't love her," he corrected. "Your mother was a victim of the system. She happened to be in the wrong place at the wrong time, and she was chosen for a job she wasn't strong enough to handle."

Jaime looked confused.

"That's pretty much what it was, princess," he admitted. "I needed a cover, and Fran Colby fit the bill."

"And me?" Jaime asked carefully. "Was I just part of the cover?"

"You know better than that," he said gruffly. "I've always loved you. I wasn't the best father in the world, and before you were born, I'd convinced myself kids didn't fit into my scheme of things. But that all changed the first time I held you. You were the one good thing that came out of that marriage."

Jaime looked away. "Mother didn't think so," she said darkly.

Lynde gave her hand a little squeeze. "Your mother was sick, princess," he told her. "It wasn't her fault she never could be the mother you needed."

"I kept telling myself that, all these years," she admitted, her voice faltering. "I kept telling myself that she didn't know what she was doing, that she wasn't responsible—that *I* wasn't responsible—"

"You weren't," her father cut in sharply. "It wasn't your

fault, your mother's illness. I suspect it was something that actually took root in her long before you were born.''

''I've always had a hard time believing there wasn't something wrong with me,'' Jaime said then. ''First Mother, then you—''

''I didn't have any choice.'' He frowned. ''It was my job. It was something I *had* to do. I'd committed myself to it a long time ago.''

''I didn't know that then,'' Jaime said tightly. ''All I knew was that my mother had left me, then my father was gone too. They told me you were dead, that you'd embezzled a fortune from Grandfather's firm and run off to Europe. I couldn't believe you'd really go off and leave me like that . . . until I found the footlocker.''

''Footlocker?''

''*Your* footlocker,'' she said. ''It was in the attic at the house. I found it one day—it was full of letters, cards, presents, things you'd sent to me over the years. They—the Harcourts—had been hiding them there. The day I found them, I left. I never went back.''

''It's your house now,'' he pointed out.

She shook her head. ''It didn't matter. It *doesn't* matter.'' She paused. ''I still have that footlocker, you know.''

''Do you?'' He didn't know what else to say.

Jaime nodded. ''I've kept it with me. It was all I had left of my father—until that night in Tripoli.''

''You have me now,'' he said.

''For how long?''

''For good,'' he answered. ''No matter where I am or what I'm doing, I'm with you in spirit.''

''You really aren't coming home, then,'' she concluded.

He shook his head. ''I can't,'' he said. ''This is my job, Jaime. It's the only thing I know how to do. It's who I am— I can't change that.''

Jaime shook her head, dangerously close to tears. ''If you're not coming back to the States with us, then where will you go?''

''Back to the Middle East,'' he answered without hesitation. ''After all these years, I couldn't go back to playing a desk jockey. Besides, I've discovered I speak Arabic better than English now.''

"How can you possibly go back to Libya?" Jaime asked.

"I can't," he responded. "But there's always Iran, Lebanon, Syria, and other countries with known connections to terrorism.''

"You're not even going to come home for our wedding?''

He smiled. "I'll be there, princess—in spirit." He looked up at Nicholas. "You take care of my little girl—or I'll come looking for you.''

"I intend to," Nicholas promised.

"I was counting on you to give the bride away," Jaime said.

He chuckled. "I could never give you away.''

Jaime rose to her feet slowly. "You won't be able to stay in touch?''

"We'll see," he said. Then, to Nicholas: "When will you two be leaving?''

"By the end of the week," Nicholas told him. "We have to make a stopover in Paris for a few days to take care of business there.''

"Take care of her.''

"I will.''

They left the room after he drifted off to sleep again. "I don't know if I can take losing him again so soon," Jaime told Nicholas once they were out in the hallway. "I wanted him at our wedding—''

Nicholas only smiled as he embraced her. "I have a feeling he will be," he told her. "One way or another.''